The DREAD DESCENDANT

LAUREN CATE LEAKE

Cover art by Jess Kuespert.

ISBN 979-8-218-32198-7 (paperback)

Starbound House.

For you, the dreamer.

And for my mother. I hope they have access to Earth's library in whatever galaxy you are dancing across.

A majority of this book is from the depths of my mind, where Malachite Puer lives and pestered me relentlessly over ten years to write this story. Some non-fiction aspects of human history such as names, places and wars are used. I didn't choose that. This is how it happened. But make no mistake, the journey you are about to embark on is one of pure magic.

This story has content that may not be appropriate for all ages such as violence, language, and sexually explicit scenes.

THE DREAD LANDS/ATERNA

REALMS

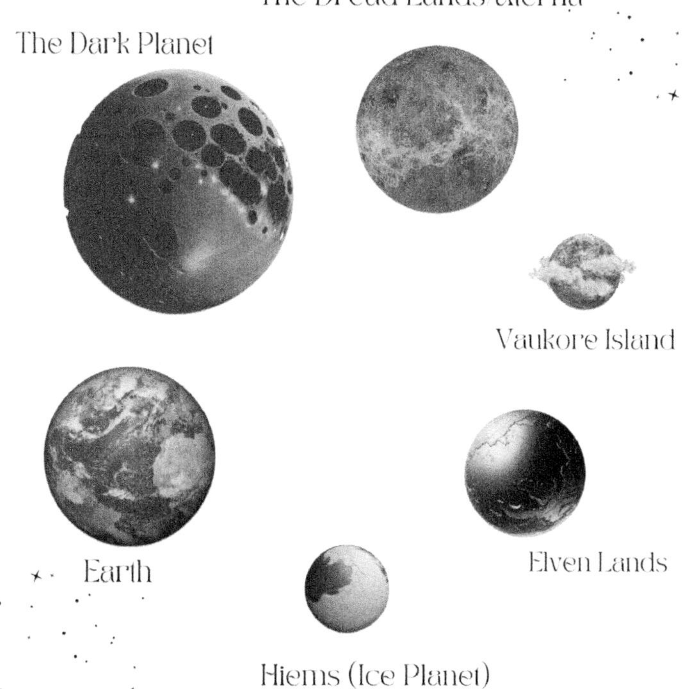
The Dread Lands/Aterna
The Dark Planet
Vaukore Island
Earth
Elven Lands
Hiems (Ice Planet)

PLAYLIST

Killer Queen by Queen
Magic by Pilot
bury a friend by Billie Eilish
Victorious by Panic! At the Disco
brutal by Olivia Rodrigo
Edge of Seventeen by Stevie Nicks
Sweet Dreams by Eurythmics
Feeling Good by Michael Buble
Believer by Imagine Dragons
Season of the Witch by Donovan
My Guy by Mary Wells
Supermassive Black Hole by Muse
Enchanted by Taylor Swift
I Have to Have You by Blue
Ain't No Rest for the Wicked by Cage the Elephant
YES MOM by Tessa Violet
Money Power Glory by Lana Del Ray
Dream a Little Dream of Me by The Mamas & the Papas
I Put a Spell on You by Creedence Clearwater Revival
Strange Magic by Electric Light Orchestra
For Whom the Bell Tolls by Metallica
traitor by Olivia Rodrigo
Golden Slumbers/Carry that Weight by Jennifer Hudson
Middle of the Night by Loveless

Chapter 43 Spiracle by Flower Face
Chapter 49 Possum Kingdom by Toadies

BOARDS

PRONUNCIATION GUIDE

Maeve *like wave*
Malachite *like kite*
Abraxas *sis not sass (though…he has that)*
Reeve *like leave*
Vaukore *vow/core*
Vexkari *vex/car with letter "E" sound*
Ambrose *like gross (I can assure you he is far from it)*
Spinel *spin/elle*
Peur *pure*
Zimsy *zim/zee*
Orator *or/uh/tor*

Chapter 1

The Orator stood outside the ornate ivory gates at Sinclair Estates, checking his pocket watch and rapidly tapping his foot. Muttering under his breath, he cursed the Committee of the Sacred for his tardiness. His leather shoes glistened in the morning sunlight, as the pale and tan pebbles crunched beneath his step. The gates elegantly opened themselves as he hastily slipped inside.

The hydrangea-lined pathway boasted vibrant year round blooms, despite the chilly year round climate of northern England. Purple, blue, white, green, and pink florals encased in vivid green leaves Magically bound to never wither.

The two-story white doors slipped open from one another, a silent invitation. The Orator didn't hesitate to cross the threshold into the glittering marble foyer of the manor.

He had been an elected official, rubbing elbows with the Magical elite for nearly ten years, and still he never stopped marveling at the luxury the Sinclairs obtained, and hold onto.

One of the Sacred Seventeen families.

The Sinclair's home contained carved statues, fine marble, golden bannisters, ornate frames, and a painted ceiling one could get lost in. The grand entryway ran the length of the house. On the far end sunlight poured through enormous glass-paned doors, which stood open, leading to the balcony.

"Ambrose," called the Orator, as the front door clicked shut behind him. His voice echoed across the hall. There came no reply.

He moved towards the balcony. The grand staircase to his left, marbled like the rest of the floor with gilded golden railings, twisted to the floors above.

"Orator Moon."

The Orator turned. The Premier came jogging down the stairs. Life in his step.

"Ambrose," said Moon. "Thought you might be on the balcony enjoying a morning cigar. Apologies for my tardiness, you know how hard it is to meet with the Committee right now. I have a better chance of an audience with King George himself."

Ambrose shook his head. "You mean the Queen?"

"Old habits," huffed Moon.

Ambrose laughed. "No need to apologize, old chap."

Ambrose spoke with London high society ease. As all Sacred Seventeen did.

Ambrose Sinclair was younger than the Orator. Which was odd for a Premier. Premiers were typically wartime generals with the most battle experience, the highest record of duel wins. Usually men in their sixties, but Ambrose had just turned forty-five with his youngest daughter in her final years of schooling at Vaukore Academy.

She was a topic of discussion Ambrose had forbidden. His daughter's memory charm skills would make her a great asset in the war, if harnessed properly perhaps she could end it all together. In truth, the Orator was far too frightened to bring the idea up again. He may have the highest ranking office in the Magical world as The Orator, but the Sinclairs had Pureblood. Ancient and unbreakable Magic ran through their veins. And while Moon was welcomed into their fold as their worldly leader, he was no fool. Ambrose could snap him in half with a blink.

And would proudly do so for his children.

The Premier was unyielding in keeping his children away from the war. Though, Moon couldn't blame him, after what happened to his firstborn. Still, he wondered. . . The Witch would be twenty-one soon. An adult in their world. Perhaps she could make the decision on her own.

Regardless of his young age, Ambrose won the Magical Militia with a landslide vote. Every year.

Ambrose Sinclair had a knack for leading the Bellator Sector, those elite Magicals who made up the Magical Militia. They rallied behind his speeches and swooned over his tomcat smile. And now, more than ever, when the Orator's Office found themselves entangled in a human war, Ambrose was needed.

The Orator straightened. "I'm here to discuss the events of last night."

Ambrose's eyes darted to the balcony, he was silent for a moment, contemplating, and then chose to answer.

Through the ornate glass doors was a lavish stone balcony that expanded over The Gardens, which, like the hydrangeas out front, were enchanted with everlasting and endless life. The balcony was suited with terraces and plants, soft plush furniture and a sunrise view.

And Maeve Sinclair herself.

Ambrose's youngest sat sipping tea in an ivory and sapphire blue teacup, well aware her father knew she was there and listening intently to their political strategy. Maeve had never expressed a personal interest in the war or politics, but she understood the value of knowledge. Information. The potential for the upper hand. All were as valuable as her own Magic.

She placed the dainty bit of porcelain on its matching saucer. The smell of her favorite tea as intoxicating as ever.

The sunrise over Sinclair Estates could have been award-winning in Maeve's opinion. Blue and violet light danced across the vast gardens.

The servants called it endless summer, but summer was ending in the human world where seasons still prevailed. Autumn was calling, beckoning students back to their studies. Which meant Vaukore, the most ancient and prestigious Magical academy, was calling Maeve to hers. Only the best and the brightest were admitted after their eighteenth birthday to train at the cherished boarding school.

The birds were barely waking as she sipped her tea. Light songs fluttered across the valley. Her lips paused against the teacup, as Orator Moon said-

"You're in the countryside, I doubt they'll come this far out, but still," his voice said lazily, "couldn't hurt to reinforce them. They've begun bombing the entire United Kingdom more and more."

Her Father's warm laughter drifted out onto the balcony. "My father would be insulted if you thought his ancient enchantments on this estate weren't strong enough to withhold a human's idea of warfare."

Maeve smiled into her teacup.

There was a light smacking sound, what Maeve imagined to be The Orator hitting her Father on the arm. "Take it however you like,

Ambrose. The reality is their bombs are becoming more and more volatile."

More laughter. It was the most wonderful sound she knew. Warm and inviting. Everything about her Father was just that.

"And stop giving those bastards money," continued The Orator. "I know you have more Gold than all of The United but find a new hobby."

"It is not a hobby, they are training exercises for my men. A single human bomb is the equivalent of a hundred soldiers' magic. What better way to prepare them?"

"And I suppose it's pure coincidence you also receive awards for protecting human civilians with those training exercises?"

"You signed off on those, Orator." She could hear the smile in his voice. "You tell me."

Maeve wondered what brought the Orator to her father's private residence so early.

The Estate answered, and a perfectly folded newspaper appeared on the white iron table beside her. She set down her teacup and glanced at the headline of the The Magical Times:

August 1st, 1944

ROGUE MAGICAL MILITIA CAPTAIN RUMORED TO BE ASSISTING NAZI GERMANY IN BOMBING HUMAN CIVILIANS

Kietel was his name. Her Father had named him Captain himself.

Moon's voice continued. "Did you decide on a number to have stationed at Vaukore?"

Vaukore.

Maeve hated that the Orator's Office passed legislation ordering that her father's men guard the academy. She despised the idea of soldiers stationed at every corner of the school. Until now, the school had remained untouched by the influence of modern human warfare.

But as their weapons grew in strength, Magic was becoming. . . breakable.

"They are already there," said Ambrose.

"German soldiers as well?"

Ambrose hesitated, but when he spoke it was with powerful ease. "All Magical Militia are under my command. Regardless of their human counterparts alliances."

He said it like it wasn't the first time.

Moon muttered something under his breath.

He was not alone in his fear. It was smart to be afraid. In war, hearts are fickle.

Hungry.

"Whatever you say, Ambrose," said Moon. "But I must ask. You refuse to have your soldiers here, refuse to reinforce your enchantments at your own home, but fought tooth and nail to have them at Vaukore."

"Maeve is at Vaukore."

"But she is here too."

"I am here."

And that was that. There was a light clapping sound, and then retreating footsteps across the echoing entryway.

"Eavesdropping?" Her father questioned.

Maeve shook her head and remained looking out over the lush gardens at Sinclair Estates. "Doesn't really count as eavesdropping if I was here first and you held your conversation on the other side of an open door."

She could feel his smile before she looked at him. He was already dressed for work. All black, which suited his silver-streaked dark hair, a high collar and a long black wool blazer. A small circular pin on his breast pocket indicated his status as the Premier.

Ambrose Sinclair oversaw the Magical Militia. Only the Orator, an elected official like her Father, held a higher rank in the Magical world.

A world hidden from humans. A world living in secret refuge on Earth. The Dread Lands were their true home.

"I'm going to miss you," he said, beaming at her.

He leaned casually on the bannister, folding his arms over his chest.

"Don't say that," replied Maeve as her cat, Spinel, rubbed against her legs.

Her father was arguably the only thing The Vaukore Academy lacked. Leaving him after such a divine summer was nearly unbearable.

"You'll probably miss that sunrise more," he teased.

She tilted her head to the side in disapproval. Ambrose's smile widened.

"Oh, please, plus jeune serre-livre," an affectionate name he used for her, "I know you are about to burst."

"Truthfully," she looked out over the garden, "yes."

Ambrose laughed knowingly. "Like father like daughter."

Maeve smiled and reached down to pet Spinel. "Perhaps because I'll be there all by myself for the first time without Arianna . . . I don't know. I just feel something. . . Different. A change in the wind. I felt it all summer."

"A Witches instinct is nearly never wrong."

Maeve's brows pulled together.

"At any rate," said Maeve, "I have to do something about my Alchemy score."

Ambrose groaned and rolled his eyes. "Still on that?"

"Wouldn't you be?"

"Not if I was already performing at an Elite level in Practical Magic," laughed Ambrose.

"I suppose," agreed Maeve after the nice reminder of her success in her favorite subject. "Still not a Supreme though."

A moment of silence fell between them. Then Ambrose spoke.

"Neither are most Magicals until they are nearing thirty."

Maeve ignored his rationale and asked:

"Do you really think your men are necessary at the school?"

Ambrose nodded. Just as he had each time she asked him about it since it had been voted on and signed into law.

"Do you think Kietel is truly assisting the humans in warfare?"

Ambrose hesitated. "He might be."

"What does that mean for you?" She asked.

Ambrose smiled softly at her concern for him. "It makes my job tricky. But it changes nothing. I don't want you using the Main Portals in London, Paris, or New York on the weekends," he said. "I'll escort you to school myself."

That was against the rules. Rules the Orator's Office made.

Maeve's eyes shot to him. "But I wanted to stop by Starlights in Paris and purchase that brooch I saw in the window the other day, before heading to school."

"You already have that," said Ambrose.

"No, I don't," said Maeve simply. "I have the brooch that matches Aunt Madrigold's pin, but not this pin. I know they do look similar."

"I know the difference," said Ambrose, smiling mischievously. "I am saying you already have that pin."

"Oh," sighed Maeve, realizing her father must have gone behind her back and purchased it.

"It's already packed for you."

Ambrose pushed off the balcony ledge and strode towards her. He tucked his hands behind his back and kissed the side of her head.

"Thank you. You didn't have to do that," said Maeve reaching for his hand.

"Have a wonderful term. Don't forget to write me."

He squeezed her hand three times.

"I wouldn't dream of it," she promised.

He pulled her out of the seat and guided her onto the clearing on the balcony. Spinel jumped into her arms, granting her a swift kiss on the nose.

Ambrose held out his right hand, palm flat. From it shot a bright white light that began circling up and down, creating an oval-shaped mass of Magic.

She dreaded the feeling to come, as she did each time she passed through a Portal. Ambrose was quite skilled at making them though, which enabled Maeve to pass through with ease.

Ambrose squeezed his daughter's hand tightly and nodded in confidence. He pulled her close, and together they stepped into the swirling blue and black void.

The blue iridescent light twisted into yellows and orange, growing deeper and deeper in shades of color until the red became violet.

The balcony behind them lagged and stretched out of vision as they moved off Earth and into a different realm. The colors before them swirled into a clear view of their destination.

Maeve didn't lose her footing as she stepped out of the Portal, but she ran her hands across her face and let out a shiver, shaking her hands slightly.

Spinel jumped from her arms and took off through the gates ahead.

Golden light flooded her eyes. She breathed deeply as they stepped out into the misty morning light of the mountain plains. The black gates of Vaukore were swung wide open, welcoming students back for the fall semester.

Before the war, everyone with the ability to create their own Portal to Vaukore was permitted to do so. Now, however, students arrived in droves through one giant Orator's Office-mandated Portal near the gates.

Magic was being disrupted, and Magical travel, which moved through time and space, was dangerous if Portals were not strong enough. Deadly even.

The massive Portal which students were excitedly filing through was held up by multiple Magical Militia. Her father's soldiers.

Bright golden S's on their breast pockets indicated their Supreme Magical status. Stronger than all the rest.

Ambrose took her shoulders and turned towards her.

"Their presence changes nothing," he said. "You study and practice just as last year."

She nodded. "I know."

Nodding at one another in understanding, he dropped his hands.

"Have a wonderful term, darling. I'll see you at Christmas."

Maeve smiled as she turned away from him, making her way to the gates. The Magical Militia didn't look or cast notice as she passed, but they knew Ambrose was there, and they all knew who Maeve was.

Headmaster Elgin stood at the gates adorned in a bright white pantsuit with a cape pinned at her shoulders. Casual and stylish clothes for a Witch. Her long, salt-and-pepper hair was slicked tightly back. She reassured a few new students who were huddled together warily, intending to ease their nerves amongst the upperclassmen.

For eleven years she had been one of the Headmasters of Vaukore, overseeing the Combative Magic program that prepared Magicals for the Bellator Sector. And for eleven years she greeted each student by name at the gates.

She smiled at Maeve as she passed. "Maeve. Where's Spinel?"

"Already hunting in the mountains I'm sure," answered Maeve with a soft smile.

The ancient Magic of Vaukore Academy shifted through her as she crossed the stone threshold past the gates. Inhaling the power deeply, she embraced the familiarity as it brushed up her leg with each step. It was solid, consistent and unyielding. Like the great stone mountains nestled around it, and the roaring waterfalls that fed the glassy lakes. Like the forest of giant trees with roots older than any Magic.

Past the gates were the stables, which held single horses, saddled and ready, and numerous horse-drawn carriages, for those students uncomfortable riding through the mountain terrain. She petted a dark black mare that bowed its head at her. Some of her silken mane was braided intricately with golden jewels and rings.

"Would you like to race?"

Maeve turned.

Malachite Peur stood gripping the reigns of a horse, his Vaukore Paragon badge shiny as ever on the lapel of his blazer. Below it was another badge of rank, showing his status as Champion of Duels. Maeve's own Paragon badge was identical to his. Symbols of their appointed positions and rank in the school.

"Must it always be a competition," she drawled as she mounted the black mare.

He was exquisi-

"Where my competition is concerned," he replied with a gorgeous, feline smile.

He was conceited. Nothing else.

"I'm honored you think of me as competition," said Maeve in a bored tone, "given that you have an absurdly high opinion of yourself."

The youngest Supreme in history. Of course he did.

His raven-colored hair fluttered in the morning breeze. Pushing a soft curl off his forehead and looking up at the castle in the distance, a soft smile pulled at the corners of his lips. Near his cheekbones.

Cheekbones that could cut a girl's heart right open-

Cheekbones that granted him anything he wanted.

She stared at him with a soft placating smile, but he merely smirked in satisfaction and mounted his horse.

"I'm sure you'll have plenty of opportunities to lose to me again this year," said Malachite.

Maeve rolled her eyes.

She didn't look back as she squeezed her legs together tightly, and the mare quickly began up the grassy dirt path. They broke the tree line quickly and Maeve smiled.

Vaukore Castle glowed like the gothic cathedrals she'd seen in France. Their dark, stone-pointed arches and stained-glass windows would invoke awe even from a human. But Vaukore, once the home of the first king of Magicals, was much more than stunning architecture.

Chapter 2

"Did you arrive in a private portal?"

Maeve looked up from her book. "What?"

"Everyone says you walked through your own portal with Uncle Ambrose."

"So what?"

"I had to come in with everyone else!"

Maeve returned to her reading. "You poor thing."

Abraxas Rosethorn snatched the book from view and tossed it onto the side table. Maeve frowned up at her cousin. His bright blonde hair was styled neatly back, his black blazer and pants were pressed with perfect seams. Abraxas had a pale boyish face, bright blue eyes, like all the Rosethorns, and the confidence of someone far beyond his years.

Spinel stretched in his sleep in her lap, curling his paws tightly across his face.

"We've been back not two hours and you're huddled in the corner of the library reading."

"I've already unpacked," said Maeve. "And I'm not huddled. This just happens to be my favorite armchair. Had to claim it early."

The Library at Vaukore was nearly a third of the castle. It held ancient knowledge from all Seven Realms, and information dating back thousands of years before Magicals fled to Earth.

Like most of the castle, it was made of grey stone and rich, mahogany wood. It had once belonged to King Primus, the long-dead ruler of all Magic. That was before the lines of Magic were broken. Before Dread Magic and Shadow Magic were at war with one another. Before the people of Aterna lost their Magic altogether.

Abraxas flipped open the book. "Is this Shakespeare? This looks terribly boring."

"What do you want, Brax?" Maeve whined.

"Just thought I'd say hello," said Abraxas, grinning.

"No you didn't," said Maeve.

Abraxas shrugged. "Perhaps I came to tell you that you should be writing detentions for a few new students just down the corridor, Miss Hall Monitor."

Maeve looked up, annoyed.

"Why, what are they doing? And don't call me that," she said.

Abraxas was slyly slipping away, her book in hand, but Maeve didn't protest. She'd read it many times and knew he'd secretly enjoy the contents.

"You'll just have to see," laughed Abraxas.

"Fine," she sighed, and set Spinel aside. "I'll see you at dinner."

Abraxas stopped and gave her a guilty look.

"What?" She scoffed. "Too busy with your chums to sit with me?

"I saw you all summer," he protested.

Maeve waved him off without another word.

She threw on her blazer and straightened the deep sapphire satin bow hanging down her blouse. She made her way down the fourth floor hall, checking each empty classroom for trouble.

"Slacking off, Sinclair."

Maeve backstepped as Malachite rounded the corner.

He placed his hands behind his back and examined her. His slender and tall frame was statuesque in the shadowed light from the candelabras.

"Not slacking. I just knew you'd have a handle on things," retorted Maeve, looking up at him sweetly.

He glanced down at her with a reproachful look, amused at her coy attempt to mock him.

Malachite, called Mal by those closest to him, was a fellow third-year student and top of their class. Top of the school truly. Even with her sister Arianna graduated from Vaukore, she was still in second place to Malachite. He shone in the spotlight.

He was a model pupil in Vaukore's Combative Magic mastery program.

The boys hung on his every word. The girls tried relentlessly, but his time with them was always short and quiet.

Private.

The way she would want it to-

The Professors and Instructors praised him just for breathing. But if she was honest with herself, which her bias prevented her from being, his scores and winning streaks earned him those accolades. But she wasn't honest with herself. She was convinced his good looks and charm were what sealed him first place.

Certainly not his status as the youngest Supreme in history.

Malachite gestured for her to walk beside him. They strolled down the corridor, Mal moving with a graceful ease that rivaled her own.

She hated that.

Her knee-length skirt swished as she kept stride with him.

"It's an honor to be a Paragon," he said. "Or have you forgotten the meaning of the word? You shouldn't disregard your duties." Malachite looked over at her. "I'm sure whatever book your nose was in can wait."

The corners of Maeve's lips turned down.

"I don't need a vocabulary lesson," she said with a placating grin.

Conceited prick.

"And how can you say that patrolling the halls and giving out petty demerits is more important than learning?"

"I didn't. I said it could wait," said Malachite matter-of-factly as he ran his long pale fingers through his raven hair.

"What were they up to anyway? Those students?" Maeve asked as they walked the hall together. "I know you sent Abraxas to find me and point out my slacking."

Mal frowned. "I did no such thing. I noted your absence. Your cousin rushed to find you. If you felt you were slacking, perhaps that's your own business."

They continued with their duties as Paragons, a prestigious title given to only the top-ranking students in Combative and Practical Magic studies. It was their job to ensure the customs and magical rules of Vaukore were upheld. Students from all across Earth attended Vaukore, not just Pureblood Magicals like Maeve.

Her black dress code approved sling back heels clicked across the floor as they walked mostly in silence. She fixed the collar of her black blazer, tossing her hair behind her shoulders.

They strolled the statue and painting lined halls, giving directions to confused first year students and reminding them of the Cauldron Ceremony later that evening. A few fresh faced students stared at the castle in amazement. Magic poured from every corner. Even the fire lights themselves burned with ancient magic.

The new students, freshly eighteen and wide-eyed, gaped at the enchanted castle. King Primus placed all his Magic in Vaukore before he died. Scenic murals felt real to the touch, some you could even enter and explore.

The brocade and scenic wallpapers even boasted the castle's magic. Butterflies glided across a field of wildflowers. Birds soared between treetops, singing their songs. There was even a pride of lions on the seventh floor, who strode along their paper world, never paying much attention to students.

Vaukore Castle's Magic was as alive as ever.

"Rumor has it The Premier escorted you to school himself, despite orders from the Orator's Office that all students use the main portal from London to travel to and from this realm."

"My father never was one for rules," said Maeve.

"A trait he passed to you."

Maeve smiled at what was meant to be a dig. "He's the Premier. He can do whatever he wants."

Mal nodded and spoke swiftly. "Must be incredible."

They reached the castle courtyard. Flowers grew in abundance there, like at Sinclair Estates. Maeve ran her fingers across the bright blooms. Green vines snaked their way along the side of the castle, climbing higher and higher against the stone to be closer to the sun. On either side of the shining archway into the valley were two Magical Militia.

She stood up straight.

Their silver attire perfectly pressed and fitted. Each of them bore that golden S. Maeve suspected each solder here would be a Supreme.

"If you told them to jump, would they?" Asked Mal lowly, no trace of jest in his voice.

"No," was all Maeve said. "I am not my father."

She may have been the Premier's daughter, but those Bellator answered to Ambrose Sinclair alone.

"That mark on your wrist means something though," he retorted.

Maeve didn't look at her wrist. Where three small pointed stars were Magically branded in black ink. Grouped together at the corner of her left wrist. A symbol of her Sinclair blood.

"All it means is that if something happens to me they are in a spot of bother." She smiled softly, thinking of her father.

Mal didn't laugh.

Chapter 3

In the Great Hall of Vaukore, named Hellming Hall, the Headmasters of Vaukore stood side by side, in complimentary black and silver velvet formal attire, stars and swirls of light shooting across the fabric. Headmaster Elgin smiled at the group of huddled new Magicals who eagerly awaited their course of study placement at Vaukore. Twenty years her junior, Headmaster Rowan's face was unreadable. That was the blank expression he wore most days. His dirty blonde hair swept his shoulders. He was Headmaster of Practical Magic studies, just as Elgin was Headmaster of Combative Magic studies.

A large black iron caldron sat on a stand before them, deep shades of green and sapphire smoke bubbled over its edge and slunk to the floor of Hellming Hall like silk.

The ancient Magic of Vaukore resonated off that holy cauldron, which held too much power over the state of young minds. There were two areas of Magic mastery at Vaukore: Combative and Practical. The cauldron's choice to place her in academic studies rather than combative had nearly wrecked her two years ago.

Carved in stone above the Headmasters was Filii Magicae Numquam Soli.

Children of Magic Are Never Alone.

The vow by King Primus that all Magical beings were welcome there, and a modern reminder to students.

Behind the Headmasters were three massive stained glass windows that represented Vaukore and the original Magical Courts of King Primus: Dread, Shadow, and Aterna. Each window vaulted upwards, coming together at a sharp point. At the center, a mix of grays and blacks and white depicted the silhouette of the castle, surrounded by clouds and a starry night sky. It was a small, but beautiful realm, after all.

Maeve stared at the stunning emerald green stained glass of the far window and the serpent that ran through it, its fangs proudly poised to kill, which represented Dread Magic.

The window for Shadow Magic was comprised of sapphire panes scattered to create a burst of light, and on either side, two bright white feathered wings spread mightily open.

The center window rose high into the vaulted ceiling. The symbol of Aterna Magic was the dragon. The violet and amethyst creature had its wings tucked tightly, a long tail snaking around its body and its head held proudly high.

The three courts of King Primus were long gone, just as Shadow Magic and the people of Aterna's ability to create Magic was.

Maeve had been devastated when she was chosen to become a master in academia, and not become a fighter like her father and her ancestors before her. She glanced over to where Abraxas sat. His tie hung loosely around his neck. Malachite next to him smirked at something he said. Her cousin practically worshiped Malachite, a fact which Maeve despised.

One by one, the new students reached their shaking, excited, and nervous hands into the cauldron. The swirling smoke would designate their placement as it changed to one single color. Some took longer than others. Some barely had to dip a finger in for their results.

Maeve had merely laid a hand on the brim of the cauldron for its decision. Sapphire blue swirls of night cascaded to her feet as panic flooded her skin.

She cried when she was placed in Practical Magic studies, terrified of losing her father's affection. Though, to anyone that knew the brilliant Ambrose Sinclair, they knew he was secretly elated and not at all surprised when his youngest daughter wound up breezing through her studies in academia.

Some Sinclair secrets run old.

A strawberry blonde-haired boy's eyes grew wide as his smoke turned bright green: Combative Magic.

The lining of his dark blazer and the hemline of his pants now had a dark green thread line running through them. He gave Headmaster Rowan and Elgin a respectful nod and suppressed his smile.

Maeve's Father, who taught briefly Vaukore before his time training the Bellator, the Supremes that made up the Magical Militia and Law, and eventually commanding them, told her that the

Cauldron's Magic was not concerned with our worldly labels, but rather with the Magic inside each student that waited patiently to be explored. Magic most freshly eighteen-year-olds were far from aware of.

Ambrose said that thousands of years ago, in the dawn of Magic, the ancient Magic of that Cauldron had been used by King Primus himself to place Magicals in their respective places in his kingdom.

After all the new students were placed, dinner was served. Tradition stated that the old King's feast included all of his courts and lasted long into the witching hour. Unfortunately for the students of Vaukore, curfew was ten o'clock.

Maeve assisted The Head Girl in guiding the twenty-one students placed in Practical Magic back to their dorm on the east wing of the castle.

"Right," said Lavinia Roberts rounding on them. "I'm Head Girl of the whole school." Her Irish accent was thick and musical. Maeve enjoyed Lavinia much more than her Head Girl from primary school. "Maeve is a Paragon of Academics. You'll all be taking Latin, but for a quick lesson: a Paragon is a model of excellence." Lavinia smiled. "Which means we're in charge." Lavinia held her hands up. "Yes, there is a Head Boy. No, you do not have to listen to him. There are also a handful of other Paragons." She paused and scrunched her nose. "Only one of them you'll want to listen to, but oh well."

Maeve suppressed a smile and shook her head. Even Lavinia wasn't immune to Malachite's natural power.

"I'll let Maeve take the lead. She knows a lot of useless information about the castle."

Maeve frowned. Lavinia grinned and gestured ahead. She ignored her comment and told the new students all about the castle's history, the Magicals that once inhabited Vaukore's realm, and even stopped to talk about some of her favorite paintings and tapestries.

Most of their faces were wonderstruck. She reminded herself that most of them didn't grow up with Magic like this. Simple Magic maybe. But not like Vaukore. Not like Sinclair Estates.

"Hello, Maeve."

A short blonde girl stepped towards her and extended her hand. Maeve shook it.

"You got in," said Maeve.

"Just as you said I would."

The girl smiled.

"Good," said Maeve. "And congrats on beginning your journey in academia."

"Practical Magic studies," she said happily. "In Primary School, you spoke so hopefully that you'd get to train in dueling and fighting."

Her words slammed into Maeve. She hadn't meant them as an insult, but they hurt all the same.

"I was."

The girl's smile faltered slightly. "I'm sorry-"

Maeve held up her hand and recited the speech she had perfected about not caring that she was the first Sinclair since Merlin who was not placed in Vaukore's school of Combative Magic. That she looked better in a blazer with pale blue stitching than emerald green anyway. That she hadn't cried at all her first night at Vaukore.

Maeve's schedule was as planned: jam-packed with every class possible. First thing in the morning was Alchemy with Professor Hummingdor. Which was perfect, seeing as Maeve wanted to ask him about extra lessons as soon as possible. Fear of losing her status as a Paragon of Academics fueled her desire to speak with him.

She made her way down from her dorm room into a gorgeously ornate part of the castle filled with books, white marble statues, and sapphire blue velvet furniture with gold trim. Maeve's own chambers at Sinclair Estates had been modeled after it. The lavish rugs and velvet embroidered material suited her style.

The dorms for the Practical Magic students sat in the East Wing, and it was Maeve's favorite part of Vaukore Castle.

And it was the closest to the Library.

"Good summer, Maeve?" Lavinia Roberts asked.

Lavinia was one of two Head students, known for their vigor and sense of responsibility. The Head Boy and Girl held the highest rank of students at Vaukore, and were handpicked by the Headmasters in their final and fourth year at Vaukore. Lavinia was also Captain of the Vaukore Chess Club and Magical Fencing Club, and considered herself personally responsible for her team having won the past two fencing tournaments at school.

"Fine. And yourself?"

"Spent most of it at a fencing camp in Ireland. Gonna be a good year," said Lavinia intensely, as her fist met her palm. "Right. Babies, listen up!"

Lavinia explained to the new students that as students in her program she better not hear about any of them sticking a toe out of line. Maeve smiled as she warned them that Maeve, being a Paragon herself, thoroughly enjoyed writing detentions for misconduct and wouldn't hesitate to write any one of them a week's worth.

That was true.

Lavinia quickly explained that the entrance to the dormitories at Vaukore were enchanted to ensure their studies were being properly absorbed. The correct answer to an educational question was required to gain entry, and the castle was always kind enough to provide helpful hints to expand the mind. A bit of light reading was required if one didn't know the answer or had fallen asleep in class and missed the lecture.

Maeve laughed softly at their apprehensive expressions and made her way down from the East Wing and into the main castle. She preferred her dorm's means of entry more so than that of the combat students. They were forced to duel and best an enchanted knight from King Primus' reign. The castle was kind to them as well. Sir Knoble was humble and helpful in his own defeat, should a student struggle with their duel.

Professor Hummingdoor was as bright and bubbly as ever, and excited to see all his favorites, bouncing on his toes from one to the next. Maeve rolled her eyes as he shook Mal's hand for well over a minute. Maeve was included amongst Hummingdoor's favorites, but everyone knew the Potions and Alchemy Professor fancied his pupil Mal the most.

The Alchemy Chamber was lined with a dense haze of smoke early that morning, as Maeve batted her way to the workstation.

There was no time wasted. The class got straight to work on brewing a set of Shrinking and Enlarging Potions. They worked silently for the entirety of the class. Despite being placed in an area of study, all students received basic Magical training across many subjects.

On her way to the supply closet to retrieve more bat fangs, she passed by Malachite, who was working calmly over his perfect looking potion.

Once finished, Maeve's potion awarded her a strained smile from Hummingdoor with encouragement to do better. Mal was awarded a grand clap on the shoulder. He was perhaps the only combat student with higher academic marks than the Practical Magic students. The last few students were exiting the classroom as Maeve made her way to Hummingdoor's desk.

"Professor, may I have a moment?"

"Of course, Miss Sinclair! Trust you had a good summer?"

"Always. Though, glad to be back at Vaukore, Sir," said Maeve with a smile.

He smiled back, as though he understood the sentiment completely.

"So," started Hummingdoor. "Is it safe to assume you are not satisfied with your Alchemy grade in last term's exams?"

"Correct," said Maeve, her voice businesslike.

"Also safe to assume you're looking to be tutored in preparation for your final exams?" The Professor spoke as though he was solving some great mystery, and was rather proud of himself for solving it.

"Also correct. I've never had to be tutored in anything, Professor. I have to admit, it feels a bit embarrassing just having this conversation."

"That's nonsense!" He laughed heartily as he rearranged random papers on his desk, "With a little guidance you'll be performing better in no time."

Maeve smiled slightly. "Thank you, sir."

"See? Not so grim as you make it." He squinted.

"I suppose so," said Maeve. She gathered her bag and started to stand, prepared to ask Hummingdoor when their lessons would begin.

"Marvelous," said Hummingdoor. "I'll talk to Mr. Peur myself."

Maeve's heart stopped as she clutched her bag tightly. "I'm sorry?"

"Malachite. I'll talk to Mr. Peur-"

"No sir, I heard you," began Maeve. "I just meant. . . does it have to be him?"

Hummingdoor laughed loudly, the sound bubbling out of him. It did not comfort Maeve.

"Pride is a dangerous emotion, Miss Sinclair. And not of an academically inclined mind at all." He smiled wisely and stood at his desk, leaning over as though he was about to tell her a secret. "He's the best in class, best in the school really. Tutors many others as well! Seems like the right choice, hmm? You begin tonight, yes?" He raised a finger in the air. "No time such as the present!"

He turned his back and began rummaging through some drawers.

With a heavy sigh, Maeve took her cue to leave.

The rest of her classes were as expected. In Healing Class, Violet Bentson hounded Maeve about why she was in bed so early last night and how she was never any fun anymore.

"I have plenty of fun," said Maeve.

"No," said Violet, her voice sharp. "All you care about is school now. I didn't see you all summer, and you went straight to bed last night!"

Maeve pretended to be intensely reading a section of her textbook to avoid conversing with Violet.

"And it's not like I get invited to see you over the summers, as if your family's mansion doesn't have guest quarters. . ." she continued babbling, but Maeve's thoughts were elsewhere. She was too busy dreading having Malachite tutor her.

At seven o'clock sharp, Maeve waited in the far corner of the library, drumming her fingers on the table. She resented Professor Hummingdoor for forcing Malachite upon her.

Mal arrived not a minute late. Maeve watched him stride between two tall bookshelves towards her. His dark hair was pushed back, perfectly in place.

"Good evening, Sinclair," said Mal, politely.

"I asked for anyone but you."

"There's no one better than me," he said without bothering to look at her.

Maeve watched him set out his parchment and books.

"Wonderful," she said with a slight grimace.

"It is true you performed on an Elite level for Charms last year? That is, to say, beyond a fourth-year level as just a second-year student?" Asked Mal without missing a beat.

"Yes," replied Maeve, lazily.

"And that you spent the summer working on the Committee of Experimental Charms at the Orator's Office?"

Maeve paused for a moment.

"Yes," she answered hesitantly, surprised by his questions. No one outside of the school Professors, and a few jealous and nosey students, knew about that.

"Because you created a new memory charm last term? With Headmaster Rowan?"

"Rowan can barely take credit for that and I'm sorry, I didn't realize I had a biography published," laughed Maeve.

Malachite's famously charming smile appeared. His silence told her he wasn't continuing without an answer.

"Yes," said Maeve, laying into her answer. She opened her Alchemy book.

"I'm sure Rowan made sure you had that opportunity at The Orator's Office then," said Mal, turning the pages of his potions book as his smile faded.

Maeve picked up on a change in his tone.

"Actually," she started, "my father did. He's very close to Orator Moon. Being the Premier and all."

"Now you're bragging," smirked Mal.

"Wouldn't you?"

His face hardened. Maeve immediately knew she had stuck a nerve. Mal didn't have parents to brag about. Likely sensing she was about to apologize, Mal spoke before she had the chance.

"Well, according to your Alchemy scores you have nothing to brag about. Let's get started, shall we?"

Maeve didn't object.

The next morning at breakfast, while reading her first edition of "A Witches Guide to a Modern World" by Evelyn Starbound (a gift from her father) when a flash of bright blonde hair appeared by her side.

"So," began the musical voice that belonged to none other than Abraxas, "am I to understand that the one and only Maeve Sinclair has actually stooped to being tutored?"

He gave a dramatic shiver.

"Shut up, Mr. Rosethorn," said Maeve plainly, taking a bite of her toast.

"Oh, resorting to formalities. You do know how to wound me."

Maeve smiled at him from the corner of her eye.

Abraxas had been her friend since they were children. In fact, Maeve couldn't remember a time that they hadn't gotten along perfectly. This was partly due to Abraxas being Maeve's cousin, as her Mother, Clarissa, was a former Rosethorn. Abraxas had been just as sour as Maeve when she wound up in a different area of study. In fact, all of Maeve's childhood friends were placed in Combative Magic.

Maeve, Abraxas, and a number of other students at Vaukore, belonged to the Sacred Seventeen, which were the only pureblooded Magical families left on record. Three centuries ago forty-nine Magical dynasties fled to Earth for protection from their home realm. Now only seventeen remained. And their Magic had seeped into this new world, presenting an entire new generation of Magical bloodlines.

"How did you know?" Maeve asked.

"Oh, well I personally knew you'd be desperate-"

Maeve shot him a glare.

"-when you scored anything other than perfect on your Alchemy exam," said Abraxas. "However. . ." Abraxas pulled his lips together tightly. "Mal was quite pleased to see you, the second best- those are his words not mine!" Abraxas was practically giddy as he continued, "to see you, needing his help."

Maeve closed her eyes in frustration.

"Bet Arianna would have a hay-day with such juicy information," said Abraxas quickly.

Maeve grabbed her book and smacked him on the arm, laughing. Her older and very successful sister would love any blow she could give Maeve.

"Don't you dare!" She gasped.

Maeve and Abraxas walked together to Summoning and Enchanting, where Professor Harquinton was already seated behind her desk. She wore a very stylish pantsuit, which Maeve recognized from a store called Witch's Wears in London.

"Ms. Sinclair, Mr. Rosethorn," said Harquinton curtly as they took seats next to one another.

"Good summer, Professor?" Asked Abraxas.

Harquinton gave Abraxas a small nod and greeted two other students who entered the room. Maeve's mind drifted back to the nauseating idea that Malachite Peur was gloating her failures to all of the school.

She glowered at him as he entered the room a moment later. Mal didn't even look their way, he was too busy enchanting Professor Harquinton.

"He's so full of himself," whispered Maeve.

"So are you," said Abraxas.

She frowned at this, but found it difficult to argue. Professor Harquinton didn't hesitate to begin preparing the class for the "next hurdle in their Magical career journey." Final Exams were still two years away, but the time to prepare was now.

It seemed every other Professor shared Harquinton's sentiment. By the weekend Maeve already knew she'd be spending every second of it in the library. Her scheduled tutoring with Mal was set for Saturday morning and needed a few hours dedicated to it alone.

When their Charms Magic class came, Headmaster Rowan sat behind his desk in a black and silver velvet suit. His feet were propped on the luxurious wooden desk, exposing his silver boots.

"Maeve," he said without a smile. "Wonderful to see you. How did the summer go?"

"It was good," shrugged Maeve. "Although, I don't much care for the Orator's Office as a whole."

Rowan nearly chuckled. "I cannot fault you there. Government suited me about the same. Did you meet Daniel Rodríguez?"

Maeve nodded. "I did."

"He seemed eager to meet you after I told him about your memory charm abilities."

"He didn't believe I could withstand a collapsing memory, Sir," said Maeve. "And still come out with the truth."

"I trust you proved him wrong," said Rowan solemnly.

"Of course, Sir," said Maeve, careful to hide her pride.

Rowan didn't respond well to arrogant and cocky students.

He gave her a militant-like nod and motioned her toward her seat.

In Worldly Studies, which was Maeve's least favorite subject currently, they had a long discussion about the current Human War. She got enough of those lessons from her Father. The Magical World stayed out of such affairs for the most part, but this war was different. There were rumors that many Magical and Immortal families felt it was the Magical's duty to extend a hand. But Politics and relations with the Human Government were tricky, as her Father ceaselessly reminded her. Nevertheless, the Magicals were intertwined in the war. And the Immortals, tucked realms away were absent.

"Has anyone found Kietel?"

Maeve's eyes moved slowly to the student who had spoken.

"The allegations that Kietel has played a role in aiding the German human army in their civilian attacks is purely speculation," said Professor Wadsworth. "Now, on with today's lesson."

Maeve knew that was a lie. The truth wasn't public knowledge, and the Magical papers like the Magical Times, which were considered the most reputable by the Double O, sure as hell wasn't going to print in the papers that a Supreme Magical had gone rogue, much less one from their own office.

That weekend, early in the morning, Maeve headed to The Wings, a letter to her father in hand. He would be wanting to know the arrangements she had made to remedy her Alchemy problem, though she decidedly left out that the plan included a handsome young boy. Arguably the most handsome one at school.

Her father had nearly fainted over the summer when she waltzed "a little too closely" at a party with Alphard Mavros, so she felt it best not to perpetuate any anxiety he might have.

She reached the base of the winding spiral staircase to what was once a tower full of owls, ravens, and hawks. Before the invention of the Letter Desk Charm, Magicals strictly corresponded through birds, or "on the wings," a phrase which remained despite the modern use of a writing desk.

At the top of the tower were a few ravens and a brown barn owl. They perched on small carved archways of all sizes that stretched high into the tower. Now most of those archways sat empty, and The Wings were filled with chestnuts stained writing desks.

Though, Magical Letter Desks were still a luxury, and many Magicals still used winged beings to correspond. Her Grandmother Agatha refused to retire her beloved birds.

Maeve placed the letter to her father on one of them. It disappeared with a POP, and realms away at Sinclair Estates appeared on her father's own writing desk.

Malachite was unsurprisingly on time for their tutoring lesson, holding open the door to the library for her. Once they were seated in Maeve's preferred corner, they began working quickly. After about an hour of nothing but Alchemy theory, Mal veered off topic.

"In terms of your Charms work, I'd like to ask you something."

"Sure." Maeve withdrew from her parchment.

"Was it a memory renewal charm?"

Maeve smiled. If there was one thing she would talk freely about, it was this.

Mal continued. "The article published in The Starlight Gazette didn't specify. And I can't help but notice there are no such credible charms."

"An astute observation," she commended him. "But no."

"Have you considered how useful such a charm could be?"

"I have. Though, I'll admit I am much more interested in false memories and how to break them… how to make them."

"And that's what you did for The Orator's Office this summer?"

Maeve nodded, proudly. Mal retreated into his own thoughts for a moment.

Maeve brought him back to reality when she spoke. "Are you in need of a memory renewal?"

"No," said Mal sweetly. "Does the Orator's Office know you can jump through minds?"

"Yes," said Maeve.

His brows pulled together. "Did you work on that this summer as well?"

"I-" she started, and then hesitated, remembering that her father had been against her demonstrating her ability to The Orator's Office.

Mal's brows flicked up. Maeve sighed.

"I did, yes," she answered finally.

"How does it work?"

"It's not entirely clear to me," she said. "It's like a door opens, and I just have to walk through."

Mal shook his head slightly.

"You don't believe that I can do it?" She asked.

"No," he said. "I'm certain you can."

"So what is it?"

He looked out the dark starlight-flecked window. "It's impressive. No one else has that ability."

Maeve's mouth fell open, a small laugh escaped her lips. "Was that a compliment?"

Mal's eyes slid back to hers. The corner of his mouth turned slightly up.

"Primus and the Gods," said Maeve. "I almost can't believe it."

"Enough," he drawled. "I want to see."

Maeve hesitated. "Alright."

"I'll arrange it," he said matter-of-factly.

They abandoned all talk of her exclusive abilities and returned to the lesson at hand. After another hour, Mal decided that would do for the day, and left her to the homework for her other subjects. As expected, she spent the remainder of her day in the Library.

As much as Maeve Sinclair hated to admit it, her lessons from Malachite were rapidly paying off. In only a few weeks, Professor Hummingdoor had noticed, and much to her dismay had applauded Mal in front of numerous students, for her improvements.

She received a letter from her father, stating how proud he was that she had found a solution. Also included in his reply was a stunning sapphire ring. Engraved on the band was the Sinclair Family Motto: usque ad mortem.

The ring had granted her an exaggerated eye roll from Abraxas and a comment about being spoiled, which Maeve chose not to hear.

Chapter 4

It quickly became colder on Vaukore Island, where all four seasons didn't exist, but the island's ancient Magic allowed them to experience them all the same on the tiny planet.

The first light snow had come, sprinkling the ground with shiny flecks of white, but inside the castle by a crackling fire, Mal and Maeve were perfectly warm.

On one of the desks was a copy of The Starlight Gazette someone left behind. The front page read:

GERMANY BOMBS MORE HUMAN CITIES AS THE WAR CONTINUES . KIETEL UNACCOUNTED FOR, SOURCE CLOSE TO THE DOUBLE O SAYS HE HAS ABANDONED HIS POST AS CAPTAIN UNDER PREMIER SINCLAIR

Maeve glanced at the headline, her stomach sinking.

"Will you be participating in the first duel tomorrow night?" Mal asked Maeve, bringing her out of her thoughts.

"Oh, no," said Maeve. "That's not exactly my thing."

"Have you ever dueled before?"

"Plenty. I grew up with it. It's just. . . not my thing."

Mal scrunched his face. "That's odd."

Maeve shrugged. "I was placed in Practical Magic studies, in case you've forgotten."

"Plenty of academic focused students participate in the duels."

"Well, I don't."

"No," said Mal cooly. "Don't shrug it off. I want to know why."

His eyes were fixed on her. They were dark as the sky between stars.

Maeve sighed. "I don't know why."

Mal was quiet, clearly thinking. "I think I do."

Maeve raised her eyebrows.

Mal continued. "I think you aren't good at it, and that's why you don't like it."

Maeve couldn't help but laugh at the accuracy with which Mal had just called her out.

"Tell me I'm wrong," he smirked.

"You're not wrong," relented Maeve.

"Your sister, Arianna, she was very good. I take it you never beat her at home?"

Maeve laughed again. "She loves to torture me come dueling time."

Mal ran his fingers through his hair and relaxed back in his chair. "That is very interesting."

"Can we go back to studying, please?" Maeve pulled her book towards her. Mal whisked it away.

"You grew up dueling and you've never won? Not once?"

"Why is this so important to you?"

"Because you're a better Witch than your sister, in every regard imaginable. I cannot fathom how someone so good at charms and spellcasting wouldn't be an amazing fighter."

Maeve's cheeks flushed hot. Malachite had bestowed her many compliments in the past, but they were always laced with some degree of mocking. He spoke genuinely now. Mal's stare was intense as Maeve regained her composure.

Mal's voice quieted. "I suppose I'm curious how that came to be. Surely your father has tried to teach you?"

Maeve smiled softly, "many times."

Mal's head cocked to the side. "And?"

"And," said Maeve, becoming annoyed, "something doesn't click."

"Hmm," said Mal. "How old were you when you started dueling?"

"Oh, for as long as I can remember."

"Arianna is, what, two years your senior?"

Maeve nodded.

"Still, that's enough for her to have quite the leg up on you as children. And if the cycle never broke. . . "

Maeve remained silent. Mal studied her response.

"You don't speak of your mother," said Mal, matter of factly.

Maeve's face hardened.

"There it is," whispered Mal.

Maeve smiled the soft smile she was best at, the smile she presented day in and day out as the face of the Sinclair name was on her shoulders. She learned this smile at a young age, when she learned all the etiquette expected from a Pureblooded Magical child.

"My sister has always held my mother's favor," said Maeve, kindly.

"But you hold your father's."

"That doesn't win duels. There's no power in favor."

Mal smiled at this like he admired her way of thinking. "I could teach you if you wanted. I've seen you fence, you move well on your feet. Dueling is not much different."

"Teach me?"

"How to fight."

"How to duel you mean?"

Mal shrugged, "however you want to name it."

Maeve contemplated him for a moment, her eyebrows drawn slightly together. She had seen Mal win many magical duels throughout their time at Vaukore. Even at a young age, he bested those much older than him.

"I think I will stick to what I am already good at, and perfect that," she whispered, pulling her textbook back from him.

When the two of them said goodnight, Maeve made her way to The East Wing of the castle, eager to crash into her comfy dorm room bed.

"Oh, thank Heavens," gasped a pair of girls as she strode towards the door.

The pair of them jumped to their feet, slamming close the book that had previously been in their lap.

"Have you read this?" Asked the blonde one, as she shoved the cover in Maeve's face.

"Yes," said Maeve with a laugh.

"I knew you would have," said her friend. "I just said maybe Maeve will be back soon from her tutoring lessons with Malachite."

Maeve grimaced. "Does everyone know about that?"

The girls exchanged an incredulous look. "Everyone is talking about it," they said in unison.

Maeve walked around them. "What exactly is there to talk about?"

"That if you are struggling to pass Alchemy we're all doomed."

"How do you get any work done around him?" Laughed the blonde as her cheeks flushed.

"Gods," muttered Maeve.

As she approached the ornate arched ivory double doors, a golden inscription was spread across the doorway.

"Here," said the blonde, handing her the book.

"I don't need that," said Maeve. "The answer is Year 604. Prince Danin."

The ivory doors clicked open and the inscription faded. The book vanished from the girl's hands with a swift howling of the wind.

Maeve slipped quickly between the double doors and grabbed each knob in her hands.

"Just for being so nosy," said Maeve with a smile.

The girls' mouths hung open wide as Maeve slammed the ivory doors quickly, locking them out in the corridor, forced to answer a different and new question without her help.

"That's cruel," said Lavinia, who was sprawled across an armchair with a book held high. "They've been out there moaning for twenty minutes."

"They're such babies," said Maeve. "Academia or pleasure?" She asked, nodding to the book Lavinia held high above her head.

She looked over at Maeve with a wicked grin. "Pleasure."

"Goodnight," said Maeve quickly, making her way towards the girl's dorm rooms.

Lavinia shot up and smiled widely at Maeve.

"You're denying yourself a good time, Sinclair."

"Reading is to stimulate the mind-"

"Oh there is plenty of stimulation-"

Maeve turned back towards her, suppressing a smile.

"See," said Lavinia. "You know you want to try."

Maeve watched her for a moment. She thought about how Abraxas would never let her hear the end of it if she started reading Lavinia's erotic novels. Spinel appeared from the shadows of the room and gave her a few chirp like meows. He stretched deeply with a wide mouth yawn.

"Goodnight," said Maeve once more.

Lavinia shook her head and laid out across the chair once more. "Your loss."

Spinel followed her up to her dormitory. Within minutes she was asleep, Spinel curled up beside her.

The next day the castle was buzzing with excitement for the return of The Dueling Club. Tonight was the first duel of the year. The duels always pulled a crowd. Maeve rarely attended. But maybe tonight was different.

There was no doubt Mal would best anyone who stepped up, as he had been undefeated since his first duel at school.

"Maeve?"

A faint voice brought her out of her thoughts and back into Healing Class, an elective she had postponed taking until now. To her left, Violet's eyebrows were raised and she was waving a hand in her face. "Have you heard anything I've said?"

Maeve batted her hand away. "No. Sorry."

The rest of the class was practicing their nonverbal spells, something Maeve had mastered last year.

Violet rolled her eyes. "I asked if you were going on the trip this weekend. Because rumor has it that Velvetina's has some gorgeous new winter wear."

"Oh. I should probably study," she said, thinking about her father's clear aversion to the main Portals.

Violet's head flung backward as she closed her eyes in frustration.

Maeve chuckled lightly."Fine. I wouldn't mind a pretty new coat."

She'd have to write him and finagle getting permission.

Violet exhaled and raised her hand to practice. "Thank you."

Maeve watched a student struggle to produce a healing spell silently as she drifted into her thoughts.

She could honestly use a day off just to have fun. Now that she was performing better in Alchemy, there was much less for her to stress over.

The only portal still available for students to use on weekends was the one to London, and the Headmasters had ensured them it was safe and guarded. Maeve much preferred the Magical shops in Paris, but London had a fine array too.

Last year, she and Abraxas managed to get banned from one shop in Paris. Something about "snobby British children."

"I won't be setting foot through that portal," said Harriet Simms from behind them.

"Good thing no one asked you," snapped Violet.

Harriet glowered at her, fixed her Combative Magic pin as though it meant something, which it did, and returned to her work.

After class, Maeve set out to find Mal. She knew he'd be leaving Combat Dueling class and waited for him in the main corridor. She spotted him rather quickly.

"Malachite," said Maeve as she reached out and touched his arm to gather his attention. "May I have a short word?"

His eyes lingered on her hand. She dropped it at once and stepped away from him. His eyes found hers, and he nodded for them to move over.

They pushed through the swarm of students heading for their various dorms and rounded a corner out of the traffic.

"Firstly," she began, "I just want to thank you for helping me with Alchemy, I know I was difficult at first."

He attempted to hide a small smirk at her admitting her own arrogance, but Maeve knew he was all too pleased with himself regardless.

"Secondly, I'm going to London this weekend so I won't be meeting to study."

Students continued passing by them in the main hallway laughing loudly.

"Thank you for letting me know," said Mal, his voice businesslike.

Maeve nodded and noticed his expression shift.

"Thirdly, good luck tonight," said Maeve, backing away. "Not that you need it."

Mal smiled softly in agreement. Maeve turned on her heel and headed to Hellming Hall.

Dinner was filled with whispers of bets for the duels. Betting was strictly illegal at Vaukore, though no Professor truly enforced this. Professor Larliesl, who sponsored The Dueling Club, usually pretended he had no idea the betting was even taking place.

Maeve ate her dinner alone, which was mostly how she preferred it. There was much more time to read and contemplate that way.

After much thought, she decided she would make an uncommon appearance at the duels.

"Did you hear a first year boy challenged a fourth year? He's got to be mental." Maeve overheard a young student say as she made her way to the Dueling Hall.

The large hall was once an amphitheater, now stage to all dueling activities at Vaukore. Layers of seating circled around the painted wood floors.

"Maeve!" Abraxas called from one corner of the room, motioning her over.

Maeve made her way through the large crowd of students, over to a group she knew quite well.

"Hi, Maeve," said Iris Astoria, a Witch who was younger than Maeve.

The Astoria family, like the Sinclair family, was a bloodline of Sacred Seventeen. Six of the Sacred families had Pureblood Magicals in school at Vaukore with Maeve. They were among the seventeen families left with only Magicals in their lines and lineages. The Magical world on Earth was now a mixture of Humans, Elves, and Magicals. The Sacred Seventeen, however, did not marry or reproduce outside of those seventeen families, as was their duty designated by the Committee of the Sacred.

Maeve took a seat in an oversized armchair, crossing her legs.

"Would you like to place any bets?" Abraxas asked Maeve, in an affected voice.

"Absolutely," said Maeve leaning over to look at the dueling sign-up list.

"Fawley is fighting Avery?" She whispered, glancing over towards Fawley.

Hendrix Fawley was a senior at Vaukore, in his fourth year. He and Maeve were two of the few Sacred Seventeen members in history to be placed in academia. A fact which they commiserated on many occasions. Fawley's family didn't take it as well as Maeve's did. The morning after he was placed his parents came bursting through the front gates of the school demanding to speak with Headmasters Elgin and Rowan.

"I'd put money on Avery, sadly," laughed Thormund Prewett.

"I dunno," said Mervyn Roswyn. "The stakes are high for Fawley."

"But Mal's really been laying into Avery lately, telling him he's got to progress," said Phineas.

"I'll bet on Fawley," said Maeve plainly.

"What?" Said Phineas, shocked.

Maeve shrugged. "You didn't see him this summer in his duel. He's gotten pretty good and we all know I think Avery is a wuss."

"I'm with Maeve," said Abraxas. "Especially about the wuss part."

They reviewed the rest of the sheet and discussed their projected winners. There were few others Maeve was willing to bet on. Abraxas bet on every single duel, even the first years.

Mal emerged from the crowd and made his way towards them. His eyes found Maeve, but his cool expression never faltered. He was dressed casually with no school blazer or badges of rank in sight.

"Evening, Sinclair. I wasn't expecting to see you here," he said, collected as always.

"What else is there to do on a Tuesday night?" Maeve said cooly.

"Read the same book for the millionth time?" Abraxas snorted.

Maeve smirked playfully and shot him a look as the rest laughed.

"I have no idea what you're laughing about, Roswyn," said Maeve. "Based on your Alchemy test I saw the other day you could stand to read at least one book."

"Oooh," said Abraxas, covering his mouth and grinning ear to ear. Roswyn scowled at her and turned away.

Presley Barton, who played on the fencing team, came around and took their bets.

"Fawley? Yikes," said Presley, shaking her head.

There were a few laughs.

"Maeve," said Presley, "We thought for sure you'd end up at try-outs finally this year. Everyone says your brother was the best fencing captain Vaukore ever had."

A cold sensation filled Maeve's stomach at the mention of Antony Sinclair.

"Hurry up Barton," said Lavinia Roberts. She seemed to appear from nowhere. "We can't start until you've taken all the bloody bets."

She pushed Presley along.

The group of students, and Lavinia, knew better than to make any comment, but their sudden silence spoke volumes about the uncomfortableness of the situation. Maeve was admittedly grateful for Lavinia's quick action and change of conversation topic.

Lavinia pulled up a seat next to Maeve, offering her a bar of chocolate, which Maeve happily accepted. Lavinia also had a large bag of sweets which was getting passed around.

Professor Larliesl made his way atop the dueling stage and urged them all to quiet down. He was a broad shouldered half Magical half Elvish man with tawny blonde hair braided down to his waist. His ears were pointed at the tips. Once a member of the Magical Militia, Larliesl was now a retired educator and Master of Duels at Vaukore.

"Welcome to another year of duels!" Larliesl clapped his hands excitedly. "The customs are the same and I trust you all know them, if not best of luck. Tonight we'll start with our newcomers and make our way up to the undefeated third year Paragon of Combat: Malachite Peur!"

There were a few hollers of praise and clapping among the students. Maeve rolled her eyes and suppressed a smile as Abraxas whistled loudly. Mal was undeniably well liked.

"Let's begin!" Shouted Larliesl.

Two first years took the stage timidly. With much encouragement from Larliesl, they did well.

As the night went on, and the skill level rose, the duels became more grand. Lavinia was very impressive against Randolf Grisham, a senior boy who, rumor had it, was always talking down to specifically the girls in his classes. The two bested each other at the same time, calling for a draw.

Avery didn't disappoint, losing to Fawley, and earning Maeve twenty rubies. She pocketed them happily. Fawley had a very strong Deterioration Hex that slowed Avery down completely.

Larliesl had even asked for Fawley to demonstrate the Hex once more on his next opponent.

"For educational purposes of course," said Larliesl.

Mal praised Fawley as he walked by and Avery sulked.

Finally, it was Mal's turn. He took his place opposite Phineas, who was his first opponent of the night. Their duel was impressive. Maeve could see that Phineas had been working hard over the summer. Though, she suspected that Mal was going rather easy on him, observing his progress.

When it seemed Mal had enough, he defeated Phineus with a quick flick of his wrist, solidifying Maeve's assumption.

There were two more that challenged Mal. Randolf Grisham and Davey Gunner, both fourth year Combative Magic students primed to join the Bellator.

As Grisham took the stage, Mal turned to Larliesl. "Sir. Would it be against protocol to, perhaps, duel Gunner and Grisham at the same time?"

There was a wave of whispering that buzzed around the room.

Larliesl contemplated this for a moment, biting down on his lip.

"I don't see why not," said Larliesl, excitedly. "If your opponents are up for it."

"Absolutely," said Gunner stepping up onto the platform, and sharing a smirk with Grisham.

Maeve and Abraxas scoffed in synchronization. There was no doubt in Maeve's mind that even if there were four of the school's best against him, Mal would still win. He beat her sister Arianna so badly the previous year she refused to duel him ever again.

The three boys stood at the ready as the room collectively held its breath.

Larliesl had a bright gleam in his eye. "Begin!"

"Vulnus!" Shouted Mal with one long slender finger pointed at Grisham.

One finger. A symbol of Mal's power.

The symbol of a Supreme. A Supreme far ahead of his time.

A Supreme Magical used two fingers, and in rare cases one single finger, to conduct their Magic. Maeve had never used less than three fingers.

With a loud bang, Grisham was knocked backward, clutching his stomach.

Simultaneously, Gunner sent Mal a hefty stunning spell from three tightly clenched fingers. Mal dodged the jet of blue light.

"Ligare!" Thick rope like strand of Magic burst out of Mal's fingertip heading straight for Gunner.

"Obstris!" Gunner blocked the spell with his palm, creating a misty shield between them. This gave Grisham time to get back on his feet.

"Concutere!" Shouted Grisham, attempting to blast Mal.

A collective gasp came from the crowd at this was a potentially brutal spell if cast well and aimed properly.

Mal blocked the spell with ease.

He sent a curse towards Gunner and then Grisham, one right after the other. Mal had stopped using verbal spells on them, firing from each pointer finger.

The pair successfully blocked him, but it brought Gunner to a knee.

Grisham was distracted and Mal sent him a stunning spell, knocking him square in the chest. He fell to the ground, unconscious.

Maeve looked to Mal, expecting a smirk of satisfaction, but he was completely focused on finishing Gunner.

There were a few jets of light back and forth, but Gunner had taken quite the hit. Mal's stunning spells were strong.

Gunner was back on his knees and Mal delivered a stunning spell with so much force that Gunner flipped over backward, losing the duel.

The room erupted with cheers. Larliesl made his way swiftly to Gunner and Grisham to ensure their well-being. They were fine, albeit a little knocked around, but contrary to the scowls on their faces as they arose, they were fine. Magically exhausted, but fine.

The goal of a duel at Vaukore was, after all, not to cause fatal harm.

Larliesl took the stage and gave Mal a pat on the back. The corner of his mouth turned up at the Professor.

"Unless anyone else would like to challenge our reining champion," said Larliesl, "that concludes tonight's duels! Off to your duties and dormitories!"

Mal gave Larliesl a full smile as the Professor gave him another heartfelt congratulations. The room began to empty.

After the duels, Maeve had monitoring duties on the second floor until midnight. She was sure that there would be plenty of students out of bed after such an exciting event.

Abraxas was boasting Mal's achievements as they made their way up the stairs.

"Well done," said Maeve as Mal appeared at her side.

His attention turned from Roswyn as he smirked at Maeve.

"I'd like to see you up there."

Roswyn hurried up a few steps and joined the others.

Maeve laughed and changed the subject. "You should come this weekend."

Mal laughed. "To London?"

Maeve nodded as he stared at her in disbelief.

"Why?" Mal's eyes narrowed, instantly locked with hers. Maeve hated when he did that.

She shrugged carelessly. “I dunno. But I’m looking forward to a day off. Maybe you could use one too. There’s a tea shop there I like to study in.”

Mal seemed to contemplate his response for a brief moment, before giving her a small sympathy smile, which she also hated. They reached the second floor. Mal continued on to the third floor for his assigned duties.

“Enjoy your day, Sinclair. I’ll be in the library should you change your mind.”

Chapter 5

The air had a chilly bite to it as Maeve, Violet, and Lavinia walked across the grounds to the Main London Portal, passing Magical Militia every few yards, their faces set in stone. Maeve didn't miss the apprehensive glances her dorm-mates gave them. Her thoughts were expectedly consumed by the amount of work she still wanted to get done, even though Violet had told her about a hundred times she deserved the day off, and she had succeeded in obtaining her father's permission to go.

For Maeve, it wasn't a question of deserving.

She would simply rather be studying with Mal.

No.

Just studying.

Though Malachite had made her quite a tempting offer. She relished the thought of seeing her sister's face in defeat. A snapping sound brought her back to reality.

"Hell-o?" Violet's fingers were in front of her face.

"What?" Maeve slapped her hand away fiercely. "Why are your hands always near my face?"

"Because you're never listening," said Violet.

"How can she? You never shut up," said Lavinia.

Violet gasped and Maeve smiled wickedly.

"That's so mean!" Whined Violet.

While Violet and Lavinia were going at it, Maeve's thoughts once again wandered back to Mal. His duels had been wonderful. Enchanting. Maeve was admittedly jealous of such skill.

Much to Maeve's happiness, the rumors about Velvetina's were true. Her new line of winter wear in the London shop was stunning.

Violet picked out a sweater, and Lavinia a pair of boots.

Velvetina's face lit up when Maeve told her she'd be purchasing the entire line, and she thanked Maeve incessantly until the girls left.

They sat in Esmarelles enjoying ice cream and tea after they finished their shopping. Maeve sipped what the humans called a London Fog, Magical's called it a Grey Sunset, while Violet interrogated her about all the time she was spending with Mal.

"He's my tutor," sighed Maeve. "And not even the one I wanted."

Violet huffed. "Still. You were at the duel last night and you never come to those-"

"What do you want me to say?" Maeve asked, becoming annoyed.

"She's jealous," said Lavinia, smiling as though she had just uncovered a secret.

The shade of pink Violet's face turned solidified Lavinia's accusation.

"Oh bloody hell," said Maeve, grimacing. "Is that why you've been up my ass lately?"

Lavinia's jaw dropped and Violet's jaw clenched.

"Maeve!" Hissed Violet, her eyes darting around the shop.

"I didn't mean to-" started Lavinia looking concerned, but Maeve cut her off with a raised hand.

"It doesn't matter. I'm not mad. It's just funny that I couldn't see it before," said Maeve in an icy tone.

Violet swallowed hard and put on a brave face. "I know you don't even like him like that. Everyone knows you fancy Alphard Mavros."

"Keep your voice down," warned Maeve as a few heads turned their way upon the mention of Alphard's name.

"But I guess you've moved on now that Alphard has graduated school," Violet whispered, looking away from Maeve.

"I doubt that's true," said Lavinia, attempting to diffuse the tension. "Besides, it's not even worth your time, Vi. In three years he barely pays girls attention for long. He's too focused on his studies. And remember what happened to. . ."

Lavinia didn't finish her sentence, for which Maeve was grateful. Violet frowned at Maeve and sipped her tea silently for the remainder of their time at Esmarelles.

In less than an hour, Maeve grew bored and made an excuse to head back to the Portal. This caused much whining from Violet, which Maeve promptly ignored.

Maeve walked in silence down the narrow alleys of Magical shops and restaurants.

Once, she was told, there was a great Kingdom that was theirs. Much like the humans had on Earth. Vast cities with Magic flowing freely. Now they were bound to a life in hiding. On a planet that wasn't home.

But the shops in London and Paris, New York, and Milan were glamoured away, undetectable to a human.

She turned down another street, which opened up into a small park with stone archways and a fountain.

The Magical Militia meant to provide the Portal back to Vaukore were across the grassy lawn. They didn't acknowledge her arrival as she approached them. They carried on with their own conversation.

"I'd like to go back to the school," she said.

They fell silent and looked at her.

"The Portal doesn't open back up for another hour," replied one of the soldiers. The tallest among them. "Miss Sinclair."

He only addressed her personally to ensure her he was aware she was Ambrose's daughter. Maeve smiled at this.

"What's your name?"

"Nigel Ferrmont," he said.

"Is that French?" She asked.

He nodded.

"But you sound British."

"Born and raised."

"Where?"

The soldiers behind him exchanged small glances.

"Here. In London," he replied. "Your Father taught me in school."

Maeve beamed. "Then you must be a Supreme."

Nigel flicked the bright shiny S on his uniform. "Are you?"

The men behind him stiffened.

Maeve was silent for a moment.

"No," was all she said.

"I have heard otherwise," said Nigel casually.

"Maeve!"

She turned. Abraxas was jogging across the grass towards her.

"I've taken enough of your time," started Maeve but Nigel held up his palm.

"Hop to it boys," he said.

The portal spiraled into existence between them as Abraxas reached her side.

"I hope you enjoy the rest of your Saturday, Miss Sinclair," said Nigel.

Maeve looked at the portal, and then back up at Nigel.

"Thank you," she said.

Abraxas linked his arm with hers and they stepped through into the uncomfortable in-between of worlds.

Portals were tricky work. Maeve's father told her that the soldiers chosen to uphold the portals between realms were exceptionally gifted in creating them and sustaining them.

After the air had been squished from her lungs, and they were strolling towards the gates of the castle Abraxas asked:

"Thank Merlin for your ability to name-drop Uncle Ambrose. I didn't want to wait another hour."

"I didn't do that," said Maeve, pulling her new coat tightly around herself.

"Liar."

"Has it ever occurred to you that maybe there is more than one way to get what you want? Demanding doesn't exactly buy me any favors."

Only then did Maeve realize Abraxas was holding himself strangely. And his coat looked rather bulky and large.

"What do you have?" Groaned Maeve.

Abraxas' pace quickened up the path and he hollered back at her.

"See you!"

Maeve shook her head with a laugh and opted not to ride to the castle, but to take the long walk along the mountain trail instead.

She was almost to the entryway of the castle when a raven swooped down and stretched his leg out towards her. She recognized the silver and black bird instantly. It belonged to her Father.

There was a small scroll of parchment attached to its leg that read:

Dearest Maeve,

I'm so glad to hear your term is going splendidly. Thank you for the invitation for tea on your next trip. I can't wait to see you- so close to your birthday too.

The annual Autumn Gala was wonderful. I do hate that you missed it. Arianna won first place in her age range for duels, with your cousin Ignatius coming in ninth in his.

I also spoke with Daniel Rodriguez, who was quite impressed with your work at the Offices of Magical Oration this summer. He will be visiting again over Christmas. Interesting.

Write me soon,

AS

Maeve walked along the main corridor of the castle absentmindedly.

Of course Arianna won.

It was nauseating really.

Maeve wondered what a duel between Malachite and Arianna would look like at one of those parties. Malachite would, of course, win, but she'd like to see it nonetheless. Maeve pictured Arianna frowning, crying practically, in defeat. Only, it wasn't Malachite that Maeve pictured defeating her, but herself.

Determination fueled her footsteps as she jogged up the stairs.

She didn't want to settle for just academics. Fighting was in her blood. The desire had been gnawing at her for years. There was only one Magical who could help her achieve that goal.

She found him in their normal spot in the Library, nose deep in writing an essay.

"I want to learn how to fight," said Maeve in one winded breath.

Malachite didn't look up at her. He was mouthing the words he was writing, and only when he reached the end of his sentence, and placed a very precise period, did he speak.

"Tomorrow then."

Without another word, Mal dipped his quill and continued writing.

Even though he never looked up from his work, Maeve was certain she saw a hint of satisfaction on his face.

Maeve met Mal the following evening in the dueling hall. Mal received special permission from Professor Larliesl to use it for practice.

"Again," said Mal coldly.

Maeve pulled herself up and readied herself for what felt like the hundredth time that evening.

She wasn't ready for him as he knocked her to the floor once more with a blast of pale blue light.

"Again." He spoke louder this time.

"Malachite-"

"Up."

Maeve pushed off the floor and pushed her hair back in frustration. She was tired. He fired on her before she was even ready.

With a smack, her knees hit the floor as his Magic slammed through her. Cold as ice and sharp as a sword.

A breath snapped out of her and the groan of pain she was suppressing slipped from her throat.

He was strong. Much stronger than her.

"You aren't even trying, Sinclair."

Maeve scowled at him and rubbed her shoulder.

"Your mind is everywhere but right here. The only goal is to block me. Empty your mind of anything else. Now," said Mal, "up."

Maeve rose to her feet once more, her hand ready to throw up a defensive shield from her palm.

"Then give me a moment to learn my focus," snapped Maeve.

Mal hesitated, then lowered his hand.

She closed her eyes. He was right. Her mind was elsewhere. She was focused on his judgment, the daunting task ahead of her that seemed impossible. Her mother's constant annoyance at her success and joy in her failure. At the forefront of her mind were the years of failed dueling attempts as a child, her Father's sympathetic, but arguably disappointed, face and her sister's smug one.

Maeve steadied her breathing, controlling each one, frustrated that Charms and Spells came so easily but not Offensive Magic.

Mal had told her once before, that if she could slip through minds and create new spells, there was likely little she couldn't do.

Just because it's a duel, doesn't make it different, he had said.

Maeve inhaled, opened her eyes, and exhaled.

A bright blue jet of light shot towards her from the tip of Mal's finger. She moved her hand across her chest in a flicking motion and shouted, "Skartum!"

Mal's jet of light slammed into the silvery mist in front of her, pushing her back a few feet. His hex made golden sparks as it bounced into the wall.

Maeve didn't smile but looked at him for approval. He gave her a small nod.

"Again," said Mal, motioning for her to ready herself.

They practiced for another hour before heading to their Paragon duties. Malachite instructed Maeve to pay close attention to his next appearance with The Dueling Club and take notes on his tactics.

Maeve's heels clicked into the ancient stone tile of the castle and echoed off the vaulted corridor walls as she patrolled the first floor with Abraxas, who wasn't the least bit concerned that he was out past curfew. He was going on about some bit of gossip he overheard

Professor Hoggart and Professor Warleton whispering about. None of which Maeve cared about currently. Her thoughts were preoccupied with the past few hours.

She had successfully blocked Mal. And while she didn't expect praise for the bare minimum, she was pleased with herself.

"I heard you left Violet crying in a tea shop yesterday."

Maeve laughed. "That's hilarious. I did no such thing."

"Well, she's told everyone you're a horribly mean friend."

Maeve was silent for a moment. "It doesn't matter," she finally said quietly.

They rounded a corner, and two freshman boys jumped and started walking the other direction.

"Hey!" Shouted Maeve, making her way towards them. "Where are you supposed to be?" She recognized them. They were new combat students.

The pair of boys turned around slowly, attempting to conceal a bag behind their backs.

Maeve held out her hand. The shorter boy punched the other on the arm.

"I knew I shouldn't have let you talk me into this!"

The shorter of the two gave Maeve the bag. She opened it fully expecting a bag of banned substances or some other form of contraband. Even liquor perhaps, which was strictly prohibited at Vaukore. Much to her surprise, the bag was stuffed full with sweets.

"Is this just candy?" Asked Maeve. "You're out of bed for candy?"

"He's out of bed too!" Exclaimed the taller boy, pointing at Abraxas.

"Excuse you, I'm Abraxas Rosethorn."

"Oh, shut up," Maeve said to Abraxas. "Detention, both of you, and ten demerits each."

"Can we at least keep the sweets?" Muttered the shorter boy.

"No," said Abraxas, snatching the bag from Maeve.

Maeve instructed them to go straight to their dorm. They scurried off, arguing with one another.

Abraxas pulled out an orange cupcake with large pumpkin-shaped sprinkles and began eating it.

“Where did they even get that?” Laughed Maeve.
Abraxas shrugged. “No idea, but I’m glad they did.”

Chapter 6

Maeve attended every Dueling Club event, as were Mal's instructions. She looked forward to her lessons with him almost as much as Charms class. Maeve was blocking his spells with consistency and becoming better at her offensive spells as well.

"You make a good teacher," said Maeve, gathering her things after their lesson.

Mal smirked at this. An expression that suited his handsome features. "You aren't a bad pupil. Believe me, I have worse."

"Oh, I'm well aware," laughed Maeve. "You mentor Roswyn as well."

"Careful, Sinclair," he said with a smirk. "Roswyn is stronger than you."

Maeve looked away from him and chewed the inside of her lip. "For now."

"You've known all of them your whole life haven't you?" Asked Mal. "Being a Sacred Seventeen."

Maeve nodded. "My family is especially close to the Rosethorn's though, as my Mother was one. Which I suppose is why Abraxas and I get along so well."

"How old were you when they put that mark on your wrist?" He asked casually.

"I don't remember," she said. "It's always been there."

"I've noticed you keep your sleeves down most of the time," he said. "Are you ashamed of those symbols on your wrist?"

Maeve stopped and lifted her left arm, letting the sleeve of her sweater fall to her elbow. Three sharp-pointed stars sat branded in Magic on the corner of her wrist.

"I'm not ashamed," she said quietly.

"You shouldn't be," he said. "Your family has ties to a lost civilization of Magic."

"I know that," she said, letting her arm fall back to her side.

And it was true. She was proud of her family. Of her father. She knew her blood was laced with ancient Magic that made her stronger.

Though, Malachite was the exception to that idea. Stronger than all of them. A supreme before he ever set foot at Vaukore. With no Sacred blood. Born unto a Witch with no name, and no Father to be found. She died giving birth to him in a cold December alleyway.

"When I look at those stars, I don't see a reverent and ancient symbol of Magic. All I see is a cage. An hourglass about to run out. Those three stars represent the three types of Magicals. Only one remains. As if we too are destined for death."

"You truly believe that Shadow Magic and Aterna Magic have ceased to exist?"

"What else would they be? The Shadow People were wiped out long ago in the Great War. Before Magicals even came to Earth. And according to my father, the Immortal people placed all their Aterna Magic in their High Lord. None of them have practiced so much as a summoning spell for thousands of years now."

Mal hesitated for a moment, as though he thought what he was about to say should have occurred to Maeve long ago. And perhaps it should have.

"There are seven realms. That we know of. One of them has been sealed for three hundred years. Two of the others are closed to us. You honestly think you know what Magic lies in those realms? In the Dread Lands?" Maeve had no reply. Mal stood tall. "You're far too clever to believe everything you're told."

On a Saturday afternoon, Maeve and Malachite were dueling. When Maeve declined to go to London with Violet, she received yet another nasty comment about how she and Mal spent too much time together. Lavinia overheard their conversation and gave Maeve an enthusiastic thumbs up, followed by a wink. Maeve rolled her eyes.

Mal was in a particularly lighthearted mood as they lazily shot spells back and forth, discussing Magic.

"Your father had you practice a Dread curse as a child?" He laughed.

"Yes," said Maeve.

"They're illegal."

Maeve shrugged as he blocked her jinx. "I've told you before. My father isn't really one for the rules. At least, not the ones in his interest to break."

Mal looked intrigued. "I have a favor to ask."

Maeve shifted her head to one side.

"I want to see you create a false memory."

Maeve's brows pulled together. "You mean. . ."

"In your mind," he finished.

Maeve laughed through her nose. "You think I'm going to let you in my mind?"

Mal smiled.

Damn. It was a sight.

"I'm so curious. Besides, I've never been in a Pureblood's mind."

"That's because Purebloods have built in mental shields."

"I know," said Mal plainly.

Maeve watched him carefully for a moment as her eyes narrowed. "Have you been in many minds?"

Mal didn't answer. "Are you going to let me see or not?"

"Are you going to answer?"

Mal's expression was unreadable. "You already know."

Maeve nodded, thankful he couldn't force his way into her mind without her permission.

"Alight," she relented under his pressing gaze. "I'll show you."

A smirk flickered across his face. Maeve held up her hand.

"But if I tell you to get out," she said gravely, "you get out. Deal?"

Mal's smirk never faltered. "Deal."

He pointed his finger at her. Maeve lowered her mental shields, allowing him to enter her mind, and prayed she wasn't making a terrible mistake.

No light emitted from the tip of his finger.

The Dueling Hall disappeared and she was watching her father demonstrate a series of spells in his study at Sinclair Estates. She was only three. Ambrose was excitedly showing her hand motions and making Maeve giggle with gold sparks.

"Is that your father?" Asked Mal's voice.

"Yes," said Maeve.

He appeared at her side. "You aren't even trying to force me out."

"I have no idea how to do that," said Maeve plainly.

Her father and three-year-old self disintegrated, and she was standing in the Dueling Hall at Vaukore once more.

"That was a real memory," said Mal with a slight disappointment. "Again. This time show me something false. I want to see these perfect faux memories you boast about."

"I do not boast-"

But Mal ignored her. He dove back into her mind, her shields still completely unprotected. He ran through thoughts it seemed. Many things, not all of them memories, flashed before her eyes.

She flung the first thing that came to mind out before them: her charms test from the previous morning. Only the room was empty, save for a giant oversized clock and a roll of parchment so long one would assume she had been writing for days without ceasing. The clock ticked away as the fake Maeve wrote hastily.

It was an odd sight. Unrealistic, but based in truth, as all false memories were.

"Finally," said Mal, his voice echoing across her mind. He appeared at her side, observing the fake Maeve as she scribbled away.

Maeve gathered herself, feeling a boost of confidence. "Perhaps we can change it up?" She said, playfully, thrilled to be in control for once.

The scene before them disappeared and was replaced by the Dueling Hall at Vaukore, a perfect replica of Maeve and Mal standing and dueling one another.

The fake Maeve hit the fake Mal with a hefty curse, bringing him to the floor in tears. Maeve stood victorious over the crying fake Mal.

"It looks completely real," said the real Mal, mesmerized.

Maeve smiled.

Her stomach flipped as Mal pulled out of her mind. She was dizzy and took a knee to the floor as the room spun.

"That's incredibly impressive," said Mal, striding towards her.

Maeve took a deep breath and relished his praise. "Thank you."

"Could you, hypothetically speaking, place that memory inside my head, causing me to think it happened like that?"

"Yes," said Maeve. "But I would just modify your memory seamlessly to appear the false way I want, not have to implant an entire false memory. Though, that is also doable. Say, for example, you were never here, and I wanted you to believe you were. But that is... advanced and I don't know that I could-"

"This is what you showcased at the Orator's Office this summer? The Headmasters have seen you do this? The Orator's Office knows you can do this?"

Maeve nodded. "And more so, break other's false memories as well. "

"You learned to do that first didn't you?"

"Yes. I studied them until I knew where all the flaws typically were, which enabled me to perfect my own. Of course, there are many factors still. You were viewing my false memories live. They're even stronger when perfected from the outside."

"How?" He questioned.

"Using a host," she answered.

Mal stared past her, nodding his head in understanding. He turned on his heel quickly. "Next lesson," he turned back towards her, "how strong are your shields when you're too weak to create such a strong memory?"

"What?" Maeve scoffed. "When would I ever need that?"

Wordlessly and without warning, a bright green light shot from Mal's finger at Maeve, which she blocked. However, it was quickly followed by another. The second spell hit her square in the stomach.

She screamed as she doubled over. A sharp, slicing sensation ran through her body. A hundred needles pressed into her throat.

She didn't get her shields back up in time.

He entered her mind a third time. It was a mess of things: the pain she felt, a conversation with Abraxas, watching Spinel chase a mouse down the hall. Everything swirled past without control.

She couldn't breathe.

She tried to bring forth a false memory to block Mal, but they all fell apart before she could create them. The pain was too much. She had no way to create the memory with her mind scattered from the burning throughout her entire body.

Her position of dominance and control had not lasted long.

Mal shifted through her mind with ease, running down everything that rose to the surface. He didn't stop to observe anything.

With a bang, the contents of Maeve's mind appeared blank for a moment.

There was a loud scream from a woman. Suddenly a room Maeve knew well came into focus. The grandfather clock against the wall at Sinclair Estates said it was well past midnight, and the foyer was illuminated with blue moonlight through the windows.

No. No. No.

There were three men, one of which was her father, surrounding a mangled and bloody body that lay lifeless on the floor. Ambrose Sinclair was kneeled over the body crying.

Maeve recognized the memory instantly and desperately began trying to force Mal out. It was no use though. She was under a hex that wasn't going to give until Mal himself lifted it. Her shields were down and staying down until he relented.

The scream had come from Clarissa Sinclair, Maeve's mother, who upon seeing her only son dead on the floor, collapsed. One of the men shot to her side to console her.

Ambrose remained over Antony Sinclair's body. His oldest child. And only son.

There was a flash of green light, and three Magical beings stepped through the fireplace in the foyer. Maeve recognized them as

Orator Moon, his Senior Secretary, and The High Lord of the Immortal Realm himself, Reeve.

Reeve halted halfway across the floor. His face stuck in a pained expression. And shook his head in disbelief.

Maeve wanted to scream for Mal to get out, but nothing happened. She struggled to breathe from the pain of his hex and was forced to watch the scene herself.

"The head of the Department of the Regulation and Control of Magical Creatures is on his way," whispered the Orator to the man by Ambrose.

Ambrose looked up.

"Maeve," cried Ambrose, looking at the marble staircase.

The sound of his voice sent a chill down Maeve's spine.

Every head in the room turned, save for her Mother's, and there on the stairs was fourteen-year-old Maeve, standing in complete horror.

Ambrose shot up from the floor and ran towards her, scooping her up in one quick motion. This revealed what was left of her brother, Antony's body.

Clarissa screamed in agony once more.

"You shouldn't have seen this," cried Ambrose, tucking her head onto his shoulder and scooping her into his arms.

The men began examining Antony's body. The High Lord Reeve placed a hand on Antony's chest and closed his eyes in prayer.

The sight became nauseating quickly, as it had been quite some time since Maeve examined this memory. She could no longer feel the burning pain throughout her body.

"No," whispered Maeve. "Get out."

She felt Mal pull away. She gathered all the strength she had and managed to break free of the loose grip he held on her as the memory slowly faded.

Mal stood silently a few steps away from where she kneeled on the floor, exhausted. She ran her shaking hands over her face.

Maeve pushed off the floor and grabbed her bag without looking at him. She headed for the door, eager to be as far away from him as possible. She took the long way to her dorm in the East Wing, so that if he did come after her, their crossing paths would be unlikely.

A golden question in swirly handwriting shot across the ivory doors with a scraping sound.

If you have it, and you show it to other people, it's gone. What is it?

"Aren't you cheeky," said Maeve.

That is incorrect, appeared in small writing beneath the riddle. It disappeared as Maeve sighed. A book appeared at her feet.

Need a clue? The door wrote.

"No," said Maeve, annoyed. "It's a secret."

The double doors clicked open. Her feet were heavy as she climbed the marble stairs to her room, already tugging at the tie around her neck. Spinel jumped into the bed ahead of her, purring loudly.

It would be easy enough to avoid Mal for the rest of the weekend, but during class might prove more difficult. Though Maeve had a feeling he would give her the distance she deserved.

Chapter 7

Maeve was in a gloomy mood as Hendrix Fawley sprinted downstairs from his dorm, across their common area, and slammed down a copy of The Magical Times.

"What?" Asked Maeve as she set her tea aside.

"Look," said Fawley as he pushed the newspaper towards her and sat in one of the bright velvet sapphire armchairs. "I looked for you at breakfast but Lavinia said you've been eating up here for a week."

Spinel crept out from under Maeve's seat and rubbed against Fawley's legs.

Maeve shot to the edge of her seat with one glance at the headline.

THE DREAD DESCENDENT ALLEGEDLY RETURNS
KIETEL CLAIMS TO BE THE PROPHESIED DREAD
PRINCE ORATOR'S OFFICE URGES ALL MAGICALS TO
DISREGARD CLAIMS THAT THE FABLED DREAD
DESCENDANT RETURNS

She snatched up the article at once.

"Impossible," she said.

Fawley laughed, a smile wide across his face. "This is insane. Oh, Lavinia also said to give you this." Fawley handed her a bright pink book.

Maeve flipped over the cover.

"Oh, Heavens," said Maeve tossing the erotic novel onto one of the couches.

She grabbed the newspaper and read over the front page.

KIETEL, the rogue German Magical Militia General, has returned to public eye with a jaw-dropping declaration: He is the legendary Dread Descendant the Magicals of Earth have waited three hundred years for.

Ambrose Sinclair has repeatedly defended KIETEL in his absence, and now the Premier is silent at last. The Pureblood Magical Militia Commander and Elected Official in the Orator's Office declined to comment this morning.

Orator Moon spoke with us briefly, excusing Premier Sinclair's dismissal of the public's questions. "Premier Sinclair's duty is the protection of our world, not to comment on politics. That privilege lies with me. Currently, there is no validity to Kietel's claims, most modern Magicals aren't even certain they believe in this prophecy, let alone a power-hungry Militia Captain's delusions of grandeur. As our friends in the PMO say, 'Keep Calm and Carry On'.

Maeve set the paper down and looked up at Fawley. He slipped off his dark grey blazer with sapphire stitching and leaned back in his chair. His fingers drummed against his knee.

Maeve's eyes scanned over the moving photograph of Kietel at the top of the page. He was dressed in his Magical Militia uniform.

Neither of them spoke.

Students were buzzing about the headline as she and Fawley walked to class. Headmaster Rowan was leaning back in his chair, his eyes down at a copy of the paper.

The class was silent. Finally, Rowan tossed the newspaper aside and leaned forward, placing his elbows on his desk.

"So then," he said, his voice devoid of emotion. "Thoughts?"

No one moved or made a sound. Until Randolph Grisham spoke. "What does it truly matter?"

Rowan's brows slowly raised. He nodded slightly. "Are you asking me?"

Grisham nodded.

Rowan stood from his desk and rounded it, making his way to the center of the room. His boots clicked across the hushed classroom.

"It matters, validity aside," began Rowan, "because we are on the verge of war. Division creates chaos. Chaos yields war."

"Is it true that he will take all of us away?" Violet asked, her voice trembling slightly.

Rowan didn't answer right away. "Some interpret the prophecy that way, yes."

Grisham spoke again. "But it doesn't seem like he's getting support. I thought the prophecy spoke about the Dread Descendant being praised by the Magicals."

"I don't believe that's exactly it," said Rowan.

"They will be drawn to him," said Maeve.

Rowan looked towards her.

"Yes, that," said Grisham.

"He makes a point, surprisingly," said Maeve.

A low chuckle bounced across the room. Grisham eyed her.

"They are drawn to him," argued Rowan. "Or have you not heard many Magical Militia have abandoned their oaths and are now under his command?"

Maeve swallowed. "I don't mean them."

"You mean us?" Asked Fawley. "Sacreds?"

Maeve nodded.

"And that's your only argument?" Asked Rowan. "Ah."

Maeve avoided Mal's gaze, burning into her from across the classroom.

"I mean, he is a very powerful Supreme. And his claims of his lineage have been verified." Said a voice.

"Actually there is a break in the line," said another.

"But isn't that to be expected?" Asked the first.

Rowan spoke over them. "Mr. Rosethorn,' he called. "Recite the prophecy to us."

Abraxas leaned back in his seat next to Mal. He swallowed and cleared his throat. He recited the words with almost boredom, like a pledge he'd memorized since childhood that no longer held meaning.

"In a desperate hour, your Prince of Darkness will return. Through a broken line of Magic, into unsuspecting veins. His life will call like to like in those where Magic blood remains. The Descendant of Dread will conquer the plague of the Promised Land, with a single finger, not a sword. Rejoice, child of golden blood, freedom shall be yours. On backs and broken necks will balance be restored."

The classroom turned eerily silent.

A shadow cast over Maeve in Hellming Hall, and a smooth voice spoke, "I didn't know."

She lowered her book and looked up at Malachite, who she had managed to avoid talking to or looking at for over two weeks. She looked back to her book. He had given her well-deserved space.

"How?" Scoffed Maeve. "It's all anyone at school acquaints me with. It's what they love to gossip about when I walk by as if I can't bloody hear them."

Mal's voice remained cool, in opposition to hers. "You know I pay no attention to gossip, Maeve."

The use of her first name didn't go unnoticed. Maeve was somehow infuriated more by his calm demeanor.

Her book vanished from sight as Malachite whisked it away, seating himself in front of her. She refused to meet his gaze and stared out over the hall instead.

"You had to have known I would find that out eventually."

Maeve's head snapped towards him, opening her mouth briefly to snap at him, but resigned, calming herself first.

"I don't want to see it," said Maeve cooly.

Mal's face screwed, looking at her almost dumbly. Maeve sighed, looking at the mahogany table as she spoke.

"You pushed past a barrier that night. A barrier even I don't go past. Antony's death. . . The sight of him like that. . . I can't have it always creeping into my thoughts. I can't have it keep me up at night, I can't have it destroy my studies and…"

"You blocked an entire set of memories somehow?"

She nodded.

"How?" Mal shot impatiently. She shot him a look back.

"Rowan did it for me."

"Of course." Mal pushed back into his seat with a sour look on his face.

"I couldn't do it myself. I invented the damn spell myself, it's just one can't perform it on oneself. He said that if I promised to spend the summer working that silly job at the Double O, he would make it so I controlled if I saw those memories. The other night when you saw that memory, it came flooding back to me like the first time."

"I broke past a charm Rowan himself put on you," said Mal, poorly attempting to hide a wicked smile.

"Yes, by all means, make it about you," said Maeve.

His eyes shot to hers, but she had a smile tugging at her lips.

"Impressive as it is," she continued. "I don't care to see it."

Mal looked her over and pursed his lips. "You are running from something, that's unlike you." He spoke lazily, pulling out a piece of parchment and a quill. "I am here to push you, not to care what memories hurt or haunt you. Face it head on or it will be your downfall I should think."

She opened her mouth to argue, but Mal was quicker.

"And don't say you aren't ready."

Maeve snapped her jaw tightly shut.

Maeve met Mal in the Dueling Hall later that evening. He was pressing her, much more so than he had been doing. His methods of triumph were becoming more and more uncalculated, which kept Maeve on her toes.

Tonight, each time Mal defeated her, she had to answer a question.

On their first duel, he asked her if she had ever used her memory charm spells to get something she wanted, but possibly otherwise wouldn't have achieved on her own.

"Wasn't it on my own, since I cast the spell myself?"

Mal commended her on this clever response.

The second time he bested her, and had her bound by thick rope-like strands of Magic, he asked her if given the choice to bring back her brother from the dead, at the sacrifice of her Father, would she?

"What a deranged question," said Maeve, her voice low.

The ropes tightened around her. Her mind slipped to those books Lavinia kept offering to lend her.

"And you haven't even heard my third question," replied Mal.

"I already know your third question," said Maeve.

The ropes grew even tighter, constricting her body. She winced.

"Is that so?"

"Yes," said Maeve. "You want to know why my brother was murdered."

Mal's face didn't change as he stared down at her, which solidified Maeve's accusation.

"My brother was a werewolf," admitted Maeve, straining. Mal's expression didn't change. "And I'm sure you know people like him aren't exactly treated kindly. It was supposed to be a secret. Very few knew. He refused the treatment enforced by the Double O to keep him from changing"

Maeve hesitated but continued when he didn't say anything.

"Of course, that was a gross mistake on my father's part: assuming very few knew. He was killed by another wolf it seemed. It was grotesque when they found him- two of my father's men found him-ripped to pieces. What you saw in my memories was what they managed to piece together of him. . ." Maeve trailed off, her voice just above a whisper now. "His eyeballs were even carved out."

"Your father recounted that detail to you?" Mal asked, his voice flat.

"No," she said incredulously. "I took a dip inside his memory jar one night when he was asleep. Not that the bloody paper didn't print that too."

Mal was unfazed as he stood above her.

"When I looked into it," he said, "the official Orator's Office statement was that it was a tragic accident and no foul play was suspected. Yet, you use the word 'murdered'."

"It's lies, Mal. They all lie. The Double O, the newspapers, it's all the same. This school probably lies. Hell, according to you, my own family lies."

The Magic constricting her disappeared with a popping sound as Mal released her.

She let out a quick breath.

"And you think Kietel is lying about being the Dread Descendant?"

Maeve looked up at him.

He extended a hand to help her up, which he had never done before. She took his cool hand, and he pulled her to her feet. There were burn marks from the ropes where her sleeves were rolled back. She stood silently, observing the marks. Her Sinclair family ring glistened in the candlelight.

Maeve stammered a response, but it caught in her throat.

Mal reached out and ran his icy, slender fingers over the spots that would likely yield bruises along her arms. Maeve shuddered at his unexpected touch. She looked up at him and he met her eyes only briefly before he turned on his heel.

"I think we're done for the night," said Mal.

They gathered their things and made their ascent out of the dueling hall. Maeve rolled her sleeves down, concealing her marks.

"You skipped my second question," said Mal, as he walked her to the fifth floor.

"That is because I do not know the answer," said Maeve.

"How old was he?"

"Freshly twenty-one, and freshly engaged on his birthday, December twenty-first. A year early for a Sacred Engagement."

"That must have been terribly sad," said Mal, his voice businesslike.

Maeve was silent for a moment as they walked.

"Does your father have brothers?" Asked Mal.

Maeve shook her head and let out a hollow laugh. "Not alive. They only had girls anyway. It's a rather large deal, actually, to lose a

Pureblood line. The Sinclair name is effectively gone, and will die with me." Maeve spoke in a way that indicated this was not her first time realizing this fact.

"Forgive me," started Mal, but Maeve cut him off.

"There's no need," said Maeve. "It actually feels good to talk about it. Not what I would have expected, but good nonetheless."

They made it to the second floor and turned the corner.

Walking towards them were Roswyn, Phineas, Abraxas, and Avery. They were laughing heartily. Maeve knew well enough that these boys needn't worry about being out past curfew. Not only were they in Mal's inner circle, but the Head Boy was a combat student himself, who looked up to Malachite just like them.

"Out for a stroll?" Asked Maeve playfully, glancing at her ivory watch. "At this hour?"

They stopped a few feet short of Mal and Maeve and exchanged looks with Mal.

"Umm," said Avery, with a chuckle. "Mal?"

Mal smirked. "I believe the Paragon asked you gentlemen a question."

Roswyn burst out laughing, stepping towards Maeve. Her smile faltered and faded at his demeanor.

"I've known this one long enough to know she's all bark and no bite."

He shoved past her, slamming his shoulder into her and knocking her to the ground.

"What the hell?" Exclaimed Abraxas, stepping towards Maeve. "She was obviously just messing around."

Abraxas helped her to her feet and picked up her bag. Maeve's mouth hung open in disbelief.

Roswyn scoffed and turned to walk away.

"Roswyn," said Mal, whose voice had suddenly become low.

Maeve looked at Mal, rubbing her shoulder. His smile had vanished and had been replaced by an unnervingly void expression.

Roswyn turned towards him slowly. Mal stared him down intensely.

Roswyn glanced at Maeve, his jaw clenched tight. She was expecting an apology, but Roswyn swallowed hard and averted his eyes back to Mal with a defiant look on his face.

Mal was still staring him down, unblinking.

"Abraxas," said Mal smoothly without breaking his stare, "continue accompanying Sinclair to her dorm." He paused. "Roswyn, let's take a walk."

"I should demerit you for that-" Maeve started at Roswyn but Abraxas took her arm hastily and dragged her in the opposite direction.

Mal didn't give Maeve another glance. Roswyn held his silent focus.

Phineas and Avery stood against the wall, picking at their own fingers, as far out of eyesight as possible, likely hoping to skirt by without issue.

"What was that all about?" Maeve asked once she and Abraxas were out of earshot.

"The ass. I assume he feels threatened," said Abraxas. "Mal's been bragging about your strengths."

Maeve scowled. "Oh, whatever. I was only joking. I ought to write him a detention myself just for that ridiculous display."

"I think Mal will handle his punishment for you but I don't think it will be in the form of detention," said Abraxas solemnly.

"What?"

Abraxas sighed. "You're too smart for your own good sometimes."

Maeve was unsure how to reply to that comment. The whole scenario had been bizarre. And she had never seen Mal look so furious.

Once they reached the entrance to her dormitory, in the East Wing, Abraxas bid her goodnight. Maeve grabbed his arm quickly.

"Wait," said Maeve. "Mal's been bragging about me?"

Abraxas smirked. "Don't let it get to your head, cousin."

He waltzed off down the corridor, leaving Maeve alone.

"Excellent work, Maeve," said Professor Elgin in Protective Magic one afternoon. "That's impressively quick improvement."

Maeve's physical Magical shields were stronger than ever. They had to be. Mal was too strong for anything less than her best.

Professor Elgin smiled and moved across the classroom, correcting and observing. Maeve looked over at Mal. His head was cocked to one side with a look of approval.

She slid onto a bench next to Abraxas as they watched the rest of the class performing their shields. Protective Magic was one of Maeve's top subjects after Charms. Headmaster Elgin was a master at the art. She covered everything from physical Magic shields and potion protectants to mental shields and shielding with powerful Magical objects.

After much convincing, and a bit of blackmail, Abraxas managed to talk Maeve into attending a very forbidden party in the Combative Magic student's dorms. She relented, much to his excitement.

She turned down every drink she was offered. Abraxas didn't even bother asking her to participate in any other substances.

Their common area was a large hexagon hall, most of it designed for dueling practice. Its arched windows faced the thick forest, illuminating the room with a pale green glow.

She watched him smoke a rolled-up piece of parchment with a fluffy green substance inside. She didn't ask what it was. She didn't care.

"Who are you looking for?" Asked Abraxas after the twentieth time she glanced around the room.

"No one."

"Liar," said Abraxas with a roll of his eyes.

Maeve scanned the room once more. Roswyn was across the common room, lips locked with a new student. A Pureblood girl three years younger than Maeve.

"That's Emerie Videntis."

She sighed. "I know who she is." A Pureblood. Roswyn's only type. "Well, this has been a joy, Brax but I'm tired."

Maeve pushed her way through the crowd and towards the narrow dark passageway that led back to the main castle.

"Wait, wait," he called after her. "It's only been an hour. Give it time."

Maeve turned on him and paused. She inclined her head and studied him closely. "Give what time?"

"Oh Seven Realms, Maeve," he whined. "Do you think I don't see what's going on?"

"What's going on?" Came a voice from the darkness.

Their heads whipped towards the sound.

Mal emerged from the crowd and into the shadowed lighting coming from the narrow doorway of the common room. Whispers circled around them at his presence. His hands slid into his pockets as he casually ignored them all.

Maeve opened her mouth to speak to him. But Harriet Simms slipped from behind him and stood at his side. The second year combat student stood too close to be there without his invitation. Maeve's cheeks burned hot against her will. She steadied her breathing and leaned against the wall, tucking her clammy hands behind her back.

"I was just leaving," said Maeve cooly. "No point in staying."

"I am as well," said Mal.

"What?" Asked Harriet with a short laugh.

"You only just arrived," Maeve argued as Harriet also said, "We've only just arrived."

Harriet's eyes finally landed on Maeve. Her light brown hair was pulled gently back with an ivory bow. "How exactly would you know?" She asked icily.

Maeve's eyes narrowed. Harriet's gaze faltered.

Abraxas bit his bottom lip and tried not to look giddy.

Students stumbled between them, giggling into their drinks.

Maeve looked away from Harriet. "Because I didn't see you for the past hour," she said to Mal.

"So you were looking for me," he said matter of factly.

Harriet and Abraxas' eyes darted between the pair of them.

"Not looking. But I think I would have noticed you at a party like this. Not exactly your common ground."

"Nor yours," he said smoothly. "Anymore that is."

Abraxas' grin faltered.

Harriet smiled softly. "You used to be fun, Maeve. I remember Alphard Mavros carrying you upstairs last year because you were too-"

Mal's eyes darted down at her like daggers. She stopped short, her face whitening and her shoulders pulled up slightly.

Maeve stared at her for a moment.

"Too. What?" She asked quietly.

Harriet looked up at Mal, ignoring Maeve. "I see Roswyn and Emerie. Let's join them."

Maeve pushed her back off the wall with a small scoff.

"Don't go Maeve," whined Abraxas.

She turned back towards them. "Come with me," she said to Abraxas.

It was a challenge. But Abraxas' face fell guilty. His mouth hung open.

"Come on, Malachite," said Harriet, slinking her arm through his. "I want a drink."

Mal looked right at her, his expression impenetrable, his voice even and smooth, no doubt in Abraxas' decision as he said, "Change of plans. We're staying. Come, Abraxas."

He turned with Harriet on his arm and walked towards the party, his hands still tucked in his pockets.

Abraxas hesitated only for a moment. Then his face snapped back into its normal smug expression. He blew her a quick kiss. "You were going to bed anyway."

Maeve didn't bother protesting. Abraxas followed Mal without hesitation back into the crowd.

Maeve holed herself in her dorm for the rest of the weekend.

Sunday morning Lavinia appeared in the doorway of the third year girls' room.

"Your room is down the hall," said Maeve, her eyes quickly returning to her book.

"What's eating you?"

"Many things," said Maeve. "For starters, I'm trying to read and there is an annoying Head Girl in my room."

Lavinia leaned against the doorway. "This was my room last year. I have better books than that if you need a distraction."

"Pass."

Lavinia sighed and pushed off the doorframe. "Fine."

Each time Maeve's stomach growled, Spinel opened one eye from where he slept at the foot of her bed and chirped at her.

"But that involves going downstairs for real food," she said to him.

Her nightstand was littered with empty chocolate wrappers. Spinel chirped at her once more and laid his head back down. Dinner would be over soon. Her stomach growled so loudly that Spinel jumped off the bed and stretched, chattering at her as he slunk into the dark hallway.

Maeve set her book aside with a sigh.

She hurried downstairs and satisfied the incessant grumbling in her stomach. The essay she had put off all weekend for Alchemy needed completing. Her mind ran through the revisions needed as she made her way back up to her dorm in the darkened castle.

Mal leaned against a pillar ahead. She pretended not to see him as she approached.

"You didn't come to your tutoring lesson."

"Oh I'm quite done with that," she said, breezing by him.

His voice was playful. "Nor your training."

"Devastating, yes," she replied without glancing back at him.

"Stop," he said with an edge in his tone.

The command caused her stomach to turn tight. Her arms tensed across her chest and her neck lifted.

Nevertheless.

She obeyed.

His oxfords clicked across the stone corridor until he was in front of her. His hands slid into his pockets as he predatorily hovered above her.

She avoided his gaze.

"Friday evening. At the party. That was cruel. And I shouldn't have done it."

She scoffed, looking up at him expecting to see his eyes mocking her.

Surprise rang through her. Her face dropped. When she looked up at him, something like remorse flickered through his expression. His statuesque features were sharpened by the dim candlelight flickering off his face, sinking into the dips of his cheeks, darkening his hair.

Maeve looked at him squarely and spoke quietly, more sadness seeping into her voice than she would have liked. "Abraxas is not a pawn. And nor am I."

"I know," he said calmly. "I said it was uncalled for."

"I suppose that's the closest thing to an apology I'll get from you."

A mix of humor and arrogance danced across his face. "It would seem."

Maeve sighed and relaxed. She suppressed a smile.

Damn his charm.

"At least allow me to continue training you," he said.

Maeve laughed softly. "You are so accustomed to getting your way."

Mal's face scanned hers meticulously. Her stomach flipped as a quick breath rose up in her chest.

When his eyes landed on hers he spoke. "No one fights me quite like you do."

The words slipped from his mouth like it made him hungry. She grinned.

"Someone has to," she said.

A small laugh escaped his lips. "And you think you're the one for the job?"

"The alternatives are grim."

His brows raised.

"Let's see," she continued, passing him by and continuing down the hall. He remained in step with her. "Abraxas, the gossip, will ever only tell you what you want to hear. Roswyn, the hothead, will react without thinking things through. Avery, Gods love him, will only ever bore you with his blind loyalty. Hendrix, though I favor him, is too much of a rule follower to follow without hesitation."

"You speak of my closest friends with certainty."

"Of them I am certain," she said.

"Ah," he said casually. "And what of my friends that have graduated? What of Alphard Mavros?"

Maeve's smile faded slightly.

Mal stopped walking and asked sharply, "What about him are you certain of?"

Maeve turned towards him. "Of Alphard, I am unable to speak poorly."

His expression was relaxed. Carefree. But behind that was the feline way he looked down at her. Like she was trapped.

"Why is that?"

"He was my brother's best friend," she replied without hesitation. "And he never laid a hand on me when I was. . . intoxicated."

He was still for a moment. Then he nodded subtly like he was determining how honest she was being. "I know that," he said finally.

Maeve opened her mouth and then snapped it shut.

"Speak," he said tauntingly with a flick of his brows.

So she did. "When you were apologizing, or whatever, were you sorry you used my cousin and I against one another or sorry for your comment that I used to frequent those parties?"

Parties that three years ago Alphard Mavros had kissed her. Where she drank. And used whatever drugs Abraxas provided. Whatever made her forget Antony.

Mal rounded her and continued down the corridor. "I never said I was sorry."

Chapter 8

"I started a new club Maeve," said Lavinia as Maeve entered the common room late one evening after dueling with Mal. Her legs were exhausted. Her arms full of lead. And her brain fuzzy.

He pushed her harder each time they met. Each curse and hex was stronger, and each time she fell to the stone ground she pulled herself back up. Red welts covered her knees. She didn't have the energy to heal them. Nor the bruises across her chest. Bruises she had a morbid fixation with in the bathroom mirror. Something about his marks on her spiked her adrenaline.

Lavinia offered her a drink. Maeve declined.

"What's that?" Asked Maeve absentmindedly, her attention on Harriet Simms across the common room. Harriet, Presley and Lavinia played all the Magical sports Vaukore offered.

Harriet sat there, her skin flushed and her laughter loud. Maeve tried to stop herself, only a little, and was unsuccessful. She argued it was wrong, unethical. But the thought of Harriet and Mal at that party was burning a hole in her mind. She could put it to rest with ease. And so she did.

She slipped into Harriet's mind. Harriet didn't even feel her there. She was weak, and the drinks Lavinia poured were strong. The memory Maeve desired to see presented itself in a flash, and Maeve latched onto it at once.

Mal and Abraxas' dormitory blurred into shape. Only the tapered candles in the wall sconces were lit.

Mal and Harriet appeared into focus. The door clicked closed behind them. Harriet stood on her tiptoes to reach him. His arms wrapped around her waist.

Their lips pressed together and Maeve's insides plummeted. Sweat pooled at the back of her neck. Mal's hands moved to Harriet's hips. And then her face. And then his hands dropped to his side. He pulled from her slightly. Harriet pressed forward, placing her hands on his face.

His hands brushed across her hips once more, gripping her tightly. She pushed their kiss deeper-

Suddenly, he shook her off and stepped away from her, turning his back. He ran his hand through his hair. Harriet took two steps backward.

"What did I do?" She asked.

With a heavy sigh, Mal leaned against the wall in between his and Abraxas' bed. "Nothing," he said weakly, his head hanging.

"Then-" she started, but Mal sighed and looked up at her, cutting her off.

"Apologies, Harriet," he said, little sorrow in his voice, never looking away from her. "But it's time you left."

She stared at him, her eyes wide with hurt. She didn't protest.

Mal's stare was intense.

Then without meaning to, Maeve slipped through a doorway. And was in Mal's mind. Harriet turned and left him without another word, slamming the door behind her. He didn't even watch her go. He stared at the opposite wall in his dorm.

Darkness slammed around her like four walls that appeared from nothing. She turned and gasped, stepping backward.

Mal stood, towering over her. His face rang with a mixture of awe and anger. The realization it was her washed over his face and the anger subsided. They stood there in that swirling silent darkness until Maeve finally spoke.

"You wanted to see," she said softly.

Their voices echoed off the void, bouncing around them.

"Incredible," he whispered.

Maeve sucked in a breath. She looked up at him. "No one has ever felt me inside their mind before."

"You might as well have been screaming at me."

"I'm sorry," said Maeve. "I shouldn't have."

He shook his head.

"Why did you stop kissing her?" She asked, regretting the words as they slipped from her lips.

His eyes turned cold.

He stepped towards her and Maeve panicked to hear his response. She pulled on that invisible doorway into Harriet's mind, flinging herself out.

Intoxicated laughter filled her ears. The warm firelight of her common room shook into vision.

She had jumped from Harriet's memory to Mal's mind. And when he realized she was there, he attempted to block his mind from her. Successfully.

Harriet was sipping another full drink with a smile. She had not the faintest clue Maeve had just watched Mal reject her.

"Did you hear me?" Lavinia's voice filled her ears.

Maeve shook her head, shaking off the lingering feeling of Mal's presence.

"Sorry, what?" Asked Maeve.

"A book club," said Lavinia. "And we have room for one more. Though, they're not your kind of books. But I know if you gave them a chance you'd love them."

Maeve tore her eyes away from Harriet and looked at Lavinia. Lavinia followed her gaze to Harriet.

"You threatened, Sinclair?" Asked Lavinia playfully.

He had stopped. He pushed Harriet away. While Maeve refused to acknowledge why this brought her joy, she allowed herself to relish it all the same.

"I've never been less threatened actually," said Maeve cooly. "When does this book club meet?"

They didn't speak of it, what she did that night. Mal didn't question or berate her, and he paid no attention to Harriet Simms as they passed her and her fencing friends in the corridor.

Maeve jumped through minds, on willing subjects, three more times in the coming weeks. Mal used their training to strengthen all her Magic, and their tutoring lessons to expand both their Magical knowledge. Other than their Paragon duties, which Abraxas still affectionately called glorified hall monitor responsibilities, they spent all of their free time immersing themselves in Magic.

Mal was as insatiable as she was.

On Thursday evenings, she studied alone when Mal was with his closest combat boys and the Master of Duels, Professor Larliesl. They had formed their own exclusive "gentlemen's only" club as Abraxas called it.

Maeve had rolled her eyes. It was really "combat school only" if they were honest.

After a week of intense classes and a draining Defensive Magic Examination, Maeve was seated in her favorite corner of the Library, tucked away from the rest of the castle. She was attempting to get as much work done as possible before the weekend because she promised Abraxas she would attend the fencing match between the third and fourth year teams. Antony had been unbeatable, a top player in his time.

Antony had learned to Obscure at a young age, making him an excellent player with the ability to disappear and reappear, teleporting around his opponent.

She heard footsteps making their way towards her.

"Abraxas told an interesting story last night," said Mal, with a hint of mischief in his voice.

Maeve didn't look up from her essay as he sat down. "Abraxas exaggerates."

Mal pulled up a chair across from her.

"He said that when you were eleven, the summer before primary school started, that you-"

Maeve interrupted him. "So what if that's true? Don't act like you haven't gotten away with plenty."

"Is that so?" Asked Mal with a conceited smirk.

"Certainly," said Maeve. "For example, you should have been expelled last year."

Mal leaned back in his chair, smiling. But Maeve noticed a sharp look in his eye as he watched her carefully. His speech was calculated.

He waved his right hand, flicking it out an opaque burst of Magic that encapsulated them. Blocking in all sound.

"Explain," said Mal.

"It wasn't all that difficult to figure out actually," said Maeve, playing with her quill. "My Father was summoned here to the school with The Orator. Headmaster Elgin asked me to take a look at Valeria Carter's memories. The Headmasters insisted it was strange that Warner confessed and yet had no recollection of hurting Valeria. My Father agreed."

Mal cocked his head to one side, still smiling at her.

"Of course, there were no memories of such an event, as Warner was innocent. I knew that the moment I entered his mind. Warner kept insisting, through tears, he must have blocked out the memories, but that he was horribly sorry for what he had done. Valeria was all over the place. Someone had hurt her, but she repressed all of it. I couldn't see anything. But I felt all of it. There was a lingering trace of Magic. Magic I was, at the time, unfamiliar with. Different from all else."

"That Magic," said Mal, quietly. "Are you familiar with it now?"

Maeve nodded and whispered. "It calls to me quite often."

A long silence passed between them, the only sound the snapping of the fire. Finally, he spoke quietly. Softly.

"It was an accident."

Mal placed his elbows on the table and bowed his head. "Why did you lie? If you knew he was innocent?"

"Because that Magic. . ." she trailed off. "I couldn't bring myself to betray it."

"You had no idea it was me."

Maeve nodded. "That's true. But all the same I couldn't do it."

"Then what did you tell them you saw? Warner was cleared of the crime."

Maeve hesitated and debated telling Mal the truth. His dark eyes bore into hers. Truly, it had been an accident. She knew that. That day, inside Valeria's head she had felt it.

Exposing her own lies was a dangerous game. But his eyes. . .they begged for her honesty.

"I lied to my father. To the Double O. To all of them," she whispered. "I said I saw the whole thing. I said that the memory collapsed as I was viewing it. That I made a mistake and broke it." Maeve felt her stomach boil as she admitted the part she was ashamed of. "I said that Valeria tried to kill herself. And Warner saw it."

Mal's eyebrows rose slowly.

Maeve's heart was racing. Mal's eyes moved to her throat. He shook his head ever so slightly and spoke softly, concern flooding into his voice.

"Relax, Maeve."

"It was all I could think of to clear him in the moment, and still not tell them the truth," she said, her voice catching.

His eyes were soft. "Do you believe that I didn't mean to hurt her?"

"Yes," said Maeve with a strained inhale.

Mal looked down at the desk between them. "I lost control. It isn't always easy to have this power flowing through me."

Suddenly Mal's constant cool demeanor made sense.

"What happened?"

Mal didn't look at her. "She was drunk. We were arguing. She and I had been. . . I told her I didn't care for her physical company anymore."

Maeve hated the hot feeling deep in her stomach that bubbled up at that detail.

"She didn't take it well. She started screaming at me. It burst from me before I could even think. I've never felt anything like it. I hope I never do again."

"If you had just told them that, everything would have been fine-"

"I panicked. And you don't know that," he said darkly. "I do not bear the last name you do. Things are different for me."

Maeve steadied her breathing and leaned back in her chair. They knew one another's secret now. Betraying one would mean betraying the other.

"Children of Magic are never alone," she recited the Vaukore motto quietly.

Mal's eyes met hers. And they understood one another.

"You are able to trace your exact bloodline aren't you?" He asked suddenly.

Maeve nodded.

"Could you trace mine?"

"Possibly."

"I've searched every book in the library attempting to find the Peur bloodline."

Maeve bit her bottom lip. "Perhaps they weren't students here. Perhaps they were from elsewhere. Your parents."

Mal stared at the table between them. Maeve thought it must be maddening to not know where one came from.

She knew from Abraxas that when Mal's mother gave birth to him, before she died in a darkened alley, she wrote his name on a dirty piece of newspaper.

Malachite was all she wrote. The name of her baby boy. She knew she wouldn't live long.

An old lady who lived in an apartment nearby said she called herself Mary Peur. That she was a delusional prostitute who insisted her husband was a powerful nobleman.

She was a whore who lived what could have only been a deprived and miserable life.

To die in an icy back alley at the age of seventeen.

Mal didn't speak of it. Ever.

Maeve only knew because she was nosey. Their first year together at Vaukore when Mal soared past her in every subject she traveled to the archives at The Orator's Office and pulled the newspaper describing his birth. The headline stuck with her:

Magic Prevails This New Year: Magical Baby Boy Born Unto Human Woman on the Dark Snowy New Year's Eve Streets of London.

Maeve pulled herself from her thoughts.

"I can research in our private library over Christmas break if you like."

"Yes," said Mal, his voice eager.

"You'll be staying here, I presume?"

He nodded. "I'd like you to bring me back everything you can get your hands on. Every book, anything."

"Consider it done."

"And this conversation never happened," said Mal darkly.

"What conversation?" Asked Maeve with an innocent expression.

Chapter 9

The castle was decorated with shades of silver and crimson silk and crystal. A large fluffy tree covered in gold and white ornaments sat at the center of the library. Snow piled up on the window panes outside as the cold mountain air slammed against the glass.

Maeve attempted to slip past Lavinia and the rest of her book club where they sat on fluffy pillows around the fire, drinks in hand.

"Where do you think you're going?" Said Lavinia.

"To bed," said Maeve.

"No one is in bed this early except boring ole Patty," said Presley.

"Patty has the right idea," said Maeve.

"Come on Maeve," whined Presley. "You said you'd come!"

"Fine," she relented, suppressing a smile.

She curled up on the couch across from Lavinia. Annacorta, a second year, leaned back near her legs.

Harriet was absent from this week's meeting it seemed.

"Spill it," said Lavinia, tilting her head backward.

Maeve's brows raised.

"Malachite Peur," said Presley.

Violet stiffened.

"What kind of book club is this?" Said Maeve with a grin.

"The best kind," said Lavinia, pouring her a cup of tea.

"The kind that gossips?" Asked Maeve.

"That's what I just said," replied Lavinia, passing her a cup of tea.

Maeve opened her mouth before taking it, but Lavinia beat her to it.

"Just plain boring tea. Just the way you like it."

Maeve took the tea and thanked her. "So what are we reading this week?"

"Pride and Prejudice," said Presley with an exaggerated smile.

"Oh good," said Maeve. "I've read that."

Lavinia smacked Presley on the arm. "We aren't reading that, Maeve. We're reading this."

Lavinia tossed her a bright red hardback book. Maeve flipped open the inside cover to the vulgar synopsis.

"Oh my," she said with a laugh.

Annacorta grinned. "I'm already halfway through."

"I don't know if this is my cup of tea," said Maeve.

"If Malachite Peur was shagging me it wouldn't be mine either," said Presley with a drunken cackle.

"Classy, Barton," said Maeve smoothly.

Presley stuck her tongue out.

"Just one detail, Maeve," said Annacorta. "We won't tell anyone you weren't a proper lady."

Lavinia snorted. "We should be asking Harriet. I heard she went up to his room."

"Where is she?" Asked Presley.

Lavinia took a swig of her drink and shrugged.

"I dunno. But I do know that she said he left her speechless."

Clever Harriet. That wasn't a lie. She had indeed been speechless at his rejection.

"Valeria said the same."

"I mean," said Lavinia, "the poor girl tried to off herself when he dumped her it must be the biggest-"

Presley's hand flew over Lavinia's mouth and the girls toppled over laughing.

Maeve felt ill at the mention of Valeria, who never returned to school after the incident, but she kept smiling.

"Just tell us!" Laughed Lavinia.

"I can't because we never have," said Maeve.

Maeve realized that they likely weren't the only ones assuming she and Mal were sleeping together.

"What about his lips?" Asked Presley. "Does he kiss with passion or so, so softly?"

"I wouldn't know," replied Maeve.

"You're such a liar," said Lavinia. She tossed back the rest of her Elven Brandy. "All I can say Maeve is enjoy Mal while you can," she slurred. "You're going to need these books when you're married to your own cousin." She laughed heartily.

Maeve's skin turned to ice. Lavinia's face dropped as her hands flew to her cheeks.

Presley and Violet and Annacorta's giggling ceased. The rest of the girls looked down at their drinks.

"Maeve," she started, "I'm so sorry I shouldn't have said that."

The next breath Maeve took felt ridiculously long.

Last Christmas Astrea Mavros and her cousin Kazir Greenbrier were engaged to be married. They weren't the first Sacred Seventeen relatives to be engaged. And they probably wouldn't be the last.

"I didn't mean that," Lavinia continued, her voice growing panicked. "It slipped out as a joke-"

Maeve's glass vanished from her hand. She pushed off the carpet and Lavinia went to grab her hand. Maeve slipped away before she could, making for the doors of the dorm.

"Maeve!" They called after her.

But she ignored them all. She steadied her breathing and rushed across the common room, throwing open the ivory and gold double doors leading into the castle with the flick of her palm. They slammed into the stone walls behind her.

The corridors were dark at this hour. It was well past curfew. The storm outside rose, lightning flickering on the other side of the vaulted windows. Thunder shook in the distance. Low and steady.

She flew down staircase after staircase. She stopped only once she was outside, in the covered courtyard where stone archways allowed the ice-cold snow to blow through freely chilling her to the bone.

There were no guards in sight. Thank Heavens.

She slumped to the stone steps beneath her, and pulled her knees up close, breathing in the toxically cold air. The storm picked up. Thunder slammed into the castle, jostling her heart.

She was a fool for letting her guard down in front of them. She should have gone to bed. Instead, she was the butt end of a joke.

"Sinclair?"

Maeve didn't need to turn to know who approached her.

Malachite's tall, slender frame appeared in her peripheral vision.

"What are you doing?" He spoke lazily, that cool drawl resonating in his tone.

"Good evening to you too, Malachite. Getting some fresh air," said Maeve, matching his demeanor.

Mal slid his hands into his pockets and looked down at her, waiting for her genuine response. She didn't care to hide from him. She might as well tell him.

"I'm not like them. I don't fit in with them."

"No," said Mal, "you're better than them."

"No," said Maeve with a frustrated sigh. "That's not what I mean. I mean they live entirely different lives than I do. Those girls have no idea what it means to be in my position."

"You envy them for it?"

Maeve didn't answer.

Malachite's brow ticked up. "You do."

Maeve stood and brushed past him. "It's not that simple." He snagged her arm gently before she could pass. Electricity shot down Maeve's arm as she jerked it away from him and stepped back.

"What happened?" He asked. His eyes darted to her hand.

She looked up at him as the Magic begging for release danced across her fingertips. Malachite felt it too. He looked down at her hand where it was twitching at her side.

"Do it," he said quietly, his eyes lifting to hers. "Let it go."

Maeve shook her out hand rapidly, attempting to suppress her anger.

"Don't do that," said Mal. "Let it flow freely."

Maeve stepped back from him once more. "I need to go."

She turned on her heel and as he grabbed her again, that surge of Magic slammed down her arm, cool water spreading through her veins, turning to electric ice.

She turned on him with two sharp fingers and fired at his throat. Malachite's shield slammed up as his fist wrapped around her fingers and dissipated the bright green spell that had just burst from them.

A concise and controlled pulse of Magic whipped towards her, blowing back her hair. Her breathing was quick and erratic.

Nothing that powerful had ever come from her.

Two fingers. She had used two fingers.

"Finally," said Mal calmly with a hint of annoyance. "Congratulations. You're a Supreme, Maeve."

She looked at their hands in disbelief. His touch became delicate as continued.

"I have watched you for months now dueling. In class, as you practice defensive spells. I feel your Magic, desperate to unleash its full strength. The only way to release that level of Magic," he ran his free hand along her middle and pointer fingers, sending ice down her arm, "is here."

"It just. . .happened," she gasped.

Mal nodded slowly. He was deep in thought with his smooth fingers running along her skin. His voice was barely above a whisper as he said, "Such a deadly weapon to be so soft."

Maeve was suddenly hot and cold all at once.

The storm outside had subsided. Light rain pattered against the castle, spilling over into the open courtyard.

He released her right hand. And kept her other arm in his grip as he stepped closer.

"Now," he said, "as for those girls, no, they will never know what it is like to be born of the Sacred. They will never know the burdens you carry for the perpetuation of Magic. They will never know or feel your fear and conflicted emotions about the life before you as a Sacred Seventeen."

"And you," said Maeve, through her teeth, "do you feel my fears and confliction?"

"Every day," said Mal cooly. "They seep out of you, slither across the table, and pierce into my very blood."

Maeve's throat caught as her cheeks began to fill with warmth.

"You wonder every day who it will be on your twenty-second Christmas. Who you will be chained and bound to. There are only so many names on the list." His dark raven eyes sparkled in the moonlight as he spoke with the ease he carried himself with endlessly. "But you don't want it to happen at all."

Maeve didn't realize she was on the verge of tears until warm wet streams saturated her face. Malachite's eyes moved down to her lips as they quivered. He released her arm.

She wiped her cheeks with the back of her hand and fixed her face proudly.

"You do not understand how it feels to be both proud and furious for something you had no say over."

"Do I not?" Asked Mal, a hint of annoyance seeping into his tone.

They stared at one another in silence. Of course he did. Maeve knew he did. He may not have been a Sacred Seventeen, but Mal had come from nothing. He was the most powerful student in history and yet he was found in a damp back alley in his dead mother's arms at only a few hours old. With only his name scribbled on the small piece of paper his mother clutched in her cold, dead hand. No family or even a scrap of clothing of his own.

"Fair enough," said Maeve.

"I know what I plan to do. The only question is what you plan to do."

"I have no intention of letting my life be decided for me," said Maeve darkly.

It was small, but Maeve could have sworn a smile pulled up at the corner of Mal's lips.

"I would expect nothing less from a Supreme."

Chapter 10

Winter holiday had almost arrived. Mirror Lake, one of the many glacier lakes around Vaukore, sat nestled between the castle and the foothills of the mountains. Its bright blue water froze solid overnight. Maeve was anxious to see her father soon. The East Wing of the castle had a perfect view of the reflecting pool of water. She had received a detailed letter from him about all their plans for the Christmas Holiday, and how he couldn't wait to see her.

There were only a few exams left to get through, and Maeve wasn't worried about any of them. However, she was concerned that she hadn't seen Spinel in a few days, which was uncommon, even for her exceptionally curious cat.

She walked the corridors calling his name early one evening with a bit of meat she had taken from dinner. Around the corner, she came face to face with Roswyn. Maeve gasped as they almost collided, but smoothly moved around him.

He stared at her for a moment.

"What are you doing with that meat?"

"Looking for my cat," said Maeve indignantly. She had not forgiven Roswyn for their last altercation. "I'd say you owe me an apology, but based on the bruises still lingering on your face, you got what you deserved."

Roswyn's temper swelled, and he tried to steady his breathing.

"I must really get under your skin," laughed Maeve.

"I guess I just don't understand it," said Roswyn, his face sour.

Maeve raised her eyebrows, and he continued.

"According to that cauldron, you weren't even worthy of studying Combative Magic, no matter how pure your blood is."

Maeve's heart rate began increasing at his comment. She changed the subject.

"You and Emerie having fun?"

Roswyn smirked. "I picked her years ago. Turns out she's as good as I imagined."

"Too bad about her Magic though."

Roswyn glared at her.

"A lineage of seers and not single prophecy made." Maeve clicked her tongue.

"Yeah," said Roswyn. "But that Cauldron still chose her over you."

Maeve's smirk faltered against her will. Roswyn smiled.

"So I don't get it. I don't get why he gives you the time of day."

"Couldn't say," said Maeve. "Perhaps he grows tired of listening to you whine."

Roswyn laughed. "He'll grow tired of you soon enough. One way or another. Clock is ticking. When's your twenty-second birthday again?"

Roswyn hit his mark. Maeve's cheeks flushed hot. Roswyn nodded in triumph. "Thank Primus and all the Gods it's not me."

"You've got that damn right." Maeve rolled her eyes and turned away from him to continue her search for Spinel.

After over an hour of searching, Maeve sat on the main stairs of the castle, just outside Hellming Hall. Roswyn's comment lingered in her mind.

From the side corridor emerged Headmaster Elgin. Her long gray hair was loose and free.

"Good evening, Maeve."

"Evening, Madam," said Maeve politely.

Elgin stopped and observed her. "What seems to be the matter?" Asked Elgin.

"My cat," said Maeve. "I haven't seen him in a few days, which is not like him."

"The black one, with the odd colored eyes?"

Maeve nodded.

"Oh, I'm certain he'll turn up," said Elgin. "Cats are brilliant creatures, and you know what they say?" Maeve waited for her to continue. "They say they take after their owners, which makes him the second brightest cat at Vaukore."

Maeve's brows raised, certain she had never heard Elgin crack a joke. Maeve smiled at this attempt to cheer her up.

"If I may speak boldly," said Elgin, "I have noticed you and Mr. Peur have become close-"

Maeve laughed. "Why is everyone so fixated on that?"

"Forgive me," said Elgin genuinely. "It's just that it can be incredibly lonely to be, so to say, above the rest. When I made Bellator straight out of school even those closest to me became distant."

"You were a Bellator? In the Magical Militia or Law Enforcement?"

"Yes," she replied. "Your Father was a Captain then. When the time came I chose Magical Law. Not the military."

Maeve smiled. "I've heard he was beloved then."

Elgin nodded. "He was a marvel. His leadership capabilities were unmatched. His Pureblood Magic was, and still is, a force to be reckoned."

"That's funny," said Maeve. "I don't see him that way."

"Of course not," said Elgin gently. "At any rate, I only meant that you and Mr. Peur are both incredibly gifted, and I hope the pair of you can assist one another in your Magical journey."

Maeve looked away. "Yes. He's helped me a great deal."

Elgin nodded. "And I believe you are capable of doing the same."

Maeve smiled. "Thank you. I think I'll head to bed now."

"Goodnight, Maeve."

Maeve stood, turned, and made her way back up the stairs, resigning to go to bed without Spinel.

On the final day of classes before the holiday, Maeve finished her History of Dread essay in record time. She sat down at a desk in the common room to write a brief note to attach to the gift she was giving Mal.

Malachite,
Thank you for all your help this term.
I hope you like this token of my appreciation.
Maeve

She rolled the note up and tied the little purple box with a green ribbon. This gift was a last-minute decision on Maeve's part, prompted by Abraxas mentioning that Mal's birthday was on the winter solstice on New Year's Eve, for which he'd be alone.

"Funny," Abraxas had said, as he copied her notes from Curses and Their Counters Class, "yours was the Autumn Equinox. Which you wouldn't let me celebrate for you this year."

Maeve had ignored him.

She placed the gift in her bag and went down to Hellming Hall.

After having a bite to eat, she made her way across the room to one of the long mahogany tables, where Mal sat.

"Going to Hummingdoor's party tonight?" Inquired Maeve.

"I am," said Mal. "He'd be devastated if his favorite didn't."

Maeve laughed.

"Well, I'm off to pack for the holiday. I wanted to give you this before tonight, even though it's next week." Maeve reached into her bag and handed him the small purple box tied up with green string. "Happy Birthday."

Mal looked dumbfounded. He looked twice from the present and back at her and then began tugging at the string.

"Oh Heavens, no," said Maeve. "Don't open it in front of me. I don't want to see the look on your face if you hate it. See you tonight."

Maeve flounced away, leaving Mal looking somewhat confused.

Hummingdoor's party was, as usual, lavishly decorated. Gold and emerald drapes with sparkling moons hung about the hall. A large table stacked with food, including a giant chocolate fountain, ran along the center of the packed hall.

"You look lovely, Maeve," said Abraxas, taking her arm. "I do always say silver is your color."

"Thank you, cousin." Maeve smiled at him.

"Bet you're ready to be home."

"Dying," corrected Maeve. "Though, this Christmas marks seven years since Antony's death. . ."

Abraxas stopped walking and looked at her, stunned.

"You. . . you never talk about him."

Maeve gave him a small smile and looked away.

"No, no, no," said Abraxas, grabbing her arms. "You can talk about anything you like, of course. It just caught me off guard."

Maeve thanked him and smiled. "I suppose I'm trying to stop running away from it."

Abraxas nodded. "Let's get some drinks, shall we?"

Abraxas poured her a full glass of Dragon Whiskey, and even though she protested, he shoved it in her hand regardless.

"One drink, Maeve," said Abraxas, clicking his goblet against hers.

"Fine," she relented without a smile.

They were seated at a table of students playing a card game, all of their cheeks flushed red as Abraxas told a hilarious story. Maeve pretended to drink her bright green beverage and poured it into Abraxas' cup when he wasn't paying attention.

"Damn it, Rosethorn," growled Randolf Grisham, throwing down his cards. "Your incessant yapping makes it hard to concentrate."

Abraxas didn't respond and pulled the money at the center of the table towards himself. Maeve laughed, tossing her losing hand into the deck.

"Phineus, you can take my spot," said Maeve.

She stood, patting Abraxas on the shoulder, and slipped away. She found a small table on the far side of the room and seated herself.

Even though it was his party, Maeve saw very little of the Alchemy Professor. He eventually got so drunk that Henry Willis had to escort him to bed while he slurred and shouted for everyone to enjoy their dinner.

She watched a few students dancing to the music, wondering if she would waltz at any of the parties over the holiday. Her father was an excellent dancing partner.

Mal's entrance immediately caught her eye. He was wearing a black turtle neck sweater, which fit him nicely, and grey slacks. She watched him make his way through the crowd. His charming nature was at its peak tonight.

After a moment, he spotted Maeve, excused himself from his conversation, and made his way toward her.

"I've noticed your affinity for sitting alone," said Mal, "but do you mind if I join you?"

"Not at all," said Maeve gesturing to the seat beside her.

He pulled out the chair and as he sat he watched her for a moment.

"Thank you for the gift," he said finally.

"It's tradition to give a Magical a watch for their twenty-first birthday. Since I won't see you on your actual birthday, I figured I would go ahead."

Mal pulled the sleeve of his sweater back slightly, revealing the gold watch with an emerald inlay. The two hands were serpents with bright red tongues, and the numbers were ancient ruins.

"You didn't have to," said Mal.

"I know that."

Maeve reached out her hand without thinking and ran her fingers over the face of the watch. The sapphire ring on her finger complimented it perfectly.

"It really is lovely," she whispered.

She froze, realizing her potential mistake. She looked up at Mal, whose eyes were already locked on hers. Maeve's fingers lingered across Mal's hand. His skin was cool to the touch, and his expression was softer than she could ever recall seeing him. He slowly turned his hand over, and Maeve instinctively ran her fingers across his smooth palm, trapped in his gaze.

"Did you find Spinel?" Asked Mal quietly.

"Yes. He came back last night," said Maeve breathlessly.

Mal didn't pull his hand away, nor did he break their gaze.

"Good. Are you packed for home?"

Maeve nodded.

"Have you contemplated staying?" He whispered.

Ice trickled down her arm as his fingers reached up, gently holding her wrist in place.

"How would I raid my father's library for you then?"

Mal inhaled slowly. "I suppose you wouldn't."

"And that's very important to you, is it not?"

His fingers constricted around her wrist.

"Incredibly."

"Then I'm afraid I must go."

His eyes dipped to her lips and back to her gaze. "Shame."

There was a loud crash as the xylophone was knocked to the ground, and the music abruptly scratched to a halt. The room filled with intoxicated laughter.

Maeve jerked her hand away and avoided Mal's eyes.

"Looks like it's time to eat," said Maeve as most of the party seemed to be making their way across the room to the larger dining table. Maeve and Malachite followed suit and took seats next to one another, and Abraxas took the seat on her other side.

The evening was enjoyable. Without Hummingdoor, the conversation actually flowed nicely. Though, with no one there to regulate the Immortally Brewed Bourbon and Dragon Whiskey intake, the night became boisterous rather quickly.

There was a definitive difference between the table of upper-level students and the table of first years who stared at the others in shock. Lavinia had threatened to start giving out detentions to a few if they continued drinking, though Maeve noticed she seemed quite intoxicated herself. Mal and Maeve were discussing an article from that morning's paper on Kietel when she heard her name come up in conversation.

"Maeve's got a dragon skin in her house," said Abraxas, his cheeks flushed bright pink. "Basement, really."

"No way," said Hermes Grandleberri. "I thought they weren't real!"

Hermes had clearly had too much to drink, but Maeve couldn't resist commenting.

"How are you even at this party when you don't realize dragons were and, more importantly, still are, real."

There was a round of laughter as Herme's eyebrows furrowed in confusion.

"Is there really a dragon skin in your house?" Asked a wide-eyed girl with glasses. Maeve recognized her as a new student, though she wasn't sure of her name.

"Yes," said Maeve offhandedly. "The skull too."

"Damn, that's wicked," the girl grinned widely. Maeve returned her smile and turned back to Mal to continue their conversation.

"You think just because you're a Pureblood whose Daddy is the Premier you belong at this table," spat Randolf Grisham from across the table.

The entire room instantly went silent. The air pulled tight around them.

Maeve looked across the table, certain Grisham's comment was directed at someone else. But based on the hostile stare she was receiving, she was incorrect.

Maeve's charming smile didn't falter as she stared him back down.

"My apologies, Grisham, I didn't realize I needed to present you with my qualifications when I arrived tonight." Maeve looked around at the others. "Did anyone else forget? No? Just me then." An icy quality began seeping into her otherwise delicate voice.

Mal folded his hands in his lap and leaned back joyfully as he watched Grisham's expression.

"But since you're so curious," said Maeve. "I'm at this table tonight because I have performed at an Elite level for years, in multiple subjects. And recently, A Supreme level. I score at the top of the school consistently and am incredibly dedicated to the execution of Magic beyond what we know of its limitations. I'm a Paragon, incredibly well organized and studious, and have written hundreds of unassigned papers over my educational time here at Vaukore simply because I enjoy learning and exploring Magic. I am the youngest witch in history to create a memory charm and, undoubtedly, one of the youngest to create any type of spell, let alone one that quite literally bends the mind. I am the only witch on record in the history of Magic with the ability to jump between minds and I would bet my father's entire fortune you don't even come close to that achievement."

She picked up her sparking water, toasting Grisham as his cheeks flooded red with anger and left him with a final seething blow.

"And for the record, I am not 'just a pureblood,' Grisham. I'm a fucking Sacred Seventeen. And you'll do well to remember it."

There were a few chuckles, the loudest being Abraxas', who applauded.

Mal sat like a chiseled statue next to her; only after a moment passed and regular conversation had resumed did she feel his slender fingers enclose around her own under the table.

Chapter 11

"Good morning!" Chimed Maeve cheerfully as Abraxas slumped into a horse-drawn carriage for the ride across the plains to the Portal the next morning.

Abraxas grimaced. He grabbed his head and motioned for her to be quiet.

"I can't imagine why you aren't feeling well," said Maeve with no attempt to lower her voice and no sympathy for his hangover.

A group of students on horseback running by singing Christmas carols at the top of their lungs sent Abraxas reeling. He laid down in the seat and dramatically threw his coat over his face.

Maeve was nestled in the corner. Her mind wandered as she attempted to read with her legs propped up on the seat. The carriage was warm and cozy. She was undoubtedly excited to see her father over the holiday, and she had never contemplated staying at school for Christmas before now. As the horses began their leisurely pace across the vast grounds, their hoofs crunching against their snow to the gates of Vaukore, she felt conflicted for the first time.

Her thoughts drifted to Mal's invitation for her to stay. . .and what that might entail.

She had other purposes for going home, though, besides just the holidays. She was dying to hear about Kietel from her father, and she had promised Mal she would bring him as much information as possible regarding his possible heritage.

This gave her enough purpose to put aside her strange and newfound desire to remain at school over the break and focus on the tasks at hand.

Everything was as expected back home. Her father, Ambrose, threw his arms around her the moment he saw her step out of the Portal in London. Maeve had coerced him over many letters to not give her a private escort again.

"Is that a new coat?" He had asked.

"Yes." Maeve grinned from ear to ear, showing it off. "Velvetina's."

"It looks lovely on you," beamed Ambrose.

Her mother, Clarissa, had given her a polite smile and nod as she and Ambrose entered the foyer of Sinclair Estates. She then immediately began ordering Maeve's maid Zimsy to put away all her things, and Maeve didn't see her mother again until dinner.

Her father, of course, wanted to know all about school and how her past few months had been. Ambrose had already arranged for tea in his study so they could properly catch up. Maeve obliged with great joy.

Her father nearly shed a tear when Maeve told him she used two fingers only a few nights ago. His youngest daughter was a Supreme.

Christmas came and went rather quickly. Maeve received quite a few lovely gifts, but her favorite was the dress her Grandmother Agatha sent her. It was a custom-made gown from Persia, silver and gold, and it was absolutely stunning.

"Mother intended for you to wear it to The Rosethorn's for the Sacred Party," said Ambrose.

The Sacred Seventeen Party, a time-honored tradition for Maeve's family, was not only thrown by The Committee of the Sacred, but it was held at the end of December, between Christmas and New Year's Day. It was exclusively for the families of the only Pureblood Magicals left and sometimes their honored guests.

The holiday season in general had proved to be a difficult day for the Sinclair family in the wake of Antony Sinclair's death.

"Of course," said Maeve, holding the dress against her body and admiring it. "I love it."

Arianna opened her dress for the Sacred Seventeen party next. Arianna smirked when it was more expensive than Maeve's. Maeve rolled her eyes.

An hour later, when all the presents were opened, Clarissa didn't hesitate to begin clearing the room of boxes and bags. Though she herself didn't lift a finger. She only ordered the Elven servants in the house to do so.

The fire between Maeve and her father danced warm shadows across the room. Maeve slipped off her shoes and pulled her legs onto the lounging chair.

"I want to ask you about Kietel," she said plainly.

Arianna's shoulders pulled up, but she didn't look their way. She was nose-deep in a new book.

"What about him?" Replied Ambrose.

"Do you think that it's true?"

"Unfortunately what I think doesn't matter," said Ambrose. "I must treat the threat with validity."

"Threat?" Asked Maeve with a quick laugh. "If he is the Dread Descendant, then is it wise to go against him? You know the prophecy of his return as well as I do."

"I do," said Ambrose. "And his claims align with that of the prophecy."

"Then I don't understand what makes him the enemy. Some made up Human line of land?"

"No," said Ambrose. "Some of Germany's Magical Militia have pulled from the treaties we have with the humans. My men. They are not fighting the same war we are anymore."

"So what are they fighting for?"

"Domination. Under a new flag. Under a new regime."

Maeve leaned back in her chair. "I read his speech. The one from this morning that the Starlight Gazette printed and you threw in the fire."

Ambrose pulled a cigar from a golden box on the side table, the tip lighting instantly as it touched his lips.

"Where did you get a copy," he asked casually.

Maeve ignored him and continued. "He seeks to free Magicals from their confinement."

"Ah," said Ambrose. "But that is not the prophecy, is it?"

"It's part of it," argued Maeve.

"It's not, Maeve. You so badly want it to be true?"

"No," said Maeve. "For what it's worth I don't believe he is the Dread Descendant."

A smile tugged at Ambrose's lips. "I figured not."

"The prophecy speaks of those with Golden Blood being freed."

Ambrose nodded.

"Purebloods."

He nodded again, all trace of that smile gone. "As you can see, that puts me in a precarious position with the Orator's Office. And the other realms. It is not my duty to protect only Magicals with Pureblood. It is my duty to protect the Magical world from evil actions, regardless of whether those actions are Magical or not."

"I know. Have you seen Reeve recently?"

Ambrose eyed her. "The Immortal High Lord," he corrected, "is not meant to make an appearance at the party."

"What does he say?" Asked Maeve.

"Alright," said Ambrose as he clapped his hands on his knees and stood.

"What?" Asked Maeve, feigning innocence.

Ambrose smiled and flicked her nose. "That doesn't work on me."

Maeve batted his hand away and he chuckled, planting a kiss on her forehead. Arianna, who had been pretending not to listen to their conversation, crossed her legs and eyed Maeve.

"What's your problem?" Asked Maeve lazily.

Arianna shrugged arrogantly and Maeve ignored her sister for the rest of the evening.

The Sacred Seventeen party was at Rosethorn Manor, which greatly excited Abraxas. He loved a good party. Maeve received many compliments on her dress, which Grandmother Agatha took full credit for every time.

After a brief, but lovely, dance with her father, Maeve was seated outside on the balcony. The grounds at Rosethorn Manor were enchanted to give off a warm fuzzy feeling, which was preferable to the icy climate they were currently in.

Up the balcony, steps came a familiar face. One that had, in the past, brought butterflies to her stomach.

Alphard Mavros stumbled towards Maeve, laughing with a younger gentleman Maeve didn't recognize.

Alphard stopped in his tracks and smiled upon seeing her. His eyes raked over her body quickly, but she didn't miss it. He stood up tall.

"Hello, Alphard," said Maeve before he could speak.

"Maeve," smiled Alphard. "How's Vaukore?"

Maeve shrugged. 'Same as ever."

His chin lowered. "You wound me so easily."

Maeve smirked. Alphard took a long swig of his drink and nodded to his friend to move along.

"Abraxas says you and Malachite have become chummy."

"Abraxas says a lot of things. He is my tutor."

Alphard clicked his tongue and eyed her. "Didn't think clever Witches like you with perfect scores needed tutors."

"You don't know anything about what I need," said Maeve playfully.

"Don't I?" Smirked Alphard.

"You're picking on me now."

"You make it so easy," he teased, taking a seat beside her.

Maeve suddenly felt like he was too close. Though she and Alphard had been much closer upon a few occasions, panic rushed through her as his arm brushed hers.

"I heard you made Paragon again as well," said Alphard.

"Checking up on me, I see."

Alphard laughed, raising his hands in omission. He looked her over for a moment. Maeve inhaled sharply as his eyes glazed into a lustful look, shifting down to her lips.

His voice changed. "Let's go take a walk," said Alphard, taking her sparkling water from her and setting it down.

Maeve glanced up at him. Alphard was like all the Mavros family boys. Dark skin and hair, ruggedly handsome, broad shoulders, full of ease, quick-tempered, and nothing but rebellion in his blood. And now, after just a few short months as a Bellator in training, his build was stronger. Not to mention the Mavros were the wealthiest Magical family in the world. Alphard and Antony's abundance of gold got them out of quite a few pickles in their glory days as young teenagers. Alphard loved to start fights. Antony loved to finish them.

But as Alphard took her hand, she pulled it away gently.

"The duel is about to start," said Maeve, making an excuse. She smiled at him as her stomach twisted.

He scoffed softly and narrowed his eyes at her mischievously. "Whatever you say, Sinclair."

He downed the rest of his drink and made his way inside. Maeve remained where she sat, feeling guilty for having turned him down.

Ambrose came through a set of double doors a moment later, motioning for her.

"The duel is starting, love."

Maeve didn't hear him. She was staring off across the lawn. Ambrose made his way over to her.

"Maeve."

She jumped as his voice pulled her abruptly out of her thoughts.

"Yes?" Asked Maeve.

"Is something wrong?"

She couldn't muster the feigned smile she would have typically given him. "I think I just need some air."

Ambrose leaned against the banister.

"We're outside, darling," said Ambrose, his face concerned.

Maeve stood. "A walk then."

Ambrose slipped off his jacket and handed it to her. Maeve slipped it on, wrapping her arms around herself. The warm scent of cinnamon cigars nestled into her bones.

"Can I do anything else?" Ambrose asked.

Maeve shook her head. "I just need to work through a few things myself."

Ambrose squeezed her shoulder and smiled at her before turning back towards the house.

She stepped onto the grassy lawn. The gardens were lit with floating candles along the pathway to the rocky shore, illuminating the colorful florals that bloomed year-round. Maeve's family used a similar enchantment in their own gardens to keep everything in constant bloom.

She took her time down the path, trying to think of everything except what was eating at her. It was no use, though.

Alphard. His attention had made her uncomfortable when it never had before. She suppressed the root of those feelings and walked in solitude with a foreign and uneasy guilt while the rest of the party enjoyed the duels.

Perhaps Mal would be participating in the duels if he were there. He'd dazzle them all.

Outside of the gardens, she reached the shoreline. It was suddenly cold, and the ground was icy and slick. She pulled Ambrose's jacket tightly around herself. The sky was clear, but the ocean was violently slamming water into the rocky beach. It pushed and pulled with great force. Each crash sent a cold burst of air towards her. A wobbling light from above reflected alone the dark water.

She looked up. Small, glistening green lights floated towards her across the sky. She squinted. It was a raven. As it approached her she held out her arm. The great bird spread its wings wide and lowered itself onto Maeve's extended arm. She took the square parchment from its leg.

Maeve,
I hope your holiday is going well.
-M

The raven pressed against her, soaring its body back into the dark night sky.

His words were brief. . .but they were his.

Her cheeks turned warm at the unexpected letter.

"How odd," she whispered with a smile as the raven disappeared in the darkness.

A sense of purpose surged through her. She turned sharply on her heel and quickly returned to the Manor with Mal's letter gripped tightly in her hand.

The duels were still in progress, which enabled her to slip into the house and upstairs without being seen. The Rosethorn's had a study on the second floor, three doors past Abraxas' room, where she could draft a letter to Mal.

She tossed open the door to the study. Aunt Beatrice Rosethorn had a large assortment of stationary to pick from as Maeve pulled open the drawers of the desk. She picked a random set of parchment and laid it flat on the desk. Aunt Beatrice also had dozens of ornate quills to pick from. Dainty blue jay quills, brown and white hawk quills, even a bright red phoenix quill. Maeve grabbed a plain white quill and dipped it in the ink well.

She stared at the blank parchment. Her mind crept to a halt as her breathing slowed. The perfect words would not come, no matter how much she begged. And so she placed the tip of the quill on the golden parchment and wrote.

Malachite,

I hope yours is as well. There's a duel tonight, and I imagine you'd be putting them all to shame.

-Maeve

She rolled up the parchment with a smile and sealed it with red wax and a gold ribbon. Cheers and applause echoed down the hallway from the duels below as she snuck quickly to the west tower where there was a small mail desk she knew would have access to Vaukore.

She placed the letter at the center of the desk, and after a moment, it burst into flames. Dissolving into nothing.

Maeve smiled.

She re-entered the party as Leslie Loxerman was taking the stage to make, what looked like, a toast. Loxerman was the current head of The Committee of The Sacred. She had short brown hair and a perpetual frown.

"Thank you all for coming to such a wonderful evening, and thanks graciously to the Rosethorns for hosting us," said Loxerman.

The room applauded. Maeve watched her Aunt Beatrice relishing the praise.

"Now," continued Loxerman, "One of the best Sacred Party traditions and something we all know to be the backbone of preserving our Pureblood lines. . . An engagement announcement." There was an exciting buzz throughout the room. Engagements were becoming more and more rare as pureblood lines died out. "Please raise a glass to Titus Iantrose and Arianna Sinclair!"

Her jaw fell open.

Maeve scanned the crowd quickly and laid eyes on her father, who was embracing Titus happily. Her sister Arianna was perfectly poised next to Titus.

Suddenly, Arianna's expensive dress made sense.

Maeve knew perfectly well Arianna barely knew Titus and had mentioned upon occasion that he looked like an oversized goblin. Yet here she stood, her arm wrapped around his, looking up at him as though he hung the moon.

It was her duty as a Pureblood, nothing more.

The whole affair was grotesquely fake and not the first time Maeve had witnessed two barely of-age friends rejoicing, or so it seemed, celebrating their arranged marriage.

No one had even bothered to tell her.

The crowd raised their glasses. "To Titus and Arianna!"

"Oh, Maeve," said Juliet, a Pureblood Witch about Maeve's age, suddenly appearing at Maeve's side. "Isn't it wonderful?"

Juliet sighed happily and squeezed Maeve's arm. "Just think how soon that'll be me up there."

Maeve nodded, not paying her much attention. Her eyes were locked on her twenty-three-year-old sister.

"Even sooner," continued Juliet, joy oozing from her tone, "you."

Maeve's stomach dropped as she plastered on a smile. "How exciting."

Chapter 12

Maeve walked up and down the rows of books in her father's library, looking for anything that might help Mal find even a hint of his ancestry. It would seem utterly unorganized to a proper librarian, but Maeve felt her father would know precisely what she was looking for.

After close to an hour of perusing on her own, she resigned and pulled her father away from his work in his study.

"What in particular are you looking for?" Asked Ambrose.

"I suppose, blood lineage?" Replied Maeve innocently. Ambrose stopped and eyed her. There was a glimmer in his eyes.

"That's very vague," said Ambrose slowly.

"It is."

"Can't you be any more specific?"

Maeve bit her lip.

"Alright," laughed Ambrose. "Come."

He guided her a few rows down and reached up to a high shelf.

"This one," said Ambrose, pulling down a wide, thick page book with no title, "has the most family trees but little additional information. You'll need to cross-reference with any of these." He gestured to an area of books on the higher shelf, also with blank spines.

"That's a mighty fine start. Thank you," said Maeve taking the large book from him and setting it on a desk.

Ambrose lingered for a moment.

"This wouldn't have anything to do with your disbelief in Kietel's Dread Descendent claims would it?"

"No," said Maeve as she opened the book and ran her finger down the index.

"Surely you can at least tell me whose blood you're looking to inspect without specifics."

Maeve laughed. "A friend from school."

"A friend I am unaware of?"

"A friend you are not unaware of. My tutor."

"Ah," said Ambrose excitedly, as though she had just confessed something. "The tutor that has you casting Supreme level spells? And how is this young wizard unsure of his bloodline? He's of human decent?"

"No," said Maeve defensively. "Well, only partly. That would be wild. He's. . . He was abandoned as a baby. He grew up in a human orphanage with no idea of his abilities."

"That's interesting."

Maeve nodded as she flipped through a few pages.

"Is he-"

"That's all the information you're getting, Daddy," said without looking at him.

Ambrose turned to leave, but he stopped. "At least tell me his name?"

Maeve grinned. "Malachite Peur."

Ambrose nodded, content with his interrogation, and took his leave. Maeve gathered all the books and carried them back upstairs to her room to browse in solitude. The last thing she needed was Arianna being nosey.

Hours and hours of research and Maeve came up dry. She ran her hands across her face with a groan.

"More tea?" Asked Zimsy.

Maeve shook her head. "I think it's making me jittery now."

Zimsy sat on the lush carpet across from her and folded her legs beneath her. Her Elven hair spiraled past her shoulders, shiny as silk.

Her wide eyes peered over the books Maeve flipped through. Her features were delicate, like those of a bird, with subtly pointed ears and glowing skin, She had only been a child herself when she came to be a servant in their house. Years before Maeve was born. But even now, Zimsy glowed with everlasting beauty, as all the Elven people did.

"Who is he?"

"Who is who?"

'The boy that keeps writing you letters."

Maeve looked up at her. "Don't be nosey."

Zimsy smiled at her. "Please. There isn't a single thing you do that I don't know about. I'm Magically bound to you and the first time something remotely interesting is happening-"

"Damn," sighed Maeve with a smile. "I had no idea your life was so boring without me."

"I've had to wait on Arianna while you've been at school."

Maeve grimaced.

"Exactly," said Zimsy desperately. "Tell me who he is."

Maeve shook her head.

Zimsy cried out in annoyance and flung her hands up. The sleeves of her pale yellow linen dress flittered up. It was a modest outfit. As all the servants wore.

Maeve's smile faded.

"What's that?" Asked Maeve sharply.

Zimsy followed Maeve's gaze to the backs of her arms. Zimsy's cheeks flushed.

"Gods be dammed," said Maeve darkly.

Zimsy pulled her sleeves down hurriedly. But it was too late. Maeve had already seen the marks of punishment on her arms. Deep red and purple lumps of bruising saturated the back of her petite arms.

"Don't get all worked up," started Zimsy.

But Maeve held up her hand. Zimsy's lips pulled into a thin line.

Maeve closed her eyes and steadied the breath of hatred that rose in her chest.

She felt Zimsy moved behind her. Her small fingers laced through Maeve's hair, beginning a braid.

Maeve opened her eyes and picked back up the book.

"His name is Mal."

Maeve and Mal wrote back and forth over the winter holiday. Each time Maeve sent a letter, she was immediately eager for Mal's reply.

The Sinclairs hosted Arianna's fiancé, Titus' family, for dinner one evening shortly before Maeve's return to Vaukore. Titus was as dull as Maeve had imagined him. He worked for the Double O in Magical Transportation Laws.

"You must see some pretty exciting things then," said Ambrose.

"Not really," said Titus dully. "I mostly do paperwork registering new Letter Desks as they get manufactured."

Maeve gave Arianna a discouraged look, who had given up on her facade of a smile twenty minutes ago.

"Sounds fascinating," said Maeve.

Titus shoved a piece of meat in his mouth and chewed loudly. "Not really," he said, shrugging.

He was as bright as he looked. Maeve looked again to Arianna, but her sister would not meet her eye. She stared down at her plate.

Titus' mother changed the conversation to their wedding, which Maeve's mother insisted on hosting here at their home. This perked Arianna up slightly.

Ambrose managed to withhold his curiosity about Malachite until the night before Maeve's journey back to Vaukore.

He and Maeve were seated in Ambrose's study playing a game of chess. There was a large fire in the middle of a black marbled fireplace, and Maeve was settled in an armchair with a fur blanket keeping her toasty.

Ambrose's study had a large mahogany desk with floor-to-ceiling shelves filled with various books, magical objects, pictures, and boxes. It smelled distinctly of the cigars Ambrose frequently smoked.

The couches and chairs were covered in elegant, dark leather.

"Malachite Peur was it?" Asked Ambrose casually as he moved a pawn.

"What about him?" Maeve asked cooly.

Ambrose shrugged. "I don't know that name. Just a curious name is all."

"You mean it's not a Sacred Seventeen name," said Maeve, cornering his king.

Ambrose looked displeased.

Maeve laughed, "I'm too sharp for those kinds of lies, Daddy."

Ambrose looked at her seriously.

"I'm being pressured, Maeve," said Ambrose. " Next year you'll be twenty-two. I want to give you as much time, as much freedom, but your duties-"

"I don't want to discuss it," said Maeve, her voice quiet and strained. "Watching Arianna stand beside Titus like that. . ." Maeve trailed off. "You should really pay more attention to your game."

Ambrose's king burst into flames as it vanished from the board.

"I think I'll head to bed," said Maeve victoriously, stretching.

"Oh now, I didn't mean to ruin the mood."

Maeve smiled. "You didn't. I'm tired and need to pack."

"Zimsy packed for you, surely."

"Well, I'm still tired," said Maeve. "I did want to ask you one thing, though."

"Anything," said Ambrose.

"I overheard you and Uncle Rosethorn talking at The Sacred Party about Reeve. You wouldn't answer me the first time. But I want to know: do you still have an alliance with him?"

Ambrose leaned back in his chair. "Yes," said Ambrose after a moment. "The High Lord is aware of Kietel's claims if that's what you're asking."

"Has Kietel been to the Immortal Lands?"

Ambrose shook his head. "Not yet."

"But Reeve would know if he did right?"

"Where is your etiquette?" Asked Ambrose with a laugh. "The High Lord-"

"I'm sorry it seems silly to call him that," said Maeve.

"You dislike the Immortal God?"

"No. I've never really met him."

"Surely you have at a party?"

Maeve shrugged. "Maybe. It's been years I think. I can't even recall what he looks like, so I hardly think that counts. Do you like him?"

"Reeve is one of my closest allies and oldest friends. I have known him my whole life."

"He is prepared to move against Kietel if need be?"

Ambrose laughed. "Since when are you so into politics?"

"Since the humans forced their war into my world."

Ambrose gazed at her, his eyes glistening with pride in the firelight.

"Sometimes I forget how grown you are... how bright. But do not forget, it is we who forced our way into theirs."

He took her hand across the chess board and squeezed it three times. This was an act of affection Ambrose had done with her since she was a child. Each squeeze represented a word in a silent "I love you."

"If you do not plan to be on Kietel's side of the conflict to come then yes, The High Lord and his army are prepared to fight alongside me and the Magical Militia."

"And you trust the Immortals to win?"

"The Immortals have an advantage and have for a thousand years. The power of the Gods being in the hands of The Senshi Warriors is beyond our own. Reeve is and has been for hundreds of years, the most powerful being alive. But I do worry- it won't be enough."

"But you have great relations with Reeve," said Maeve. "You just said so."

"Yes," agreed Ambrose. "But the High Lord is not the only one at play here."

"The Elven lands have been sealed shut for three hundred years-"

"They are not of whom I speak."

Maeve studied him for a moment, then her jaw fell slightly open as she asked:

"You don't think the Humans pose an actual threat do you?"

Ambrose's eyes narrowed, as though he was calculating how to respond to his daughter.

"Have you seen what those bombs can do?" He asked.

Maeve shook her head. "No, but-"

Ambrose interrupted her. "They are only the beginning. They are killing each other by the thousands. It's only a matter of time before Magicals are in danger too."

Maeve sat back in her seat, brows pulled together, and spoke calmly.

"But, what you are insinuating, that can't happen. Our numbers are already too few, especially ones like us."

"With Pure Blood?" Asked Ambrose, pointedly.

"Yes," said Maeve with a small exhale.

"How many Half Bloods are there now Maeve? How many babies are being born each year with no Magical lineage at all?"

When Maeve didn't answer, he continued.

"Do you not know?"

She shook her head in defeat. Ambrose continued.

"Pure Blooded Magic is dying out and has been for quite some time. When our people fled to Earth there were over fifty Sacred Families that made it out alive. Now there are seventeen. Magic is finding a way to preserve its existence despite our failure."

The word failure hit Maeve in the chest like a train.

Ambrose sensed it and gave her a soft reproachful look. "I mean our failure three hundred years ago. My forefather's failure to defeat the darkness that drove us here."

Maeve nodded, eager to shift topics. "One more thing. Zimsy."

He sighed. But not in frustration at her.

"I know." He said.

Maeve waited a moment before she spoke. "Do you?"

Ambrose bowed his head. "I don't have a say, Maeve.'

"This is your household," she fired back.

"And Zimsy and the other Elven servants came from the Rosethorn's with your Mother. Do not forget the Sinclair's never held a slave."

Something slimy trailed down her arms at the word.

"Don't call her that," said Maeve slowly, her voice laced with ice.

Ambrose's eyes softened. He stood and moved towards her. He cupped her face between his hands. He spoke warmly. "My darling daughter. I'm sorry."

When he released her, her head fell back against the leather armchair. "After my twenty-second. When I leave this household. Does she come with me?"

"Her enslavement curse lies with your Mother."

Maeve nodded. That was all she needed to know. So she made her way to bed after she stood and kissed her father's cheek.

The Sinclair house was dark and quiet. Once she was inside her room, the candelabra on her desk was shining down on a letter from Mal. She opened it at once.

Maeve,

I wonder so often if Kietel travels to the Dread Lands. I also wonder why or when or if he will go after the Orator's Office. I'm certain your father keeps a tight lip on those affairs.

I heard from Abraxas that your sister is engaged. Congratulations are in order. The paper printed it on the front page as well. Sacred engagements become rarer and rarer it seems. Perhaps one day, if Kietel truly returns us to our ancestor's home realm, such forced arrangements won't be necessary.

Eagerly awaiting your return,
M

Maeve folded up the letter and stowed it away in her ivory leather bag. Knowing she would see him the next day, Maeve didn't reply.

She curled up under her dark blue velvet canopy bed, which had its ceiling enchanted to span over various stars and constellations. They twinkled faintly as Maeve reflected on Mal's words, eager to bring him the the first step in his journey to the past.

Chapter 13

"Was it absolutely necessary for you to go telling all of my business to Alphard?" Maeve asked Abraxas in the tearoom at Sinclair estates early the next morning. Ambrose was Portalling them to Vaukore. Abraxas insisted on being included.

Abraxas rolled his eyes and leaned back in the armchair. "No, but it was fun to watch him get all worked up."

"Oh, shut up. Alphard adores Malachite like the rest of you pricks."

Spinel jumped into Abraxas' lap as Maeve took a seat opposite him.

"It's interesting to have watched you grow fond of Mal."

Maeve scowled. "Fond?"

"Don't mistake me. I understand why. You're suddenly more powerful than ever." He petted Spinel absentmindedly. "It's just you used to chastise me for looking up to him."

Abraxas' tone was unfamiliar. His normal drawl vanished.

"I suppose I did," said Maeve looking out the window. "Apologies."

Abraxas smiled softly.

There was a snapping sound from the foyer as Ambrose popped through the oversized fireplace, a costly means of travel between households. It required more Magic than Obscuring.

"Come," he called as he passed the tea room door, clapping his hands together. His boots clicked across the marble tile.

Maeve and Abraxas met him on the balcony. He was suited as the Premier. After quick goodbyes, Maeve and Abraxas were in the snowy foothills of Vaukore Island, looking up at the glowing castle in the distance.

Maeve carried all the books she brought for Mal down to Hellming Hall. She nearly tripped down the stairs as the heavy stack knocked her off balance.

The Magical Militia had moved inside the castle. No longer were they just stationed on the grounds, but they lined the Grand Entry Way. A pair of them stood stiffly on either side of the stairs on each landing. Four of them were stationed at the dormitory doors.

They ignored every student. Even the Premier's daughter.

Mal was seated at the farthest table.

"Hi," said Maeve, sliding onto the bench across from him.

His gaze lifted up at her.

"Hi."

Perhaps it was Maeve's imagination, but it looked like a breath of relief escaped his lips. And a small smile was being suppressed.

Her imagination. Surely.

"This is everything I thought you'd be interested in reading." Maeve set down the stack of oversized books. "However, these three on top will probably prove the most useful."

"Thank you." Mal peered at her over the stack. "You didn't search yourself?"

Maeve pursed her lips. "Well, I did. But. . . I think you will have a better chance than me. Like calls to like."

Mal raised his brows.

"Have you never heard that?"

He shook his head slowly. "Only in that prophecy."

"My father used to say it all the time," said Maeve, pulling a plate towards her. "Magic calls to magic. Darkness calls to darkness. Blood calls to blood."

Mal considered this for a moment. "Like calls to like," he repeated, his eyes on her.

Maeve's stomach flipped. She managed to nod and said, "Do let me know if you need anything further, though."

He pushed the stacks of books aside. "I have something for you," said Mal. "I had an idea for us to communicate more efficiently."

Mal handed her a rather small piece of parchment. "I have one as well. I've bewitched them. Whenever one of us writes the other, the message will appear instantly. Once it has been read, it will disappear."

Maeve turned the slither of parchment over in her hand and smiled. "That's quite clever."

Mal nodded. "Now, I can reach you whenever I need you."

Maeve's stomach plummeted this time. "Even outside of Vaukore?"

Mal nodded. "Wherever you are."

Maeve couldn't tear her eyes away from his. Dark flecks of light swirled through their chocolate color, sparkling at her.

The gesture was so genuine. So personal.

So. . .

Maeve pocketed the parchment. Mal thanked her for the books and immediately got to reading.

Classes resumed. Maeve got high remarks from Headmaster Elgin in Defensive Magic for her counter curses, and from Headmaster Rowan for transfiguring Abraxas into a snowy white owl. No others besides Mal successfully transfigured their partners in class into animals. It was a temporary illusion, but still advanced Magic.

The Headmaster commented to Abraxas after class that he made quite a beautiful owl. Maeve bit her lip to keep from laughing. Abraxas didn't appreciate the comment.

"It's your complexion," said Maeve with a grin.

It was weeks before Mal brought up his heritage to Maeve. She was seated in the farthest corner of the library by a crackling fire when he appeared in front of her with an open book pointing to a line.

"Read this."

Maeve took the book from him.

"Gagner, James: Human: father to one unknown Human son and unknown Magical daughter. Gagner Farm and unknown Magical Daughter sold to the Peur Family in 1913. Debt settled."

Maeve looked up at him.

"Holy Merlin," said Maeve.

Maeve looked back down at the entry. There was a small hand-drawn map of the Gagner Farm property lines. Beside it was a black star with Ragsling Village scribbled next to it.

He found a connection.

That was all the information the book contained. The next line moved to the Gaurteel family.

She opened her mouth to speak, but Mal cut her off.

"When term ends," he said. "I will be going to find them."

"Do you think they are still there? This information is from thirty years ago."

"Like calls to like," said Mal.

Maeve couldn't argue with that.

After a moment, she spoke. "What if you do find them? What if the Gagner's are still there and know where the Puer family is? What if they knew your mother? They could help you find your family."

"A family that doesn't want anything to do with me. A family that left my mother to die-"

"Have you considered they may not know you exist?"

Mal hesitated and then nodded.

Maeve sighed. "Your curiosity must be bursting. It'll be months before summer."

"All too true." His voice had that dark quality to it when his mind was racing. "You're in here, you know?" .

"Yes," was all Maeve said.

"You have blood going back to Merlin."

Maeve laughed, "Father doesn't believe that. He was at Vaukore you know? He studied Practical Magic for a time."

She was quiet for a moment watching his expression. "I don't know anyone with the last name Gagner."

He nearly rolled his eyes. "They were no one of importance. The daughter was sold as a slave it seems."

"Slave to the Peur family. Your family."

"I don't need to hear about how you don't like that term right now," said Mal. "We aren't talking about Zimsy."

Maeve bit her lip. Mal was tense.

"Why is there no record of the name Peur anywhere? Not one single book? No lineage. No list of names. It's like they simply don't exist."

Maeve had been waiting for him to bring it up. "Because it's possible she wasn't a witch Mal."

Mal stared at the table between them. And didn't speak for many long moments.

"I always wondered how could she have died. How did she come to be who she was, what she was, if she had Magic at her fingertips? But after years of searching the name Peur, and finding nothing, I suppose I already knew." He leaned back in his chair. "If she had been as powerful as me, a Magical like me, she would have been able to beat death."

"That would be quite the accomplishment," said Maeve.

Mal didn't look at her. He was deep in thought.

The next day Mal was distant, reserved, and quiet. In classes, he didn't raise his hand to answer questions. He didn't even ask questions himself.

At dinner, a bright green light illuminated from her bag, whose contents spilled out onto the bench beside her. She dug for the small slither of parchment and on it was Mal's elegant handwriting.

Meet me in the library before monitoring duty.

Maeve looked around the Hall to find him, but he wasn't there.

Maeve paced in the darkened corridor later that evening with her hands tucked behind her back outside the Library, waiting on Mal. He appeared a few moments later with Abraxas and Hendrix Fawley.

"You two get promoted, or am I missing something?" Asked Maeve.

"Missing something," said Fawley sweetly.

"Hendrix and Abraxas will be patrolling the halls for us tonight," said Mal matter-of-factly.

Maeve's mouth fell open. "What?"

Mal held open the door to the Library. "Come, Sinclair. On your way, boys."

Abraxas gave Maeve a wink and sauntered off with Hendrix. Maeve looked after them, her mouth still hanging slightly open.

She turned back to Mal, ready to protest.

The look on his face stopped her. His expression was more serious than she could recall ever having seen him. "This must be important if you're willing to blow off Paragon duties."

He didn't reply. He merely gestured his head towards the Library.

She walked past him without further protest. The door snapped shut, and he brushed past her. All the fires were out. The lanterns and chandeliers above them hung still and dark. She followed him to the far end of the Library, where there was a locked door that read:

RESTRICTED AREA

"Oh, it's that kind of night, is it?" Whispered Maeve, grinning.

The Restricted Section of the Library was for staff and approved and monitored visits only. Getting permission for access was nearly impossible. And the door was magically sealed shut by order of The Double O.

"Only a librarian of Vaukore can-"

With the wave of his palm, the door clicked open. And Maeve fell silent.

"That old Witch is in love with you," she said, referring to the sculpture of Marybelle Marsen, the first librarian for King Primus thousands of years ago.

Mal smirked softly in triumph.

"Don't smile. She's a sculpture. It's weird," she said brushing past him.

Once they were on the other side, he shut the door behind them quietly. The Restricted Area wasn't lit.

A beam of bright light swirled from the gold-linked bracelet on her wrist as they entered the darkness, lighting their way. It floated alongside them, its light wafting and waving between white and blue.

"Let me guess," he said. "A gift from your father."

"It's a lux charm," said Maeve. "Everyone has them."

She looked away from him as it slipped from her mouth. Those charms were expensive. "I'm sor-"

"We only have the hour," said Mal. "Hendrix and Abraxas will cover for us, and then we need to be on our way."

Maeve didn't argue. "And what exactly are we doing here?"

"Looking for something that would be, to quote you, 'quite the accomplishment'."

Maeve's eyebrows raised and she frowned slightly. "You want your Magic to be immortal."

"Sharp as a thorn."

Mal was not smiling. He was not attempting to charm or manipulate her. "The Immortals of Aterna figured it out. Why can't I?"

"Well," said Maeve. "We should start right away then."

Between the two of them, they took three books each that proved promising, based on titles alone. The plan was to read them, find any and all useful information, and return them to the Restricted Section. And continue that pattern until Mal had his answers.

"Did you enjoy being me last night?" Maeve asked Abraxas on the way to Alchemy the following day.

"No offense, Maeve, but I pretended to be Mal, not you."

Maeve pushed him as they laughed together.

Hummingdoor paired Maeve with Roswyn to brew together, which delighted neither of them.

"Was Mal with you last night, like Abraxas says?" Roswyn asked Maeve.

Maeve measured out snake venom on a set of scales. "I don't see why that's important to you."

Roswyn snatched the bottle of venom from Maeve, his temper swelling to the surface.

"Watch it," warned Maeve, her voice low. "I don't intend to fail the day because you want to throw a tantrum."

Roswyn stared her down, huffed, and placed the vial back on the desk.

Despite his sour attitude, Hummingdoor passed their potions, and the rest of the day was quite nice.

Maeve came across some interesting concepts from her Restricted Section books, but not exactly what they were looking for. A few days had passed since their initial visit, and Mal proposed they swap the books out for more.

While both Mal and Maeve learned quite a bit from their illegal readings, they visited the Restricted Area of the Library for weeks with no success. Maeve assured him if they came up short, her father's library, or even the basement library, would provide answers.

But summer was too far away for Mal.

"Have you ever heard of a Lethifold?" Mal asked Maeve one night in the Dueling Hall.

They were mindlessly sending spells back and forth over conversation.

"I don't believe so."

"They are considered a highly dangerous dark creature."

"Derived from lethum, Latin for 'death' possibly."

"They're said to be nothing more than a thin dark cloak, levitating off the ground with a carnivorous appetite. Only attacking at night. They suffocate their prey and then digest them."

"Ah," said Maeve. "So more likely 'lethi' as in levitate, and also lethal."

"Thank you for the Latin lesson." Mal sent a hefty hex her way.

"Anytime." Maeve blocked it with ease.

He lowered his arm and stared at her.

"You're going to duel tomorrow night."

Maeve laughed.

"You're ready."

Her face flattened. "Oh, you're serious?"

Mal crossed the circular dueling platform towards her. "Tomorrow. I'm putting your name down."

In a swift motion, Mal dismounted the platform and made for the door.

"Hurry up, Sinclair. You've got Paragon duties. I know you wouldn't dream of blowing those off."

"Cheeky,' whispered Maeve, with the hint of a smile.

Chapter 14

As she made her way to the Dueling Hall for the weekly duels, Maeve ran into Mal.

"You know, you were right about something," said Mal.

"I'm certain I'm right about many things."

He rolled his eyes and ignored her. "In one of those books you gave me, it talks about Dread bloodline being able to use Magic others cannot. I wonder if Kietel can? I wonder if he could be immortal?"

The Magical Times wrote about Kietel every day. Every day he was a murderer, a traitor, a bigot, and a liar. He wrote a speech the Times refused to print. The Starlight Gazette did though.

He defended his actions, calling out The Orator's Office and her father even for conspiring against Magicals to obtain power. It was a call to action for all Magicals. And a threat to Magicals who opposed him.

"What do you think?" Asked Mal.

"I don't know. I don't understand it all."

"I never thought I'd hear you say those words."

"Shut up," said Maeve.

Mal looked down at her with a satisfied expression.

The hall was already jammed full. Freddy Jones, coordinator of the dueling club, made a beeline for Mal and Maeve when he saw them.

"Oi! Malachite," said Freddy, holding out a clipboard with a list of students on it. "You mean to write down 'er name?" His head jabbed towards Maeve.

"I did," said Mal.

Freddy's face scrunched up. "But she ain't never even dueled before."

"I know that, Freddy," replied Mal calmly.

Freddy ran his fingers through his hair and looked sideways at Maeve. "Alright, but the lineup fell for 'er to duel Grisham, so you'd better be certain."

Mal clapped Freddy on the shoulder. "Even more so now."

They made their way through the crowd.

"I see Abraxas," said Maeve, heading in his direction.

"Did you see?" Abraxas asked as they reached him, his eyes wide.

"Yes." Maeve nodded.

"I can't wait to watch you destroy him."

Abraxas was eagerly writing down his bets for the night. When Lavinia came around to collect them, she smiled at Maeve.

"I placed my whole wager on you," said Lavinia.

"I did as well," said Abraxas.

Maeve smiled and relaxed back in the chair. It was common knowledge that Mal had been training her for months, and apparently, everyone was eager to see what she was made of.

Halfway through the night when word spread that Mal's pupil would be fighting Grisham the dueling hall was filled with nearly every student and Professor at Vaukore.

Headmasters Elgin and Rowan made an uncommon appearance.

It wasn't long before it was Maeve's turn. Professor Larliesl was practically giddy as he announced her name. Grisham was already making his way onto the platform. There was a buzz through the room as Larliesl invited them to take their places.

Mal grabbed Maeve's arm, bringing his lips close to her ear.

She exhaled sharply. Cool, refreshing Magic pressed through her blouse and into her arm. It tricked down the side of her neck as he spoke.

"Grisham loses his temper easily. Use that to your advantage," whispered Mal.

Maeve's eyes never left Grisham as she nodded and took the stand. Grisham looked annoyed that he had to duel Maeve. Like it was beneath him.

They joined in the middle and bowed.

"Don't think because you're new, I'll go easy on you," seethed Grisham.

Maeve took a low curtsy and looked up at him.

"How about because I'm a girl, then?" She said sweetly. Maeve let go of her skirt with a flourish and turned on her heel. She walked the length of the platform and turned to face Grisham. He readied his left hand at his side. Maeve tossed her hair over her shoulder and followed suit.

"Begin!" Shouted Freddy.

Green light shot from the tip of Grisham's two fingers, Maeve ducked down, took a knee, and fired back without hesitation.

Maeve's hex hit Grisham square in the chest, sparks of blue splattering across his shirt, ripping the fabric as he grunted in pain.

A hex she sent with two fingers. An audible gasp rang through the room.

Maeve could hear Abraxas cheer loudly.

Grisham's body was already reacting to the hex; his two front teeth were getting longer every few seconds. His face turned bright red. He reared his arm back and sent her a bright green hex. It completely missed her. A group of girls screamed and had to slink to the floor to avoid getting blasted.

Grisham reared back again and sent Maeve another hex. She blocked his advance with her left palm. His teeth were still growing rather rapidly, and he looked furious.

Maeve lowered her right hand to her side, at the ready, just as Mal had taught her. Magic barreled down her arm, building and begging for release.

He fired on her again, the sparks as bright as his angered face. She blocked with her left once more, power swelling at her right side. It pulled her eyes to a close.

A third, furious curse flew from Grisham's fingers as it slammed into Maeve's shield.

She opened her eyes. Pulled her two fingers into her palm, reared her arm back, and fired, two fingers flinging bright sharp light across the dueling platform.

His shield shattered. He was too focused on his offensive Magic to create a proper shield. And her magic encompassed him entirely. He slammed to the floor with a loud smack in a silent cry. His mouth hung open, teeth pushing past his bottom lip.

He was down for one, two, three seconds as Maeve crossed the platform towards him. He pushed into the floor and made to stand. But he stopped as Maeve pressed two fingers into his throat.

He looked at her with a hatred that rivaled the way her sister looked at her.

The room erupted in applause and cheers. Maeve sighed with relief and dropped her hand. She stepped away from him. She allowed herself to meet Mal's eyes. He gave her a slow nod of approval. He was subtly smirking and politely applauding. His behavior was in complete juxtaposition to Abraxas, who was losing his mind with joy. He and Hendrix Fawley were jumping up and down, their fists in the air.

She looked back down at Grisham and extended him her hand. He slapped it away without a thought and pushed off the dueling platform.

"Thornburg!" Shouted Larliesl. "Take Mr. Grisham to the Healing Hall to have those teeth retracted at once."

Grisham was one step away from foaming at the mouth. His two front teeth were already past his chin. He glared at Maeve.

"Fucking bitch," he muttered, but Larliesl didn't miss it.

"Fifty demerits for foul language, Grisham," his face suddenly stern. "And another twenty for being a sore loser."

Thornburg escorted him away before he could hurt his reputation and school rank any further.

"Brilliant hex, Maeve," said Larliesl, his smile returned. "That one isn't easy to successfully cast."

"Thank you, sir," said Maeve, jumping off the platform with the assistance of Freddy.

"Nice job, Maeve. I 'ave to say I wasn't expectin' that," said Freddy.

Maeve smiled at him.

The rest of the night was just as enjoyable, and, of course, Mal remained the undefeated champion. No challenges.

Later that evening, when she entered the common room, Lavinia punched her arm with such gusto Maeve almost sent a spell her way before she realized Lavinia was merely excited. Maeve rubbed her arm.

"I knew you'd pull that out!" Yelled Lavinia. "I've already told Freddy to put us together next week. And I really think you should consider coming to the Magical Sporting Expo this summer. I think you've probably got that in you too."

"Are you mental?" Maeve shook her head and ascended the spiral staircase to her dorm as quickly as possible.

Violet and the other third year girls were not there. Once she settled in bed, Spinel came lurking out from the shadows.

"Where have you been?" Asked Maeve reproachfully.

Spinel chattered at her briefly before jumping on the bed. Maeve hadn't seen him in quite a while.

"You look like you've had your fair share of food," said Maeve, rubbing his fat stomach.

Spinel wasn't listening and was already curled up asleep at the foot of her bed.

A green light suddenly emitted from her bag on the nightstand. She grabbed the small piece of parchment hastily as, letter by letter, a message from Mal appeared.

Well done. You made me proud.

Something deep in her chest swelled.

Maeve grinned. She grabbed her quill as his words disappeared and wrote back.

All thanks to you.

Word spread quickly about how skilled of a duelist Maeve had become. And that she was performing at a Supreme level. Abraxas told her he heard two fellow third-years whispering about how she could probably move up to even beating Mal. They both got a laugh from this.

Grisham's teeth were back to their appropriate size, but his hatred for Maeve, which was already evident, was only growing. Reiner Gupp, Head Boy, found Grisham lurking about the fourth-floor corridor after hours. Reiner informed Maeve he could only assume Grisham was attempting to ambush Maeve during her Paragon duties on the fourth floor.

Mal's jaw tightened when he heard this. Reiner assured Mal he was given detention and a stern talking to.

Abraxas was sorting through his stew in Hellming Hall next to Maeve. Mal was across the hall with Roswyn, Avery, Phineus, and Hendrix.

Abraxas wasn't talking. Which meant he was thinking. Which meant at any moment-

"What's going on between you and Mal?"

Maeve forgot how to chew and swallowed a whole slice of potato. She coughed loudly and grabbed her chest. "What?"

Abraxas let his spoon fall into his stew. "I've known every secret of yours since before we could talk. And now you're going to start hiding from me?"

"There's nothing," she began to insist once more.

"He's looking at you."

Her head snapped up. But Abraxas was a dirty liar. And Mal was not so much as glancing her way. He was listening intently to Hendrix.

Abraxas grinned. "Nothing, cousin?"

Maeve exhaled, long and tight. "I'm in over my head aren't I?"

Abraxas shook his head slowly and grinned. "You have no idea. Go on, ask me if he talks about you."

Maeve pushed her plate away and swung her legs around the bench, leaving Abraxas without a word.

Final exams were just around the corner as the school year was coming to a close, and Maeve had never felt more confident in her abilities. She was performing at a Supreme level in all her Practical Magic courses, and Defensive Magic as well. Rowan spent the whole day lecturing on her latest essay on Experimental Charms. He was impressed, to say the least.

In Alchemy, Abraxas slid across the desk from Mal and Maeve. Maeve watched as he made what looked like a shady exchange with another student.

The class paired off. The current assignment was brewing a poison and its antidote of their choice. Maeve was making the poison, and Mal was making the antidote. They had been brewing these particular potions for almost three weeks. It was a large percentage of their final grade.

Halfway through the brewing process, Abraxas turned to them both and said, "Going to the fencing matches tomorrow?"

"No," said Maeve and Mal in synchronicity. Neither of them looked up from their work.

Maeve could feel Abraxas' frown.

Once finished, Mal inspected Maeve's potion, which had a pink aroma wafting around it. He gave her a nod. Mal bottled their potions in preparation for Hummingdoor's assessment.

"I daresay these look, smell, and feel perfect!" Hummingdoor cheered from the other side of the workstation. "No doubt one would be cured instantly with this antidote, Mal, my boy. Well done."

Mal stood leaning against the edge of the tall work table.

Hummingdoor set the vial back on their work desk.

"Could we see, sir?" Mal asked casually.

Hummingdoor looked at him. "See what?"

"If it would cure one instantly, as you said."

Mal's eyes slid slowly to Maeve.

"I don't think anyone is willing to poison themselves in class today just to see how sharp your antidote is, Mr. Peur," he said lightheartedly.

Maeve spoke before she could think.

"I will," said Maeve cooly.

The Professor's smile faltered slightly as his head shot towards Maeve. He stuttered a few broken words.

Maeve wasn't sure exactly what came over her. She grabbed the poison she made, which she knew to be absolutely without flaw, pulled out the stopper, and locked eyes with Mal. He stared back at her with a vacant expression that danced on excitement.

"Maeve!" Screamed Violet.

Maeve downed the contents of the vial in one gulp. It tasted sweet, like crunchy sugar and honey.

Professor Hummingdoor stood across the table from her with wide eyes. His hands were stuck in mid-air.

"Miss Sinclair, what did you just do?"

"You said yourself, sir. I'll be cured instantly with the antidote. I have no doubt either," said Maeve, her head becoming light.

Mal took a step towards her.

The Professor stammered. His eyes were glossy round spheres. "What if we're wrong? It would take me weeks to brew the antidote, by which time you'll be surely dead."

Maeve's legs were giving out under her. She stepped towards the wall, bracing herself. Mal moved closer.

"Heavens! Primus and the Gods! Merlin and all Seven Realms! I'll be hung, the Premier's daughter-" started Hummingdoor.

"As I said, sir, I don't doubt-" she slurred.

Mal was suddenly all that she saw, and then the room around her went black.

When Maeve awoke, she was lying in the Healing Hall. The crisp white linen bed sheets were warm against her skin. It was late, as the only light in the room came from her bedside candle. She propped herself up and looked around for Healer Kimmerance, the head healer at school.

"I told her she could go to bed," said a familiar voice. Maeve looked towards the foot of her bed, where Mal sat. "Kimmerance, that is," he said.

Maeve pulled herself completely upright. "It's that late? I've just been asleep?"

Mal nodded. "I suppose that's what happens when you down an entire bottle of poison, Maeve."

Mal's voice was low. It was quiet in the castle at such a late hour.

"What happened after I fainted?"

"Well," said Mal, closing the book in his lap, which Maeve recognized as one they had nicked from The Restricted Area of the Library. "I caught you before you smashed your head on the stone floor, Hummingdoor and the rest of the class rushed to your side, and I administered my antidote as your face and hands were turning a palish green color." Mal crossed his legs and continued. "You came to for a moment when I was carrying you here, and then you became unconscious once more. And now here we are."

"But your antidote worked."

"Of course it did. You knew it would."

Maeve sat silently with Mal studying her.

"Why did you do that, Maeve?"

Though Maeve could only see a glimmer of his face, she was certain he was completely satisfied and knew quite well what her motive was.

His approval consumed her.

The desire for his fixation, his attention, for his dark eyes to be on her alone was enough.

"Does my father know?"

"Oh yes," said Mal. "I've never seen those Magical Militia move so quickly. As soon as they saw you, they bolted into action. He was here before I laid you on this bed."

"You met him?"

"Yes," said Mal.

"Was he mad?"

"At you?" Asked Mal. "Of course. Cursed up a storm." He smirked into a cocky grin. "Thrilled to meet me, though. Already knew my name and everything."

Maeve's cheeks turned hot.

"His position is more powerful than I realized. The world seemed to stop when he arrived."

Maeve leaned back against the soft headboard, her eyes tired once more. "He didn't stay."

"Kimmerance assured him you were perfectly fine."

But Maeve wasn't concerned with that. She knew her father well enough to know that under normal circumstances, he wouldn't have left her side, entrusting no one with her well-being except himself.

But Mal was there. And her father had.

Once her strength returned, Maeve found herself sitting in the Headmaster's office, explaining to them that she merely made a mistake and thought the assignment was to ingest the potion. Headmaster Elgin was delighted that she was alright, and they laughed off the entire situation. Rowan frowned at her as said that Hummingdoor nearly had a heart attack at her actions.

One afternoon the following week, Maeve informed Mal she was finished with her stolen library books and had no valuable information to share.

"I have a bit more of one to look through," said Mal, still desperate to find answers in his quest for beating his mortality.

The week dragged on, and Maeve's school workload was endless. She promised Abraxas she would attend the fencing match with him and immensely regretted that decision.

She was the last to leave the common room for bed, finally satisfied with her History of Magicals essay.

Spinel was happy to see her climb into bed. She was almost asleep when she noticed the pulsation of a faint green light coming from the pocket of her cloak. She was careful not to disturb Spinel, got out of bed, and made her way to the wall where her coat hung. She reached into the pocket and pulled out the small scrap of enchanted paper she and Mal used to communicate.

There on the parchment was one unfamiliar word scribbled out:

Vexkari.

Chapter 15

The library was completely abandoned save for Mal and Maeve, who were spread out across a table in the back corner. Madam Florence, the Librarian, went to bed an hour ago and allowed them to stay past hours. This was primarily due to the dazzling smile Mal flashed her.

The Paper folded on the table between them had a giant headline plastered across the page:

THE DREAD DESCENDANT RESPONSIBLE FOR THE DEATHS OF FOUR MORE MAGICAL MILITIA.

Maeve ignored the implications of the report and focused on Mal's explanation of Vexkari. The text read:

VEXKARI-scarred with Magic.

Magic transferred from one being to another, between Magical worlds and objects.

"It seems like incredibly advanced magic," said Maeve as they were in a deep discussion about his recent discovery. "This book doesn't mention anything about how the process will feel. I can't imagine it's easy to move Magic that way. And how do you even know this will accomplish your goal?" She asked, reading over the very brief entry on Vexkari. "Though, I have no doubt you can do it."

They read all they could on Vexkari, little that there was. Maeve rested her chin on her hand and looked up at the wallpapered landscape. The field of flowers blew in the wind, wafting sweet scents towards them.

Maeve sat up straight.

"What?"

"King Primus put all his Magic into Vaukore," she recited.

Mal looked over at the wildflower painting, realizing as Maeve spoke that they'd been around such Magic all along.

"The paintings, the castle, all of it," she said excitedly.

"It's all his Magic. It's all Vexkari," finished Mal.

He looked over at her as she smiled.

They theorized the endless possibilities of Vexkari late into the night, long past Maeve's eyes wanted to remain open. Mal suggested moving on to their academic studies in preparation for final exams.

"I need to get some sleep, actually."

"You still need to know this," he tapped his pointer finger on the parchment in front of her.

"We spent the entire night discussing other things," she snapped.

Mal's eyebrow raised. He frowned.

"I'm sorry," said Maeve, resting her chin on her hand. "I'm just tired."

"And ungrateful."

"Oh please," she narrowed her eyes at him. "You love having something to hold over me."

"Admittedly."

Mal leaned back in his chair and stretched. She took a moment to scan his long torso. Something in her stomach flipped over as his button-down slid up, exposing his skin. She shook it off and closed her book, which landed her a stern face from Mal.

She ignored him. "I have to get some sleep. I have a Charms exam in the morning."

"Seriously, Sinclair? You could take that exam in your sleep."

Maeve smiled. She stood and began gathering her things. He followed suit, and they walked silently down the corridor. They reached the staircase, and Mal started ascending with her instead of making his way down to his dorm.

She stopped walking. "What are you doing?"

Mal continued up the stairs and spoke plainly. "Walking you to your common room. I worry that idiot Grisham still holds a grudge over you."

"Even so," said Maeve. "I could take him."

"I don't doubt that. I would, however, love to sink my claws into him as well."

He looked down at her with an eager dominance.

Maeve laughed. Admittedly she'd like to see that.

"Miss Sinclair," came a voice behind them.

They turned quickly and saw Headmaster Rowan standing in midnight blue robes. His expression was stern.

"Sir, we were just finishing studying-" started Mal.

Rowan held up a hand, signaling they weren't in any trouble for being out at such a late hour. "Only a moment of your time, Maeve, if you'll allow it."

"Of course, sir." Maeve strode off towards Rowan quickly, bidding goodnight to Mal over her shoulder. She caught a glimpse of Mal's face as he turned away. He was irritated by Rowan's interruption, but he hid it well.

She walked silently alongside Rowan until they reached The Headmaster's office. The door was password-protected behind an ancient and glorious mural of a knight from King Primus' reign.

"Good Evening, Headmaster Rowan," said the knight sleepily. "Miss Sinclair."

"Hello, Sir Kale," said Maeve sweetly.

Her newfound understanding of Vaukore's Magic and power caused her to marvel at the knight.

The knight's eyes widened as though he hadn't expected her to know his name. He yanked his sword from its sheath and kneeled before her.

Maeve smiled.

Rowan flicked his wrist in the air, and Sir Kale moved to the side. A ways behind him was a door. As she and Rowan walked forward into Sir Kale's painting, the door came closer and closer until Rowan pulled its handle and held open the door to the Headmaster's Office and Suites.

Elgin stood in the dark-tinted glass window. She looked over his shoulder at Maeve. Maeve anticipated her smile. But it didn't come.

Rowan gestured for Maeve to have a seat. She sat in an oversized, squishy armchair, eyeing the Headmasters curiously.

"I hope I won't keep you long, Miss Sinclair." Elgin's smile was forced, "Though since I know how well you'll do on your Charms exam in the morning, I don't feel too guilty."

Maeve welcomed the compliment. Elgin continued.

"I am, however, sorry for what I, what we, need to ask of you."

She stared her down from behind reading spectacles. "And ask that it stay between us."

"What is it? Am I in trouble?" Asked Maeve.

Elgin took a seat behind the large mahogany desk and folded her hands neatly in her lap.

Rowan turned towards them and spoke. "It is we who need a favor from you this time, Miss Sinclair."

"Of course, sir," said Maeve politely.

"I am sorry to keep you from a good night's sleep, for this may take some time."

Rowan pulled a vial swirling with silver and black fog from the pocket of his robes. Maeve knew instantly what it contained. She leaned forward in the armchair as her eyes grew large. He moved away from the large stained glass window and crossed to her.

"What am I looking for?" She asked. "You think it's a lie?"

Elgin spoke now after a quick glance to Rowan. "The memory is truthful."

They were silent for a moment. Rowan wouldn't meet Elgin's gaze.

"Who's memory is this?" Asked Maeve.

They remained silent.

Maeve tensed. "Whose is it?"

Rowan started. "It belongs to-"

"Rowan," snapped Elgin, "I think we're making a mistake."

"She has a right to know whose mind she is about to enter."

He stepped towards her, but Maeve threw up her hand. "Stop." She sunk back into her seat. She wasn't there to verify a memory.

"You want me to jump."

It wasn't a question.

Elgin sucked in air. Rowan stared at her tersely.

Rowan lowered the vial and set it on the oversized desk.

He didn't look at his counterpart as he spoke. "It seems it is time for me to confront the past, which I have long ignored."

Maeve stayed silent.

"If I am to be a part in the war on our doorstep, I need some answers."

Maeve looked to Elgin. Her face pulled taunt.

"This is to do with Kietel?" Asked Maeve.

"Yes," said Rowan. "I'll admit Maeve it is purely for personal and selfish reasons that you are here."

Maeve hesitated. "I owe you," she said finally.

From the corner of Maeve's eye, she saw Elgin shake her head.

Maeve swallowed and looked at Rowan. "Into whose mind?"

"This memory is mine," he said. "From the summer. There will be a man with dark black hair sitting across from me playing chess. I need you to get into his mind. I need to know where he is."

Maeve took a deep breath. "It would be better if I just used the memory straight from your mind."

Rowan's eyes narrowed, a silent rejection of that idea.

She pushed back from the edge of her seat and leaned into the soft back of the chair. "I'm ready."

Rowan picked up the vial of swirling substance, pulled the topper off, and stepped towards her.

She and Mal had practiced this dozens of times now. She anticipated the falling sensation that was about to drift through her as Rowan poured the silvery black mist onto his fingertips.

Maeve closed her eyes.

He moved before her and braced her face with his unused hand, tilting her head to the side. The memory was warm as it trickled into her temple.

Slowly the feeling of the chair beneath her vanished. The pale blue hues of the headmaster's office through her eyelids turned to black light. She straightened her legs as she fell in a slowed motion. She heard her feet touch down before she felt it. The sound echoed across the void.

Light flickered in the distance, like a single burning candle flame. She pushed towards that light, and it flew at her in one blink.

Rowan and the black-haired man came into vision. They were blurred and muffled at first. Then in another blink, they were fully formed, and a tense voice filled the space.

"Damn, Ezekiel," said the dark-haired man. "I forgot how well you played."

Each of them stared at the chessboard between them.

Rowan didn't laugh or smile. He moved to touch a piece and then didn't. The dark-haired man leaned back in his chair.

Rowan then reached forward and moved a piece with confidence. The dark-haired man looked across the board, realized what Rowan had done, and frowned.

They stared silently at the chessboard.

Maeve circled around them.

They continued to play until Rowan won. The dark-haired man shook his head. "Another game?"

"No," he said curtly. "I prefer to leave on a high note."

The pair stood and shook hands and then they dissolved into darkness. As quickly as they disappeared, they reappeared, and the scene replayed itself.

Again.

And again.

And again.

No doorway opened for her to slip into. Nothing happened at all. She paced around the small space, yawning occasionally and stretching. On the tenth replay of the memory, something snagged her attention. During one of their moves, the dark-haired man had two pieces disappear, as though Rowan had taken two.

"Oh no," said Maeve as she realized why no doorway was opening, why there was no option for her to slip into the dark-haired man's mind.

This memory was, in fact, a lie. It was not entirely truthful like the Headmaster claimed. Maeve brushed it off as Rowan's memory of this chess game not being sharp.

The scene began a final time, and Maeve prepared herself to break through the "crack" in the memory. Rowan moved his piece, knocking the dark-haired man's knight aside. Maeve reached for it at once.

"Concurred," she whispered.

The memory around her silently exploded. Rowan, the dark-haired man, the chessboard, the table, everything blasted into the darkness and began collapsing around her, trying to suck her down with it.

Maeve held her footing as Rowan's false memory disintegrated. She slipped, faltering slightly as she too began to fall and pulled back out of the memory.

She planted her mind in the darkness, refusing to fall, and the air beneath her became hard once more. The darkness beneath her barreled up, air whipping through her.

She closed her eyes and calmed her quick heart.

When she opened them, Rowan and the black-haired man sat before her, playing the same game of chess.

"Damn, Ezekiel," said the dark-haired man. "I forgot how well you played."

Rowan moved with certainty, no hesitation, and took one of the dark-haired man's pawns.

She looked at the man-

And slipped into his memory of their chess game.

"How could you?" Said Rowan. "Or do those German radicals you associate with not play?"

The dark-haired man laughed. "They play. But we are busy with more important things."

"Like genocide?" Asked Rowan plainly.

The dark-haired man moved his piece. "Like fixing this world we are forced to inhabit."

Rowan didn't respond to that. Maeve looked at the board. He was two moves away from winning.

"When is your next meeting?" Asked Rowan.

"You considering joining us? You aren't in the Militia. You weren't even a Bellator."

"No," said Rowan lazily. "But I have other skills."

"Like being a spy?"

Rowan looked across the table at him.

The dark-haired man scowled now. "Yeah, mate. People talk."

"They say I'm a spy for the Double O?"

The man nodded. "For Ambrose himself. No one trusts a spy. Not even the man who's got him doing the spying."

Rowan laughed. Maeve had never heard him laugh. He made his final move. The game was over.

The dark-haired man shook his head. "Another game?"

"No," Rowan answered curtly. "I prefer to leave on a high note."

The pair stood and shook hands. Maeve let go of the memory and held onto what she could of the dark-haired man's mind. The memory misted into a void and a man's voice rang out across the darkness.

"Death before dishonor," said the voice. It bore a thick German accent.

Bright red light pulsed around her.

There was a scuffle around them. Many voices.

"Rolf," said the German.

So that was his name.

"Chancellor," replied the dark-haired man, Rolf.

Maeve felt the dark-haired man's fear. She felt his insides quiver under this German man's gaze.

And suddenly he appeared. Yellow blonde hair and pale blue eyes. A large nose with a bluntly trimmed golden mustache. A red and grey uniform with that black human symbol. The one like a distorted cross.

She looked up at Kietel, the self-acclaimed Dread Descendant, through the dark-haired man's eyes.

Panic raced through her. This was happening in real-time. She was seeing him as he was. Rolf looked to their left, where the bodies of a man and woman lay sprawled across a set of chairs. Dead.

Maeve recognized the man.

There were Magical Militia there. Men with Orator's Office insignia on their cloaks.

Rolf's attention shot back to Kietel, who was looking at him sternly, with his head cocked to one side.

"Chancellor," said another voice, addressing Kietel, but he held up a finger to the new voice and remained staring straight at Rolf. Straight at Maeve.

"Sir?' Asked Rolf.

Then with a terrifying realization she saw across Kietel's face his own realization that she was there. She exhaled sharply as fear flooded through her. She yanked on the doorway to Rowan's memory, but it was too late. Kietel flung himself towards her. He slammed both hands around Rolf's neck.

Maeve screamed as she felt the contact. Air flow through her lungs seized up. His hands constricted around her neck, pressure building up in her face.

"Who are you?" Spat Kietel, his pale blue eyes bore into hers with a dangerous fury.

Maeve gripped at her neck, her fingers desperately clawing at his nonexistent hands. Water flowed from the corners of her eyes. Her chest tightened.

"Who are you?" He spat each word as his hands grew hot. Magic pooled on his palms.

No no no- she panicked and pushed against Kietel, desperately trying to find her doorway out.

Maeve.

Mal's voice echoed in her ears. Distant and muddled.

Her head grew fuzzy.

Something cold pressed against her back. She leaned into the familiar Magic as Kietel's face blurred and she felt her own Magic fading out of existence.

Let go, Maeve.

Mal's voice said again.

Icy tendrils wrapped around her from behind.

Let go.

His voice said.

But I'll fall.

She said back.

Cold pressed into her temple.

Let. Go.

She obeyed.

The ground beneath her feet swallowed her fully as she heard Rolf's mind snap out of existence. Air, sweet air, flooded her lungs with a shrill scream as she plummeted into nothing, falling endlessly through darkness.

Chapter 16

Maeve sucked in a tight gasp as she was slammed back to the Headmasters Office. Her breathing was sharp, in and out, in and out. With a death grip on the arms of the chair, she forced her breathing to even as her vision refocused.

She felt the floor beneath her feet. The fabric of the chair beneath her legs. She was out.

So many things occurred to her at once. One, Rowan had tricked her. Two, the war was about to turn ugly. Three, the human leader of the Germans was dead.

And four, her father should know.

Then. . . Five. . . The worst realization of all. They had purposefully not included him tonight.

She felt ill. No one had ever felt her presence in a mind before besides Mal. And that's because she was in his mind. She wasn't in Kietel's mind.

But he grabbed her like he saw her, like he felt her. She felt him. Her hand moved to her throat, where his hand had felt so real only a moment ago.

No matter how she strained her vision remained completely blurred.

"He's dead," said Maeve with a shake in her voice.

"Who is?" The voice was familiar.

It was Orator Moon.

Goosebumps scattered her arms and legs. Sweat pooled at the back of her neck and under her knees.

"Kietel was there," she said.

"Who is dead Maeve?" Came his voice again.

"The human leader. Hitler. Kietel was there. He-he. . ." Her voice broke as she said, "Does my father know about this?" She was aware of the fear that dripped from her voice. "I need to talk to him."

"I'm here, Maeve."

His voice was warm, filled with a strength that was unmatched in terms of comfort. Her vision shifted to her left. A blurred Ambrose stood a reach away.

"Are you alright?" He asked.

He didn't move to touch her. Maeve nodded. Warm salty tears reached the corners of her mouth.

A hand came into vision from her right. Cool knuckles brushed across her skin, gathering her tears. She looked over at Mal.

She wanted to dive into his arms and bury her head against his neck.

Maeve stifled the cry that threatened to erupt from her throat. "They aren't stopping. Kietel is in control now. His war is only beginning. And. . ." She looked to the Orator. "You have spies in your office, Orator Moon."

"I have been telling you, Lenny-" started Rowan.

"Magical Militia as well," said Maeve, her voice dead.

Ambrose didn't reply. No one said anything except Maeve.

"And you," she looked at Rowan. "You are a spy as well?"

Her Father spoke now. "Rowan has been aiding me-"

"You tricked me," said Maeve, hot tears streaming down her face.

Rowan looked away from her.

Mal ignored her statements like he hadn't heard it at all. His gaze moved to where she gripped at her throat, and his hand trailed down her cheek until it wrapped gently around her fingers. Her own grip relaxed and her fingers melted into his.

His eyes bore into her, pushing her to speak.

Ambrose was leaning against the desk, his arms folded across his chest and a scowl plastered across his face.

"He saw me," said Maeve shakily.

Mal's fingers ran across her throat and spoke calmly and quietly. "He grabbed you."

She nodded through tears.

"I couldn't breathe. I was about to die- I think Rolf is dead and I saw-"

"Enough," said Ambrose. "Congratulations, Rowan," said Ambrose. "You got your information."

"Ambrose-" started Elgin, her face pale.

He pushed off the desk and walked to Maeve. Mal dropped her hand and his and stood. Ambrose took her hands and pulled her to her feet. The room spun. But Ambrose steadied her.

He linked his arm around her and made for the door. Where Arman, Captain of the Bellator, stood with his arms folded. The Premier's second looked to his direct superior and held the door open. Mal followed them.

"Moon," said Ambrose. "Get to the Double O. I'll be there shortly."

The Orator stalked towards the oversized fireplace and vanished into the flames with one last disappointed look at The Headmasters.

"Premier Sinclair," said Rowan. "I had to know. We needed to know. I had no idea this would happen. She's jumped a dozen times and never been in danger."

"She's jumped a dozen times through minds of students her age and rank," seethed Ambrose. "Not into the minds of Magical Militia Supreme. If it was by your arrogance, you put her through it you are still to blame."

"Your daughter agreed, Premier. If you will not put her powers to use in this war then I will-"

The room darkened. Rowan's face paled. The floorboards groaned and creaked. The fire in the corner rose, its flame now bright blue.

Ambrose turned sharply and said darkly, "Don't you ever come to her behind my back again. You no longer work for me. And if I had the authority, you'd be stripped of your titles and ranks and sent to the Dread Lands to die."

"But you don't," said Rowan. "You do not run the Committee. Nor are you even on the Committee. And I am not your Bellator."

Ambrose gave him one last disgusted look before slamming the door behind him.

In the corridor, Maeve leaned against the cold stone, resting her head back. She flexed her fingers and then shook them out.

There was something still pulling her. Pulling her towards someone's mind. She couldn't shake the feeling of unwanted magic. Like it lurked over her shoulder.

"Did they call for you?" She asked as Ambrose ran his fingers through his hair in frustration.

"No," he seethed. "Malachite did."

Maeve's eyes flicked to Mal. His expression of concern remained.

She knew he didn't trust them. Perhaps rightfully so. Elgin hadn't wanted this to happen, as if she knew what was to come.

Ambrose began walking and Maeve and Mal followed him. His pace was quick, anger filled every step. Arman followed them in the rear. Maeve struggled to keep pace. Her legs were begging for rest.

"Those fucking pricks," said Ambrose through his teeth.

"I agreed to it," said Maeve.

Ambrose shook his head and laughed darkly. "Did they tell you you'd be jumping to Kietel's right hand? Straight to one of the most powerful dark wizards to date?"

"No," said Maeve quietly.

"Furthermore," said Ambrose, "if you had known whose mind you were entering, who you would be engaging with, would you have done it?"

Maeve sighed. "Probably."

"No," said Ambrose. "I didn't raise you to be that careless."

Maeve opened her mouth to speak, but Mal spoke first.

"Premier, if I may speak?"

"Ambrose," corrected her father.

Mal placed his hands behind his back. "Ambrose. You are not concerned with the information Maeve obtained?"

"The information Maeve obtained was useless. We have spies in that room. We would have known within the hour. Now Kietel has been made alert of those spies, we will likely lose them and he is aware there is someone out there with the ability to jump minds. A fact that I have spent the last ten months denying for my daughter's safety. So the war remains, and the worst is yet to come."

Maeve and Mal exchanged a look. Maeve's hand crept to the back of her neck.

At the foot of the stairs were two Magical Militia. They remained astute as Ambrose neared them.

"You're coming home with me," said Ambrose over his shoulder.

"For tonight?"

"Until this war is over."

"No," said Maeve, coming to a halt.

Ambrose didn't stop walking. "I didn't ask."

"Neither did I," said Maeve coldly.

Mal looked between them.

"I won't go," said Maeve. "I'm sorry Daddy but I won't. You'll have to drag me out of this castle by force."

Ambrose turned back towards her. A soft smile pulled up on his lips. He sighed. And looked up at the vaulted ceilings.

"Poxley," said Ambrose.

One of the soldiers pulled to attention, slamming his right fist against his chest.

"Premier."

"Does it surprise you my daughter is so headstrong?"

"No, Premier."

"Are you prepared to fight that stubbornness in order to obey me?"

"Sir."

Maeve stood tall.

"Good," said Ambrose. "Because she's your top priority now. You too Karpent."

The other soldier made the same motion across his heart.

"Premier."

"Arman," he said, stepping closer.

"Premier?" He said.

"You're now stationed here until further notice."

Maeve and Mal looked back at him. He was older than them, but younger than Ambrose. Green eyes, dirty blonde hair and a shiny C badge on his chest.

He didn't look at them. Only at Ambrose.

"If you insist on staying here," said Ambrose as he stepped back towards her, "I'll have them breathing down your neck."

“Fine,” said Maeve. “I can handle them.”

Ambrose loosed a laugh. “I have no doubt.” He turned to Mal and extended his hand. “Malachite.”

Mal took it and their grip lingered.

“You are welcome at my table anytime. I am grateful for your service to my daughter.”

Chapter 17

The Captain of the Bellator's presence at Vaukore certainly didn't go unnoticed. Rumor had it the Headmasters protested his post, but Arman reminded them that it was The Premier's legal right to station his soldiers at Vaukore. Any of them.

They couldn't argue.

Students huddled behind newspapers lined with that which Maeve already knew. The Human leader of Germany was dead. And Kietel was in full control. Maeve unintentionally slept through her first class, missing her charms exam.

When she woke, there was a scroll beside her bed, sealed with the Vaukore crest in red wax. She peeled back the seal, popping it loose from the ivory parchment, and pulled the oversized scroll open with both hands.

Gold letters in a swirling handwriting glittered across the page.

On the first of May in the year one thousand nine hundred and forty-five, it is hereby declared that the third child of Ambrose and Clarissa Sinclair named Maeve is excused from her third year Charms examination by order of Ezekiel Carlton Rowan, fifty-second named Headmaster of Vaukore Academy of Enchantment.

Rowan's swirling signature slashed across the bottom of the page.

She dropped the scroll onto her lap, it curled back under itself at once.

She didn't care about the exam. She didn't care about the newspaper that sat on her bedside table. She didn't care that anyone was dead. There was only one thing on her mind.

Her hand crept to the nape of her neck. Where an unfamiliar and unwanted feeling still lingered.

And she knew it meant trouble.

Down the spiral staircase of her dormitory sat Mal. He was lounging along a sofa, knees pulled in and a book resting against his legs. One hand lazily propped on the side of his head.

She crossed the common area towards him.

"Tell me you didn't stay here all night."

"Of course not," he said, turning a page. "Arman had the night shift. I slept like a baby in my own bed."

He finished the next page and then closed the book, swinging his legs to the ground. His eyes traveled from her face to her stomach to her toes and back up. Maeve shifted her weight.

"How do you feel?" He asked.

"Fine," she lied.

His mouth pulled tight. It was difficult to lie to him.

"You pulled me out, didn't you?" She asked, hoping he wouldn't press her.

He nodded. She looked away towards the windows that lined the common room. Sunlight poured onto the plush sapphire floor. "How?" She looked back at him. "How did you know I was in danger?"

Mal answered with certainty. "Like calls to like."

Even though Mal was satisfied with his discovery of Vexkari Magic, he insisted they continue to visit the Restricted Area of the Library to learn as much as possible about what they weren't being taught in school. Maeve, of course, agreed wholeheartedly.

She held up her hand, her lux charm illuminating the spines of books along the tall shelves. Many of them didn't have titles or authors, even. They were visiting during their normal Paragon duty hour, and tonight Abraxas and Hendrix were covering for them.

She heard Mal remove something from the shelf and went to peek over what he was reading.

"Have you noticed how many of these Magical experiences happened on the Dark Planet?" Maeve asked Mal.

Mal nodded. "I have."

"Father says that was the origin of Shadow Magic."

The pair continued pulling books and reading for close to an hour. Maeve spent most of that time nose-deep in a poorly handwritten book on memories and magic. Most of it was hard to decipher, as it was also written in French.

"How many detentions do you reckon Abraxas has given out so far?" Asked Maeve.

"Probably not enough. Come look at this," said Mal. "'The army of Di Inferius.' Do you know that word?"

"The Latin would roughly translate to 'underneath' or 'below,'" said Maeve. "What's it referencing?"

"It's not very specific. It's some kind of list."

Maeve scanned it over. "Those are Gods or something. 'Dis Inferius' she repeated twice over "God's below," she said finally. "That's it."

"God's of the underworld," said Mal.

"I think so," said Maeve. "Oh no," said Maeve. Her face dropped, and she grabbed his arm. She shook her wrist quickly, the lux charm at her wrist extinguished.

They heard the distinct sound of a door opening just a few shelves over, followed by the rapid clicking of heels on the floor.

Mal placed the book back swiftly, but there was no time to escape.

"Lux," said a high-pitched voice Maeve hated as light popped into the air. Madam Florence stepped towards them, her mouth in a thin line.

"How unbelievably unacceptable. Two Paragons in The Restricted Area of my Library. You both should know better."

"Madam-"

Florence cut Mal off quickly. "I have no time for excuses this late, Mr. Peur, as disappointed as I am to see you of all students here. To the Headmaster's office, both of you."

Mal didn't look Maeve's way, but she could see his wheels turning.

The walk to the Headmaster's office was silent, save for Florence muttering under her breath about naughty children and the rhythmic click of her kitten heels. Maeve felt they suited Florence as they were incredibly tacky. She remembered her father once told her Madam Florence and himself butt heads quite frequently.

They stopped before the large floor-to-ceiling mural of a sleeping knight.

"Evening Sir Kale," said Florence sharply.

The man in the painting awoke with a snort. "Heavens, Betsy," he crooned. "Don't you know it's bad luck to wake a sleeping knight?"

Sir Kale shifted his armor and shook his head sleepily.

Florence ignored him. "I need to speak to the Headmasters about these two."

"Password?" Asked Sir Kale as his eyes fluttered shut.

"Sir Kale!" Screeched Florence.

The knight startled angrily and huffed at her. "The Headmasters are away!" He snapped. "You can harass them when the sun rises."

Florence's lips pulled into a thin line. "Where are they?'

But Sir Kale was already snoring.

Florence stormed down the corridor, commanding them to follow.

"Come," she said sharply. "I suppose your Professors will have to hear of your disobedience."

After a long and silent walk across the castle, they reached the Staff Quarters.

Florence swung open the double doors of the suite, revealing Professor Larliesl, Hummingdoor, and Harquinton.

They followed Florence into the living area. It was decorated with layered rugs and mismatched armchairs of deep tones. The candelabras across the room dripped yellow wax onto the wood below them.

Larliesl's face fell flat when he saw Mal and Maeve. Hummingdoor's face lit up.

"Mr. Peur!" He shouted. "And Miss Sinclair!"

Florence frowned.

"What is it now, Florence?" Asked Larliesl lazily.

"Evening, June," said Harquinton as he excused himself with polite nods to everyone.

"Good evening, June," said Hummingdoor in a singsong voice. "Miss Sinclair, Mister Peur, shouldn't you be on Paragon duty? Has something happened?"

Madam Florence stepped forward. "Indeed they should be and indeed it has. I found them in The Restricted Area of the Library, Clifford. My library!"

There was an awkward silence. Hummingdoor looked back and forth between Mal and Maeve; his brows pulled together. Larliesl took a swig of his dark-colored drink.

"Whatever for?" Asked Hummingdoor, laughing nervously.

"I know!" Madam Florence said, raising her finger. "They don't think the rules apply to them, Clifford."

"They are Paragons, June," said Larliesl sounding bored. "Two of Vaukore's finest."

Madam Florence cleared her throat.

"Pardon me," she started, "but I believe they are entitled children who've never gotten in trouble for anything they've done wrong. They likely never imagined standing here, having been caught for breaking school rules. Never in all my years of education at Vaukore has a student dared to enter the Restricted Area of my library. I don't even understand how! No doubt the Orator's Office will be furious."

The room remained silent. Hummingdoor's face had grown quite serious. Maeve knew it was now or never. The time to pull them out of this disaster had arrived.

Florence pointed at Mal. "They were simply up to no good."

"No, ma'am, I'm afraid that's simply not true," said Maeve, her voice breaking.

Mal's head shot towards Maeve, where she stood crying.

"Professor Larliesl, I'm terribly frightened, you see," said Maeve, addressing the dueling Master.

Larliesl's attention shot to her as he quickly set down his drink and moved to the edge of his seat.

"My dear!" Hummingdoor flew to his feet and rushed to her, helping her to a seat in one of the squishy armchairs. "Whatever has caused you such distress, Miss Sinclair?" He looked over his shoulder at Larliesl. "Grab a hanky from my bag, will you?"

Maeve wiped the corner of her eye. "You see. . . surely you heard about my meeting with the Headmasters a few nights ago. And while I can't divulge the details of that privileged arrangement, I was weakened after using my memory-" she wiped her face with her palms. "I even missed my exam the next morning," she cried. "I've been weak for days now. But I was in the library studying, and I heard someone coming towards me loudly. It was already past curfew, and I was scheduled to meet Mal to begin our Paragon duties together. See, I've been scared to do them alone lately."

Maeve took the handkerchief from Larliesl, thanking him. She dabbed her eyes gently.

"Heavens, why?" Hummingdoor asked her.

"Well, I'm afraid there's someone who holds a grudge against me," cried Maeve. "See, I beat him in a duel a few weeks ago, you remember sir, and we may have exchanged a few unpleasant words since then, and he's been very hostile and trying to get me alone." Maeve dabbed her eyes again, growing more frantic in her speech. "And I just knew he was coming for me in the Library! I ran as fast as I could and hid in the restricted area. I was terrified! The enchantments on the locks must not be up to date, but thank goodness they weren't."

Madam Florence's jaw was practically on the floor. Hummingdoor patted her hand gently. Maeve continued.

"He followed me inside." She sounded frantic now. "It isn't very tidy in there, did you know, Professor? It's rather unkempt. And since it's so unorganized and dark, I lost my lux charm and lost my way at some point. If Mal hadn't come looking for me, Grisham might have gotten to me."

"Randolf Grisham?" Asked Larliesl.

Maeve looked him dead in the eyes, a perfectly turned down frown on her face, and nodded.

"Reiner wrote Grisham a detention last week for hanging around the entrance to the East Tower curfew," said Larliesl. "And I personally witnessed his hostility."

"My word," said Hummingdoor. "I wish you would have come to us sooner, Maeve."

Larliesl walked over to a painting of a short man.

"Leopold, visit your other painting, the one in the East Tower, not the one in the dungeon, and see if the boy is there now."

The short man left without a word, leaving his portrait empty. Maeve understood Vexkari further. The portraits of her brother that sometimes lay empty on the walls at Sinclair Estates. . .were a part of Antony's Magic.

Larliesl crossed back to them. "Mal, my boy, always so selfless, always helping others. Vaukore is lucky to have you."

Mal looked at Maeve. "I'm just glad she's safe."

"Such comradely between students And studies divided! He's saved you twice now, Miss Sinclair!" Said Hummingdoor with a wide smile and a wink.

Maeve took a moment to survey Madam Florence, who refused to meet her gaze.

"Larliesl," the short man named Leopold reappeared in his portrait. "He seems to be lurking behind a pillar."

Maeve had to suppress a smile as her heart swelled. She had not been expecting Grisham to solidify her lie himself. She glanced at Mal, whose face was as innocent as an angelic statue.

"Primus and the Gods," said Larliesl under his breath. "Miss Sinclair, I'm off to deal with it myself." He made for the door.

"It's rather late, Lar," said Hummingdoor. "Perhaps these two should be off to bed."

"Of course," he replied. "Mr. Peur, please escort Miss Sinclair to her dorm room safely."

He Obscured out of the room hastily, teleporting himself across the castle. It was advanced Magic, and only staff were permitted to use it.

"Goodnight, Professor," said Maeve, laying Hummingdoor's handkerchief on the desk and turning towards the shocked Librarian. "Thank you, Madam Florence. I'm sure your coming to the Library scared him off."

Madam Florence scowled and stormed out of the room.

Hummingdoor smiled softly. "Goodnight, Maeve, Mal. I'll ensure your light charm is returned to you by morning, Maeve."

"Thank you, Professor." Maeve smiled at him.

Mal held the door open for Maeve. "Goodnight, sir."

They made their way out the door. They glanced around, ensuring their solitude.

Once in the corridor, Mal spoke as they walked.

"You lied," said Mal. "You lied brilliantly."

Maeve nodded and stared at him confidently, her tears dried. "Yes."

Mal came to a stop and stood with his head cocked, analyzing her. Maeve laughed and began walking towards her dormitory. A small yawn escaped her lips. She continued with dramatic flare, "It must be so difficult to be Malachite Peur," she teased, laying into his full name," always having to save poor, weak, Maeve Sin-"

Mal caught her wrist and spun her around with force. She inhaled sharply and looked up at him as their bodies nearly slammed together, ready for him to reproach her. She swallowed and calmed the adrenaline that spiked from his unexpected touch.

"Have I displeased you?" Asked Maeve genuinely, as she wondered how he could possibly be angry with her after she single-handedly pulled them from trouble.

But his face was not angry. In fact, he looked completely in awe.

"No." Mal's voice hummed in the empty corridor. "Quite the opposite."

He stepped towards her, never releasing her wrist, and brushed her hair behind her ear with his other hand. Maeve inhaled quicker than she would have liked for him to notice. His fingers sent ice down the back of her neck, down her spine, and spiraled into her stomach.

"Where is your light charm?" Asked Mal.

"I stashed it as we were leaving."

Mal looked down at her; his hand still lingered on her face. "You don't even need that thing."

"I was frantic, frightened. Weak. Of course, I did."

Mal smiled down at her. "Clever girl."

Maeve was stuck. She had never been this close to him.

And Gods. He was captivating. His features were so bold, his lips perfectly sculpted and full.

"Come," said Mal, causing her to startle slightly. He dropped both his hands and crossed around her. "I promised to return you safely to your dorm, Miss Sinclair."

The next morning Maeve found her light charm at her bedside with a note from Professor Larliesl.

I took the liberty of retrieving your light charm myself. Remind me to teach you not to need it. I am not entirely sure how a Supreme missed that lesson.

My eye caught this book I think you'd appreciate. Oddly enough, it was sitting on the ground right by your lux charm. Very unkept indeed.

Larliesl

Maeve looked down to see the French memory charm book from the Restricted Area. She shook her head and smiled triumphantly.

Chapter 18

Maeve was so busy studying that she hadn't seen Mal, except in passing, since the night they were caught in the Restricted Area. The previous night when she finished her Paragon duty, she spotted Mal and his usual gang of ever-worshipping combat students entering Larliesl's office late in the evening.

This was a regular occurrence for Larliesl and his favorite dueling boys. With Mal being, arguably, at the top of the list.

It had, however, been pleasing to find out that Grisham lost his spot on the fencing team, was given detention until the end of term, and was banned from the Dueling Club for his attempted attack on Maeve.

"Have fun at your little boys' club last night?" Maeve asked Mal, feigning a smile as he sat opposite her in the library.

Mal smirked back. "We talked about you, actually, Sinclair."

"Oh?"

"Yes. I believe Larliesl called you 'a waste in Practical Magic.' That you belonged fighting and dueling."

Maeve frowned at the satisfied look on Mal's face.

"I took up for you, though."

"Right," laughed Maeve, dipping her quill in her inkwell.

"I told him you weren't a waste in anything."

The scratching of her quill stopped. Mal's voice wasn't arrogant. He wasn't gloating over her. Maeve was taken aback by the genuine way he spoke. His face was stoic but sincere.

"Thank you," was all Maeve could muster.

"You're welcome."

A moment of silence passed between them, but Maeve couldn't help herself from continuing to pry.

"What else was said about me?"

"Abraxas said he was certain you'd win Head Girl next year. Larliesl agreed," said Mal. "He also said he was certain he had seen more growth in you this term than most any student in his recent memory."

This satisfied Maeve greatly.

"He spoke fondly of your brother."

Maeve's breath caught.

"I'm sure." Maeve resumed her writing once more. "Those boys hang on your every word. Follow your every whim. You jump and they don't even ask how high they just start flinging themselves in the air, hoping to be the highest. You'll do great in the Bellator Sector."

He smiled. She didn't.

"It's fucking annoying," she finished.

He didn't hesitate to say with a velvet tone. "Don't be bitter because I stole your sweet Brax."

"Don't call him that, only I can call him that, no you didn't, and don't say I'm not right."

"I never said you weren't right."

"And Merlin forbid they not adore absolutely every little thing about you. That's why you're always dressed so-"

perfect

-"neat," she finished.

He hesitated. "Neat?" He repeated dryly. "Have I offended you, Sinclair?"

Maeve looked back down at her work. It vanished with the snap of his fingers.

She looked up at him. "I'm studying."

"You're studying spells you already know. Magic you can already dominate."

"And?"

"How old were you when you first jumped minds?"

"I was four."

"Four," he repeated. "Four years old performing unheard of and unprecedented Magic that there is no record of. And even with the knowledge that it is doable, you are the only one able to perform it, no matter how hard the rest of us may try."

"Do you have a point?"

"Don't you think you should be trying to do more?"

"I didn't try to jump when I was four, it just happened. My mother was screaming at Zimsy and I wanted it to stop."

"And you think that means you can't do more now? Because I disagree-"

"Is that what you tell your boys?" She muttered.

"Don't interrupt me," said Mal. "And yes. It is."

Maeve placed her hands in her lap. "And what do they say? What do they care?"

Mal's eyes were dark and calm, like deep midnight waters. "They see you, Maeve."

She was silent for a moment and answered his earlier question. "I am trying other things."

"I'm not talking about that little memory spell you already published."

"I know," said Maeve. "I'm not either."

"Good," said Maeve. "Tell me about them."

And so she did. She told him what little she could. What little ideas she had. Practical Magic Charms were dependent on many factors. She told him what she had dabbled in, what she was confident she could accomplish.

Once he was satisfied, he looked at her with a proud, but challenging expression. And then he changed the subject entirely.

"I'd like for you to come with me to search for my family."

She knew the weight of such a request.

She nodded silently.

"Good." He leaned back into his chair.

"I wonder, though," started Maeve. "If your Mother lived there, perhaps your father did too."

Mal had, of course, already thought of this and merely grimaced.

Maeve spoke softly. "That's why you want me to come."

"If he's there, Maeve. . ." She had never heard Mal speak quite so darkly. "If my disgusting father is there, I will need the best memory alteration there is."

"Well," said Maeve. "There is no one better than me."

Mal met her gaze and returned the smirk that lingered on her lips.

"Alright. I have an idea," said Maeve, offhandedly, as she and Mal walked from the Herbology and Alchemy Greenhouses back down to the castle. "What if you come spend the summer at my house?"

Mal couldn't hide the surprise on his face.

"Think about it," continued Maeve. "All the parties my father throws, all the high-ups, wealthiest Purebloods, and Double O officials- it could be your introduction to them. A way into that world. Not to mention Father's expansive knowledge of the Magical Arts, his library, and the entire basement of the house- dedicated to Dark Magical artifacts, objects, and readings."

Mal stopped walking. She turned back to him. "Basement?" He asked.

"Oh, yes. Thrilled me as a child. I snuck down there all the time."

"What's down there that can't be in his office or his library?"

"Mostly family heirlooms, banned books, things the Double O has deemed 'illegal.' No one is allowed down there, or so says my Mother. Like I said, it didn't stop me."

Mal scoffed. "So, what makes you think I'll step foot anywhere near it?"

"Is being the most powerful and youngest Supreme alive not enough? No, you'll make your way down there on your charm alone, I figure."

Satisfied with this answer, Mal badgered her no more about the basement at Sinclair Estates and gladly accepted her offer. Maeve wrote to her father On the Wings that afternoon asking permission for Mal's stay.

"Where will you tell him you're going when we go to Ragsling Village?" Mal asked her the following day in Defensive Magic.

Maeve shrugged. "Nowhere. I'll say you and I are making a quick stop on the way in, and it shouldn't take but an extra day to get it done."

Mal eyed her.

"What?

"Nothing." He smiled. Not a real smile.

Maeve shrugged flippantly. "I mean, you don't intend on sticking around, do you?"

"No," he said grimly.

Every Professor seemingly felt the need to cram in as much new information as possible in their final week of schooling. Maeve had a stack of essays to finish on top of preparing for the final exams in the coming days.

In Defensive Magic, Headmaster Elgin decided the last minute was the perfect time to teach them about the most dangerous creatures one could encounter while battling the dark arts of Magic. Thanks to their Restricted Area readings Maeve already knew about most of them.

"Manticores are actually capable of human speech," said Elgin.

Maeve recalled reading that hundreds of years ago, a manticore escaped its execution because of how horribly vicious it was. Not even the most trained Bellator could hold it captive.

"The Black-fanged Fire Ground Viper," said Elgin, "often referred to by Bellator as 'little viper,' due to its small and innocent appearance, yet venomous nature and deadly bite. . ."

Mal leaned towards her, his lips close to her ear. "Perhaps that's what I should refer to you as," whispered Mal, "little viper."

This caused an involuntary twist inside Maeve's stomach. She attempted to act unaffected. She bit her bottom lip as his nose brushed against her cheek.

She resisted the urge to grab the back of her neck as warmth slipped from her skin and that reoccurring eerie feeling slipped into her spine. The sensation came and went quickly. But there was no doubt in her mind: it was the same Magic from the night she last jumped minds.

She didn't mention it to anyone. Not even Mal. And certainly not her father, whom she knew would react dramatically.

On the final dueling event of the term, the Dueling Hall was filled with students celebrating the end of another school year. Maeve dueled Lavinia and won. Lavinia swore rather loudly upon defeat, for which Larliesl took ten merits from her. And then an extra five when it occurred to him that she was Head Girl.

Maeve and Abraxas were seated in two large armchairs near the middle of the Hall, drinking lemon fizzles. They were currently cackling at two second-year twins, who hit one another simultaneously with the Lingualigatum Spell. This effectively glued their tongues to the tops of their mouths, making each spell they cast after that absolutely ridiculous.

Professor Larliesl called their duel a draw and sent them to the Healing Hall.

It was Mal and Jake Pile's turn to duel and close out the evening. Larliesl called them to the stage. Mal took his place, but Jake was nowhere to be seen. Larliesl called for him again. And once more.

"He was 'ere earlier, Professor. I know I saw 'em," said Freddy Jones.

A few other students agreed they had seen Jake only moments ago.

"Drat," said Larliesl.

"If I may make a suggestion, sir, "said Mal charmingly. Larliesl waved his hand, signaling for Mal to continue.

"Sinclair," said Mal matter-of-factly.

There was a collectively excited gasp from the room.

Maeve's head whipped to Mal, who stood smiling handsomely at her.

"OH!" Larliesl nearly jumped. "Miss Sinclair?" He called for her.

"Here, sir," Maeve called back, her eyes still on Mal.

A smile tugged at her lips. She was disappointed in herself for not having seen this coming. She stood and walked towards Larliesl.

"Would you mind?" Larliesl asked her, extending his hand to help her up onto the circular platform. She met eyes with Abraxas, who gave her a wink.

Maeve tossed her hair behind her shoulder and locked eyes with Mal. "It would be an honor."

News traveled quickly about their duel. So quick, in fact, that by the time Maeve arrived in the East Wing, she was bombarded by questions from students who didn't even attend the duel. Arman had slipped through the doorway of the Dueling Hall just in time to silently watch them.

"No one has ever dueled with him like that! I thought for a moment you might win," said Lavinia.

"I really should get to bed," said Maeve, trying hard not to smile.

She entered her dorm room just in time to see Violet roll over away from her with a huff. She tucked herself into the sapphire velvet sheets in her dorm room. Her cheeks hurt from grinning. Mal had orchestrated the entire duel flawlessly. It was like a dance. He even allowed her to show off.

A green light emitted from her bag on the nightstand. She grabbed the small piece of parchment hastily as, letter by letter, a message from Mal appeared.

Beautifully done, Little Viper.

Maeve held the parchment close to her chest and fell back into the pillow as she bit her lip with a smile.

Chapter 19

"Did you hear?" Asked Abraxas. "Jake Pile's in the hospital wing."

They took a seat at breakfast together.

"Whatever for?" Maeve asked Abraxas, grabbing some toast and jam.

Abraxas shrugged, with his signature mischievous look on his face. "Seems he doesn't even remember anything about last night. He didn't even know he was supposed to be dueling."

Maeve froze. "Mal."

Abraxas was grinning wickedly.

"You knew!" Laughed Maeve, smacking him on the arm.

"Perhaps."

Maeve shook her head. "I should have known, honestly."

She continued spreading jam on her toast as something soared across the hall, snagging her attention. Her father's hawk swooped down, landing on the table in front of them with violent flair.

"Hello, Rumple," said Abraxas, feeding the evil-looking bird a bit of sausage.

Maeve grabbed the parchment from Rumple's leg. "Why didn't he send it through a desk?" She asked quietly.

Dearest Maeve,

I'm terribly sorry for the delay in my response. We would be thrilled to have Mal for the summer. You mentioned making a day stop before your arrival? I'm sorry I can't be there to Portal you home first. But I can arrange to have your things picked up in London and brought home. Mal's as well.

I can't wait to see you.

Don't use the desks.

A.S.

Maeve tossed down her toast and shot up from the table.

"What the hell?" Abraxas shouted after her. "Not even a 'have a lovely day, Abraxas'?"

"No yelling in the hall, Mr. Rosethorn," said Professor Webelton. "Five demerits."

Mal was not at breakfast in Hellming Hall, but she had a good idea of where he would be. She climbed the stairs to the Library, flying past the Magical Militia stationed at every landing.

Mal was, as she expected, sitting in their favorite reading nook.

"Guess what," said Maeve, seating herself opposite him.

He scrunched his face at her happy demeanor and waited for her to answer.

"My Father absolutely cannot wait to have you at Sinclair Estates." She dramatically tossed her hair, flashing him a smile.

Mal again looked incredulous.

Maeve sighed. "You are happy, yes?"

He laughed subtly. "Oh, yes."

"Good." Finally satisfied with his response, she pulled out "A Look into the Modern Mind" and began reading where she had left off. "Oh, and my father says not to use the letter desks. Have you heard anything?"

"Probably just his mistrust of a certain Headmaster," said Mal as he eyed her.

Maeve retreated into her book, then looked up once more. "Oh, and I heard Jake Pile can't remember a thing from yesterday," said Maeve with a smirk. "In case you were curious."

"How odd," said Mal.

Maeve crossed her legs and relaxed into the armchair, reading her book.

After a moment, she looked up to see Mal eyeing her down. "What's the matter with you today, Sinclair?"

She lowered her book and gave him a pity smile.

"Mr. Peur, I don't think you even realize the summer that you are in for." She leaned towards him. "The parties, the duels, the dinners. The people, the hours spent in my father's study discussing Magic, his prized library literally at your fingertips." Her grin widened. "You're going to love it."

The weather on Vaukore Island finally allowed for a nice sit by the lake.

On her final weekend before their journey to Ragsling Village and then home, Maeve took full advantage of the mild temperatures and sprawled out in the warm sun, reading. Maeve was not the only student who chose to spend their Saturday outdoors. Several students were hiking in the mountains with Professor Larliesl.

Her peaceful afternoon was interrupted by McKenzie Barlett shoving his fellow student Tyler Drume into Mirror Lake. Which consequently brought a few of the merfolk that lived in the lake to the surface in curiosity. Both boys screamed upon seeing the captivating creatures, scaring the sirens away. They were the only Magical creature still inhabiting Vaukore's Realm. Though, there were parts of the mountains sealed off. And Maeve often wondered if there were other creatures deep behind those walls of Magic stone.

Maeve wrote McKenzie a detention. When she turned her back, Tyler punched him in the face.

Maeve whipped around. "Did you just punch him?"

McKenzie's nose was bleeding heavily. The boys around were covering their mouths to keep from laughing.

"He deserved it for pushing me," said Tyler, trying to wring out his soaked sweater.

Maeve was astonished. "Yes, he did."

The group grew silent as McKenzie's mouth fell open at a Paragon saying he deserved to be sucker-punched.

"What's in your hand, Mr. Drume?"

"Nothing. I swear!" Tyler yelled.

"Yes, there is."

Tyler Drume looked confused. "There's really nothing-"

"Nothing," said Maeve. "So if I ask you to cast a spell for me, can you?"

Tyler nodded.

"Show me," said Maeve.

Tyler looked sideways at McKenzie, who was equally confused as blood dripped from his nose. He did as Maeve said and performed a shield charm perfectly.

"Wonderful," said Maeve. "Do you truly still believe there is nothing in your hand?"

Tyler looked down at his fingers.

"You're a wizard. You shouldn't resort to human fighting with all the power you could possibly need quite literally at your fingertips. Next time you feel the need to break someone's nose, 'confrontus' will do the job the right way."

Tyler and McKenzie looked both embarrassed and confused.

"To the Healing Hall, Mr. Barlett."

The boys rushed down the hill towards the castle immediately.

Maeve returned to her reading spot, lying back in the grass. The sun kissed her arms, her neck, her legs. It pressed into the small bit of her stomach that was exposed when she laid back.

It wasn't long before she spotted Mal strolling across the valley towards her.

"Afternoon," his velvety calm voice greeted her.

Maeve looked up at him, squinting in the sunlight. "Hi."

He took a seat on the grass. "What are you reading?"

"This book from the Restricted Area on memory charms."

"Any better luck translating it?"

Maeve sighed. "Not really. It's not just the translation, though. The handwriting is abysmal too."

"Do all spoiled Witches grow up learning French? Or just the Sinclairs?"

Maeve frowned.

"Don't fret. Merely being playful."

Maeve smiled softly, returning to her reading. Mal was silent for a moment.

"Set aside your book."

She looked up at him and obeyed. Pulling herself off the grass and crossing her legs beneath her. He was silent for another moment.

"I'm going to do it tonight."

Maeve sat up straight, her eyes wide.

"Are you sure?"

"Yes."

Maeve exhaled loudly. "Wow."

She stared at a spot in the grass that was slightly brown.

Mal was going to perform a Vexkari. A dangerous and dark bit of Magic. Her mind flooded with concern. What if it went badly? What if he got hurt? Was it even wise to perform the spell in the castle?

"Maeve." His smooth voice pulled her from her thoughts. "This castle is Vexkari. I don't know if it will work, but I need to try. There is something in this place that calls to me. My Magic yearns to be one with it. It holds ancient power, a protection over all of us. It's-"

"The safest place to do it," she finished for him.

Mal was not present in Hellming Hall for dinner, but shortly after she came across Roswyn running his monitoring duties for him on the fifth floor.

"Mal would have given you this, so I won't be doing anything less. You're lucky he's not here, though. You know he'd be disappointed in one of his trainees breaking the rules without asking him," said Roswyn. "Now, get."

The boy hurried past Maeve. Roswyn saw her and laughed.

"Bet you can't stand me doing your prized Paragon duty," he said.

"You're putting far too much stock in my feelings towards you," said Maeve walking past him.

"I figured you'd be with him tonight. Guess he didn't deem you important enough to be included in whatever it is he's up to."

Maeve stopped abruptly, turning towards him and dramatically dropping her jaw. "He didn't tell you?"

Roswyn's face dropped. Maeve smiled wickedly, throwing her head back as she laughed.

Magic fluttered across the back of her neck, knocking her off balance. She stopped laughing and gasped.

"What's the matter with you?"

"Dammit," muttered Maeve as she shivered. It was the second time this week she felt that unwanted Magic.

Roswyn rounded her. "I asked you a question."

Maeve's legs trembled. She reached for the stone wall of the castle as she braced herself. Roswyn opened his mouth once more, but Maeve cut him off.

"Don't pretend I suddenly matter to you."

"You don't," he said darkly. "But it's not my interest in you that concerns me."

"What a good dog," she said with a smile.

The feeling released her and vanished completely. She let go of the wall and walked around him. "I didn't eat dinner is all," she lied, knowing he would report to Mal.

She left Roswyn without another word.

Once in her common room, Maeve attempted to read one of her favorite books to shake the uneasy feeling. Mal consumed her thoughts.

Was he alright? How had it gone? What if he was still in the process because it took hours? Each line she read blurred, and worry and curiosity reappeared at the front of her mind.

The backs of her eyelids forced themselves into vision. . .

She awoke with a hefty sigh and felt Spinel shift and stretch on her chest. She was curled up on one of the ivory couches in the common room. It was late. The fire at the center of the hall had all but burned out, and the candlelights floating down from the rafters were out.

She resolved to go to bed. With heavy feet, she climbed the spiraling staircase to the dorms. Violet and the other girls were fast asleep when she reached their dorm room. Spinel scurried around her ankles and jumped into bed with a girl named Patricia, curling up with her long-haired tabby cat named Marcel.

She pulled out the small piece of parchment she and Mal communicated with. She scribbled a few words:

How did it go?

She stared at the words. They remained on the paper. Another minute passed, and they still had not faded. Maeve set the parchment on the bedside table with a small sigh.

She knew he'd be disappointed in her worry.

She laid awake for quite some time, her mind wandering across all sorts of things in an attempt to not fall asleep, desperate to hear from him.

Her eyelids were winning. Sleep was ready to claim her once more. Just as they were beginning to close, she saw her writing on the parchment paper disappear, and the paper glowed green. Mal's reply came:

Perfectly.

Maeve smiled and pulled the covers up tight, allowing herself to fall quickly asleep.

The next morning, Maeve packed her trunk and suitcases for the journey home. Spinel kept packing himself in Maeve's trunk, even though Maeve removed him many times and assured him he wouldn't be left behind. A faint green light emitted from the bed, where Maeve had books and clothes strewn about. The tiny piece of paper read:

Come outside.

Maeve set the parchment aside, flew down the stairs and out into the corridor.

Mal stood leaning against the wall. He looked quite well. The corners of his mouth turned up upon seeing her.

"Tell me everything," she said hastily.

He laughed. "Let's take a walk."

They walked the halls as Mal recounted his night prior. He admitted it was excruciating and exhilarating. He described it as the most powerful and euphoric rush of Magic he had ever controlled, and that at times it had control of him. He had successfully merged part of his Magic, his life, and forged it with the ancient Magic of Vaukore.

Maeve was in awe.

"And you feel alright?" She asked him.

"This is the best I've felt in a long time. Perhaps since I came to Vaukore." He had a pridefulness in his walk today. "I proved to myself that I can control my Magic. And it will bend to my will." He looked over at her. "What's that face for?" He asked her.

Maeve felt a flush in her cheeks. "Honestly. . . I'm so impressed."

He seemed to enjoy her praise more than usual as they walked.

"I think you could be one of the most powerful beings there ever was," said Maeve quietly. "More than the High Lord of the Immortal Realm."

Mal stopped walking and turned towards her. Maeve mirrored him. His face was calm and contemplative as he reached out and touched her face, running his thumb along her jawline. A large sigh rose and fell in her chest. She relished the feeling of his cold fingers on her flushed skin.

"Don't just stand there, boy," said an old wizard in the enchanted mural behind Maeve. "You know what to do."

Maeve's stomach dropped, and she felt her cheeks burn hot. She knew they were bright pink.

Mal dropped his hand, placed it back in his pocket, and gave the old wizard a reproachful look. They avoided one another's gaze and continued down the corridor, pretending the previous moment hadn't happened.

"Uncle Ambrose, or Premier Sinclair to you I suppose, will adore you," Abraxas said to Mal on the horseback ride across the grounds to the gates of Vaukore. The Portal to Earth awaited them. Spinel and Julius, Abraxas' silver cat, ran ahead of them, tumbling over one another.

Summer glistened across the wooded mountains that encased the island. The sun beamed down on them, casting golden light from clear blue skies. Mal's sleeves were rolled back. Maeve found herself staring at his grip on the reins.

The veins in his arms.

"And I'll be there with Mum and Dad for all the parties," continued Abraxas. "You have warned him about the parties, haven't you, Maeve?"

"Yes," she said quickly, pulling her gaze from him. "He's been warned."

"I, for one, can't wait for you to duel some of those preppy Orator officials," said Hendrix Fawley with a grin, as he pulled up next to Maeve.

Mal looked like he had already had this thought.

"Alphard and The Mavros Family will be there too," said Abraxas, with far too much mischief in his voice. Maeve reprimanded him with her eyes, but neither Mal nor Hendrix noticed.

Maeve explained to Mal days ago that after The Summer Solstice party long into the night and the next day, a handful of men gathered privately for cigars, maybe some Magical sporting games, and conversation. It was by invitation only.

"Your Father allowed you to sit in on these meetings as a child?" Mal had asked.

"Oh no," said Maeve. "I listened through the door. Some of the most important leaders in the world will be in that room. It's your best opportunity to charm them."

In London, they bid the others farewell and paid the train to send them to their destination.

Chapter 20

They arrived in Ragsling Village well past sundown. It was a charming village with cobblestone streets and little pitched-roof cottages. The main road that led them straight to town, a mile from the train stop, was lined with quaint shops with hand-painted CLOSED signs in their darkened windows.

She felt no Magic, not even a trace.

Ragsling Village was purely Human.

They moved into a narrow alleyway between two shops, heading for a flickering light ahead.

Maeve halted and strained her neck. Her hand reached back and grazed the nape of her neck.

"What?" Asked Mal in a hushed voice.

That uneasy and unwelcome feeling trickled down Maeve's spine. Barely there. It had been a week since she felt it. She sighed, having hoped it was gone.

"What's wrong?" He asked.

Maeve didn't look at him. "Nothing."

"It's not nothing," he replied. "What are you feeling?"

Maeve looked down the cobblestone alley. A cool breeze pushed around them, blowing a newspaper past that had been littered. She relented and finally admitted what she had kept from him.

"Like someone is watching me," she whispered.

She could feel Mal's immediate reaction of panic. Then disdain.

"For how long?"

"A month," she admitted.

"A month?" Mal asked incredulously.

Maeve looked up at him. "It comes and goes."

Mal shook his head. "Why didn't you tell me?"

"It seemed, well, irrelevant."

Mal's eyes were darkened by the moonlight-less alleyway, but Maeve knew there was anger flitting across them.

"Come on," said Maeve, and restarted their walk. "We need to find a place to stay."

"We're Magicals. We can stay anywhere we see fit," said Mal.

"But don't you think it's much more adventurous this way?" She asked, wringing out her hands in an attempt to dull the creeping sensation running across her skin. "Besides, if you have Magical Family near, it's best they don't feel our Magic first, in case a surprise visit is necessary."

"I know," said Mal, clearly still annoyed at her secret-keeping. "I'm the one who suggested that."

"I don't remember that," said Maeve playfully, glancing over at him.

He shook his head.

The narrow path opened up into a square. There was a small brick fountain in the middle. It was dry, barely a trickle of water running down the center. Across the square was a tall, skinny brick building with a large sign that read: RAGSLING KEG AND QUARTERS. It was the only building on the street with light shining through the windows.

"Maybe they have a vacancy and we can stay the night," said Maeve.

They crossed the square in silence, their cloaks whipping in the summer wind. The steps to the pub creaked as they approached the door. Mal reached for the knob, and Maeve's arm shot out in front of him quickly.

"I think you should wear your hood up. This village is small, and if you bear any resemblance to your family, they'll know who you are. It's best you aren't seen, given our business here."

Mal cut her a look but pulled his hood around his face. Maeve stopped, mesmerized by the dangerous look it gave him. He pushed open the door with one long arm and Maeve crossed inside, brushing off the smile threatening to betray her thoughts.

The bar smelled strongly of beer, a smell Maeve detested. Behind the bar was an older man with a large grey mustache that covered his whole mouth. It was as dreary on the inside as it was on the outside.

"Excuse me, sir," said Maeve with a smile. "We're traveling through and hoping to find a place to stay for the night."

She placed her hands on the counter. They stuck. Her smile faltered as she peeled them up and looked at them. They were now covered in a thin, sticky film.

She held her hands awkwardly in the air.

The barman looked her over. "I got two rooms, but I don't know about renting them to teenagers. You traveling alone?"

"We are, sir. If it's any consolation, we aren't teenagers. I'm twenty-one-"

"What's a pair of kids doing traveling alone?"

Maeve sighed and smiled once more. She reached into her bag and pulled out a stack of Human currency, hating that she was touching her things with dirty hands. She slid eighty pounds across the counter at the man.

"Are the rooms upstairs or down?" Maeve asked him.

The barman's eyes grew wide, and he choked on the swig of beer he had just downed. Scrambling to gather the money, he nodded and pointed towards the stairs on the opposite side of the pub.

"Thank you," said Maeve curtly.

Up the rickety stairs, there was a small landing with two doors opposite one another. Maeve snapped her fingers, instantly cleaning her palms.

"What happened to 'no Magic'?" Mal asked.

"Oh," she said, never having realized how habitual Magic was. "I suppose that didn't last long, did it?"

"Where did you get that human money?" Mal asked lowering his hood.

"One must always be three steps ahead of one's self. The possibility for plans to go awry is almost certain."

"Hmm," said Mal. "It's likely you overpaid. Or we could have done it my way."

"What's your way?" Asked Maeve.

"Goodnight," said Mal with a wicked grin as he pushed open the door to one of the rooms.

Maeve smiled softly and retreated into her own room. There was little to it. A twin bed with a metal frame and pale sheets, a small dressing table, and a wooden chair. In the corner was a black stove of sorts for heat or cooking.

She clicked the door closed quietly and leaned against it. It would be difficult to sleep knowing he was so close. She slipped off her cloak and laid it across the chair. She ran her hand over the set of candles on the nightstand, flames bursting at their wicks.

The Pub was so quiet she was scared Mal could hear her thoughts as she lay on the feathered bed.

Wind tapped against the window.

She ran her finger along her jawline, thinking about how his hands felt on her skin as she drifted off to sleep.

The bed shook. In the distance was a faint whirring sound, followed quickly by another shake. She sat up slowly. The candle stand on the bedside table clattered quietly, its flame extinguished.

The next whizzing sound was louder. Maeve moved quickly to the window as the glass shook. In the distance, bright lights were flashing across the horizon like distant lightning.

Then a loud and shrill sound filled the streets below. It was a blaring siren that ascended and descended in pitch.

It was a chilling sound.

A warning.

Maeve gasped and grabbed her nightrobe. She threw it on as she ran towards the door. She flung it open and startled as Mal was already standing at the threshold. His hair was disheveled, and his robe was carelessly covering his exposed chest.

The landing outside their rooms was dark, but Maeve could see his finger was pointed, ready, and his eyes were wild.

The creaking of steps from the third floor caused Maeve to shove his hand away. She placed herself between Mal and the barman.

"You kids alright?" He asked.

Maeve nodded quickly.

"Yes," answered Mal.

"They aren't getting us tonight," said the barman. They're bombing over in Maidstone, by the looks of it. Much larger metropolitan nearby."

Mal and Maeve stood silently as the barman stood awkwardly.

"Still, there's a bunker a few blocks down," said the barman. "You two might want to make your way there for the night, in case."

"We're alright," said Mal. "We'd prefer to stay here, sir."

The barman shifted nervously as a flash of light from Maeve's room illuminated the hallway.

"I feel responsible for the two of you," said the barman. "You look like well-off kids, and I ain't trying to have some rich snot coming after me for not getting you to safety-"

"You do not care who we are," said Mal plainly. "You'll go back to sleep and leave us be."

Maeve glanced down, but Mal wasn't pointing at him. She looked back at the barman, expecting another argument. But the old man nodded, turned, and made his way back up the stairs without another word.

Maeve looked up at Mal as the inn rumbled once more.

"Your way, I see," said Maeve.

"Don't know what you mean."

Mal stepped past her into her room and stalked to the window, observing the bombing on the horizon. Maeve closed the door behind them.

"How far away do you think they are?" Asked Maeve as she stood beside him.

"Far enough," said Mal.

They watched for a moment. Maeve looked down, and there were humans in the streets hurrying towards the bunker the barman spoke of.

"I have to admit," said Maeve. "That's quite the invention of theirs. Massively destructive."

Mal didn't respond.

"Father says one bomb matches the strength of a thousand Magicals. And they keep making bigger ones."

She pressed her palm against the glass. The panes vibrated despite their distance from the bombs.

Mal asked. "Do you still feel that Magic from earlier?"

Maeve nodded. "It's so faint. Makes me doubt its existence."

Mal was quiet for a moment as they watched and listened to the distant rumbling. Then he spoke lowly. "Don't keep those kind of things from me."

Maeve didn't respond.

"We should place protective enchantments," said Mal, as another larger quake shook through the village.

Maeve agreed. Together they cast enough protective barriers to prevent them from being harmed should the bombs make their way over to Ragsling Village.

After another moment, the sirens fell silent, and Maeve yawned. Mal looked her over.

"You should go back to sleep," he said.

Maeve nodded and made her way towards the bed. Mal seated himself in the small wooden chair in the room.

"What are you doing?" Asked Maeve.

"What does it look like I'm doing?"

Maeve frowned.

"Go back to sleep, Sinclair," said Mal, running his fingers through his hair. "Morning is only a few hours away."

Maeve's eyes lingered on his exposed chest for a moment before she felt her cheeks become warm. She slipped under the covers quickly.

"What about you?"

"I was finding it difficult to sleep anyway," he said.

Maeve propped up on her side. "Because of the anticipation of tomorrow?"

"No," he said. "Because you've had a feeling you were being watched for a month and didn't bother to tell me."

Maeve rolled to her other side. "You're just nervous is all."

She stared at the blank wall, her back to him, and wondered if she'd be able to fall asleep with him so close.

Chapter 21

Maeve slept better than she could remember having slept in ages. It was still dark when they departed Ragsling Keg and Quarters the following morning. The sun was only beginning to make its rise. Hues of purple and orange lined behind the trees.

They made their way through the village, just as the earliest shops were showing signs of life. Fresh newspapers were being dropped on each doorstep by a young boy. At the edge of the village, the cobblestone turned to dirt. The trees became scrawny. The path darkened and narrowed into a dense wood.

"Is this the way?" Said Maeve, with a glance over her shoulder.

Ragsling Village had nearly disappeared behind them in the morning mist.

"Of that I am certain," said Mal. He pointed ahead, where thick fog lingered over the path. "It's calling to me."

Maeve squinted ahead, and through the mist and wood was a flickering yellow light. As they drew closer, the outline of a small stout house came into view.

Once through the fog, Maeve could feel there was magic close by. Nature had mostly reclaimed the Gagner's home, which was overgrown with vines and its frame sinking into the hill on one side.

A rickety low-lying fence scattered before them, with a metal mailbox nailed to a post. It was covered in dirt and cobwebs. Maeve snapped her fingers to clear the dirt.

Carved in primal writing was GAGNER.

"This is it," she said.

Mal looked back at the house and continued up the winding path. Maeve followed closely behind. The house looked nothing short of abandoned. Shattered windows, rotted boards, and a slumping frame. Without hesitation, Mal opened the front door of the house. Maeve's hand shot to her face at the smell. It reeked of death and rot.

There was a ripped chair in the corner. It was occupied.

"Who are you?" Said a voice.

A brutish man leaned forward, his eyes slipping back into his head.

"My name is irrelevant. I'm assuming yours is Gagner?"

The man smacked his jaw together a few times, drool slipping out at the corner. He didn't answer.

Maeve looked at the picture frames that ran along a small table. They were covered in years of grime and dirt. She bent close to one. Written in elegant handwriting was "Thaddeus Gagner, age twenty."

She looked from the photo and then to the man. It was him.

"Your name is Thaddeus," she said.

He tried to push himself out of the chair, and failed, resigning himself to his position. He lay limply in the torn chair.

"Thad. Me Mum called me."

Mal moved towards him calmly. He took a seat in the chair opposite Thad.

"I'm not here to harm you," said Mal. "I'm looking for someone."

Empty bottles of Human liquor littered the floors. Maeve glanced back down at the photos. She blew on them, dust flying up into the air. There were many pictures of the Gagner family. They had been living in squalor for some time, it seemed.

Thad shifted in his chair to get a better look at Mal. "What time is it?"

Mal flicked his wrist up and looked at the watch Maeve had given him on his birthday. "Six forty-two in the morning."

"What year is it?"

Maeve looked to Mal, who remained calm and patient.

"1945."

Thad shook his head and lifted his hand, like he was going to strike himself, then lowered his hand.

Maeve looked back down at the pictures. There was a picture of Thaddeus, much younger, with a young girl. Maeve blew hard on the frame as more delicate writing appeared.

Thaddeus Gagner, age 14. Mary Gagner, age ten.

Thad moved to the edge of his seat and squinted at Mal.

"You look just like that rat Peur boy my sister Mary was sold to," said Thaddeus.

Maeve's eyes shot to Thaddeus. Then to Mal.

"What?" Asked Mal quietly.

Thaddeus pointed at him, his finger shaking and his mouth turning into a scowl. "You the spittin' image of that filth across the valley."

Maeve's heart was roaring to a racing speed. She moved a step towards them.

"You come 'ere to take more from me family?" Asked Thaddeus, his aggression boiling over. "My sister wasn't enough?"

"What's his name?" Mal asked calmly.

So calmly it terrified Maeve.

"What is this man's name I resemble?"

"I won't never forget it," said Thaddeus. "The rat's name was Malachite Peur." Thaddeus spat on the floor.

Fear flooded through Maeve's mind all the way down to her toes. Mal didn't move an inch. He stared at Thaddeus with a controlled serenity.

Thaddeus continued. "No, I won't ever forget it. She thought he hung the damn moon. But after a while, he sold her to some Englishman up in London. I never saw her again. She died, that's what that paper said, giving birth. That was twenty years and some odd change now." Thad scowled. "You looked about twenty and some change."

That slither of paper found in Mal's mother's hand after she died giving birth to him. It was a desperate attempt for his father to be found. Alerted. For Mal to be delivered to safety.

"She wasn't naming you," said Maeve quietly. "She was naming your father."

Mal had already realized it as well. That Thaddeus' sister was his mother.

"She was a human," he said. "Your sister?"

Thaddeus' face contorted. "She was special, but there was nothing wrong with her. I told those mens in fancy suits that too. Just strange things happened sometimes. Things she didn't mean to do."

"What men?" Asked Mal.

Thad's shoulders pulled up. "Some pricks that came asking about her after she died. Called himself a funny word I 'ad never heard of."

"The Orator?"

Thad snapped his fingers and smiled at her. "That the one."

Maeve shook her head, smiling weakly back at him. She looked back down at the photographs. Mal's ten-year-old mother smiled up at her.

"They came after she died and I tried to kill that rat meself."

"Are the Peur still here?" Asked Mal.

"Oh, they're still here alright. Towards the Manche."

"The what?" Asked Mal.

"He means the English Channel," said Maeve. "'The Manche' is the French title." She stepped towards Thad. "Do you know much French Mr. Gagner?"

"Only what me sister taught me before she went to London. She said the Peur was French."

Mal stood and extended his hand to Thaddeus. "Thank you."

His voice was short. Curt. Void of all emotion.

Thaddeus looked up at him, and then at his hand. "You my sister's boy?" Thaddeus' eyes returned to Mal.

"So it seems," said Mal.

"I tried to find you," said Thad, his face soft and discomforted.

Maeve's heart tightened.

"But you was long gone. No trace. I didn't think you'd have his last name. . ."

Thaddeus raised his arm to strike himself. Mal snagged his wrist swiftly. Thad looked up at him, shocked.

His arm relaxed and Mal released his grip.

"Where is she buried?"

"Here. Down the hill."

Mal nodded and extended his hand to his uncle once more.

Thaddeus reached for Mal's hand and made to stand. As their fingers brushed, Thad fell limply back into his chair, his large belly rising and falling in a deep slumber.

Through the forest and across the southern valley was a large manor. It sat in perfect opposition to the Gagner House. It was clean, with planted flowers sitting in the windows. The painted white wood shone in the morning light. It was a slim manor with two stories. Its windows sat open, yellow linen curtains flowed in the breeze.

The pair silently climbed the pale stone steps to a large white door. Mal opened the front door with a flick of his wrist, the locks clicking. The door fell open silently.

Muffled voices and music came from inside the house. Once inside the foyer, it was clear the sounds were coming from just one room over. She heard a man's voice, followed by a woman's, followed by laughter.

Light jazz music flowed through the house.

Mal waltzed through the large archway, lowering his hood. The woman screamed. Maeve stood back in the shadows as she heard the sound of glass breaking.

"Who are you?" Said a man's voice.

"Is it not obvious to you?" Asked Mal. "I am told we favor."

Maeve made her way into the drawing room. It had expansive windows that faced the valley, allowing sunlight to pour into the room. They were wealthy.

Nothing compared to her own family's wealth, but extremely wealthy nonetheless.

The men were on their feet, the woman cowering behind the older of the two men. There was a teacup shattered across the black and white tiled floor. It seemed they had interrupted their morning tea.

Maeve gasped upon seeing the man who was undoubtedly Mal's father. He was just as handsome as Mal, only older. The pair were almost identical. The other two, Maeve surmised, were Mal's grandparents.

"I don't have much time," said Mal, "but I do want to know something. Why did you abandon my mother when you found out she was pregnant?"

His father's eyes were wide.

"I don't suppose you have an answer that would please me or change my mind about killing you."

The woman began sobbing, clutching onto the older man. "It's alright, Cherie," said the man, his French accent thick.

Mal laughed in an unsettling way. "I desired to know you for so long. I blamed you for so long," said Mal. "Now, I want nothing except your human existence erased."

He pointed a slender finger at the woman, and then at his grandfather. They fell to the floor, limp, smashing their heads on the glass table in the process.

That was the first time Maeve had ever seen Magic kill. It was illegal, deemed so by the Orator's Office, to use any Magic to kill, let alone a dark spell designed just for that. That was ancient and feared Dread Magic. They were redacted from the curriculum at Vaukore long before Maeve's time, but it seemed Mal found the Dread Curses in one of their stolen Library books.

Or maybe Magic was more instinctual.

Maybe Mal wanted to kill. And his Magic obeyed.

Mal's father looked at his parent's dead bodies in disbelief. His skin turned pale. His voice was broken and shaking as he turned back to Mal.

"You're my son."

In a flash of red light, Mal's father's face sliced open, spewing blood across Mal's own face and robes. His father's face contorted in agony.

Maeve's stomach twisted. Her hands flew to her face, covering her mouth.

His father lifted off the floor with the slightest movement of Mal's fingers. His body tight against Mal's magic.

"Did you know she was pregnant?" Mal's voice was unsettlingly calm.

Blood spewed from his father's mouth.

"No," he cried.

Mal watched him for a moment. "Maeve."

Maeve's heart kicked. Her breathing was quick. She stepped towards Mal. Her hands shook at her sides.

"This is Maeve," he said. His father's bloodshot eyes moved to her. They begged her for help.

She swallowed hard.

"She's going to enter your mind. And see if you are lying."

Mal's father began sobbing, choking on his own air.

"Unless you've had a change of heart?" Asked Mal. "And have found the truth?"

His Father nodded. Mal's hand fell to his side and his father to the floor.

"Did you know?" Mal repeated.

His Father nodded. "I-left-her. . .in," he heaved, "London. I couldn't- I shouldn't have been with her-"

Maeve's eyes were burning. Her throat was tight.

"And you didn't care if I lived or died?" Asked Mal.

His Father bowed his head. "I was-a- child-"

Rage pulsed from Mal. Maeve took a step back as it flared towards her. He stepped towards his father, who was crawling towards the bodies of his dead parents, gasping. Mal stood in his path.

"Did you know she was a Witch?" Asked Mal.

His Father made to nod his head. "That is why my parents purchased her. I beg of you, believe me, I had no choice. I did what I was told-" His Father looked up at him shaking with fear. "Please, my son."

Mal pointed his finger down at him. "I am no son of yours."

"Wait!" He wailed. "Do you have the locket?"

Mal didn't move. "Locket?"

"The locket I gave her-the-the locket!"

Mal took a deep breath. "She had nothing of value on her when she died giving birth to me."

His Father's eyes sparkled over. "You-you don't have it?"

"No," said Mal darkly. "What significance is that to you?"

"I gave that locket to her, to protect her," he said softly. Blood pooled on the floor beneath him. "To protect you."

Mal crouched before him, their faces nearly touching. "What would you know about protection?"

Maeve couldn't tear her eyes away from Mal's father. Mal would look just like him in twenty years. Same chiseled jaw. Same sharp cheekbones. She almost hated to see his stunning and dangerous face brutalized in such a way. He looked too much like Mal.

"That locket was a Peur heirloom. For hundreds of years, that locket guaranteed safety and fulfilled lives. It was my only chance to. . .keep her alive." His gaze traveled to a portrait that hung above them.

Maeve followed his gaze up to the painting of a dark-haired man with a long beard and dark eyebrows. Around his neck was a gold ornate oval locket.

Magic speared through her. She grabbed her chest and her eyes snapped shut.

"Maeve," said Mal.

Maeve's eyes shot open. Something called to her. Something old and ancient and forgotten. Her head whipped to Mal's father, who was on the verge of dying.

"Like calls to like," she whispered.

"What is his name?" Asked Mal, pointing to the portrait above them. The man with dark hair, beard, and eyebrows frowned down at them. He wasn't a moving portrait like some at Vaukore or Sinclair Estates.

"Orion," wheezed Mal's father.

"Artemis Orion The Dread," said Maeve.

"Yes," said his father. "My ancestor."

"The last ruler of the Dread Lands," said Maeve weakly as all heat drained from her body. "Before the plague."

"The what lands?" Mal's father asked. They ignored him.

The hairs on her arm stood up straight. The words slipped from her without a second thought as she looked at Mal and realized-

"You're the Dread Descendant."

Maeve flinched as Mal's hand jerked to one side, and a loud snapping noise came from his father's neck, and he lay dead. Mal stared at him blankly. He didn't look at Maeve.

Thoughts barreled across her mind. She couldn't stop them as they blurted from her mouth.

"Peur. At the root of your name. I'm so bloody stupid," said Maeve. "It's French. They came to France and made a new life. In hiding. Of course- the name broken down means-" She was shaking her head quickly, as though the thoughts were impossible.

"Means?" He said quietly, never tearing his eyes away from his father's body.

Maeve's heart was kicking. "It's fear."

"Fear?" His voice almost sounded sad.

"Synonymous to Dread."

Mal leaned forward and took his father's hand in his own. Sitting on his finger was a black stoned ring. Mal's head turned to one side, examining it.

He slipped the ring off his finger and looked at it closely.

"You've known," said Mal, without turning towards her.

Maeve's breath caught. His tone was laced with danger. The image of Valeria snapped to her mind.

Mal stood and looked down at his family, slipping the ring inside his pocket. "Is that why you wanted to get close to me?" He asked.

Maeve scoffed, insulted at his misplaced anger. "You are remembering things quite incorrectly."

Malachite turned towards her, his face drained of all color and set in stone.

"I suspected," relented Maeve under his intense stare.

He set towards her; she gasped as his face was suddenly close to hers. She stepped backward, but he continued his pursuit.

"And you never thought it prudent to share your suspicions with me?"

Mal pressed her against the wall, pinning each shoulder beneath his hands. The small set of paintings behind her slammed to the floor. Maeve jumped as the glass shattered beneath them.

"You never felt it?" Retorted Maeve. "You never thought there was a chance-"

"Of course I thought there was a chance," seethed Mal. "I have always known I was something bigger."

"Good," snapped Maeve. She swallowed hard and her voice grew quiet. "Good. Because you are something bigger. You are the true Dread Descendant."

He didn't speak again until his breathing returned to his normal pace. His eyes darted around her, studying her face. His expression was lost.

"How is that possible?"

"The line will be lost," recited Maeve. "There is Magic in his veins. It just lies dormant."

"Was," corrected Mal quietly.

She nodded.

"I killed them," he said. He said it as though it was just occurring to him.

He looked up at the portrait of Artemis Orion. His cheeks slowly turned a light shade of pink. His eyes glassed over. His hands flexed at his sides.

He walked past her out the open doors of the back of the manor. He sucked in a sharp breath. Maeve took a few steadying breaths and followed him. He stood with his back to her, hands clutching the railing of the terrace with white knuckles.

Maeve stepped to his side. "The one to free your golden blood will come when the Dread line is restored."

"Sacred blood." Mal didn't look at her.

Maeve gently reached up and wiped the tears that slipped from his eyes and wet his cheeks, forcing him to face her. "Mal," she whispered, feeling her own tears forming. "You were sent to save me."

He cupped the back of her head and pulled her close. She brushed her fingers through his hair as his other arm snaked around her waist.

His dark chocolate eyes shimmered with flecks of light, like sunlight illuminated in a dark lens. Magic resonated from him, drawing her to the balls of her feet with a deep inhale.

His forehead pressed against hers.

His thumb trailed across her bottom lip.

She tilted her head up to him. His breath was cool against her face.

He looked down at her, scanning her face. A small laugh, like one of relief, escaped his lips. In a rare moment, Mal smiled fully. It was a glorious sight to see his sharp face light up like starlight.

"I think it is you who has saved me," he said.

Without hesitation, he lowered his lips to hers. White light erupted in her vision and cool, refreshing trickles of Magic slithered down her neck and arms and legs.

She wanted to be drenched in the long-awaited feeling.

She wanted his all. His silent shadow and his passive protection. His unwavering and unnerving calm. There was no feeling but him. He was all consuming.

She twisted her fingers through his raven hair, pulling herself into him with a sharp breath, instantly aching for more.

The kiss was firm, but his lips were smooth and soft.

Mal was the Dread Descendant. He was her savior. But none of that remained in her mind. All she knew was his hands on her body. His lips on hers.

She kissed him with all the power she could muster in an attempt to make up for all the times she had dreamed of his lips on her. The nights she lay awake wondering how long she'd have to wait to know how he felt. If she would ever know.

Now, finally, it felt like the world around her was no longer burning. He doused her in his chilling power.

Their kiss deepened as her lips parted and his tongue flicked across her bottom lip. His magic brushed through her, making her legs weak. His grip around her waist tightened. She held his head firmly, desperate for him to not pull away.

Finally, their lips parted and Maeve gazed up at him with adoration. He brushed his knuckle across her jaw. Maeve reeled at his touch, tossing her head back and pushing her cheek into his hand.

"Now, Little Viper," the husky way he called her brought a smile to her lips, "the reason I brought you here."

Chapter 22

Maeve's composure returned, her face poised as she stepped over the bodies of Malachite Sr. and his parents. Her job was done, and she was fairly pleased with her work. As she strode past Mal, who leaned on a pillar in the drawing room, she lingered near him for a moment before continuing towards the door.

He gave the manor one last look. It was unspoken that they needn't dawdle there. Mal followed her out the door, whipping it closed with his hand, and together they began crossing back down the valley to Thaddeus Gagner's shed of a home. She watched out of the corner of her eye as he twisted the ring now placed on his finger. It was a silver band, with two minuscule silver skulls holding the black stone on either side.

Maeve wasn't absent for Mal's second time using Vexkari. She watched as he added his own Dread blood and Magic to the ring. Neither of them could deny the power radiating from the ring. He didn't understand how he knew, but Mal was certain the black stone was filled with ancient Dread Magic.

She had never seen such a powerful display of darkness. It blew out the walls of the Peur House, destroying what the Humans called electricity. They had learned about it in Human Studies at Vaukore.

It was a curious invention on their part, though. Almost like Magic.

The act of Vexkari appeared excruciating, just as Mal described. He was on all fours by the end, panting. As he performed the spell, Maeve attempted to illuminate the tip of her fingers. They produced no light. There was a faint circle of wispy black smoke that fully surrounded Mal. An ancient and unfamiliar tongue resonated from his mouth.

When Mal screamed the loudest, swirling black clouds of magic cracked from his mouth, barreling into the ring. Maeve attempted to take a step towards him through the smoke, only to be shot backward and hit the wall. She grabbed her head in pain, kept her distance, and watched in awe until it was finished.

The black smoke disappeared through the open window, and Mal's breathing began to regulate itself. He ran his fingers through his hair, pushing it back, and took a few deep breaths. He leaned back on his knees and looked up at the portrait of Artemis Orion, exhausted. His face was pale.

Maeve squinted through the haze. She would have sworn his cheekbones sat higher, more pronounced now. His head hung once more.

"Mal?" She called.

Maeve looked down at him with a questioning look. He looked up at her triumphantly. She sighed with relief and returned his satisfied smirk.

Mal's pace was routinely fast, as they had already reached the woods once more. They entered The Gagner House to find Thaddeus just as they had left him.

Unconscious.

"That's not surprising," commended Maeve.

The compliment didn't go unnoticed, though Mal's expression remained cold.

Maeve positioned herself in front of Thaddeus. Placing her fingers at her temple, she pulled forward the false memory of The Peur family's murders she created. The silvery black substance hung from her fingertips like dripping glue.

"You are certain?" She asked Mal. "I hate to do it to him."

"I am certain." Came Mal's voice from behind her.

She didn't argue. She knew they had to cover themselves. The Double O had been here before. They had suspected Mary Gagner was Magical in some way. And Thad made it easy for them to incriminate him. He admitted he had already tried to kill Mal's father once.

She closed her eyes, reached out with her free hand, and touched Thad's forehead. His mind was like butter, and all his memories blurred in and out of focus.

She worked swiftly in what felt like record time, planting the false memory in his mind. She erased all memories of herself and Mal meeting Thaddeus. She released his mind for a moment, only to return and extract the new memory herself. She opened her eyes and looked up at Mal.

"Would you like to see?" Asked Maeve.

Mal merely raised his eyebrows, but Maeve was used to reading his silences by now. She rose from her knees and pressed the black, hazy substance hanging on the tip of her fingers into Mal's temple.

He submerged for only a minute before coming back. Maeve had to suppress her anxiousness, even though she knew the charm to be without fault.

His eyes opened as she pulled the memory out. It dangled at her fingers.

"Brilliant," he said.

With a confident swish of her arm, she tossed the memory into Thad's muddled brain.

There would be no confusion about who murdered Malachite Senior and his parents. If anyone cared to search his mind for evidence, they would see no trace of Mal or Maeve, only Thad himself. When Thad awoke, he would think nothing other than that he himself had killed them.

With a wave of Mal's hand, the door to the Gagner shack of a house slammed shut. Maeve didn't follow him down the hillside to his mother's grave. He stared at it only for a moment before traveling back up the hill and the pair began their journey to a summer at Sinclair Estates.

Chapter 23

"Alright," said Maeve as they ventured deeper into the woods, away from the Peur's manor. "You're certain you can-"

"How many times must I reassure you I can Obscure both of us safely there?"

She grinned. "At least once more," said Maeve.

Mal didn't smile. "Take my hand."

"I can just go separately-"

"Take my hand."

"Show me," said Maeve. She pointed. "There."

Mal nearly rolled his eyes. "I studied Obscuring last term, Sinclair."

"Well, I've never seen you do it. I don't enjoy the idea of getting dismembered when you only teleport half of me to-"

Mal vanished with a SWISH and a mist of pale Magic. He reappeared behind her. She jumped and spun around. He looked smugly satisfied.

"Ok now-" she started.

Mal lunged for her and grabbed her wrist. She gasped as her body compressed and swirled next to his. She spun loose from his arms ten feet from where they had just been standing.

She had only Obscured with her father. But Mal successfully moved them both safely.

She looked up at him.

"Satisfied?" He said.

Maeve breathed deeply as Mal smirked down at her.

He extended his hand to her once more. She swallowed and took it. He jerked her towards him.

She collided with his chest with a quick gasp.

"What's that tea shop in London you adore?" He asked. His free hand brushed her hair behind her ear and she was certain he could feel her heart slamming against his chest.

"Esmarelles? The one with the pink door?"

"That's the one."

"You're certain you know where to go?"

Obscuring was only possible on realm and required certainty. They couldn't just jump through space to some place they'd never been.

Mal nodded.

They twisted again, compressing together. The sensation lasted longer this time. Maeve gripped his arms tightly and tucked her head into his chest.

Solid ground appeared under her feet and Mal's hands braced her sides as she tilted backwards. He released her gently as she leaned against the stone-walled alleyway he dropped them in.

"This isn't the tea shop," she said.

"I have a quick stop I need to make," he replied, taking a step towards her.

The alley was dark and abandoned. A main street was close by. She could hear the distant buzzing of people and life. Maeve lifted her head up to meet his gaze, tucking her hands behind her back.

His eyes traveled quickly to her lips.

"We're late," said Maeve quietly, a small smile on her lips. "Father expected us," she flipped her wrist over and looked at the dainty ivory and gold watch, "thirty-three minutes ago."

Mal was an inch from her. "They can't know who I am."

Maeve nodded and smiled softly. "I know that."

"Not even your father. Not yet. There is still too much at play."

Maeve pushed off the wall and closed the gap between them. She couldn't resist. She tentatively placed her hands on his chest. "When the time is right. Until then, you have my word."

Mal held her there for a moment. His eyes locked on her lips.

"Can your father infiltrate minds as easily as you can?"

"No," answered Maeve.

"Good," said Mal. "Otherwise you'd be erasing my mind from the events this morning."

"You don't want him to know you framed a man for murder?"

Mal took her face between his hands. "I don't want him to see the thoughts I have about his daughter."

Maeve wobbled slightly, and her lips parted with a sharp exhale. Mal's hand moved to her chin, gripping it between his thumb and forefinger. He pulled her to the tips of her toes, their noses nearly touching as he bent over her.

"I keep things discreet-"

"You don't have to tell me, Mal." She interrupted in a whisper. "It's all our little secret." She grinned.

Mal's lips were nearly on hers. But it wasn't a kiss that pressed into her lips. His teeth sunk into her bottom lip. Maeve's eyes grew wide as she pushed against his chest, ripping her lip free from him. She swallowed as a small laugh escaped her.

Mal smirked.

"Thoughts like that?" Maeve asked.

She suddenly understood Lavinia's interest in those novels.

Maeve shook her head. But she couldn't hide from him. The satisfied look on his face told her he knew she enjoyed it.

He gestured his head towards the street. She followed him out of the darkened alleyway.

They were in north London. He turned promptly to the right. The strip of buildings across the road were completely demolished. Some of the building's facade stood, while its insides had been seemingly carved out. Piles of their remains flooded out onto the sidewalk.

Between two strips of destroyed buildings stood a three-story building. Perfectly intact. As though the bombs somehow missed it all together. Maeve looked over her shoulder. No buildings across the street had survived either. The road they crossed was torn to shreds, nothing but broken bricks and piles of dirt.

The building that stood tall and clean had a black iron fence that ran the length of the sidewalk. A matching gate at its center said Finchley Orphanage in fat iron letters.

Maeve stopped. Mal continued towards the gates. A couple carrying bags of produce passed between them, bidding Maeve a good day, but she didn't hear them.

"You did this," she stated.

Mal stopped and turned towards her. His fingers wrapped around the bars of the gate. A pulse of Magic whipped towards her, shooting into the sky against an invisible wall.

"Mal!"

They looked past the gates, towards the front doors of the orphanage. A boy no more than seven years old ran down the smooth sidewalk towards them.

Tulips lined the pathway, vibrant color in striking opposition to the desecrated and colorless lots on either side of the iron fencing.

Mal smiled.

Maeve's heart soared.

He pushed open the gate with one hand and stepped inside. Maeve moved closer as the boy reached Mal. He kneeled before him. The boy threw his arms around Mal's neck. Mal wrapped one hand around his back.

"Jude," he said.

Jude looked over Mal's shoulder at her. "Who is that?" He asked.

Mal pulled away from him and stood. "This is my friend Maeve from school."

Maeve smiled softly at him.

"Are you an orphan too?" Asked Jude.

Maeve's stomach twisted. "No," was the only word she could muster.

The boy didn't look phased. He looked up at Mal. "Mal, two men came here after the bombs a few months ago! They were asking Sister Lilly about you, but it was so funny- they couldn't get the gate to open." The boy laughed, his cheeks red. "We were all watching. Sister Lily was able to use the gate just fine and step in and out into the street. But they couldn't. They weren't very happy about it, Mal."

Mal tucked his hands into his pockets and looked at Maeve. "I imagine not."

Maeve reached out and pressed her hands against the shield of Magic protecting the orphanage. Mal's Magic. It was like solid steel. Completely impenetrable. She wasn't stepping inside. No one was. Not even a bomb.

"Sister Lily says it's a miracle from God that the orphanage was spared when everything around us wasn't."

Mal looked back down at Jude. "You've gotten taller."

"Sister Caroline says I'll be as tall as you at this rate." Jude grabbed Mal's hand and pulled him towards the orphanage. "We already had lunch, but I can find you something in the kitchen. Your friend too." He looked back at Maeve, a perfectly innocent face. "Sorry, I forgot your name."

Mal tugged gently back on his hand.

"Jude," he said, his voice smooth. "I'm not staying."

Jude turned. His joyful spark gone. "But I thought you were going to stay and work here, like last summer."

"I was," said Mal. "But things have changed."

Jude's mouth twitched, turning into a slight tremble. "But you said."

Mal reached towards him and brushed the top of his head. "I know. I'm sorry. I just wanted to make sure everyone was ok."

Jude nodded. He blinked rapidly, trying to keep his tears away. "Okay."

"Bye Jude."

"Bye," the boy said, his voice shaking.

Mal released him and turned sharply on his heel, walking back towards Maeve.

"It was lovely to meet you, Jude," said Maeve with a soft smile.

He never tore his eyes away from Mal, disappointment ringing from his face. Mal didn't look back at Jude as he passed Maeve. She took a few steps back and then turned and followed Mal back to that darkened alleyway one block down.

The owner and curator of the fine teas at Esmarelles was delighted to see Maeve. After a courteous conversation, and Maeve purchased a box of new tea leaves, Maeve and Mal stepped towards the white brick fireplace. It was decorated with rosy shades of flowers and vases.

"Have you moved through the fire before?" Asked Maeve.

"No," said Mal.

"It's not real fire, but all Magical fire like this is connected. Each point of entry is like a locked doorway. Only those with a key are able to pass through. And our individual Magic is our key. You need only know where you want to go."

"And I have a key to Sinclair Estates?"

"To the foyer fireplace, yes," said Maeve, placing the tin can of tea in her bag and pulling out a handful of money. She dropped them in the hanging teapot next to the fireplace, which was the fee for using the fire. "See you on the other side."

She smiled widely and stepped onto the marble base of the fireplace. The warmth from the fire vanished, and the flames turned cool.

Maeve stepped in the cool flames. The fire's Magic melded with her own and whisked away from the tea shop. Another step and she was home. It was her preferred form of travel.

Though Obscuring with Mal did put her in a desirable position.

She stepped out onto the glistening white marble floors in the grand entryway of her home. There was a large sweeping staircase and double high ceilings. Sinclair Estates had been built in the late 1800s and was decorated lavishly with the time.

"There she is."

Maeve turned as Ambrose Sinclair came down the stairs with favor in his stride. She met him at the bottom and threw her arms around him. She inhaled his familiar scent of cigars, filling her with an immediate sense of safety.

"Hi, Maeve," said Arianna, who ascended the stairs slowly behind her father. Maeve nodded politely in her direction.

The sisters didn't embrace, but it was uncommon for the pair to show affection.

The fire crackled loudly, and Mal stepped into the foyer as Maeve's Mother, Clarissa, rounded the corner.

Mal stepped towards Maeve.

"You remember my sister," Maeve said to Mal, gesturing to Arianna.

"Of course. Hello, Arianna."

Maeve could have sworn she saw a flush come to her sister's cheeks. This was no surprise.

"This is my Mother," said Maeve quickly, not meeting her gaze.

Mal extended his hand to Clarissa, who smiled and took it. "Lovely to meet you, Mrs. Sinclair. Your home is beautiful."

Clarissa averted her eyes to Ambrose.

"And of course," beamed Maeve, "you remember my father."

Ambrose ran his fingers through his silvering hair before extending a gracious arm to Mal.

"Good to have you," said Ambrose.

"Thank you for having me, sir." Mal smiled softly, humbly.

"As I said at Vaukore, the invitation is open-ended."

"I hate that I missed your teaching at Vaukore. The other professors speak so highly of you."

Ambrose grinned and gave a wink, "Ahh- nonsense."

Mal gave Ambrose his award-winning smile.

"We'll let you get settled then," said Ambrose.

"Trudy," snapped Clarissa."Show Mr. Peur to his quarters."

"I'll show him," interjected Maeve.

Trudy, an older Elf, Obscured with their belongings without a word.

"Just in time for dinner, too," said Ambrose. "Anything you fancy, Malachite?"

"Oh, no, sir. I'm only honored to be here."

Ambrose clapped him on the shoulder and strode off down the corridor. Maeve and Mal began ascending the winding staircase to the mansion's upper floors. The guest suite was on the third floor, one floor above Maeve's room, at the center of the landing.

Mal looked up at the painted ceilings.

"I told you it was over the top," muttered Maeve.

"You love it here," he retorted without hesitation.

They stopped on the first-floor landing, looking over the bannister to the south side of the foyer below. Through the two-story windows that arched into the ceiling was the stone balcony and the gardens.

She was certain Mal had never seen a home like this.

On the third floor, he let out a chuckle as they entered the massive guest suite, which was ornately decorated in emerald and black. All his belongings were already in place. His clothes were put away, his books neatly placed on the shelf, and his Vaukore badges were on the bedside table in a crystal case.

Two emerald green leather armchairs sat on either side of the black marble fireplace. The four-poster bed was trimmed with silver and emerald fabric, too.

"The room's enchanted," explained Maeve. "It decorates itself to match the aesthetic of its guest."

Mal picked up a brown-wrapped package on the bed and looked at her questioningly.

She laughed. "My Father can't help himself."

"Yes," said Mal absentmindedly, pulling back the paper. "I've noticed his affinity for giving you gifts."

"Oh, look-" said Maeve. "it's a first edition."

Mal held up a copy of "Vaukore: the Legend of Magic."

"Am I being bought?" Mal asked, smirking.

"Perhaps," shrugged Maeve.

Mal turned to the inside cover. There, in sparkling gold letters, was a swirly signature.

Cressida Juniper Felixx

It took Maeve the entire evening and most of the next morning to not be sour that her own father had gifted Mal a first edition, signed copy of "Vaukore: the Legend of Magic," and not his own daughter.

They spent their mornings practicing in the Ballroom. A full-force blow from Mal was impossible to fully deflect, though Maeve nearly blocked a few spells quite well without completely losing her balance. Spinel was asleep on his back, sunbathing by the windows.

"I have an idea," said Mal. "If you want to try."

"Alright," said Maeve.

He strode towards her. He slipped the Peur ring off his finger. He ran his fingers over it a few times before instructing her to hold out her hand. She obeyed.

The ring fell into her palm. A cold sensation dripped down her whole body as the ring made contact with her skin, causing her to shiver.

"You want me to-"

"Put it on, yes."

"It's too big."

It was, truthfully. Mal sighed and looked at her in frustration, as though it was her fault. He studied her for a moment.

"Your necklace," he said.

Maeve grabbed the ivory cameo pendant hanging around her neck. "Ah," she said.

She removed the chain and replaced the pendant with Mal's ring so that it hung around her neck. Mal nodded and circled back around the room.

"Touch it," commanded Mal cooly, "and close your eyes."

Maeve, again, obeyed.

"Now," he said, "feel for the Magic it holds."

She inhaled deeply, letting her mind fall blank. The cool feeling of Magic turned to deadly shards of ice. Agile and fierce. The sensation started to grow, only sparks of Magic at first, but with each inhale, she felt a flame of ice wafting- surging with each breath. Soon, the feeling was a current moving through her body. It felt like spellcasting, but it was constant. Sturdy and unmovable.

The feeling was so exhilarating, so captivating, that not even Mal's velvet voice broke her connection with it.

"I'm going to attack; I want you to deflect."

Maeve nodded. Mal unleashed on her. A bright light slammed towards her.

Maeve opened her eyes and, with an easy swish of her hand, deflected his curse with such a potent burst of Magic that he took a bracing step backward.

Maeve gasped. She looked at her right hand in disbelief- she had never been able to do that before- and certainly not with ease. Mal had the most victorious grin on his face. Maeve laughed.

"I've never done that to you. What was that?"

"That was me," said Mal piously.

He strode towards her. He grasped the ring hanging from around her neck, incidentally pulling her closer.

"Oh," whispered Maeve as it made complete sense. Part of him was inside that ring. "You."

His smirk turned to a wicked smile. "I wondered if that would work."

His face was inches from Maeve's. She was quickly becoming addicted to being this close to him. She looked down at the ring in his hand. An idea struck her-

"Do you think I could duel Arianna like this?" Maeve asked, her eyes wide.

"You don't need me to beat her."

"I don't want to beat her," said Maeve. "I want to demolish her."

Mal smiled down at her in a feline way.

"That's my girl."

That weekend, the Sinclairs hosted an intimate dinner party for a few of their friends. Mal and Maeve spent the days prior dueling non-stop as she adjusted to the power of Dread Magic hanging around her neck.

They were careful to never discuss Mal's heritage. Magic was a tricky thing, and there were few secrets that stayed secrets in Magic houses. But Mal devoted all his spare time to reading, studying new Magic, and experimenting with his abilities.

Dinner was filled with lighthearted conversation. Clarissa always ensured the wine flowed heavily at her functions. Maeve and Mal politely declined the alcohol.

"I heard you've had quite the year, Maeve," said Egor Rupertill, a Professor at a primary school for Magicals, who had a short-lived career teaching at Vaukore. He was one of Ambrose's closest friends.

"Says who?" Asked Maeve charmingly.

"Larliesl," said Rupertill. "Told us you made top ranks in the Dueling Club. Finished second in the whole year."

Maeve smiled. "I had a good teacher."

"Of course," said Egor. "Everyone knows that!"

The men laughed. And Egor continued.

"Malachite Peur. Youngest Supreme in a millennium, top of the class in every subject and the heaviest recruited third year I've ever seen. Who hasn't offered you a job yet? Quite an achievement. Larliesl doesn't shut up about you. Guaranteed to make Optimum in the Bellator."

Mal smiled with pride. "That's very kind."

"And rumor has it a Maeve Sinclair has been added to the list of recruits for the Bellator." Egor eyed Ambrose with a grin. "Bet you never imagined your youngest in those ranks."

"But surely Larliesl is just being biased," said Arianna quickly. "And The Double O."

Maeve looked across the table at her sister. "What's that supposed to mean?" Asked Maeve.

Arianna smiled at Maeve with pity. "You know exactly what that means. A year ago, you couldn't even block a stunning spell. Now I'm supposed to believe you're second best to him?" She pointed at Mal, who was seated next to Maeve. "Offers of Bellator. Since when are you a soldier?"

"Would you like to see for yourself?" Asked Maeve, cooly.

"I would actually," said Arianna with a scoff.

"Oh now, ladies-" started Egor, but Maeve cut him off.

"Shall we?" Maeve asked her father, turning sharply across the table towards him for approval.

There was a wildness in Maeve's eyes her father was likely unfamiliar with. Admittedly, Maeve was unfamiliar with it too. She felt Mal suppressing a smirk next to her.

Ambrose looked at his youngest daughter questioningly, but she gave him a small nod. Ambrose was, undoubtedly, confused by her eagerness to duel Arianna, given Maeve's record of defeats.

"We're in the middle of dinner-" started Clarissa, but Arianna smiled sweetly at her mother and cut her off.

"No worries, Mummy," said Arianna, turning to Maeve with a scowl. "This won't take long."

Maeve didn't give her sister the satisfaction of a response.

Clarissa tossed her fabric napkin on the table with a grand flourish and a look of disgust on her face. She refused to look at her husband as he stood up next to her.

"Gentlemen," said Ambrose. "If you would accompany us down the hall, it appears my daughters are eager to prove themselves in front of such impressive company."

Maeve followed Arianna out of the Dining Hall.

The Dueling Hall at Sinclair Estates was empty except for a settee and a small gold bar. Clarissa and the rest of the wives placed themselves around the settee while the men helped themselves to more Dragon Whiskey.

Three floor-to-ceiling windows lined the far wall and opened up to the balcony over the gardens. They were covered in white sheer drapes that were as still as Maeve. She was calm and collected, her arms folded across her chest.

Maeve found Mal's eyes and took his ring in her hand. She inhaled sharply as she felt his energy pulsating at her chest.

Only the two of them knew what was coming.

Maeve could feel his pride for her somehow. It resonated into her fingertips. She stood like the champion she was, eager and ready to claim her prize. And they both knew that she would. The only question was how far she would go in her victory.

Maeve had played this scenario over in her head many times in the past few days.

"Are you ready, little sister?" Taunted Arianna.

Maeve took two steps forward, bowed at her sister without a word, and waited for Arianna to do the same.

Once both of the girls finished their formalities, Arianna raised her arm and sent Maeve a stunning spell with three pointed fingers. The spell was strong, as Maeve expected. But Maeve was stronger.

Maeve blocked the spell with the faintest flick of her wrist. Magic blasted back towards Arianna. Arianna's Magic was weak compared to Mal's. Maeve had been training with a Supreme with Dread Magic in his veins. Her sister's strongest spell might as well have been a light breeze of wind, especially with Mal's Dread Magic around her neck.

To the human eye, it would have seemed Maeve hadn't moved at all when she blocked Arianna's spell. A small strand of hair had escaped its place in Maeve's barrette in the pulsation of the spell. She tucked the hair into its proper place and gave her older sister the most wicked look. Arianna's face fell flat.

The room was frozen, all eyes eagerly watching Maeve.

"My God," whispered Ambrose as Maeve reared back, two fingers extending from her hand. She exerted a full-force blow on Arianna that shook the windows and sent the curtains whipping violently.

The new, cool Magic that spiraled through her whole body felt as though Mal was next to her, feeding her Magic. It was exhilarating and refreshing and-

Maeve moved so quickly and with so much force, that the whole room was uncertain of what happened. She held nothing back.

Arianna lost control and was unable to block the blast. She was down on all fours, trying to breathe. Maeve need only signify that her next strike would be fatal, effectively winning their duel with one spell.

But she wasn't satisfied.

"Get up," ordered Maeve.

This was the moment she had dreamed about for years.

She had pictured it every time her knees hit the hard floor when Mal had struck her with all his strength.

He had made her stronger with each blow. With every bruise. Every mark. And now, with a part of him around her neck, she was going to beat her sister as hard as she beat Maeve in the past.

Maeve looked to Mal, who was looking at Ambrose. They were both curious if he would allow his daughters to continue.

The awe on Ambrose's face signified he had been waiting for this moment just as much as Maeve.

"Get. Up." Maeve hissed quietly at her sister.

Arianna slowly carried her gaze to Clarissa, who offered no emotion to her favorite child. In fact, Clarissa was looking at Maeve with her lip quivering. It looked like she could cry at any moment as she clenched her jaw tight. Her mother had never looked at her with such devastation. Such inferiority.

"Daddy, we barely got to duel tell her-" began Maeve sweetly in a loud voice, but Arianna was quickly on her feet at such a low blow.

"Again then," sighed Arianna, out of breath.

Maeve stepped backward and gestured openly to her sister. "Give me everything you've got, sister."

It had been days since Maeve's duel with Arianna, but she was still relishing it. She wasn't sure what she liked more: the look on Mal's face, the look on her father's face, or the look on Arianna's face in defeat.

Mal met Titus Iantrose, Arianna's fiancé, a few nights later. Maeve didn't dare look at him when their engagement and wedding were brought up.

The Dread Ring, as they called it, was on Mal's finger as they played with new Magic back and forth, which guaranteed his triumph over Maeve. They practiced nonetheless. "If I recall correctly," said Mal, "you were called by another name at our Cauldron Ceremony, the night we arrived at Vaukore ."

"That's quite the recollection," said Maeve with a laugh.

"What was it?" Asked Mal.

He was in a sprightly good mood today.

"Amaranthine."

"Ah," he said, circling her. Maeve countered him. "I was curious about your personal lack of the letter 'A.' Given the rest of the Sinclair's have it."

"An astute observation and mystery solved."

Mal blocked the jinx she sent silently with a small smirk.

Maeve blocked his returning spell, but he used a great deal of force, sending her sliding back a few feet. Mal pointed his single finger a second time before she was ready.

Thick white light, like a rope, shot from the end tip of his finger, encircling Maeve tightly. Her hands pinned to her sides as Mal tugged the light forward, bringing Maeve to her knees. Maeve frowned.

Mal smiled in victory, licking his bottom lip as he kneeled in front of her playfully. "So why don't you go by that name?"

"Why do you care?"

The ropes binding her constricted more, making it harder to breathe.

"Answer," said Mal plainly .

"You really like holding me captive to your questions," said Maeve smiling.

"Answer," he repeated.

"My brother couldn't pronounce it as a child. So I went by Maeve, my middle name."

The mention of Antony caused Mal's triumphant smirk to falter slightly. He flicked his fingertips, and the ropes of light disappeared with a pop.

"That wasn't so hard, now was it?" Asked Mal as he rolled back his sleeves for more.

The summer was flying by. It was only days before the Summer Solstice Party, and Maeve was eager for Mal to meet the most influential Magicals in the world. Rumor had it they were eager to meet him too.

On a stormy evening, Maeve was tucked away in her favorite reading nook, a circular alcove on the top floor of the house. She leaned back in a window seat, which was covered in small claw marks from Spinel. Evidence she spent much time here.

Footsteps grew louder down the hallway. Mal appeared in the doorway.

"You finally found me," said Maeve.

"A nice hiding spot."

Maeve set her book aside. "How did your tux fit?"

"Like a glove."

Ambrose took Mal to Wizard's Wears in London to be custom-fitted for what Maeve could only assume was his first-ever luxury piece of clothing. Ambrose also purchased him an assortment of other fine clothes.

Mal sat in an armchair close to the window, staring out over the estate. Lightning slammed into the horizon. "Your world is so very different than mine."

"I imagine so."

Mal's head snapped towards her as though he wasn't expecting such a blunt response.

"I'm not boasting. I, in turn, envy you in ways you can't imagine."

"You can have anything you want here."

"It comes at a great cost," said Maeve. "My clothes may be fine, and this house stands above all the rest but you. . . Your future is so much more free than mine."

Mal looked away from her, playing with his ring. "You make your own future, Maeve. I will ensure that. Besides, I heard a rumor that you are now being scouted for Bellator."

He smirked. Bellator had seemed unattainable, undesirably even until recently. To be at the top of the Magical Chain. . .

She smiled sadly. “I believe that’s true. But it’s not that simple. What is coming won’t be an easy. . .transition. There are things expected of me. Those in power who do not wish to be dethroned.”

Mal didn’t press the subject. That was as much as they could safely speak about Mal being the true Dread Descendant. Maeve figured there was a large part of him still processing the implications of his reality.

He changed the subject.

“How badly did I bruise you yesterday?”

“Not terribly,” said Maeve.

They were silent for a moment before Mal spoke again.

“Let me see,” said Mal in a low voice.

Maeve hesitated and then stood, untucking her blouse from her skirt, and pulling it up a bit. There, on her stomach, just below her ribs, was a deep purple circle from a curse that hit her straight on.

She had screamed when it made impact. Mal’s curses burned deep. Especially Dread Magic.

Maeve took a step towards him as his head cocked to the side. His cold fingers reached out and slid across her exposed skin, sending chills across her entire body. He was unable to look away from the bruise, and Maeve was mesmerized by his expression.

“Your father complimented my watch today,” he said quietly.

Maeve tried to steady her breathing as his fingers glossed over her skin.

“It suits you,” said Maeve, trying to control her voice.

“Did he know you gave it to me?” Asked Mal.

“No.”

Mal looked up at her and dropped his hand. She let her blouse fall down, concealing the bruise.

“This is a Sinclair family watch?”

Maeve nodded.

“You honor me, Little Viper.”

“The honor is mine,” she said quietly. “And has been for quite some time now.”

Chapter 24

Trudy, the head of the servants, appeared in front of Maeve and Zimsy, where they sat playing cards on Maeve's bed.

"Miss has a visitor," said Trudy.

"That means you forfeit," said Zimsy with a smile.

"No it most certainly does not," replied Maeve. "I'll be back, and don't look at my cards."

She made her way downstairs and pushed the double doors into the sitting room off the foyer. There was her father and a man with his back turned to her.

"Miss Sinclair."

The man, Daniel Rodriguez, turned to face her. He was her instructor last summer when she interned at The Double O, and he was the newly appointed head of a Magical Minds task force.

"I'll leave you to it," said Ambrose, clapping Daniel on the shoulder.

"Mr. Rodriguez," said Maeve politely as her father passed her, closing the door behind him. "Please have a seat."

She gestured to the chairs to her right. Once they were seated, Maeve folded her hands in her lap and spoke.

"What can I do for you?"

"I know you are about to enter your final year at Vaukore and will be taking your exams to place you for your post-education career."

Maeve smiled and nodded.

"To be candid, I am here to offer you a job before anyone else does."

Maeve had not been expecting that.

"You seem surprised," said Rodriguez.

"I am," said Maeve.

"I believe that after you perform your exams, there won't be a department that doesn't offer you a job. I happen to know where your heart's work lies, though." Rodriguez smiled.

Maeve thanked him for the compliment.

"I hope you'll consider what I have to offer and know that due to the nature of The Department, there is very little detail I can give you of the job. Only that I know you'd be doing what you already do so wonderfully now."

Maeve was silent and let him talk.

"I made this packet for you. It has as much information as I am allowed to give you. Of course, should you choose to come and work with me, you'll be cleared on all the secrets."

Rodriguez pulled a black leather binder from his bag and placed it on the table between them. "It goes over the pay, title, and all-"

"And what title is that?" Asked Maeve.

Rodriguez laughed. "Assistant secretary."

"Under your Senior, Junior, and a dozen other assistant secretaries?"

Rodriguez smiled at her. "I'm sure it doesn't exactly appeal to someone as high achieving as you are, Miss Sinclair, but those witches and wizards have been working for the Orator's Office for years, some even decades."

Maeve didn't touch the binder he had placed on the table. She stared at him, thinking.

"Look," said Rodriguez, "just think about it. You'd fly up in the rankings, and I just know you'd enjoy yourself more than on The Committee for Experimental Charms, who I know is going to be able to offer you a higher pay-"

"The pay doesn't matter to me," said Maeve curtly.

"Ah," said Rodriguez, glancing about the room, "of course."

"I will think about it, yes. Thank you."

Rodriguez gave her a nod and stood to take his leave. Maeve walked him to the door.

"Oh," he said, turning towards her, "I almost forgot." He whispered now. "Did you really jump through minds straight to Kietel himself?"

Maeve stepped back slightly. She didn't smile triumphantly, though Daniel was looking at her like she should be.

"I did," was all she said.

“Damn,” whispered Rodriguez. “I knew it was true.” He stood rubbing his chin for a moment. “Head Assistant Secretary then. Just consider it as you enter your last year at Vaukore. The offer is valid until you graduate.”

Maeve mustered a smile. “Thank you, Mr. Rodriguez.”

Chapter 25

The most anticipated party of the summer arrived, and lucky for Maeve, it was the Sinclair's turn to host it. Abraxas whined as Maeve was still changing her hair in her enchanted vanity. It was pulled up in a loose twist.

"Come on," said Abraxas. "I want to hear about your duel with Arianna."

"Patience," said Maeve.

She looked in the mirror once more and envisioned her hair pulled back in braids, with soft curls falling to her shoulders. The Magic of the vanity took effect and adjusted her hairstyle perfectly. She wondered if Mal would like it that way.

"How's Mal doing down there?" Asked Maeve as she observed herself in the mirror.

"Charming everyone, as expected," said Abraxas.

Maeve smirked and started to change her hair once more.

"No. That looks fine," said Abraxas snappily. "Don't change it again. The party started an hour ago."

Abraxas pulled her downstairs and into the drawing room. They took a seat as Maeve recounted every detail of her duel with Arianna to him.

"About time," said Abraxas, slapping her on the leg. "Sure Mal was proud."

Maeve shrugged, though she knew he was.

"Miss Sinclair, Mr. Rosethorn."

They looked over as Mr. Carroll Iantrose plopped himself down opposite them. He was utterly intoxicated by the sluggish look of him.

"Mr. Iantrose," said Abraxas. "Good to see you." Abraxas turned his attention back to Maeve. "Oh- I almost forgot. We have tickets to the Pro Fencing Finals at the end of the month-"

"I see you brought a boy home," said Mr. Iantrose, smacking his lips together in such a way that Abraxas recoiled at the sound.

"Well, when you put it that way, it does sound a certain type of way, doesn't it?" Maeve said, cooly.

She had little interest in conversing with Mr. Iantrose, who was known to spew nonsense once he had one too many drinks.

"Anyway," said Abraxas, "if you want to-"

"I'm saying I wouldn't-t-t tado that," interrupted Mr. Iantrose.

Much to Abraxas' annoyance, Maeve entertained the conversation.

"Why is that, sir?" She asked.

"Because of the curse!" Slurred Iantrose dramatically.

Maeve chuckled lightly. "What curse it that, sir?"

"The one between sapphire and emerald- Dread and and sh-sh-sh-" he coughed on his brandy as he dozed off.

"And who cursed this particular union?" She asked jolting him back awake.

"Unrequited love!" Iantrose laughed loudly, becoming more inebriated by the second.

"I see," said Maeve.

Iantrose's eyes were slowly closing, and he sunk deeper into his seat. After a few moments of silence, Maeve turned her attention back to Abraxas.

"Continue," said Maeve.

Abraxas looked to Iantrose once more to ensure the drunk was out cold.

"Right. I was saying if you'd like to-"

With a loud gasp, Iantrose shot up. "HE MURDERED HER in cold blood, after all. Rightfully so stills wears the chains of his-er-um..crime."

Iantrose's face was inching back towards the side table. His eyes rolled in the back of his head.

"Who?" Asked Maeve.

"WHO?" Iantrose startled, his eyes wide.

"Oh Seven Realms, I'll talk to you later," said Abraxas with an exaggerated sigh as he stomped out of the drawing-room.

"Who murdered whom, sir?" Maeve asked, frustrated.

"No, he killed himself after!"

"Yes, ok, but who is he?"

"Oh- the- bloody-"

THUMP!

Iantrose was out and snoring as though his head hadn't just slammed into a slab of marble. A few people nearby chuckled at the old drunk.

"Bloody hell, indeed," whispered Maeve as she stood.

"Interesting conversation?" Asked Mal, arriving at her side.

Maeve's breath caught. He looked exquisite. The tux Ambrose purchased was tailored to every part of his body. The black pressed pants accented his long legs, and the crimson velvet overcoat clung to him in a dazzling way. His hair was combed neatly back, but the few dark waves that had escaped their place around his face was what caused Maeve's knees to buckle slightly.

"Oh, quite," she said sarcastically. "Mr. Iantrose has been slurring nonsense at my father's parties for years. A few years ago, he told Arianna that he was descended from Herpo the Foul himself." She laughed. "How are you making it?"

"Fine."

She could tell, however, that he was not fine. Something had angered him. He guided her out onto the balcony.

"Your father is bragging about you left and right. You surprised him this summer."

"Surprised myself, really."

"Not me. I knew you had every bit of that in you. Besides," he traced the ring around her neck, "you had a little help."

"From the very best."

She looked up at him. His fingers were cold on her chest. She felt disappointed as he moved his hand away from her.

"What's happened?" Maeve asked. "Abraxas said you've been charming everyone all evening."

He sighed deeply, and his lip curled. He turned and looked out over the gardens, wrapping his fingers around the banister.

"You are a Scared Seventeen. They look at me differently."

"Stop it," said Maeve plainly. "Mal. None of it will matter soon once they see what you can do and come to understand your desires. Who you are-"

"It matters now," he retorted quietly.

"Because you are letting it," argued Maeve. "You are unbelievably charming, and my father already adores you. This is a party with a bunch of drunks that you've barely gotten to spend any real time with. Tonight is an introduction. It isn't the end goal. You have time. They will all see in the end. Don't forget most of them look down on us automatically because, in their eyes, we're just children. They haven't even seen you duel."

"According to many of them, it's your duty to continue your pureblood line. With another pureblood."

"Like my sister already. Like poor Astrea. Cousins. First cousins."

Mal ignored her comment. "Do you think I don't know why they feel the need to remind me of this fact?"

Mal's voice cut through her as they tiptoed on a topic they never discussed. In fact, since their arrival at Sinclair Estates, Mal's physical affection had vanished entirely.

"I have no desire to lead the life that is expected of me," Maeve spoke quietly, looking out over the party. "And I had decided that long before you."

"I know, Little Viper." Mal turned towards her and looked her over. His voice became soft. "I know."

"Then smile," she said, mirroring his movement, "because my father and The Orator are coming this way."

"Maeve," Ambrose's excited voice rang out over the music. Maeve turned, acting like she hadn't seen him coming.

"Hello, Daddy!" She leaned toward her father and accepted a kiss on the cheek. Mal smiled at her sweet demeanor. Maeve knew she was good at playing the game. And she used it.

"Leonard, you remember my youngest, Maeve."

"Orator Moon, so good to see you," said Maeve.

"Ah, yes! Of course, I do- of course, I do," said Moon, taking her hand and kissing it quickly. "I must apologize for the nastiness at Vaukore back in April."

"It wasn't your fault, sir," said Maeve kindly. "Orator this is my friend Malachite Peur. Paragon of Combat, Dueling Captain, and top of our class," said Maeve as she smiled at Mal adoringly. Mal extended his hand to Moon.

"An honor to meet you, sir."

Mal had charm still left to spare evidently.

"No introduction needed on my part, Mr. Peur. Every Magical in the Orator's Office knows your name. Youngest Supreme in history. Rumor has it you'll have top pick of any job straight out of school and then perhaps the highest ranking Bellator there ever was."

"I have no doubt," said Ambrose. "Just wait until you see him duel."

"Mal is quite the companion to have, sir," said Maeve, smiling at him.

Mal met her eyes with appreciation for the compliment.

"Peur- interesting name, I think I heard of the Peur-," started Moon, but Maeve was quicker, as though she had seen this particular change in conversation coming, her crystal glass slipped from her fingers and shattered at their feet.

"Maeve," Ambrose reproached her quietly, clearly seeing through her rouse.

She looked at him innocently and ignored his tone. Maeve apologized for her finicky fingers and quickly began guiding the Orator to a set of iron-scrolled settees to reconvene their conversation.

"Oh dear," said Maeve, holding back a smile. "Mummy will be sour over that one."

She gave a small wink to her father. There was a loud POP, and the mess was gone, and four new glasses appeared on the small table they sat around.

"I'm pretty sure that was your Great-Grandmother's crystal," whispered Ambrose.

"I'm pretty sure it's not anything anymore, is it?" Teased Maeve.

Maeve looked across the table at Mal. He was already watching her. He had an uncommon look on his face, one she had seen before. A look that made her stomach flip in circles. A look of hunger. The first time she had seen it in weeks.

The conversation continued to flow until it was time for the party's duel events. Mal excused himself to prepare. Maeve couldn't take her eyes off him as he vanished into the crowd.

Ambrose walked Maeve back up towards the house. Moon walked ahead of them. "Everyone is very taken with Mal," said Ambrose.

"As expected," said Maeve, suppressing a smile, "and they haven't even seen the best of him."

She froze. Unfamiliar Magic swirled around her. Solid as steel. Foreign. But a sister to her own. To Mal's even. Like called to like.

"Ambrose!" Moon quickly gestured for him to hurry.

Ambrose quickened his pace up the stone steps and into the ballroom. Heads turned towards the house, eyes lit up with excitement.

Maeve's brows pulled together.

Buzzing whispers flitted into the air. Maeve hurried up the stairs and rounded the corner into the ballroom towards that Magical power.

"Can you believe it?" Came Abraxas' voice beside her.

She pushed onto her tippy toes and grabbed Abraxas' arm for support. "No way," she breathed.

Across the ballroom, in full black, was an Immortal.

But not just any Immortal.

Reeve, The High Lord of Aterna.

The most powerful being alive.

His smile dripped with swagger as strode across the ballroom towards Ambrose.

Magic shot across the floor with every step he took, cracking towards her. More magic than she had ever felt from another. It was ancient and holy and thick.

The Power of the Gods, they called it. The power of tens of thousands of Magicals all wrapped in one broad-shouldered, striking man.

He was well over six feet, as most Immortals were, with skin kissed by the sun and shining black hair. Tattoos peeked out from his velvety ornate tunic up his neck. They ran across his knuckles as well.

They weren't sleek or elegant. They were harsh, jagged marks of ancient Magic. Familiar and unfamiliar to her all at once.

Vexkari.

He looked to be in his thirties. But Immortals were gifted eternal beauty. They stopped aging in their second or third decades.

"I think I may faint," said Abraxas.

Reeve and Ambrose embraced happily.

"That may be the most attractive man I've ever seen," Abraxas said under his breath.

Behind Reeve was another man, but he was slightly shorter, with the same glowing skin but with long features. His platinum hair fell past his waist. Tipped Ears, like Zimsy. He was part Elven.

He did not caress the crowd with the same confidence as his High Lord. He eyed them all ruefully. Maeve didn't blame him.

"What a surprise, Reeve," Ambrose laughed. "It's been years since you visited Earth."

"Four years actually," Reeve corrected.

"Has it been that long?" Asked Ambrose. "My my. Come- the duels are about to start."

Maeve looked over at Abraxas, who was in a trance, nearly drooling. She pushed him playfully and linked her arm with his. "Let's go watch Mal."

Twenty minutes later, Ambrose and what would be considered the most influential witches and wizards in the Magical World, stood with their mouths hung open as Mal defeated a Bellator with Supreme status and a Magical Militia Captain twice his age. Then another. Then another. They were the toughest duels Maeve had ever personally witnessed. There were spells shooting back and forth so rapidly it was difficult to keep up. And Mal took them all down without breaking a sweat.

When Mal's deadly finger was placed on Arman's throat, the party erupted in clapping and cheers for him. Ambrose's second's face was set in emotionless shock.

Mal helped him to his feet, and they shook hands. Arman shakily stepped into the crowd and Mal bowed his head at the applause and cheers.

He raised his hand up in the air, and the crowd fell silent and still at his silent command.

"If I may," he said. "You've all been so graciously welcoming. It is an honor to duel here tonight. If you will indulge me, I'd like to share this spotlight with another Magical. I'd like you to see the power of two new age Supremes together."

Maeve's cheeks burned hot.

Mal gestured his hand towards her. "The Premier's blood runs strong. Maeve Sinclair."

A buzz lifted through the party.

Mal smiled fully.

It was an intoxicating sight. She would drown to see it never fade.

"Indulge me," he said softly.

Those in front of her parted and she took her place beside him. He took her hand and kissed her fingers gently.

He was putting on quite the show.

"I don't have your ring," she whispered through her smile.

"You don't need it, Little Viper." His fingers slipped down her pointer and middle finger. "Let it all flow."

It had been a dance. So intertwined. It was like they had rehearsed it a thousand times. Each step was so natural, so instinctual, so passionate that she nearly cried as he circled around her, one hand on her throat and his pointer finger at her temple in victory.

He released her quickly and pulled her to her feet. The pair embraced and pulled away from one another. Mal's eyes were swimming with a wild desire. Maeve panted as they shared one breath.

Larliesl's cheers boomed over the rest. Maeve's jaw soon hurt from smiling. Mal was surrounded by Bellator who were part of the Magical Militia, not much older than them, as soon as he broke away from Maeve. They looked at him in admiration, offering him drinks and praise. He accepted them all with elegant ease. Each one desperate for him to know their name.

Perhaps high-ranking Double O officials were not all that mattered in the game to come. The boys that surrounded him looked up at him like Roswyn and Hendrix and the rest did. Pure admiration.

Her Father appeared at her side.

"What do you think?" Maeve asked Ambrose, her hands behind her back as she watched Mal.

Ambrose stared forward. "I think. . ."

Maeve's head shot to Ambrose, expecting some light-hearted comment from her father. It was quite the opposite. Ambrose's face was serene.

Ambrose didn't answer. Maeve changed the subject.

"Is it odd to see your men drinking and dancing?"

Ambrose smiled. "Not at all. I would be worried if they didn't engage in some revelry."

"Reeve is here," she said plainly.

"The High Lord is here," he corrected her. "A very unexpected visit."

"The war is about to turn ugly," said Maeve. "I can feel it. You can feel it. And I guess The High Lord felt it despite being tucked realms away."

"I imagine that is exactly why he is here." Ambrose looked over at her. "You were otherworldly up there."

Maeve bit her lip through a smile.

"How did I do?" Asked Mal, appearing before them.

Ambrose smiled and shook his head. "Bloody brilliant, my boy, brilliant."

Maeve gave Mal a slight nod.

"Later this evening," said Ambrose, grabbing a drink from a floating tray, "come to my office after the party." Ambrose gave him a wink and left them alone.

"Well done," said Maeve.

Mal played with The Dread Ring around his finger absentmindedly.

"Though," continued Maeve, "I figured once they saw you duel, you'd receive an invitation. Seems like your introduction to The High Lord of Aterna will be sooner than anticipated."

"The most powerful Magic in the world runs through his veins," said Mal. "It's strange. I felt his presence the moment he arrived."

"I did too," said Maeve. "But I think we are alone in that."

Maeve looked across the Hall just in time to see a girl named Isabella Zaichosky meet her gaze and look away immediately. Maeve frowned.

"Mal!" Abraxas appeared at their side. "Come, I want you to meet my parents."

They disappeared into the crowd, and Maeve wandered out of the Hall. She crossed The Ballroom, where distant conversation drifted across the foyer.

Her father's infectious laughter filled the air.

She turned the corner into the Bar.

Orator Moon, her father, and Reeve were pouring themselves oversized glasses of Immortally Brewed Bourbon from the bar.

"Maeve," called Ambrose. "Come and join us."

Maeve smiled.

Reeve looked over his shoulder at her casually, his eyes tracing down to her toes and back up. A grin pulled up at his lips.

Maeve reproached him with her eyes. "Your Grace," said Maeve.

"Maeve, the Sinclair youngest," said the handsome High Lord.

Ambrose slapped his arm around her shoulders with a grin. Reeve leaned against the bar with royal ease. He was finely dressed in a black suit with amethyst embroidered swirls of fire. His silken dark hair grazed his shoulders, soft waves billowing throughout.

He was stunning. Not like Mal, whose chiseled and tall face was smooth as moonstone, his slender and built frame a perfect match to Maeve. But Reeve was different. Where Mal was the most gorgeous boy she had ever laid eyes on, Reeve was pure man. Even the thick velvet of his suit couldn't conceal the muscles underneath. His tan tattooed hands gripped his goblet in such a way she was certain he could shatter her whole with one movement of those fingers. Her eyes snapped away from his frame as he spoke with one brow raised.

"Dueling like that, surely you'll be offered a top spot out of school," said Reeve.

"She already has been offered it," murmured Moon into his glass.

Maeve grinned.

"Then congratulations are in order," said Reeve.

Ambrose clicked his tongue.

"Thank you," said Maeve. "But I didn't accept the offer."

Ambrose spoke proudly. "Maeve is also being offered a spot as a Bellator."

"I'm still considering that one," said Maeve coyly.

Reeve grinned again, and his head cocked to one side. He looked to Moon. "Is that so?"

Moon nodded and jabbed his chin towards Ambrose. "You expect anything less out of his blood?"

Ambrose loosed a laugh and Moon continued.

"He's been a pain in my ass for years!"

Maeve caught Reeve breaking his attention from her father and the Orator to survey her. She was not intimidated by the power he held, though she could feel it pushing across the floor towards her, feeling for just how much power she had.

"Moon, are you calling this lovely warrior a pain in the ass?" Asked Reeve playfully.

Moon sputtered on his brandy, and Ambrose let out a hardy laugh.

"Reeve I do enjoy your company," said Ambrose.

"Warrior?" Asked Maeve.

A female Immortal that was as tall as Reeve slunk behind him and laced their elbows together. She was stunning, like all the Immortal women, in a way that agitated Maeve. Graceful beauty oozed from her every move, her every breath, and every pore as she was pure perfection. She looked not a day over twenty-five, another perk of the Immortals Maeve envied. Reeve gave the girl a look of approval at her touch.

"Yes," he continued. "In Aterna, the Immortals that make up our defenses are called Senshi Warriors. Like your Magical Militia. Only with weapons of Magic."

"Are you one?" She asked.

Her Father's hand tensed on her shoulder, a cue to let him be. A cue which Maeve ignored.

"I am," said Reeve proudly.

"An army of Immortals," said Maeve playfully. "What could you possibly need that for?"

Moon tensed, but Reeve remained casual, a smile ticking up at the corners of his lips. One Maeve returned.

"Is that school neglecting to teach you history?" He asked with a laugh.

The golden-haired Immortal on his arm inclined her head and spoke sweetly.

"Would you like to dance before the night is over, High Lord?"

He had not introduced her. She was no High Lady or Queen. She was just his date. The High Lord's mate died centuries ago, according to her Father. Apparently, Reeve was quite the bachelor now. Much to Maeve's pleasure, he ignored his date and continued addressing Maeve herself. She wasn't sure why it satisfied her that the Immortal goddess on his arm was second to her at the moment.

"Go read about the War of Shadows. Three hundred years ago."

"I have read about it," said Maeve.

"Not well enough apparently," said Reeve.

"Apparently," said Maeve, taking a look up at her father.

"Get on," he said playfully with a gentle shove and released her shoulders.

Maeve smiled and gave Moon a curt nod.

"Your Highness," she said, bowing her head towards Reeve.

"You do not live in Aterna," he said cooly. "You need not bow as though you were a subject."

Maeve's smile relaxed. She looked up at him solemnly with a soft expression. He was not at all like she assumed. "How about as a lady showing respect for a powerful Immortal? Or perhaps warrior to warrior, as you would call it."

Reeve smirked and inhaled sharply. His date tensed on his arm. Ambrose's eyebrows raised slightly.

"You have quite the contender on your hands, Ambrose."

Maeve beamed, took the compliment, and turned on her heel, leaving them with a dazzling smile.

"You don't know the half of it," she heard her father say.

The night was almost over, and the hour was late. Maeve, Mal, Abraxas, Hendrix, Iris, and Juliet stood at the edge of The Ballroom, laughing about something Abraxas said. Roswyn and Emerie were dancing rather close, drunk off Dragon Whiskey.

The music ended, followed by soft applause.

"Ladies and gentlemen," said the conductor, "what a spectacular evening!"

The group made their way closer to listen to the evening's closing moments.

"And now, the last waltz of the 1945 Summer Solstice Party," said the conductor, turning back to the musicians.

"Looks like the night is over," said Iris with a yawn.

"Maeve," said Mal.

She looked over at him.

"Take my hand."

"What?" Asked Maeve incredulously.

The music began to swell. Mal grabbed her hand and pulled her into the center of the ballroom quickly.

"What are you doing?" Asked Maeve excitedly.

Mal wrapped his hand around her back, and Maeve placed her hand on his shoulder.

"You know exactly what I'm doing," said Mal, giving her a quick spin before pulling her closer.

She gasped as their chests collided.

He moved her gracefully across the room. Much to Maeve's surprise, Mal wasn't a bad dancer. In fact, he was quite skilled. Her dress whisked behind her, sparkling in the lights perfectly.

A few onlookers oohed and awed at them as they passed by.

"I didn't know you could waltz," said Maeve.

"I'm sure I didn't either," replied Mal.

"How does it feel to just naturally be good at everything?"

He smiled without answering.

His hand moved slowly until it rested on the small of her back. She tried to disguise the fact that this made her breath catch sharply. Maeve looked up at him.

"If we add a few flourishes, I think every eye will be on us," whispered Maeve.

They widened their steps as they moved across the room faster. Mal spun her out and twirled her under his arm as they danced around the Ballroom.

The music began to swell as it was coming to its climax. He spun her out away from him, letting go of her completely. Maeve laughed with enough joy to ensure all eyes were on them.

He took three strides towards her, cupped the back of her neck with one hand and her waist with the other, dipped her backward, and kissed her. His lips tasted smokey, like a cinnamon cigar, one of her father's, which Maeve had not been expecting.

Her hands held his face.

There were exclamations and cheers at what appeared to be a romantic gesture, but Maeve knew it to be far from romance.

Mal was staking his claim on her in front of every Pureblood in the room. In front of the entire Committee of the Sacred and The Double O.

She played her part perfectly. He pulled away from her with his signature smile, and she followed his lead. Over his shoulder, Maeve caught a glimpse of her father just as he lit a cigar and exited the Ballroom. Maeve could have sworn there was a mischievous smile on his face.

Perhaps it was her mother's objection and displeasure alone that gave her this fire, but she had been prepared from the start for Clarissa's disapproval. The purpose of tonight was to bring Mal into their world. To prepare them all for his glory. These were the elite that he needed to win over.

And Maeve was the key to making that happen.

"So much for discreet," she muttered through her smile.

Chapter 26

". . . I saw her last night."

"And?" Said a female voice

"She was a vision of power." Said the first voice again. It was familiar.

"Does she know?" Asked the woman.

"She hasn't the faintest idea."

"That is good then?"

"No. . ." He said. "That is a storm waiting to be unleashed."

The curtains in Maeve's sapphire and gold bedroom inside Sinclair Estates were already drawn, spilling morning sunlight into her room. She stretched, rolling onto her back.

The dream had already faded. The unfamiliar voices were gone. Spinel jumped off the bed and staggered over to her enchanted window, which was showing a stunning apple orchard.

She suppressed a smile as she remembered the previous night's events, reaching for the ring around her neck. Mal placed it there before she bid him goodnight.

His bold kiss had been unexpected. But Maeve relished it all the same.

Maeve slept on cloud nine. Mal was lucky to have gotten any sleep. It's likely he had stayed long into the night in her father's study. She was eager to hear his experience.

Downstairs, Maeve found a complete breakfast spread waiting for her on silver serving trays and carafes. A copy of the Starlight Gazette sat on the table. Maeve was in too good of a mood to read about Kietel and so she ignored the newspaper entirely. She sat alone on the long mahogany dining table, happily spreading cream across her cinnamon bagel.

Her mother was undoubtedly furious about the whole ordeal, but Mal had charmed many of the guests prior to their waltz. Their adoration of him would make it difficult for Clarissa to scold her.

Arianna appeared in the dining room and stopped short, standing awkwardly.

"What are you doing?" Maeve asked her in a bored tone.

Arianna rolled her eyes and made her way to the table, sitting across from Maeve.

They ate in silence until Arianna finally spoke.

"You mortified Mother last night," said Arianna.

Maeve smirked. "What did she say?"

Arianna's mouth fell open. "You're proud? You're actually proud of embarrassing our family like that?"

Maeve laughed. "Embarrassing? I think we awed the entire crowd."

Arianna's lips formed a thin, tight line. "I would have never done something like that."

"And look where it's gotten you," said Maeve. "Speaking of, how is Titus?"

Arianna's cheeks flushed. "You're delusional."

Maeve sipped her tea for a moment. "I'm sure Mal is still sleeping after being up so late with Father and the rest."

Arianna's eyes went wide. "Don't tell me he got invited back to Father's study." She laughed haughtily.

Maeve smiled. "Why wouldn't he have?"

Arianna shook her head as she sliced her biscuit open and spread butter angrily.

"Haven't got a reply?" Asked Maeve. "Well, there's a first."

Arianna glowered at her, slamming her biscuit back together.

An unrecognized bright white owl swooped through one of the large open windows and landed on the arm of the chair next to Maeve.

She recognized the bright red Vaukore seal immediately and grabbed the letter. It felt heavy, but Maeve tried not to let herself get excited. There was also the chance that Tilly Cardinal, another Paragon of Academics, would snag the vote for Head Girl at Vaukore over her.

The bright white owl helped itself to a strip of bacon and flew out of the room.

Maeve didn't hesitate to peel the wax seal and lift the envelope flap open. A black and bronze pin fell into her lap. She sighed and smiled from ear to ear as she picked it up. Engraved across the bronze were the words:

HEAD GIRL

Maeve tossed her napkin on the table and left the dining hall without another word to Arianna. She skipped up the stairs to the third floor, her new badge held proudly in her hand.

She rounded the corner as Mal's door flew open. He stood with his own letter in hand. His hair wasn't combed, and his eyes were bloodshot. He was still in his pants and button-down from the previous night. He had barely slept it seemed.

"Did you get it?" Asked Maeve breathlessly. "Of course you did. What am I saying?"

"I got it," said Mal with a smirk. "And you?"

Maeve nodded happily, presenting her badge.

"Well done, Maeve. Well deserved."

"Thank you." Maeve rocked on her feet.

Mal leaned against the doorway with a sigh.

"You should get back to sleep," said Maeve.

"I can't," said Mal. "I've been invited to fence this morning at Doggbind's. I promised your father I would accompany him."

"The Head of Magical Law?" Asked Maeve.

"The very one," answered Mal.

Maeve smiled. "Best of luck, Mr. Peur."

"Come and watch."

Maeve shook her head. "That sounds terribly boring,"

Mal reached out and ran his fingers across his ring that draped across her chest. His fingers hooked around the chain and tugged her close to where he leaned in the doorway.

His mouth hung open. "I didn't ask," he said with a raised brow.

Maeve attended without complaint.

Before their return to Vaukore, Ambrose Obscured them to various cities to purchase school books for their final year and new uniforms and cloaks. Ambrose insisted on buying Mal a tailored set of Vaukore combat attire from Wizard's Wears, the most expensive Magical Shop in Paris.

Maeve knew Mal would have secretly liked to decline, but Ambrose's love language was gift-giving, and Mal was wise to gratefully accept.

Ambrose also purchased them both new cauldrons and vial sets. Mal eyed a black leather-bound journal in the window of Hobs and Hyde Bindings. Ten minutes later, Mal's name was burned across the back cover in gold inlay.

"Ambrose!"

They turned, and one of Ambrose's colleagues was striding towards them.

"Maeve," he said, nodding at her curtly.

He then turned to Mal with the most excited look on his face.

"Malachite, my boy," he said, extending his hand.

"Hello, Mr. Beaux," said Mal, shaking his hand with a smile.

"I cannot tell you enough how amazed I was at your dueling skills," said Mr. Beaux. "And your dancing." He nudged Maeve with a wink.

Maeve pressed her lips together and avoided her father's gaze.

"Thank you, sir," said Mal. "That's too kind."

"And London," said Mr. Beaux, "hasn't stopped talking about you either."

Mr. Beaux looked at Maeve and laughed. "I told her, as her husband, it was making me a little jealous!"

Maeve smiled softly at Mr. Beaux. They were already falling for him. And they didn't even know the greatest secret of the century yet.

He was their salvation.

On their final summer afternoon before returning to Vaukore, Maeve had a surprise for Mal. They saddled up two horses and began a journey north. They rode a few times over the summer, exploring cliffside caves and the forest, but they had never traveled as far as where Maeve was taking them.

The ride was just short of an hour, and they took turns setting the pace. Sometimes they traveled quickly, wind blowing violently around them. Then Mal brought them to a slow trot, where they admired the cliffside sunset and talked about their final year at Vaukore.

Mal decided that until the Human War conflict was resolved, and his studies at Vaukore complete, he would be making no claims as The Dread Descendant.

Maeve understood. There was too much happening. The Orator's Office was occupied. The Magical Militia was now fighting in a human war they were never supposed to be in. But as civilian death tolls rose in the spring, Ambrose felt he had no choice but to lend his army to protect the innocent.

Mal's secret protected him too.

There was still so much they didn't know.

And Kietel was becoming violent, rash, and out of control. With an army to back him.

"Did you see the paper this morning?"

Mal nodded.

"Kietel is calling for the Orator's Office to surrender power to him within a fortnight. He called my father by name."

"Your Father has the entire Magical Militia at his command. Not just the British. He isn't threatened."

"I know," said Maeve. "Still, I worry."

"He worries about sending you back to school."

Maeve looked over at him. "Oh?"

"It's to be expected."

They rode in silence for a moment. The sounds of the North Sea slamming against the cliffside and the horses' hoofs against the grass were the only sounds.

"I had that feeling again," said Maeve quietly.

"It's been weeks since you felt that," he said.

Maeve nodded. "But I felt it last night. Late. It woke me up."

"Anything different?"

"It felt. . .close. And then suddenly very far. It was like cold slime trailing down my back, moving farther away with each inch."

"Have you told your father?"

"Primus and the Gods no. I know he doesn't want me going back to Vaukore right now and I'm not about to give him a greater reason to lock me in that house."

They reached the tree line of the woodlands at twilight. Sinclair Estates was far behind them. Mal raised a brow at Maeve, and she nodded him along and took the lead. They moved into the forest slowly and quietly.

"It's the perfect time of year to see them now, as it's getting a little cooler," said Maeve in a hushed voice.

"You still haven't told me what we're seeing."

"That would ruin the surprise."

They had not traveled far into the forest when Maeve grabbed Mal's arm, silently pointing ahead of them.

He followed her gaze between two trees. There, in the opening, was a bright white and gleaming unicorn. Its silvery hair was silky, and its horn was long with a pale peach color.

Maeve was delighted with Mal's amazed expression.

"Do they ever leave this forest?" Asked Mal.

"Not usually," said Maeve. "But father's Aunt told him there was one who she gained the trust of and that she would come close to the house and eat out of her hand."

They watched as a second, smaller unicorn joined the first.

"They travel in families," she whispered. "Father says their blood is incredibly powerful," said Maeve.

"Drinking it prolongs life," stated Mal.

"Not just that," replied Maeve. "When Father was a child, my Grandfather Alyicious killed a unicorn with the sole purpose of curing Father of a nasty curse as a baby."

"He gave him unicorn blood?"

Maeve nodded. "Grandmother says it worked. She said she'd heard many stories of the Sinclair's using unicorn blood to live longer lives. Though, it's considered a heinous act to kill something so pure, an act of dark magic to corrupt something so beautiful, especially when there are so few left. Not that any of that stopped my ancestors from hunting all kinds of magical beasts. But these were brought to Earth by the Sinclairs that fled the Dread Lands three hundred years ago."

"They brought others," Mal stated plainly.

Maeve nodded. "They did. And some dark creatures slipped through as well."

They watched the unicorns for a few minutes until something spooked the beautiful creatures, and they took off running. Maeve and Mal left the forest and stopped, overlooking the seaside.

His eyes burned a hole in the side of her face. He spoke suddenly.

"What do you know about The High Lord?'

"Not much. He's a Senshi Warrior. And he's been on the throne since shortly after the Shadow War. Which he inherited, power and all, from his father. Father says eventually he will pass that power onto his own inheritor, and he will die. That is the way of their Magic."

"And how long has your father known him?"

"The Immortals were not our allies until my father made it so when he was first elected as Premier over a decade ago. But he's known him his whole life."

"Because they refused the Magicals entry when they sought refuge from the blight three hundred years ago."

"Where did you read that?"

"Hummingdoor told me so."

Maeve looked out over the seaside. Reeve had insinuated that she needed to read up on the Shadow War. Maybe she did.

"He holds the Power of the Gods. Every man in that room the other night knew he was the most powerful of us all. And at any moment, it could belong to another, and his existence gone." Mal's face was stoic, perfectly poised, and held, not a hair out of place.

"For now," said Maeve. "He is the most powerful for now. That shield you made around the orphanage? It blocked a bomb, Mal. Father said a single bomb is the strength of a thousand Magicals. And that Magic came easy to you. So, for now, Reeve is the most powerful."

Mal took the reins on her horse from her hands and pulled her horse closer to his. She looked up at him.

"Do you know that entire evening I was consumed by the thought of you in that lavender dress?"

Maeve breathed deeply. "You did look distracted in your dueling."

Mal grinned softly. He pulled her forward and kissed her forehead with a chuckle, then released her reins.

"Would you like to race back?" Asked Maeve.

"Only if you'd like to lose," said Mal.

The final night of summer was traditionally an intimate dinner party among only the Sacred Seventeen families, a celebration send-off for those returning to school on August 1st. Roswyn's family was hosting them in their mountainside villa in Switzerland.

Ambrose bought Mal another tailored suit with a new set of black robes. Maeve could think of no one who deserved nice things more than the boy who grew up with nothing but a name.

She delighted in seeing him woo the crowds once again. Irma and Peitro Mavros, Alphard and Astrea's parents, were so happy to see him that Irma was beside herself with joy when Mal asked her for a dance.

Maeve was having a delightful evening. She and Abraxas were seated above the garden on a settee, giggling over Mr. Iantrose knocking over an entire statue and mistaking it for a party guest in his drunken state.

Maeve was the only one not drinking, but that wasn't out of the ordinary. Alphard was cracking jokes with Roswyn.

The mountain air was cool and thin. Refreshing.

"Look, look," crackled Abraxas, "he's trying to help it up."

He grabbed Maeve's arm and tried to calm his breathing. Arianna appeared and snapped her fingers for Maeve's attention.

"Mother wants you to come inside for the cake cutting," said Arianna.

"Why," grimaced Maeve, laughing. "That sounds terribly boring."

"As the women of Sacred in the Sinclair household-" started Arianna, but Maeve cut her off.

"Yeah, not going."

Abraxas swirled around the ice in his drink, looking up at Arianna. She huffed and walked away, muttering under her breath.

Maeve and Abraxas turned their attention back to Mr. Iantrose.

"You should go," said Roswyn.

"What?" Maeve said, turning towards him.

"To the cake cutting," he said in an affected voice. "Where the women belong," he spat.

"Shut your mouth," said Alphard calmly.

"What the hell, Al?" Asked Roswyn, clearly thrown off.

"Nothing to get worked up about," said Alphard, "just can't have you talking to her like that."

"I don't need you to defend me," said Maeve, cooly. "You'd think after Mal's last warning to him that he'd learn to keep it to himself."

Abraxas suddenly looked away, hiding behind his drink. Roswyn glowered at him nonetheless. Abraxas could never be trusted with gossip.

Roswyn stormed inside without another word.

"What on earth did you do to that poor bloke?" Asked Alphard with a laugh.

"Nothing," said Maeve. "Nothing intentional, at least."

"He does not like you," said Alphard.

Maeve noticed Leslie Loxerman, the current Chair of the Committee of the Sacred, was slowly making her way over towards them.

"Merde," muttered Maeve.

Maeve turned around to where Abraxas had been only moments ago, but it appeared that he had already fled. In a desperate attempt to escape, Maeve turned to Alphard.

"Would you care for a walk?" She asked.

Alphard finished off his drink with a long swig. "I'd be delighted, but let me get another-"

"Let's go now," said Maeve, standing and shoving him along.

Once they were out of sight on a secluded dirt path, beneath the hillside, Maeve relaxed.

"So, who are we running from?" Alphard teased.

"Shut up," said Maeve.

Alphard laughed, and they walked silently for a moment.

"My parents are up there," said Alphard, gesturing towards the house, "eating out of the palm of Mal's hand." He chuckled.

"Everyone is," she said with a laugh.

"Even you," he said without looking at her. "He's brilliant, no contest," continued Alphard. "He has all the leadership qualities, all the charisma, and charm. I'm sure your father and the Double O already have him marked."

Maeve kept her face emotionless, knowing just how different Mal's future was than anyone here could predict.

"He's smart to pick you as his closest," said Alphard, more serious.

"I'm hardly-" started Maeve, but she was cut off.

"Please," said Alphard with a scoff. "It's clear to everyone paying attention, especially my dear friend Roswyn."

Maeve didn't meet his gaze. After a short round through the garden, they were almost back at the house. The coast was clear as Loxerman was nowhere in sight.

"The three of you," she started. "You were close."

She was referring to her brother Antony, Roswyn, and Alphard.

"Thick as thieves," he said.

Maeve swallowed the knot in her throat and looked up at him. She forced herself to smile softly.

"Thank you for the company," said Maeve sweetly, beginning up the steps to the house.

Alphard laughed.

"What?" She asked as she turned towards him.

Alphard shrugged. "It always throws me off when you do that."

Maeve looked at him quizzically.

"When you switch into that perfectly polite way of interacting that you were taught," said Alphard. "And it's. . . not you."

Maeve looked away from him. No one had ever called her out on that before.

"I mean no offense," said Alphard kindly. "I know that's how we were raised. You just don't have to do that with me."

Maeve looked back at him and studied his face. He was genuine.

She nodded and gave him a smile before starting her ascent up the stairs once more.

"Sinclair!" He called after her.

She reached the top and looked back at him.

"Antony would be proud of you."

Maeve beamed and bit the inside of her cheek, heading back inside. She grabbed herself a sparkling water at the bar when Abraxas' mother, Beatrice, appeared at her side.

"Hello, Maeve," she said sweetly.

"Aunt Beatrice," smiled Maeve, "you look lovely."

Beatrice smiled and took a drink off the bar. Her long blonde hair swooped into large curls.

"Would you care to walk with me?"

Maeve obliged her.

"What I'm about to say won't bring you joy," said Beatrice. "Let's step onto the balcony."

They walked silently through the glass doors and towards the corner, away from the other guests.

"Now you have me worried," said Maeve cooly, sipping her drink.

Beatrice pursed her lips and sighed. "Your father is in denial about the wheels that are rapidly turning for you, Maeve. I want to speak candidly."

Maeve's eyebrows pulled together. "Then speak."

"Abraxas is so fond of you, and I have always been fond of you as well." Maeve could tell Beatrice was choosing her words carefully, though they were genuine. "I suppose sometimes I think of you as one of my own. I was there when you were born, you know. After all, there are so few of us Pureblooded Witches. Boys are born all the time. . . But we are not. . .we are more than family."

Maeve was silent and let her speak. Beatrice took a long sip of her drink.

"I know your twenty-second birthday isn't until October, but if you do not want a betrothal to sneak up on you, then you need to speak to your grandmother soon to postpone like Arianna was able to."

Maeve's stomach dropped, and she broke their gaze. She looked out over the vast valley below, sandwiched between two mountain peaks.

"I know," said Aunt Beatrice. "And I know that you don't want to hear this, but they're never going to let Malach-"

"Stop," interrupted Maeve. There was a likely chance Mal would see these memories at some point as his favorite dueling tactic was swimming through her mind.

"I'm sorry, dear," said Beatrice sadly. "I truly want what is best for you, and I know you dread this terrible duty that is ours. But if you want to have at least some semblance of control over your future, talk to your grandmother. She has power and can assure you marry a pureblood of your choosing. They'll want to announce it at The Sacred Party this Christmas, after Arianna's wedding."

Beatrice placed a hand on Maeve's shoulder and attempted to comfort Maeve, whose insides felt like a boiling pit.

"Thank you," said Maeve, taking her hand and looking her in the eyes. "Please do not mistake my sudden exit for being unappreciative of you."

She descended the stairs into the forest paths in search of isolation.

It was a beautiful evening for such grim news. The sky was clear, exposing all the stars. If she listened carefully, she could hear the distant waterfall pouring off of the mountain, feeding the lake below.

She followed the sound of the water until the dirt path turned to rock. Water, calm and bright in the moonlight, pushed and pulled gently on the rocks. The twin mountain peaks above glistened, their snowy white tops stood tall in the sky.

They had no worries of duty or inheritance or reputation. They were a marvel without ever moving, simply by existing. No one wanted to change them. It would be foolish to try. So it was never even a thought.

Maeve envied those mountains.

"I wonder what Mrs. Rosethorn could have possibly said to drive you all the way out here," said Mal, coming up beside her.

Maeve turned towards him. He looked so handsome dressed up. His hair was perfectly in place, and the black suit elongated his tall figure. He was built for finery. She could picture no one better suited for luxury than Mal.

"You may look, for I do not have the strength to tell you," said Maeve sadly.

He stepped closer with a concerned look and invaded her mind, only for a moment, and withdrew. He held Maeve steady as the sensation made her falter.

Maeve, who was on the verge of tears, looked up at him.

"Please, promise me-" she pressed her palms into his chest. "I-cannot-"

Her voice broke as she bowed her head.

"Destiny is knocking," said Mal, his voice velvety dark.

It was her battle to fight. She looked up at him.

"And I will not open the door," replied Maeve fiercely.

He grabbed a fistful of her hair, pulling her head back and her mouth open. He kissed her deeply, and with such force, her knees buckled. Their bodies slammed together, and she kissed him back desperately, throwing her arms around his neck.

Maeve was no mountain and had no idea what she would do, but none of it mattered. Mal was all she wanted, and she would sacrifice everything to stay by his side. Every ounce of her inheritance. Her last name. It was all on the cutting room floor now.

All the fortunes of the world couldn't buy her loyalty.

No offer of power could buy her love.

She wanted to be drenched in him. In his scent and his skin. Suffocated by his Magic.

They pulled away from one another, Maeve's breathing quick. Mal ran his thumb over her bottom lip.

"They will not take you from me," he assured her.

Maeve nodded, looking into his dark eyes. He meant it. Beatrice, The Committee, Her Father- none of them knew who he was. None of them understood.

He kissed her once more and bit gently into her bottom lip.

She was glad they would be leaving in the morning and looked forward to escaping from all of this at Vaukore.

"What time is it?" Asked Maeve as they walked back towards Roswyn's family home.

He glanced at the watch Maeve gifted him. "Nearly eleven."

Maeve nodded and was grateful the night was coming to an end.

The pair returned to the party as the final waltz was being danced. Maeve grabbed a glass of lemon juice off a floating tray and met eyes with Aunt Beatrice and Irma Mavros, who raised their glasses at Maeve and smiled softly.

She returned the gesture.

Halfway through the room she stopped walking suddenly.

"Why the sour face?" Asked Mal.

Maeve took a long sip of her drink. "Do you see that girl there?" She pointed with her glass. "The blonde? She was meant to marry my brother."

Mal hadn't been expecting that. "Oh."

"Yes. But her family didn't approve, to begin with."

"Did she love him?"

"Does it matter?" Answered Maeve, cooly.

Mal pressed her with a frown.

"No. She did not," relented Maeve.

"Have you ever considered-"

"I have actually," interrupted Maeve. "And tonight is not the night."

Maeve had no interest in delving into the most likely theory that Isabella Zaichosky's family had been the ones behind her brother's murder.

Chapter 27

Ambrose Portaled them, and an insistent Abraxas, directly into the Entrance Hall at Vaukore. Maeve and Mal stepped into the warm castle with their new Head Girl and Head Boy badges pinned proudly to their uniforms.

Thunder rumbled in the distance, vibrating the floors beneath them. Ambrose shook Mal's hand and kissed Maeve on the cheek. He wished them a good term at school.

At the foot of the Grand Staircase, The Headmasters stood. Rowan looked at Ambrose in disapproval.

"Milites!" Ambrose shouted, never breaking his gaze with Rowan.

The soldiers of the Magical Militia in the Entrance Hall all slammed their fists to their chests at once.

"Mundi!" They called out in unison.

"Memento," said Ambrose softly, and the soldiers relaxed once more.

The Headmaster's received his message fully. They eyed one another briefly. Elgin gave Rowan, Ambrose's ex-spy, a subtle look of judgment.

Ambrose turned on his heel. The Portal vanished behind him.

"Well, no surprise there," said Hendrix Fawley, gesturing to their badges as they entered Hellming Hall.

"Suppose everything will be terribly different now," said Abraxas dramatically as Spinel rubbed against his legs.

Abraxas reached for him, but he took off into the castle.

Maeve laughed. "As if you've ever gotten in trouble for anything."

After the traditional back to school banquet and Cauldron Ceremony, Maeve and Mal made their way up the stairs, assisting new students in finding their class schedules and settling in their dorms.

The castle was quiet just before curfew. Mal and Maeve strolled the darkened corridors in solitude. Head Boy and Head Girl had no curfew.

As they reached the third-floor landing, a Paragon of Combat ran towards them. Her face was flushed and her mouth was pulled in a thin line.

"Hi," she said, winded. "I'm Grace. I'm a-"

"What's happened?" Maeve interrupted her.

She sighed loudly, "Well, there was a party in the combat dorms. I came to find you two, and something's got out of hand and-"

Maeve and Mal listened to Grace no further, and they flanked her on either side and quickly made their way to the seventh floor.

"Surely Larliesl is already there," said Maeve.

"Let's take the passage off the fourth floor," said Mal. "It'll be quicker."

They rounded the corner and slipped behind a tapestry of Primus, where there was a narrow spiral staircase. Wordlessly, light flickered into existence before them, guiding them in the darkness. The stairs led straight to a secret door on the seventh floor, which appeared to be a painting. It was much quicker than taking the grand staircase of the castle.

They hastily pushed through the painting and rounded the corner. There were several new students outside in the corridor crying.

Mal strode towards the door and demanded entry from Sir Knoble. The knight bowed at the waist and stepped aside.

Maeve asked the girls if they were alright. They nodded and wiped their tears. One of them hiccuped. Maeve surveyed them all one by one. They were drunk.

As soon as the door swung open, yelling and screaming from inside the Common Room filled the corridor behind them. Mal emerged ahead of her, and they immediately spotted the issue.

There was a boy on the ground, unconscious. Another, named Henry Rowle, was screaming with his fingers drawn, pointing it at various students. He was shaking.

Mal stalked over to him and placed one hand over his fingers, curling them into a closed fist. He placed his other hand on the back of his neck.

"Stop," was all Mal said.

Shock rang across Henry's face. He relaxed, and Mal grabbed one of his shoulders and forced him to his knees.

Maeve kneeled beside the one unconscious student on the carpet and felt for a heartbeat at his throat. The boy was, at least, alive.

"What happened here?" Mal asked quietly.

A few around them fell silent. Those farther away hadn't heard him.

"I asked what happened here?" He repeated louder.

The room went silent. Maeve stood up and walked over to Henry. He was a Pureblood boy she had known her entire life. He had only been at Vaukore for a year, but he was considered one of Mal's boys.

"He's drunk," Maeve whispered to Mal.

"He used an illegal curse on Simon," said a voice from the crowd.

Maeve and Mal turned their heads towards the source. It was a small, blonde-haired girl Maeve recognized from the Cauldron Ceremony earlier that evening. She was freshly eighteen and held her composure with grace. Her accent was Russian.

"Is that true?" Asked Mal.

She nodded. Some of the others in the room murmured in agreement.

"And. . . broke her nose." The girl's gaze traveled to a brunette-haired girl sitting in a chair with her head bowed, and another girl rubbed her back soothingly.

"What provoked him?"

"Henry said something nasty about. . . her. . ." The girl referred to the brunette, who still didn't look up. "He said she didn't deserve to be here. He said she had dirty blood. And that Kietel was killing dirty-blooded Magicals like her every day."

Maeve looked at the brunette with a broken nose. Human born.

The blonde girl continued, her voice unwavering. "And then pointed right at Leela, saying he'd just do it himself."

Leela, the human-born girl with a broken nose, looked up at Maeve for the first time. Her face was stained with blood, and her eyes were red to match. She looked horrified.

Her first night at Vaukore and this is what she was greeted with. Maeve turned quickly back towards Henry and opened her mouth. Mal's eyes stopped her. The girl continued.

"He attacked her, and then Simon jumped between them, and the two started dueling one another."

Maeve realized behind them was a long table full of contraband. Immortally Brewed Bourbon, Dragon Whiskey, and Bubbling Brandy. The brandy was expensive, as she recognized a bottle from her father's top shelf.

"Where did you lot even get all this?" Asked Maeve.

No one answered.

Mal looked down at Henry Rowle with perfect composure, but Maeve was certain his insides were burning.

There was a loud commotion at the entrance to the Common Room, and all heads turned in that direction.

Larliesl, Healer Kimmerance, and Headmaster Elgin stepped into the room.

Kimmerance gasped upon seeing Leela's blood-stained face and rushed towards the girl. Maeve averted her attention to the unconscious boy on the floor, which caused her to yelp and instruct two others to help her get Simon to the Healing Hall. Leela's friend walked her behind them.

"You stay put," Mal muttered to Rowle before he strolled over to the Headmaster. Mal explained the situation to them in a hushed voice.

Headmaster Elgin sent everyone to their dormitories, save for Rowle. She and Larliesl escorted Rowle gravely out of the common room.

Maeve and Mal walked silently down the grand staircase, heading back towards their dorms.

"What an idiot," said Maeve.

Mal's face was stoic. "I have taught him better than that. To use Dread Magic I gave him the privilege of learning. . ."

"I wonder if he'll be expelled?"

Mal raised his eyebrows as they reached the sixth-floor landing and continued down. "Why wouldn't he be?"

"His money. His parents give so much money to the school. To the Committee. The Orator's Office."

Mal scoffed.

"Seven Realms," said Maeve. "His parents are going to lose it."

They reached the fifth floor, where Maeve would be heading to her dormitory to check on things there and get to bed herself.

"What an eventful first night as Head Boy and Head Girl," said Maeve, turning towards Mal.

He gave her a small smile, one that didn't meet his eyes. "Goodnight, Miss Sinclair."

He departed and didn't look back at her. Maeve resisted the urge to slip into his mind and see what was really eating at him. It didn't take her long to speculate it was Henry's loyalty to Kietel that occupied Mal's mind.

Chapter 28

Maeve was already swamped with schoolwork. She took on seven Supreme level classes and was feeling the weight of every single one. She'd even been given special permission to take Combative Magic classes, despite her Practical Magic placement at school.

"Did you hear Larliesl is ill?" Abraxas asked.

"No," said Maeve. "But I suppose that explains why his classes are postponed."

"He's insistent on having his beginning of term celebration at the end of this week though."

"Of course he is," said Maeve.

Mal appeared at her other side in the hallway and slipped a book into her bag.

"What's that?"

"Something for you to peruse later," he said.

She reached for her bag, but Mal clicked his tongue.

"I said later."

She looked up at him. "Fine."

"Rowle's parents came and got him late last night," said Abraxas.

"Did you get all of that contraband into the dorms the other night?"

Abraxas avoided her gaze. "Not sure what you are talking about."

Maeve rolled her eyes. He was lying. "Abraxas," whined Maeve.

"Look," said Abraxas, "It's done all the time, and nothing like that ever happens. Don't go blaming me for Rowle's stupidity."

Maeve eyed him but found it difficult to argue.

"I can't believe he did that," said Maeve.

"Yeah," agreed Abraxas. "That poor girl."

They passed the blonde combat student from the party, the new girl who spoke up. She was sitting on the stairs looking through sheets of parchment with an aggravated look.

Maeve stopped walking. Mal and Abraxas continued on.

"Do you need assistance?" Maeve asked.

She looked up from her papers. Then back down. "Just confused as to why I have two classes at the same time."

Maeve held out her hand. The girl's eyes flicked up in annoyance. But she handed them to Maeve nonetheless.

Maeve flipped through them. And then handed them back.

"You don't," she said. "You have Introduction to Spell Casting on Mondays and Wednesdays this term, and next term that becomes Charms."

"Thank you," said the girl, glancing over the parchment.

"What's your name?" Asked Maeve.

"Belvadora."

"Where are you from?"

"Russia. What's your name?"

"Please," said Maeve. "Spare me."

A smile kicked at the corners of Belvadora's otherwise bored expression. "Maeve Sinclair. Pureblood daughter of the Premier. Head Girl. Why do you care who I am?"

"Because you are the only one in a crowd of cowards who wasn't afraid. Not of Henry. Not of your fellow students. Not of Mal."

"Why not of you?"

"Are you afraid of me?"

"I'm not an imbecile," said Belvadora dryly.

"Maeve!" Abraxas called from behind her.

"A few of us train on Saturday mornings. You should come."

"You've never seen me fight."

"I don't need to," said Maeve.

Abraxas appeared at her side, looping his arm through hers. "What about this first year could be so interesting, cousin?"

"Shut up, Brax."

Belvadora looked Abraxas up and down, slowly and meticulously. Abraxas' expression shifted to one of interest.

"Well, well," he said lowly. "Suddenly I'm intrigued."

Belvadora didn't miss a beat. "From what I have heard, I'm not your type."

Abraxas smirked. "Darling, everyone is my type."

Maeve slipped out of his arm and threw her hands in the air in omission. Mal was waiting for her a few feet away. He joined her in step.

"That's the girl from the party?"

Maeve nodded. "I invited her to our Saturday morning sessions. I hope that's okay."

"Campaigning for me already?" Said Mal with a grin.

Maeve smiled as her hand moved to the back of her neck. Mal's carefree grin turned to a look of displeasure.

"I'm fine," she said and looked back over her shoulder. Belvadora was walking in the opposite direction as Abraxas watched her.

Mal looked back and raised his brows. "Flavor of the week?"

"Eventually he has to actually fall for someone," said Maeve under her breath. "Maybe it's her."

Mal shook his head. "It's not her."

Maeve perused the book Mal slipped her that evening. The book confirmed what they already suspected. The ring Mal took from his father and the locket he spoke of were powerful Magic objects. They were made with Dread Magic, and they were two of many Magical objects.

"Seven of them," said Maeve with a surprised exhale. "The Dread Armor."

Mal nodded. The Dread Ring sat atop his finger, glimmering in the candlelight. The two silver skulls that held the black stone in place had deep ruby gems for eyes.

"I think it's safe to say this locket it speaks of is the same one your father did," said Maeve.

Mal nodded. Maeve flipped back a few pages.

"So the ring, the locket, the dagger, the goblet, the spell book, the stone, and the crown," said Maeve.

"How do we even begin to search for these things?" Asked Mal. "There's only one other object we know that even made it to Earth. The rest could be scattered across the seven realms for all we know."

"Two," corrected Maeve.

Mal's brows raised.

"The goblet was once on display in the Double O. Until they scrubbed the place of any mention of Dread Magic. It was auctioned off privately. But I bet we could figure out to who."

They were silent for a second.

"Where did you get this?" Maeve asked.

Mal hesitated. "It was in my room at your home."

Maeve nearly dropped the book. She exhaled a quick burst of air. "That's not a coincidence."

"I'm aware of that," said Mal. "Someone knows."

Maeve chewed her bottom lip. "That house is Magic. It is Vexkari. There's a chance the enchantments of the guest suite delivered this to you. Or someone saw you duel and thought if you had these powerful objects, you could defeat Kietel."

"Reeve could easily do that," drawled Mal. "Why hasn't he?"

Maeve continued perusing the mystery book. "I don't think Kietel has done anything my father or Reeve deem defeat worthy."

"The papers are saying he's murdering Human-born Magicals who refuse to declare him as the Dread Descendant," said Mal.

"Wouldn't surprise me," she said. "But the papers also lie. Father and Uncle Rosethorn were arguing before we left about it. Abraxas' father wants to support him. A few other Pureblood houses do too. They are tired of our current government."

She looked up at Mal. His mind was distant, far from her words.

"Mal," she said softly.

He slowly looked at her.

"What are you thinking?"

Mal looked out the window. "I'm thinking my priority needs to be finding these objects so I can be who I claim to be. They aren't just symbols. They are power. They are me."

Maeve leaned back in her chair. "You're thinking of leaving school." It wasn't a question.

Mal looked over at her guiltily. "How can I find them here?"

"Like calls to like," recited Maeve. "You weren't trying to find that ring on your finger. It found you. I have a feeling the rest will too." She smiled. "Don't look so grim. I have an idea."

Emilia Brighton looked up at Maeve with wide eyes in Hellming Hall. The daughter of Walter Brighton, the head curator at The Magical Antiquities Museum, dropped her fork as Maeve sat across from her.

"Alright if I sit?" Maeve asked.

Emilia nodded quickly.

"Hello, Emilia," said Abraxas as he slid onto the bench at Maeve's side.

Her mouth dipped open. "Hello-"

"Emilia," came Mal's voice from Maeve's other side as he took a seat.

Emilia's mouth fell completely open. She snapped it shut quickly and then looked at Maeve, but her face was already pink.

"We'd like to invite you to join our weekly training sessions," said Maeve sweetly.

Emilia sat up straight and leaned towards them. She sputtered for a moment and then said. "It would be an honor!"

She beamed at Maeve.

"Wonderful," said Maeve.

"I'd also like to train you privately," said Mal. "I see a lot of potential in you."

Emilia's hands flew to her cheeks. "I don't know what to say."

"Say yes," said Abraxas. "And then thank you."

Emilia did.

It had been Maeve's idea for Mal to train Emilia privately, but as the two of them walked out of the Dining Hall together, her stomach twisted.

Abraxas snorted. "You should see your face."

It didn't take long for Emilia to spill what little she knew about her father's search for the Dread artifacts. But the tiny lead she did divulge was a start.

The Dread Crown had been lost for two hundred years since the Double O was created and took power. The Crown vanished at that time, but Emilia bragged to Mal that her father had solid reason to believe it had been stowed and protected deep inside the Black Forest. She rambled on quite a bit about his life's work there.

Maeve had numerous maps strewn out across a large table in the Library. She reached for an encyclopedia.

"That's in Germany," said Abraxas from the head of the table. He was reclined with his feet propped up.

Maeve and Mal looked over at him.

"I soak up information like a sponge," he said with a wink.

Maeve pulled out a smaller map from under the pile. "That forest is massive. And not exactly where I want to go," she muttered.

Mal looked over her, his eyes lingering on her neck, and leaned over the map.

"So are either of you going to tell me what's going on?" Asked Abraxas.

"No," they replied in synch.

Abraxas huffed and kicked his legs off the table. He crossed behind Mal to make his exit. Mal smiled softly and met eyes with Maeve.

"Abraxas," Mal called after him. "Soon."

Abraxas waved his hand in the air dismissively.

Maeve and Mal stared at the map between them. Somewhere, buried deep in that forest, was a crown forged in holy power. Maeve couldn't get the image of it atop Mal's head out of her mind.

"Off subject, but are you dueling tonight?"

Mal nodded. "You are as well."

Maeve nodded.

Mal eyed her. "Does that displease you?"

"No, not at all, but I just wonder should I wear your ring?"

"Why wouldn't you?"

"Isn't that cheating?" Asked Maeve with a smirk.

"No," said Mal, matter-of-factly.

Maeve smiled at him.

Later that evening, Maeve arrived in an already packed Dueling Hall. She made her way over to Abraxas, who was whispering something to one of Mal's boys, newly appointed Paragon, Finnian Bell. Finnian ran out of the room hurriedly.

"What was that all about?" Maeve asked Abraxas.

"Nothing you need concern yourself with, Head Girl," said Abraxas cooly.

"Of course."

The list of duels was passed around. Abraxas snatched it up to wager his bets, but Maeve didn't feel like placing any.

"Maybe if you and Mal weren't keeping secrets, I wouldn't either," said Abraxas.

Maeve scoffed. "Please. I'm only keeping the secrets I've been asked to keep. Do not act as though you wouldn't do the same."

Abraxas mimicked her silently and avoided her gaze, flipping through the pages on the clipboard.

Emilia wasn't the only one Mal was training. After Professor Larliel suggested Mal give lessons at the first duel, the parchment sheet to sign up was full by the end of the evening.

"Damn," Maeve had said, glancing down at the paper. "Looks like I didn't make the list."

Mal had smirked. "Don't think you're getting out of your regular training so easily."

Maeve leaned against the archway of the Dueling Hall early in the morning, keeping her distance as Mal instructed two students. They shot spells hastily back and forth.

Mal stopped them and corrected one of the boy's wrist movement.

"Again," said Mal.

The boy's jinx was much stronger the second time. He watched them for a moment until one of them faltered.

Mal circled the center of the room and demonstrated the proper deflection needed. His shields were so strong it blew a small strand of Maeve's hair back. She watched him in admiration. Mal stepped back, and the boys resumed their duel.

He coached them as they dueled, forcing them to be better with every spell cast. After barely dodging a spell, one boy became flustered and lost control. Sputtering sparks began flying from his palm.

"That is one of the worst disservices you could do to yourself in a fight," said Mal calmly. "You must never lose control. Your Magic is a part of you. It isn't an external force. It responds to your body, to your mind. Training yourself to stay grounded is crucial."

The boy shook out his wrist and nodded.

"Take Maeve," said Mal, gesturing behind him.

Maeve didn't think Mal knew she was there. But as she played with his ring around her neck, she smiled softly. Part of him was inside that ring. It only made sense that he could feel her presence through it.

"Which one of you can tell me how Maeve counters a spell she doesn't want to block with magic?" Asked Mal.

The taller of the two boys didn't hesitate to answer. "She takes a knee."

"Correct," said Mal. "Which she can get away with because she's shorter, and she takes advantage of a spell aimed slightly too high. You and I, Sam," he looked to the taller boy, "wouldn't be smart to attempt a dodge like that. It's why you lost control. So, what can you do to dodge a spell and allow yourself to fire back quickly?"

Sam contemplated this for a moment, concentrating intensely.

"I can't, can I?"

"Not wisely, no," answered Mal.

"So she has an advantage because she's shorter."

"I wouldn't call it an advantage," said Mal. "It's part of how she duels, but do I use it?"

Sam shook his head.

"Has she ever beaten me?"

Sam, again, shook his head. Mal nodded.

"Find your advantage. Find what keeps you from losing focus. Once more, and then we're done for the day," instructed Mal.

Maeve pushed off the archway and made her way up the stairs. She wandered down the corridors on the first and second floors, admiring her favorite paintings.

On the third floor, she slipped into the Trophy Room. Large glass casings and shelves that towered over her filled the room. She passed Mal's three years' worth of Dueling Club Awards. He'd win this year without question, too.

She traveled back a few rows to where the Vaukore Sporting awards were.

On the far wall was a large portrait of her brother Antony in his Fencing Captain's uniform. He was smiling and holding a trophy. His crystal blue eyes were lighter than hers. But they were just like Arianna's.

A golden plaque was above his portrait, with a serpent etched into the stone. It read:

In loving memory of Antony Ambrose Sinclair
Usque ad Mortem Sinclair

The actual trophy was on a stand. He had been captain of the Harpastum and Fencing Teams. Under the trophy was a glass case with all the fencing swords he won his Championships with during his time at Vaukore, and his Emerald Green and Silver Captain's badge. Each one had the date engraved on it. There was a vase of flowers on a stand next to the case. Maeve reached out and touched the green and white hydrangeas. Hydrangea was the Sinclair family flower.

"Is this the first time you've allowed yourself to look at this?" Came Mal's voice from behind her.

"It is," replied Maeve.

Mal stood beside her, looking up at Antony. Maeve fiddled with his ring around her neck, pulling it closer to her.

"I'm sorry, Maeve," said Mal quietly.

Maeve remained silent, admiring Antony's portrait. He was just as she remembered him.

Chapter 29

Larliesl was, as promised, back on his feet the next day teaching dueling lectures and preparing to host a back to school gathering for combat students. Mal asked Maeve to accompany him. She delighted in accepting his offer.

Larliesl decorated the Dueling Hall with black and silver lanterns and midnight blue sheer curtains swooping across the wide space.

Maeve was seated at a table with Abraxas, Mal, and the rest. Dinner had been served, and the boys were arguing about a section of the Astrology assignment from that morning.

"Well, what did Maeve put?" Asked Avery.

"I already took that class last year," said Maeve.

Avery frowned.

Hummingdoor appeared next to their table.

"I trust you've all had a marvelous night?" Asked the Alchemy Master drunkenly.

Larliesl appeared at Hummingdoor's side and took his glass from him.

"Always the best, sir," said Mal.

"We've missed our meetings with you, sir," said Abraxas to the Master of Duels.

"Oh yes, I have as well," said Larliesl. "Summer is lonesome here."

"Well, you appear to be much better," said Mal, smiling.

"Oh, you know Healer Kensington," said Larliesl. "She wasted no time fixing me up! Though I was hoping I would need a trip to the Circle Healers. Paid vacation sounds glorious," he said with a wink.

The table chuckled.

"Trust I'll see you boys in my office next week then? As usual?"

"Of course, sir," said Abraxas.

Hummingdoor beamed and fell into Larliesl, sloshing some of his drink to the floor.

"Oh, and Maeve," started Larliesl as an excited breath rose in Maeve's chest. "You look wonderful."

Hummingdoor clapped his hands together and bounced away with Larliesl on his heels. Maeve sunk back into her chair and let a small sigh escape her lips.

"I am still not included," said Maeve, under her breath.

Mal didn't miss it. "What?"

"I said I'm still not included," she repeated loudly.

Mal's eyes grew. "Are you joking?"

"No," said Maeve. "You heard him. It's still your little boy's club."

"Do you need to be included in that?" Mal asked her.

"You tell me," she retorted sharply.

His eyes narrowed, and his head cocked to one side. "What's the matter with you?"

"It's obvious," said Roswyn. "She's all turned around about things now."

"What's that mean?" Shot Maeve.

Abraxas downed the rest of his drink quickly.

"We were all there at your house this summer," said Roswyn nastily.

Maeve laughed.

"It's not a joke," he said. He looked to Mal. "Just some silly girl's emotions getting the best of her."

Maeve scowled. Abraxas started to interject, but Mal cut him off.

"This doesn't concern you," he said to Roswyn.

"Oh, it concerns me a great deal," he replied.

"Enough," said Mal. "Get up."

Everyone, including Maeve, obeyed.

Mal grabbed her by the wrist and yanked her back down to her seat. His face was searching hers. He was silent until the table cleared.

"That's what this is about?" Mal asked her.

Maeve scoffed and snatched her wrist away from him. His face turned stern as she pushed her chair away from the table and made her way angrily towards the door.

Certain that he was on her heels, she didn't look back. Once they were in the corridor, he called after her.

"You're angry with me?" Mal called after her. "Why?"

She didn't stop as her blood boiled.

"Speak your mind, Sinclair!"

"Because," Maeve turned on her heel and faced him boldly. "You misunderstand me still! I have proven myself to you again and again, over and over, and my frustration with the fact that I do not stand at your side and they do is perceived as 'silly, girlish emotions.' I have given you everything. Every ounce of energy and pushed myself to the edge for you willingly. I have held your secrets and you mine. I can perform Magic in circles around those boys, and you know it. I have won every duel and have proven a loyalty to you they can only dream of."

She let herself breathe for a moment to take in his face. It was set in arrogant stone, as it always was, but something was different. Maeve had surprised him with her outburst.

She waited for his look of disgust or his lip to curl upwards and his eyes to devour her. With her last ounce of courage, she finished her speech.

"I worship you."

A noticeable breath rose in Mal's chest, and the exhale escaped his lips quicker than he probably would have liked. As Maeve's adrenaline faded, she quickly became aware of the cold evening air chilling her skin.

Mal lowered his proud chin, and she caught a glimpse of what looked like a smile tugging at his lips. His eyes lifted to hers. "Say that again."

Maeve's lips pulled into a thin line. Mal's eyes darkened. His smirk vanished.

"I said, 'Say that again,' Sinclair."

Maeve swallowed.

She obeyed.

"I worship you."

A soft chuckle escaped his lips, one of satisfaction. He removed his jacket that was slung over his shoulder and walked towards her. He brushed against her lightly, rounding behind her and placing his coat on her.

"Pay attention, Maeve, for I'll only say this once." His voice hummed in the silent corridor. His hands slipped into his pockets. "I do not control the actions of others. If you want a place at Larliesl's table then take it. Demand it. But if you think you do not stand at my side, then you are not at all the clever witch I thought you were."

Maeve opened her mouth to fire a retort.

"Goodnight, Miss Sinclair," whispered Mal, his cheek mere inches from hers. He turned promptly and made his way towards his dormitory.

Maeve looked over her shoulder at him as he strolled away.

Chapter 30

At breakfast, Maeve scribbled ideas in her journal. Thoughts about memories, the mind. Anything to ease her own mind. She hadn't been able to jump in months. And nothing was helping. That strange sensation still lingered across her spine from time to time. And if she focused, she could feel Kietel's hand around her neck. Choking her. Killing her.

She was desperate to jump again.

Abraxas took a seat across from her without speaking. They sat silently until Abraxas could stand it no longer, and he inhaled to speak.

"No," said Maeve. "We're not talking about it."

Abraxas let out a loud sigh. "I wasn't even going to."

Maeve eyed him and returned to her writing. Abraxas crossed his legs one way and then the other way. He fiddled with his fingers and played with a groove in the mahogany table, sighing a few times.

"Sweet Seven Realms, what is it?" Asked Maeve. "You're in knots."

"What did you and Mal talk about after the party?" Asked Abraxas hurriedly.

"I knew it! I knew that's all you wanted to talk about. You're so nosey."

Abraxas rolled his eyes and waited.

Maeve scowled at him and shook her head.

"Fine then," said Abraxas. "Suppose I won't tell you what he told Roswyn back in the common room then."

Maeve's head whipped up from her paper. "What?"

"You heard me," said Abraxas haughtily. "You first."

"You're evil," said Maeve.

"Yes."

"Shut up or leave," said Maeve.

Abraxas sulked out of the Hall.

Maeve hated that she wanted to know what Mal had said to Roswyn so badly. That smug prick.

She stood, forgetting her breakfast, and hurried out of the hall. She rounded the corner and Abraxas was already there, leaning casually against the wall waiting for her.

"I told him I was tired of being excluded when I'm better than all of you at everything," said Maeve quickly.

"He told Roswyn if he stuck his nose in yours and his personal business like that ever again, he'd break it." Abraxas exhaled loudly.

"Did he really?"

"Roswyn hates you. What's that all about, you think?"

"I don't care," said Maeve cooly. "He's an idiot with a temper."

"He was the second strongest until you came around. It seems he feels you're a bit of a usurper." Spinel appeared at their feet, chirping loudly. Abraxas picked him up. "For what it's worth," said Abraxas, "I wish you were there, with Larliesl and the rest, I mean."

Maeve sighed. "Thank you. I know it's silly, but it's so frustrating. All I wanted when I was younger was to be in the fighting ring. But I understood why I wasn't. And now, things have changed so much, I thought I would be offered a seat at the table."

"You want to be in the limelight with him."

"Yes," admitted Maeve, playing with his ring around her neck.

"Did we go to the same Summer Solstice Party or not?"

"What?"

Abraxas shook his head with a laugh. "And you're supposed to be the cleverest of us all."

Maeve snatched Spinel away from him and walked away.

"Everyone needs to stop saying that," she muttered to Spinel.

After her daily classes, Maeve laid back on her dorm room bed reading a particularly good chapter of a book Lavinia left for her as a surprise. It was waiting on Maeve's nightstand, what used to be Lavinia's nightstand as Head Girl, when she arrived at school. The note read:

I knew you'd come around.
-Lavinia

Spinel was batting at her bag, meowing. Maeve gently removed him and opened her bag. A soft green glow was emitting from the bottom.

Maeve grabbed the piece of parchment and looked at Mal's handwriting as it scrolled across the page.

After dinner, after duties, meet me on the first floor.

When Maeve arrived, Mal was already waiting for her on the landing.

"Hello," said Maeve curtly.

"We must not be seen," said Mal quietly.

"I think we've mastered that," mimicked Maeve.

He began walking, and Maeve followed.

They crossed the grand entryway and began the ascent into the dungeons of the castle. Mal looked over his shoulder as the corridor turned darker. The charm on Maeve's wrist illuminated, lighting their way.

Ahead in the distance, light spilled into the corridor from the south stairs of the castle. To their right was the descent to the old dungeons, which were only used for storage now.

"What are we doing-" started Maeve in a hushed voice, just as Mal leaned his shoulder into the solid stone wall.

It gave beneath his weight, opening in a perfect rectangle and revealing a narrow set of stairs carved into the stone. Mal gestured towards the staircase that lowered deep under the castle. Maeve stepped towards the stairs and held out her arm. The charm shot light down into the uneven and steep stairs.

She looked back at Mal apprehensively. The hidden stone door was already closing behind him. There was only enough room for the two of them to stand on the top step. Mal snapped his fingers. A beam of hazy light dropped below them.

Mal offered her his hand. She looked down at it and back up at him. She placed her hand in his. His skin was smooth and cool. His fingers wrapped around her own.

He led her down the slick and narrow stairs. She braced her free hand on the stone walls as they made their descent.

"We're going into the mountain?" Maeve asked.

"Yes," he replied.

The air grew colder every few steps. Maeve's grip on Mal's hand tightened each time the uneven stairs caught her off guard. Maeve slipped behind Mal, her low heel slipping off her foot. He whipped towards her, grabbing her by the ribs and bracing her against the wall of the stairwell. Maeve winced as her back slammed into the stone.

She looked up at him with quick breaths.

"Wonderful," she sighed. "More for you to hold over me."

Mal's dark chuckle filled the tight space. Maeve relaxed into his grip.

Mal didn't release her. He moved his face towards her shoulder, brushing her hair back from her neck with his nose. Maeve reclined her head as her arms drifted to grip his forearms. He inhaled her scent slowly. His chest rose, pressing into her own.

He pulled back, gently setting her down on the steps. She held her shoeless leg foot the cold stone ground beneath them. She balanced herself on the wall. Mal stepped away and reached for her shoe, kneeling in front of her on the step below. He turned back towards her with the shoe in hand.

Maeve held out her hand.

Mal looked up at her. His beam of light fluttering between them. The sight of him on his knees was electrifying. Maybe it was just the dangerous way he looked up at her, like she was cornered prey and he was prepared to strike, that enticed her. Maybe it was something more.

Mal grabbed the back of her knee, pulling her leg forward as he slipped the shoe back on her foot. She placed her foot on the floor, but his hands remained. They slipped up her leg past her knee and rested on the back of her thigh. She was certain he felt her shake at his touch.

His eyes moved back up to hers. They were filled with satisfaction.

"Careful on the stairs, Sinclair." He stood and took her hand once more. "We're nearly there."

Maeve's charm on her bracelet began to fade as light lifted up into the winding and narrowing stone steps from below. The light grew consistent and bright as the steps opened into a cavern.

Maeve let out a disbelieving sound as Mal dropped her hand. Green and blue and white light swirled between the sides of the cavern. A portal. This was a doorway between worlds.

But it was old. Permanent portals between realms were mostly all destroyed or weakened by now.

Maeve stepped towards the portal. The shifting colors bounced light across the cavern, like rippling water.

She looked back at him. Above the way they came, there was a carving into the stone.

Filii Magicae Numquam Soli. Children of Magic are Never Alone.

"Does this portal go where I think it goes?" Asked Maeve, her eyes on the Vaukore motto.

Mal took her hand in his once more, pulling her forward.

She was right.

Her heart swelled in her chest. The Dread Lands. Where no Magical had set foot in three hundred years. Adrenaline kicked as he pulled her towards the portal. She gripped his hand tightly and stepped closer to him.

"Have you been through it before?" She asked nervously.

He nodded. "Come."

"Are you sure we should? It's safe?"

He looked over his shoulder at her. "Trust me, please."

The words were so soft, so genuine, that they were almost desperate. She tossed all fear to the wind in order to ensure his desire was obtained. He pressed forward into those swirls of colored light. The portal enveloped them, squeezing them tightly. Sound and light disappeared.

And then the ground beneath her was smooth moonstone.

She looked up.

Mist and shadow covered the land beyond, but before her were two giant serpent statues, each winding their way around the other in a towering archway. Their fangs were bared and their eyes filled with ruby stones.

Maeve gasped at their beauty.

Magic cracked through her lungs, down her chest. Her eyes went wide. She summoned a breathing spell, placing the palm of her hand over her mouth. But no Magic flowed.

Another painful inhale, knives across her throat, and Mal's hands grabbed her shoulders, pulling her back. The serpent pillars vanished as she moved back through the portal.

The caverns below the castle were warm in comparison. Mal dropped his hands, and she stepped away.

"I couldn't breathe. And my Magic-"

"The land is plagued with a darkness that only I can conquer."

Maeve looked up at him, dumbfounded. "I can't use magic in the land where I am promised a future?"

"For now," said Mal. "But I will make it so that you are all that you are on Earth and more in the Dread Lands."

"You can use your Magic there? And you can breathe?"

Mal nodded.

"How many times have you been there?"

Mal hesitated. "Many times. Each time I come back stronger."

She looked over at the portal.

Mal's hand tucked under her chin, drawing her focus back towards him.

"There's a reason the Dread Lands were never occupied by other forces. Magic alone can set foot in those lands."

"But we can't breathe there-"

"We once could," interjected Mal. "And we will again. I will make it so."

Maeve stared up at him. "I have no doubt."

Mal brushed the back of his hand across her cheek. "It is I who doubted you."

Maeve leaned into his touch like a cat as her eyes fluttered closed.

"I'm sorry I misjudged you at the party."

She opened her eyes. "It was a misunderstanding. I was thinking foolishly. And I lost my temper."

Mal continued the smooth motion back and forth across her cheekbone. "I don't want you to ever be sorry for that. Your rage is valuable. It's the only time you are truly honest."

He smiled softly. It was a smile that doused his eyes in swirls of glowing night. Darkness illuminated behind tiny flecks of galaxies.

She batted his hand away and stepped closer. "It is not."

Mal bent over until they were face to face, sharing one breath. His head cocked to one side.

"Don't you ever dare to push my hand away again," he said quietly.

"What will you do?" She asked with feigned innocence.

Mal shook his head. "You are so very wicked."

In the next breath, he pounced on her. His hands were wrapped around her waist and his lips slammed into hers.

She inhaled all of him happily.

In the breath after that she was against the stone wall, her hair balled in his fist, forcing her mouth open for him.

She gripped his arms, letting out a small moan as he pulled tightly on her hair. He pressed his body against hers. The cold stone behind her seeped through her clothes, sending chills down her body.

His foot pressed between hers, pushing one aside and spreading her legs. He pushed into her harder. His teeth scraped across her bottom lip. She rose on the tips of her toes in response, a silent plea for him to do it again.

And he did. His hands moved down her arms, finding her wrists. Fire erupted between her legs as he pinned them against the stone. Her leg bent, begging him to be closer.

She inhaled sharply, breathing in his scent. It was dark and dangerous and invigorating-

He pushed against her harder.

And then she realized.

He was hard.

He was rock hard against her.

He released just one of her hands, slithering across her ribs, then her waist. His fingers halted at the band of her skirt.

His hands did not shake. His breaths were long and deep. Maeve was the opposite. Every part of her was trembling, shaking beneath his touch.

His fingers meticulously gathered the fabric of her skirt while his lips never left hers.

Her heart slammed into her chest over and over. It drowned out the fear in her head saying to stop. Saying that his palm shouldn't graze her thigh like that. Saying she shouldn't feel his smooth fingers on her hips with nothing between them. That she shouldn't feel his fingers pull her panties to the side and-

"I want to feel you," he murmured into her lips.

And in the next move, he would have.

But the world exploded instead.

Their hands shot to their heads as an excruciating and violently piercing sound filled their heads. Maeve dropped to her knees, dizzy and disoriented. Mal tried to cast out a shield. But it vanished into nothing. Maeve screamed as she pressed her hands against her face. Her insides were on fire. Every ounce of blood in her body was pulsing.

He grabbed her shoulders. His face contorted in pain. He pulled her off the stone floor and ran, dragging her along as she stumbled behind him. Maeve looked around them as they ran. The caverns were whole. Not a single rock or crumble of stone shook.

Her vision blurred in and out of focus as they ascended the winding rock stairs out of the mountains. Waves of paralyzing nausea crashed over her. She pulled on his arm, desperate to just breathe for a moment.

"We must keep going, Maeve."

She didn't want to. Her back slid against the stone wall. Mal's hands slammed to either side of her face.

"Look at me," he said sternly.

His hand twitched, and his teeth were grinding. He was in pain, too.

"We don't know what that was," said Mal. "We can't stop."

She nodded, and he took her hand tightly in his own.

Once they reached the dungeons, they bolted to the foyer. The castle was in pure chaos. All the fire lights were dark. Screams and cries filled the nighttime air. Mal's grip on her hand was still tight.

Fear crept into her bones and settled there. It was everywhere.

Chapter 31

By the time they reached Mal's dorm Maeve's body was no longer on fire. A dull pain lingered at her temples, but she was otherwise fine. She and Mal had not been the only ones to experience the unexplained pain.

Abraxas and Maeve embraced firmly.

"You're alright, Brax?" Maeve asked.

He nodded. "You?"

"I'm fine now. What the hell was that?"

"That was the worst pain I've ever felt," said Roswyn. "And I've been in some nasty fights. "

Maeve sat on the arm of one of the black leather couches and heaved a sigh. The emerald green common room was lit only by the moonlight pouring past the water of the lake against the vaulted windows that surrounded the circular room. In the dim green darkness, Maeve looked to Mal.

Roswyn and Abraxas continued talking. He watched them silently.

Her arms felt heavy.

Other students gathered there as well, most of them asking Mal what was happening.

Headmaster Elgin's voice rang out over the common room and presumably the entire castle.

"All students must report to Hellming Hall at once."

Hummingdoor waltzed through the doors of the common room a moment later.

"Mal, my boy good," he said hurriedly. "I'll need your assistance ensuring all students are accounted for. Miss Sinclair," he looked to Maeve. "Larliesl will need yours. To the Grand Hall, dear."

She had never seen Hummingdoor without his bubbly smile and bright eyes.

Maeve looked to Mal, not wanting to leave him. Mal gave her a nod of assurance. Maeve pushed off the arm of the chair and made her way up the stairs to the first floor. Her lux charm flittered light before her, but it was dull.

"Maeve," called Larliesl.

The Professor appeared in front of her from a dark side corridor.

"What's happening, sir?"

Larliesl shook his head and looked behind her. "Where's Mal?"

"He's with Hummingdoor," she said.

He sighed. "You shouldn't be separated," he muttered gravely.

"Sir?" Maeve asked.

Larliesl wouldn't look at her.

"Sir," said Maeve sharply, her voice breaking.

Larliesl's eyes snapped to her and then softened slightly. "Apologies, Maeve," he said. "I know you're scared."

She clenched her jaw.

Larliesl took her arm in his and led her towards Hellming Hall, a waft of fire he created guiding them.

Hellming Hall was filled with huddled students. The castle's lights were completely depleted it seemed. The only light was what they created themselves, and the moonlight that shot through the stained glass windows. Some students carried a lit taper candle, others had a continuous flame bouncing off their hands. The younger students held their lux charms, the tips emitting a soft white glow.

Headmasters Elgin and Rowan stood at the far end of the hall, under the Vaukore crest.

Maeve spotted Mal and Roswyn. Abraxas was holding Julius, his silver cat. Spinel was at his feet. He trotted over to Maeve. She bent over and scooped him up, and held him close. He brushed his face against hers with a soft purr. She rubbed the back of his head in appreciation.

Larliesl nodded towards Mal. "Stay together," he told her and disappeared into the swarm of figures.

Maeve watched him go. He hadn't asked for her assistance at all. He had only been concerned that she wasn't with Mal.

Maeve pressed towards them and arrived at their side.

"Did Larliesl say anything?" Asked Mal.

Maeve shook her head.

"Nor did Hummingdoor."

Frightened whispers filled the hall until Elgin's voice rang out.

"Our Magic has been damaged," she said in that calm and comforting voice. "Rest assured the Orator's Office is working diligently to correct the issue. Remain calm, and know we are here to ensure your safety. I am personally here for each one of you." She hesitated a moment. "The Portals to Earth have collapsed. We cannot allow you to travel home at this time. Nor can anyone travel through the Portal here."

"That's ridiculous," said Roswyn under his breath.

That buzz of fear through the crowd grew in volume. They were stuck here.

Rowan stood silently next to Elgin. He was truly void of any expression or emotion next to Elgin's concerned face.

Elgin continued. "The Healing Hall is filled with students, some of them completely unconscious. If you have taken at least two Healing Classes please join Healer Kensington in the Healing Hall," said Elgin. "For now that is all."

"That's all?" Repeated Abraxas incredulously. "Is no one going to tell us what's happening?"

Students around them expressed the same concern.

"Did Kietel do this?" Screamed out a voice from the shadowed crowd.

Headmaster Elgin cupped her hands together. "Please understand, we do not know what has caused this. I know you are scared. But Vaukore is the safest place for you right now."

Roswyn and Abraxas began speaking up as well. Maeve didn't say a word to any of them as she turned away, their bickering fading into the background. A cool, slender hand wrapped around her own, drawing her attention over her shoulder.

"I'm sure he's fine," said Mal calmly. "But let me know when he replies."

Maeve nodded, and he let go, turning back towards the rest as Maeve practically ran to The Wings. She wasn't the first one to run to the Wings. She shoved past a younger student who was already there.

"It's not-" the student protested.

"Shut up."

She grabbed one of the complimentary pieces of paper and quill and hastily wrote her father.

Are you alright? What is happening?

She sealed the envelope with the provided wax, not bothering to take the time to use her own family crest wax seal. She pushed off the desk and headed for the enchanted desk at the head of the room. She placed her letter, addressed to the desk of Ambrose Sinclair, on the desk and sighed. Nothing happened. She grabbed the letter hastily and put it back down. It still remained. She raised it and slammed it down with a slap once more. The letter remained.

"The portals are damaged," said a voice from behind her.

She turned, and Headmaster Rowan stood in a maroon, and gold velvet embroidered suit. He clasped his fingers tightly together, his face taunt as he spoke to Maeve.

"Which means the magic that desk uses is too."

"Then I'll use a raven," she said sternly.

"You won't successfully make a Portal for it to slip through."

Maeve ignored him. He continued.

"But there is no need. Your Father managed to get you a letter through my own personal portal."

"What?" She snapped.

A smile almost pulled at his lips. "Come, Miss Sinclair."

"I don't trust you," she said.

"A wise choice," said Rowan. "Given that I've betrayed you before. But I have never betrayed your father. And I don't intend to start now."

He was still a spy for her father after all.

"You're still his spy?"

"Always was."

Maeve scowled at the deception. "He knew you were going to make me jump?"

Rowan turned from her without a reply. She picked her letter up off the desk and followed him silently down the stairs of The Wings. They didn't walk towards the Headmasters Quarters.

Rowan slipped down a back corridor and opened the door to an old and unused classroom. She followed him inside, against her better judgment, and on her father's. Her lux charm barely lit the room. It was covered in cobwebs and dusk and filled with old versions of textbooks.

The door snapped shut and Rowan cast a silencing charm around them, ensuring their discussion was private. He pulled a small letter from his pocket and handed it to her.

"When did he send this?" Asked Maeve, clutching the brief letter from her father.

"Before everything went to shit," replied Rowan.

Maeve looked down at the quickly scribbled words from her father. It read:

Something of otherworldly proportions is going to happen at any second. Hang tight. Stick to Malachite. I'll be fine. You'll be fine.

Maeve felt like his last sentence had more been written to reassure himself than anything else.

"What is going on?" Asked Maeve.

"I don't think I'm at liberty to say," said Rowan.

"That's ridiculous and you know it," retorted Maeve.

Rowan gave her a reproachful look. "The Orator-"

"Fuck the Double O," said Maeve, a quiver in her voice. "And fuck whatever organization has surely double-crossed us at this point."

Rowan's eyes darted around the room nervously. "Be careful."

"And fuck you too if you're on their side," she seethed.

Rowan almost looked pleased at her tenacity. "Do you trust your father, Maeve?"

"More than anyone," she said.

"Then trust me. As he does."

Maeve shook her head. "This isn't fair."

"The Orator will be here within the hour to speak-"

"So he can come and go, but we are stuck here?"

"The Orator has special and authorized means of travel to and from this realm. We cannot simply move hundreds of you-

"Why can't you just-"

"You ask too much at times," snapped Rowan. "You are too bold."

Maeve ran her hands across her face and looked back down at his letter. He hadn't even bothered to sign it. Not as the Premier, not as her father. As if there wasn't time.

"He pretended to be mad at you that night when I jumped?" She asked quietly.

"There was no acting on your father's part. None of us intended for you to jump to Kietel."

Maeve looked up at him. "Then who?"

Rowan sighed and shook his head. She would get no answers that mattered from him.

"Where are the Magical Militia?" She asked quietly.

"They are securing the grounds," he answered. "You should go find your little boyfriend and do your duty as Head Girl."

Maeve glared. "He's not my-"

Rowan yanked the door open and disappeared into the darkness without another word.

Maeve walked silently back to Hellming Hall, relying on other's lights to guide her way.

The hall was now filled with long benches, and a small stage was positioned at the head of the room. She stopped in the entryway the moment she laid eyes on Orator Moon. Her eyes darted around him for her father, but he was not there. The Orator had come alone.

"Are you alright?" Mal asked.

His steady and even voice was a greatly welcome and soothing sound. Maeve turned and faced Mal. They stood barely more than a breath away from one another, hands rigid at their sides. Firelight flickered off his face as students passed.

Maeve nodded.

His eyes scanned her face and the way his eyes narrowed told Maeve he wasn't buying it.

They took their seats. The hall was quiet under Orator Moon's presence. He smiled at all of them. It made her feel queasy.

"Hello," said Moon. "I am sorry to have to visit our world's best and brightest under grim circumstances. However, I am here to tell you that, as Headmaster Elgin already expressed, Vaukore is the safest place you can be right now," said Moon, "until the situation has been further assessed."

Maeve crossed her legs and ran her hands over her face. Mal's frequent glances over at her indicated he had never seen her so ruffled.

"Do you think he's seen my father?" Whispered Maeve to no one in particular.

Mal remained silent, but Abraxas to her right answered quietly.

"Probably," he whispered. "But you can bet he's going to bolt out of here before you make it up there."

"Shhh!" Hissed the girl in front of them as she turned around to Abraxas.

Her face turned hot pink when she realized who she was shushing and turned a deeper red as she met Maeve's glare. Maeve held up a finger and made a circular motion. The girl slouched over and turned back to the front without another word.

Maeve's leg started shaking, bouncing nervously on the ball of her foot. Mal's hand inched closer to her leg, and she pressed her foot into the floor. His hand slowly retreated.

Abraxas had been correct, for when Moon finished his speech, of which Maeve heard none, he was immediately whisked away before Maeve could even stand.

"Damn it," said Maeve. "I want to get out of this bloody realm."

She produced a bright blue flame silently that hovered ahead of them as they walked. Maeve hadn't argued when he'd insisted on walking her to the East Wing. The walk was silent, but Mal and Maeve never had an issue with being quiet together. When they reached the large ivory double doors to her Common Room and Dorms, they simply clicked open. Maeve placed her hand along the wooden frame. The Magic was there, but weak. Like a dwindling flame.

The castle's Magic was being depleted.

"Do you feel that?" She whispered.

Mal moved slowly and placed his cool hand over hers, their breathing in sync. He lingered there only for a moment before removing his hand.

"Like you wouldn't believe," he replied quietly.

Maeve turned towards him, her voice shaking. "I can't-"

He hushed her. "Come with me," he said, wrapping her hand in his. He walked her back across the castle. The common area was occupied by students sitting in groups. Their voices were hushed and dull.

Mal led her across the hexagon room and to the stairs that led to his dorm. Silently, they climbed the narrow, creaking, wooden stairs and crossed down the corridor to his room. His private room as Head Boy.

Maeve walked inside without hesitation. Mal closed the door behind him. She turned towards him and buried her head in his chest. His arms snaked around her, one hand gently tracing up and down her back.

His scent was intoxicating, taunting her with every breath she took.

"Whatever happens, promise me you'll listen to me," he said softly. "If I tell you to run, you run. If I tell you to-"

Maeve couldn't wait any longer. She pushed up on her toes and gripped his shirt, slamming her lips into his.

He kissed her back gently. His hands found her face, and he pulled away from her.

"Maeve," he started softly.

"I don't want to think about anything else," she gasped. "I just want you to kiss me."

She pressed her lips desperately into his once more. Her hands traveled down his shirt and her fingers slipped through his belt loops, grinding him against her.

She wanted what she had been denied by all this. Before something came for their Magic. Her hands traveled lower.

Mal snatched her hands swiftly in his own, holding her wrist apart, breaking their kiss, and putting space between them. "Stop it," he said sternly. "Or you're going to get yourself more than kissed."

"So?"

Mal tightened his grip, keeping her body from his as she pushed forward. Maeve's brows pulled together.

"Is this how you really want it our first time? Is this how you think I want it? A distraction from your fear? So that you don't have to think about if your father is even alive or if the fabric of our society has completely crumbled?"

Her vision went blurry.

And his grip loosened as she fell into his chest.

Tears fell silently down her cheeks, dripping into his shirt. Her pride swallowed the sobs in her throat, desperate for release.

Mal's arms wrapped around her back, but Maeve shoved off him. She hastily turned her back on him. Wiping the wet from her face.

Mal crossed in front of her.

He tilted her chin up with his knuckle.

"Don't you dare run from me," he said quietly.

Cooly.

Like always.

Emotions in check.

Maeve's were always the opposite.

He looked down at her, studying her, his lips pursed slightly.

"I am unaccustomed to feeling fear from you," he whispered, his thumb traced over her bottom lip.

"I'm fine. Just shaken."

His hand traveled to the back of her head. "Don't lie to me."

"Why? You always know anyway," she said with a small cry.

"I don't want you to lie to me," he said, "only for me."

Maeve laughed for the first time all day.

Mal offered her a small smile in return, one that didn't meet his eyes. "It's late," he said. "You need sleep."

Maeve didn't argue. Mal pulled her close and laid them on his bed. They were a tangled mass of arms and legs. Mal's hands traced up and down her back, making soothing circles at the base of her scalp.

She tucked herself as close to him as possible, and let the cool Magic radiating from him lull her to sleep.

Chapter 32

"You look terrib-" started Abraxas. He winced, and his eyes went wide. "I mean, you look like you slept terribly."

Maeve sat across from him at one of the long dining tables the next morning.

"Yes," drawled Maeve. "Your second attempt was much better."

Abraxas placed eggs and toast on her plate. She made no move to eat them. "Couldn't sleep?" His eyes flicked up mischievously.

"I slept fine." She said dully.

"That all?"

Maeve glared at him. Abraxas rolled his eyes and picked back up his fork. He speared a piece of sausage and muttered. "Clearly that is all based all your foul mood."

Maeve fiddled with her hands in her lap. When she woke, Mal was gone. On his nightstand was a brief note explaining that he wanted to walk the grounds and assess the castle's protective shields himself.

Abraxas continued. "On the bright side, classes are canceled."

"How is that the bright side?" Asked Maeve flatly with a shrug. "That would have been a welcome distraction."

Distraction.

Gods be dammed.

She had thrown herself at Mal, and he rejected her.

"Ugh," groaned Abraxas.

Maeve took a sip of juice. "Now what am I supposed to do all day?"

Mal slid onto the bench next to Abraxas. "You'll be training all day."

He looked well-rested, but the worry in his eyes remained. For the world, for her, for himself too.

Abraxas rambled on, complaining. Mal propped one elbow on the table and looked at Maeve.

"I'm sorry," she mouthed to Mal.

A waft of his Magic slithered across the table and brushed up under her chin.

Mal drilled her relentlessly all morning, harnessing all of her trepidation into her Magic. All her energy was depleted by the end of their session.

Mal's finger was under her chin, having just bested her.

"So close, Maeve," called Abraxas tauntingly.

"I need some air," she panted.

He lowered his hand and nodded. "Roswyn," he called. "You're up."

Maeve left the dueling hall with heavy legs. She shook out her hands and stretched her arms as she walked across the foyer of the castle.

Refreshing sunlight and crisp mountain air greeted her outside the castle. The trees in the courtyard were starting to show their golden colors.

Maeve squinted, certain her eyes were deceiving her.

Reeve stood between two spiraling maple trees.

The High Lord was there. At Vaukore.

Chapter 33

Maeve bolted for Reeve, but with the slightest flick of his eyes, she froze. With just a look she understood.

Don't look so eager, his eyes said.

Students walked around him without a glance. They couldn't see him. She slowed her pace, and he walked deeper into the busy courtyard, disappearing around the corner.

She followed him.

He stood, arms casually at his side, staring up at a stone statue of King Primus. This was not the friend of her father, not the man who she had seen wine and dine at her house over the summer. This was a High Lord, with a wartime stance. He wore black Senshi Warriors Armor, tight leather and steel with amethyst stamped embellishments.

The finest uniform a warrior could wear. The tattoo-like scars of Magic across one side of his neck and face were still visible, peeking out of the solid silver armor. Across his back, a long broad sword was strapped. A straight sword hung from his hip. His brown hair was pulled halfway up. It rippled slightly off his shoulders in a breeze that drifted by.

"Qu'est-ce qui se passe vraiment?" She asked.

What is really going on?

Reeve glanced down at her with a single eyebrow raised.

"Les américains ont décimé le Japon." he answered in perfect French.

Maeve suspected he spoke many languages.

The Americans decimated Japan, he had said.

"Les immortels? Ou les Magiciens?"

The Immortals? Or the Magicals? She asked.

Reeve's face tightened slightly. "The humans."

"What?" Asked Maeve as her mouth fell open. "How many bombs did they drop?"

Reeve rolled his neck and spoke so quietly Maeve had to strain to hear him.

"Just one. So far. Thousands are dead. Not just humans."

The heat drained from Maeve's body. One single bomb had disrupted their Magic and killed thousands of people in an instant. That force was as great as their own magic, as powerful as the Supremes that made up their defenses, perhaps even Reeve himself, being "kissed by the Gods" as they said.

"Stop that," said Reeve softly. "I see your thoughts brewing."

"Don't lie to me," seethed Maeve.

"The situation is under control now," he replied.

So political.

"What if there are more?"

"I'm sure there are more, but right now they've ceased fire."

"Right now?"

Reeve didn't answer her. She pressed him further.

"Ou est mon pere," said Maeve, quietly.

Where is my father?

"Evaluer la situation," he answered.

Evaluating the situation.

Maeve's heart was kicking in her chest. "How did you get here? No one can portal-"

"There are other ways to travel, Miss Sinclair."

Maeve frowned.

"I flew."

Her lips parted, and her brows pulled together. "You flew?"

Reeve flashed his teeth. "You've never seen my full Aterna form. How could I forget?"

Maeve had wondered if the rumors about Reeve's less-than-human shapeshifting were true. She brushed it off, understanding now.

"He sent you."

Reeve nodded once. "It's too dangerous for him to portal. They're all being tracked. The Portals and the Fires are being compromised on purpose."

"By who?"

"Wouldn't that be nice to know."

Maeve's head kicked back. She ran her hands across her face. "Can you take me home to him?"

"No."

"Why not?" She snapped.

"Because," he sighed, "your little Magical body can't handle the duress of the Magic it would take."

Maeve frowned. "You didn't fly here."

"No," said Reeve. "I promise your father is working ceaselessly to get you home."

"All this time, our eyes were on Germany. But they aren't even responsible for this."

"There is no one man or alliance or country responsible for this," said Reeve. "I have been alive a long time. It takes the coming together of many great minds to do something so disastrously evil."

"How did the Orator get here last night if he didn't use a portal?"

Reeve's face dropped. He didn't know. The Orator had traveled here without her father's knowledge.

Maeve began shaking her head. "This is all fucked, isn't it?"

Reeve was silent a moment.

She was right.

"You look like you haven't slept at all," he said.

"You pick that up from your godly wisdom?"

Reeve's warrior front fell only for a moment when he looked at her like he might smile at her. Truly smile.

But the High Lord returned a blink later.

"Sleep. Eat," he said. "You need your strength. Now, you've lingered by my side for too long. Walk back inside, Maeve," said Reeve. "Trust no one here except your little Dread Descendant friend Malachite and your own blood. Walk back inside now."

Maeve's heart kicked. "What did you just say?"

Reeve glowered at her.

He knew.

How could he possibly know?

She stepped towards him, ready to argue.

He let out a soft growl and his teeth smashed together as he turned fully towards her.

"Inside the Castle. Now."

The command was so stern, so passionate that her mouth snapped shut. His eyes burned with intense fire, demanding and fierce. A bit of that Immortal power whipped from him, tossing her hair behind her shoulders and buckling her knees slightly.

"I don't obey you, remember?" She said challengingly. "I am not of the Immortal people. I am not a subject of Aterna."

"Inside."

"How do you know about Mal?" She said lowly.

"Sinclair," he started, his voice laced with threat.

"No," she shuttered. "How dare you come to me and say such a thing and then demand I walk away."

"Do not feign as though you aren't aware."

"Of course I am aware," she hissed. "I just don't know how you are."

"If I tell you, will you go inside?"

"Maybe."

Two Magical Militia were making their way into the courtyard through the topiaries.

Reeve watched them with narrowed eyes as she spoke. "It screams from him. His Magic. Dread Magic is engraved in my memory."

Maeve opened her mouth to speak, but Reeve spoke first.

"Leave me."

Those Magical Militia were heading towards them.

She huffed and turned on her heel.

"Fucking brat," he murmured.

Maeve swiveled on her heel. "Excuse me?"

Reeve stepped towards her. The mountains beneath them trembled. The sky darkened, and the temperature turned hot. Flaming hot.

But her blood ran cold. She glanced aside as the trees in the courtyard seemed to yearn for escape. Loose fragments of stone rolled beneath their feet.

Her jaw fell slightly open and she looked up at him.

His voice was barely audible as he said, "Turn the fuck around and go inside."

And she obeyed with no argument to stay. She turned and left the courtyard. The sky lightened and the ground beneath her stilled. She looked back over her shoulder. The courtyard was calm and Reeve was nowhere to be seen.

"You're pacing," said Mal, not looking up from his book.

Maeve walked back and forth across a flat edge of roots and rock against Mirror Lake, her boots squishing lightly in the muddy earth. They shouldn't be getting dirty, they cost too much money- her mother's nagging voice echoed in her mind.

But she paced anyway, pressing her boots carelessly into the mud between the trees with each step.

Mal lowered his book and stared at her. "What's eating you?"

Maeve continued back and forth, balancing on small roots as she contemplated.

"Reeve," she said.

She had already told Mal everything Reeve told her.

"His knowledge of you," she said.

"It only makes sense," said Mal. "We felt him too."

She watched as the water rippled as drops of dew fell from the tree canopy above. Mal straightened and set his book aside, frowning.

"Now, what are you thinking?" Asked Maeve.

"Reeve said there were other ways to travel here. He said your father sent him, but I don't think that's entirely true. I think he came without permission."

Maeve had stopped pacing now, as she looked at him with a brave face. Her voice was barely above a whisper as she spoke. "Does that matter?"

"I think it does," said Mal. "It means no one is trusting anyone else. Your father doesn't trust Reeve, or vice versa. The Double O doesn't trust either of them."

"Reeve was eager to get away from those Magical Militia in the courtyard," said Maeve. "But the students couldn't see him."

"Has Arman talked to you?" He asked.

Maeve shook her head. "I wonder if he even knows what is going on."

A cold breeze shot across the lake, slamming into her and cutting through her sweater. She gripped her arms tightly and scowled at the wind.

Mal stood and slipped off his own long black coat, closing the gap between them.

"You don't have to," said Maeve, though she didn't really mean it.

She happily inhaled his scent and warmth as he slid the coat around her.

"If it comes to it," he said, "I just so happen to know a way out of this realm."

It began to sprinkle as they walked back up to the castle. The Magical Militia that surrounded the castle didn't glance at them as they passed. They hurried through the courtyard as the rain began to fall harder, rounding the archway into the foyer of the Castle.

Maeve collided hard with something.

She stepped back and apologized to the Magical Militia soldier. She recognized him a moment later.

He was a Pureblood Magical in his late thirties.

He stared down at her with a cold expression. It was almost laced with contempt. He looked over at Mal. And then pushed between them.

She barely heard it, but the soldier muttered, "Blood traitor."

They whipped around.

"What did you say?" Mal said without hesitation.

The soldier didn't reply. He didn't turn back towards them. Mal moved to step towards him, his face darkened in a scowl. Maeve grabbed his wrist quickly and blocked his path.

"Move," said Mal so quietly she barely heard him as the pulse on his wrist accelerated rapidly.

He pushed against her. She placed her free hand on his chest.

"Look at me," she said calmly.

Mal peeled his eyes from the soldier's back and looked down at her. His jaw clenched tightly shut.

"Sometimes in war," she whispered. "We keep our cards close. Up the sleeve even."

Mal's eyes slid down to her.

Mal swallowed. His eyes flicked back up to the soldier, who rounded the corner out of sight. "He shouldn't have talked to you that way."

"I imagine worse things are said about me, and will continue to be."

Mal looked back down at her as she dropped her hands. "Not if they don't have tongues."

A smile began to blossom on Maeve's lips. Mal's jaw relaxed.

He had called her a blood traitor. Maeve continued to smile at Mal, but her insides twisted. That hadn't just been an insult to her. It was also directed at Mal, whose Magical blood was considered less than her own.

"Rummy," said Maeve, placing her final cards down on the blanket between her and Abraxas.

"Damn it," he muttered, looking down at his mistake that gave her the win. "I hate playing this with you."

Mal smirked slightly from behind his book.

After dinner, the Headmasters announced all students would be sleeping in Hellming Hall, and not in their dorms. The hall was lined with sleeping bags and blankets of various colors.

Maeve let out a forced breath. Mal's eyes lifted from his book. A card game was not enough of a distraction.

Mal eyed her for a moment, his book still between his hands. "You could jump, you know."

Maeve looked up at him. "Jump to who?" She asked quietly.

"Your father."

"Yes," said Maeve. "I know you've been keeping that thought to yourself for days now."

Mal's expression was unreadable. Annoyingly so. As it was much of the time she needed to decipher his emotions.

His book dipped into his lap. His long fingers gripping its cover.

"And I know exactly how you get there."

Maeve ran her hands across her face, the feeling of Kietel's grip on her throat tightening as she spoke, just like the last time she jumped. "How?"

But it was Abraxas who spoke.

"With Arman being here, your father will have a man named Timothee at his side. Roswyn's father trains with him weekly."

"Three jumps?" She said in disbelief. "You want me-" she stopped and sighed.

"The only thing in your way, Maeve, is you."

Mal spoke with a soft encouragement, no disdain or condemnation in his voice. He said it as though it were simply unemotional facts.

"Like Roswyn is going to let me in his mind," said Maeve.

"He's already agreed," said Abraxas.

She stared at Abraxas for a moment. Annoyed. They had already talked about this behind her back.

She shook her head and looked down at the cards between them. "You don't know what that felt like last time."

"No, I don't," Mal replied calmly. "But I felt you that night in the Headmaster's office. I felt the pain and the fear when you returned. I feel the lingering effects of it more every day coming from you. You let something in your mind that night."

Her eyes whipped to his.

"You opened a door," he said.

"Yes I did," she said. "And you know who stepped inside. I know who stepped inside. And you think the best thing to do is take him straight to my father? Who could be in the middle of discussing this war? Discussing their plan? Brilliant idea, the both of you."

Chapter 34

A prickle shot down her spine. But not the exciting kind. Not at all the way Mal's Magic felt when they kissed. The kind that whispered from the cold shadows of her mind to run. The kind that had her witches' instinct pooling sweat on her palms.

She opened her eyes as the feeling grew. The dark hall was eerily still in the middle of the night. The prickling was faster now. Like running footsteps-

or a portal barreling open

or magic collapsing-

She sat up slowly in the dark hall, feeling for the danger that lurked close by. Abraxas was snoring lightly next to her.

She looked across the row of students.

Mal was already sitting straight as a board. Something warm and slick rested above her lip. She touched her face, pulling her bloodied fingers back.

Mal's eyes grew wide as the prickle down Maeve's back dug in deep and ran down her arms. He lunged for her as the doors to the Hall sprung open.

"Students!" Screamed Rowan, awakening them all.

Mal's body slammed into hers as a deafening crack sounded through the hall like two boulders colliding together. The sound ensued panic. Screams flooded the hall as the ground beneath them began to violently shake. The stained glass windows depicting the original courts and the three branches of Magic shattered. Colorful glass musically fell to the floor.

Mal gripped her face in his hands.

"You stay close to me. Do you understand?"

Maeve placed her hands over his and nodded.

"To the foyer now!" Yelled Rowan.

Chandeliers of candles crashed to the floor. Paintings and tapestries dulled into nothing. Rubble and bits of stone and wood fell from the ceiling, stirring dust and debris and bursting the floor open.

Abraxas was there suddenly, helping Maeve to her feet with his eyes locked on Mal. "Maeve is the target!" He yelled over the screaming students. "They're here for Maeve!"

The realization slammed into her. "That soldier the other day-"

Abraxas cut her off, "The Magical Militia is no longer under your father's command."

Mal's arm slipped around her waist, pulling her back to him.

And this time, she didn't pull away from his touch. She melted into his protection, into the cool electricity that shot down his arm and circled around her.

"They are under Kietel's." She said.

The blinding light of a portal was pouring into the hall from the foyer.

They ran across the hall. Sparks and blasts of light of many colors illuminated the foyer. Magical Militia were fighting Magical Militia. The portal was barely large enough for two or three students to get through at a time. Larliesl and Arman held the portal open, urging students to hurry.

A burst of red light ricocheted towards them. They dodged it and kept running.

Rowan was dueling multiple Magical Militia at once. Maeve had never seen the stoic spy so violent. Curses whipped from him with passion as he guarded Larliesl and Arman's portal.

Maeve's anger flared as she watched the betrayal.

With the point of two fingers, a black light burst forth from her, spiraling across the hall and slamming into one of the soldiers Rowan battled.

"Go Abraxas," said Mal. "As soon as you are on the other side of that Portal trust no one except Ambrose."

Abraxas took off towards the swirling light. Students hurled past them. There were too many soldiers swarming the foyer from the courtyard.

Headmaster Elgin flew down the castle stairs, Magical Militia hot on her heels.

They didn't fire at her.

"Take down that portal!" She yelled, pointing towards Rowan.

The remaining two soldiers fighting Rowan dropped to the floor at once. Maeve's head whipped towards Mal, whose single finger was pointed at them.

Elgin made her way across the hall, her eyes on Mal and Maeve.

"We needn't spill Golden Blood, Sinclair," said Elgin. "I will not harm you."

"I cannot guarantee the same," seethed Maeve.

She looked to Rowan and understood things instantly from the lack of surprise on his face.

"It was you who Rowan wanted to out that night I jumped to Kietel," she said.

"Your father is too trusting," said Elgin. "But you will see, the both of you, in time," she said.

"You are out of time," said Mal.

Elgin looked to him. "So be it."

She pointed two fingers towards the Portal and adjusted her aim at Arman. Bright blue light shot towards him, slamming him square in the chest.

The Portal faltered as he was weakened, shrinking in size. Magical Militia now swarmed him and Larliesl. Harquinton and the rest of the staff stood fighting them off.

Rowan stood tall and faced Elgin.

"Rowan," she said. "I tried to tell you."

His fingers sparked at his side. "I do not listen to traitors."

Their fight exploded across the foyer as their hexes slammed into one another. Students screamed at the sound. Maeve turned towards Mal.

"There are too many of us to make it through the portals before this place collapses."

Maeve looked up at Mal, whose eyes were already on her.

"We can do it," he said.

She nodded.

Without hesitation, without thought, and with a thunderous clap, they grasped each other's forearms. Light shot down their shoulders, banding along their arms and joining with the other. Had Mal's grip on her arm not been iron-tight, she would have gone flying backward and slammed into the floor.

The bright green and blue whirls of light began circling between them, growing brighter and brighter and wider until the stone floor beneath them was swallowed by the light. A bright golden light erupted from their gripped forearms and latched itself onto the oscillating shape of the portal.

Mal nodded, and they let go and stepped away.

Scrambling students nearly shoved past them to gain access to the portal, their screams frantic and scared.

Arman was scrambling back to his feet, clutching his wounded chest. Larliesl's attention was on the Portal. The Magical Militia moved towards Arman relentlessly as he threw up a shield.

Maeve narrowed two fingers on her right hand and a silver spiral shot towards one of the soldiers. He slouched to the floor in agony. Mal took care of two more, and Larliesl took out the next. Arman pulled back his bloodied hand and pointed one singular finger at the diminishing Portal.

With a guttural scream, he poured his Magic back into the Portal. It expanded in size instantly. He turned, and with his other hand produced deadly and precise Magic, defeating the enemies swarming him in one fell swoop.

He was the Premier's second for a reason.

A student flew around them. A hex from Elgin, aimed at Rowan, clipped his shoulder. He rolled to the floor, gripping his arm. Maeve stepped towards him. The castle quaked once more, knocking her off balance. Chunks of the ceiling smashed into the floor. Maeve looked up. The castle was going to fall completely.

"Come, Darian!" Screamed another student, grabbing the wounded boy's hand as she went by, dragging him towards their portal.

"Where's it go?" She asked.

"Sinclair Estates," Mal and Maeve answered together.

They hadn't even discussed where the portal would lead to.

Roswyn appeared at Mal's side, assisting him in his fight. In one step, she could be home. With her father. Safe.

Rowan and Elgin's duel continued. Maeve watched as the Headmasters of Vaukore fought with deadly intention. Elgin, who had welcomed students with open arms. Who had promised them safety and peace. Who had vowed to protect Vaukore and its students with her life. . .was now an enemy.

Sparks of red swarmed Maeve's fingertips.

She stepped towards the Headmasters, the floor beneath each step trembled and shook more.

She pointed at Elgin and fired. Red light ripped into her side, blood spewed from the wound.

Rowan's eyes grew wide.

Only Dread Magic drew blood.

Elgin writhed on the stone floor as Maeve and Rowan met eyes. She pointed her finger at Elgin as it shook.

"Don't," said Rowan. "You don't need her on your conscious."

"She already is," said Maeve as Elgin's blood pooled. "The bleeding won't stop."

Larliesl appeared at Maeve's side. "Rowan," he gasped. "There are more coming."

They were being surrounded. And outnumbered. It appeared that there were more Magical Militia here against them than with them. Rowan stepped towards Elgin. A bright white shot of light knocked her unconscious. He looked to the Portals.

"Everyone is almost through. We can hold them off Larliesl." He looked back at Maeve. "Take Mal and get to your father. We cannot lose our Dread Descendant."

Maeve stepped away from Rowan and Larliesl, her head shaking.

"There's no time, Maeve. You must protect him-"

A second burst of magic slammed through the hall, sucking Maeve's hair back as Magic withdrew from the castle.

And everything went dark.

And cold.

Larliesl and Rowan ran towards the last few students, shooting spells at the soldiers, attempting to stop them.

Massive pieces of the castle cut loose from the ceiling and slammed to the floor, Maeve narrowly removing herself from their path. The last few students crossed their Portal where it stood beckoning them to safety.

But she froze. That prickle down her spine stilled. She turned back to look at Mal, her face struck with horror. She could feel the stalling breath of prepared Magic.

Without warning, the floor was yanked from beneath them as the Magic holding up Vaukore Realm snapped in half.

The tiles beneath them were tilting, inch by inch, rubble from the castle's destruction sliding down sideways across the floor. Her reflexes caught her and a hard wall of air stopped her from slamming into the floor. She pulled her feet under her, quickly balancing herself. Mal slid to her side gracefully and gripped her tightly, one taunt leg holding them steady. His face mangled with distress.

The stone archway behind them cracked under pressure. Mal flinched at the sound. Anger flooded his veins. It pulsated towards Maeve.

Fury like she had never felt from him.

"Don't," said Maeve, beginning to realize his intentions. They were sliding faster now, the Portal mere feet away. "Don't-"

His grip tightened, and his lips slammed into hers. Too quickly. That had been too quick of a kiss to be the last. But he kissed her like it was.

"Go," was all he said as he released her.

Mal Obscured to the center of the hall, walking on air as Maeve was nearly to the portal. The green and blue waves of mist ready to take her home, to her father. Behind her, white light was pouring into her shoulders.

Rowan and Larliesl had told her they couldn't lose Mal. Even Reeve told her to stay with Mal.

She looked at the Portal before her and, as easy as cutting a ribbon, she let go of the flow of Magic between it and herself. The Portal collapsed with all students safely on the other side.

The circle pulled and twisted in on itself, making a cyclone-like shape until it compacted so tightly it was gone. Maeve steadied her breathing and turned to Mal at the center of the Hall. He was barely three feet off the ground, both his palms extended wide. His eyes white as all his Magic poured from him.

She wouldn't leave him defenseless.

Arman and Larliesl and Rowan had pushed the traitorous soldiers out of the castle and onto the grounds. Only she and Mal remained in the foyer.

The castle twisted to its upright position. The ceiling didn't fall. The walls shook into stillness and the room grew calm. Maeve stared up at Mal in awe as he took control of Vaukore's Magic and she remembered that his Magic was fused with Vaukore's.

Air swirled around her, unsettling and. . .familiar. Her hand crept to the back of her neck as her fingers shook.

"Maeve Sinclair."

The voice behind her was burned into her mind. She turned over her shoulder. Kietel stood across the foyer.

His icy blue eyes glowed in the darkness. His hands were tucked behind his back.

Mal was holding up Vaukore. Maeve was on her own.

She pulled two fingers together, resting at her side. Kietel looked down at them.

"A Supreme." He said, his German accent thick. "Let's see what you are made of."

Panic raced through her.

"I came prepared for you," he said. "You won't find your way into my mind."

Maeve lowered her chin.

"You disagree?"

Mal lowered to the ground behind her, his eyes white. He gently collapsed onto the floor. He didn't move. She felt for the Dread Magic around her neck. She felt him.

He was breathing.

Kietel stepped towards her, and Maeve stepped back towards Mal.

"I don't think your friend is going to help you."

She stepped back towards him again. If she could get to him, she could attempt to obscure them away. She had never done it successfully, but she could try. Or at the least put a protective shield on him.

"I see," said Kietel. "You are protecting him." His pursuit towards her continued. "I'm disappointed. You aren't even trying to enter my mind. I'm afraid your father is going to be rather disappointed too."

Maeve stopped. Kietel opened his mouth to continue.

But his eyes went wide. Magic slammed into the foyer with a fury. Black and amethyst fire swarmed around them. Maeve's knees gave way, slamming her sideways into the ground.

From the violet flames erupted Reeve.

Lethal rage poured from his eyes, and all of it directed at Kietel.

Maeve's attention shot to Mal. He was still unconscious on the other side of the foyer.

Reeve's face twisted into something unholy. She felt the raw Magic that was seconds away from bursting from him.

She made to move for Mal but. . .

Her jaw fell open as Reeve transformed.

The Aterna power held shapeshifting. She nearly forgot.

She had never seen those fearsome wings and claws herself. In an instant, Reeve was part man, part mist and shadow. Great black dragon wings unfurled from his back. His fingers were scaled and sharp.

He was incredible.

He was Holy.

The castle shook beneath them. The floors snapped under his new form.

He was nothing like the dragons she pictured, nothing like the paintings and tapestries salvaged from the Dread Lands depicted. He was horrifying. His teeth were oversized, his features twisted. Black and blue and violet scales glittered in the darkness. His jagged tattoos somehow remained across his dragon form, carved into his scales.

Reeve snarled and deep amethyst fire flared from his snout. Maeve jumped and remembered Mal.

But Kietel's attention was not on Reeve.

Sharp blades locked into her arms, pulling her backward. She pointed two fingers, but it was too late. Maeve winced as her back slammed into a hard chest. Kietel stood behind her. One hand gripping her right wrist high, and the other flat across her throat, power flickering from his palm, threatening to slice at any moment.

Reeve snarled in divine hatred.

He, and the foyer at Vaukore, vanished before she could blink.

Chapter 35

The floor was cold, wet and slimy. But it was the scent that filled Maeve's nose before her eyes opened that caused her to gag. She tried to bolt upright, but her whole body felt full of lead, and her head spun as she lifted it off the grotesque floor with a groan. It was completely black save for a small slit of light pushing its way through a tall slit in what appeared to be a door.

Another inhale and that retched smell hit her again. Like rotted meat that had melted under the heat of the sun. Her hand shot to her face to cover her nose, and something steel and cold bristled her jawline.

Tight metal cuffs wrapped her wrists, each one set with three white stones.

No.

Fear spread through her, so intense she didn't notice the droplets of water falling to the floor from her soaked hair, nor the dirty brown water that flowed in from the corner behind her, soaking through her pajamas and wetting her skin.

Her sapphire ring on her finger was gone.

She gasped-

She gripped at her chest. Mal's ring lay still. Cool, magic radiating from it.

Mal.

She searched for him, to feel any pull of his Magic, but the white stones had dulled nearly all of her Magic. Merely trying to push out a search for his life force made her stomach flip again and again.

Muffled voices filled the tight space. She looked towards the metal door. Shadows moved on the other side through the small slit between the floor and the door. The door to the cell creaked open.

A Magical Militia soldier stepped inside. He was in a different uniform. One of red. But she recognized him. He had called her a blood traitor.

"Up," he said.

Maeve looked him down from head to toe. "You're a Nicklefrost." She said.

"I am," he said. "Something I'm proud of."

Her brows pulled together.

He frowned. "It will be beneficial for you to remember your pride."

Maeve leaned back against the wet wall. "I have never forgotten it."

He glared at her. "Up."

Maeve took a deep breath and pushed off the ground. She followed Nicklefrost out of the cell and across a wet dungeon. She shielded her eyes as bright light blurred her vision at the end of the dungeon hall. They walked across a long dining hall, its floors a dark wood and pale grey walls.

Nicklefrost led her to a study. The smell of a roast hit her nose as he opened the door. There was a small table with a smoking pot of strew and a variety of bread.

Maeve's stomach growled.

Nicklefrost shoved her down into a seat, his grip on her shoulder tight. Maeve refused to wince.

"Manners, Nicklefrost."

They looked towards the desk. Kietel appeared from a doorway across the room. He placed a file of papers on the desk and took off his glasses.

"You're dismissed."

Nicklefrost saluted Kietel. And left without another word. Kietel crossed towards her. He sat across from her, unrolled a set of silverware wrapped in a black napkin, and set his plate.

"Please," he said, gesturing towards the food between them, his tone businesslike.

Maeve didn't move. "How long have I been out?"

"Two days." He poured himself a bowl of strew.

Maeve's stomach cried, begging to be fed.

"You drugged me?" She asked.

"Elixir of Somnum. Nasty what that does to a Magical. The ancient ways of keeping us enslaved."

Maeve didn't speak.

"And," he said, "gave me enough time to bind those on your arms. Did you know humans in the realm actually build moonstones into their houses to ward off our kind? Or they wear it on their bodies fashionably. Clever little creatures, don't you think?"

Maeve remained completely silent.

"Of course," said Kietel, "most of you pious Purebloods think you are as special as it gets. When in reality, the humans are surpassing you at every bend. Something I cannot seem to make your father understand."

Maeve's eyes widened and lifted up at him.

Kietel smiled in an evil way.

"The last of the Sinclair line," he said.

She scowled at him. His icy blue eyes were cold and flat.

"Reeve will be in deep shit for letting me slip away with you. Did you see the horror on The High Lord's face? I'll cherish it forever. Perhaps now your father will finally hear my terms. It seems a blast of magic powerful enough to destroy thousands of lives wasn't enough to dissuade him. Perhaps his flesh and blood will be."

Maeve released a tight breath. He was alive then.

"What is making you smile?"

"Nothing," she answered.

She looked down at her clothes, still clad in a matching set of sapphire and ivory pajamas. They were wet, sticking to her skin like glue, the skin underneath turning to mush. The ivory lace trim was now stained brown, and the sapphire blue velvet was matted and dirty.

"Drink," he said as he ate spoonfuls of his stew.

Maeve shook her head. "Where's my ring?"

"Usque ad Mortem," said Kietel, quoting her family motto that was engraved on the ring. "What a lovely inscription on a fine jewel."

Maeve longed for the bread before her. Her stomach growled, begging her to eat. He continued.

"Until death, I believe, that means correct?"

Maeve didn't answer.

"Are you prepared to die for your Sinclair blood?"

Her eyes snapped to him, and his disgusted expression grew. Maeve mustered a slight scoff as her eyes narrowed.

"The Sinclair family motto has nothing to do with charging to one's death like a nervous soldier on the front line, begging for a quick release or naively thinking their name will be honored in death. It means that Sinclairs fight to the death, we fight to protect our own, to the death. I will fight to the death for my father, and he for me. I will fight until I die."

"Fight, fight, fight," drawled Kietel, his face set in stone. "And your companion, Malachite?"

Maeve smiled, the smirk growing as she thought of Mal shredding Kietel and Nicklefrost and the rest to pieces when he got to her.

"You may have evoked horror from Reeve, but Mal will kill you calmly and without so much as a fluttering heartbeat."

"I was impressed with him holding Vaukore together like that. I can't help but wonder what kind of blood runs through those veins."

Maeve glared at him. He continued.

"Those part human veins."

Maeve's stomach growled once more, loudly this time.

"For fuck's sake, eat," he said.

Maeve sighed and reached for a roll, forcing her fingers to calmly rip the bread apart and place it in her mouth, determined not to look like the starving, desperate prisoner she was. She spoke with disinterest, and just enough disdain to let him know she thought ill of him.

"You dropped those bombs on Japan?"

Kietel gave a half-shrug. "The Magic used for them may have been my doing, but the Americans bought it without convincing."

"Why did you want to destroy Vaukore?" Asked Maeve.

"So inquisitive," he said, "and so unwilling to answer any of my questions."

"Fine," said Maeve, moving a piece of meat to her plate and stabbing it with a fork. "A question for a question."

He sipped his wine and nodded. "I've already answered one of yours. Now it's my turn to get answers."

Maeve waited for him to continue.

He let his spoon fall into his stew. He entertained his fingers, his elbows pressed into the table. "Where does your friend hail from?"

"You mean Malachite?"

He nodded.

Maeve answered plainly. "He was an orphan in London."

"No idea of his bloodline?" Pressed Kietel.

"That's two questions," said Maeve cooly.

Her captor smiled, but Maeve could see he was fighting a temper. "You're a clever girl from what I'm told. Surely you understand quite plainly why your school had to go. The government has had its hand in our Magical Educational System for far too long."

"That's what set him off, you know," said Maeve quietly.

Kietel's brows raised, and Maeve answered his unspoken question.

"He loved that school."

His brows were now pulled together. "I arrived just as the last of you made it through. I think he loves more than you are willing to admit. Because you're in denial, or because you want to protect him. But either way, I did luck up with you as my bargaining chip."

Maeve leaned back in the chair, completely unwilling to acknowledge what he said, but now fully aware that she was bait for both her father and Mal.

He continued. "Answer my question."

Maeve contemplated her answer. She had two options to consider, and either one could be beneficial or potentially hurt Mal.

"If you lie to me," said Kietel, "I'll know."

Maeve scoffed. "No, you won't. My shields are not part of my Magic, they are indestructible. As all Pureblood children's are. No one gets in my mind without my permission."

"We will see." No smile laced with venom. A simple threat.

Maeve sighed and looked at her dirty nails with boredom as she answered. "Mal's bloodline is irrelevant."

"Not to me it isn't," said Kietel, a little too honestly.

Maeve's eyes flashed to him. Her jaw fell open slightly as it hit her.

"You are doubting if you're the Dread Descendant, aren't you?" She smiled. Kietel looked as though he was scolding himself for speaking so boldly. She remembered Reeve, and how he knew about Mal just by being around him. How she herself had known there was something there. Rowan and Larliesl knew somehow. “And now you have seen him. And now you doubt. . .because you can feel that power in him too.” Maeve smiled. “You may be a powerful dark wizard who commands the German Magical Militia, but you know nothing of civilized conversation or holding your cards close.”

“Yes,” he said in a mocking tone. “You Pureblood bitches are all the same.”

Maeve laughed audibly, feeling more and more like herself with every bait he took.

“That may be the case, but at least I’m not desperately hoping to be someone that I’m not.”

“Then he is of the Dread House,” said Kietel, the color slipping from his face.

Maeve folded her dirty hands in her lap and straightened. One pointed smile was all she needed to answer his question.

“It matters not,” said Kietel. “Soon I will have control of the Magicals and the Humans.”

“And you want the Humans because you think they are creating weapons you need?”

“I don’t need their weapons. I need the wars they create. War creates chaos. Chaos yields power. War sustains power.”

“War ruins everything. It is why we are here at all.”

“You need a history lesson, girl.” He nearly laughed. “Where did you get that ring around your neck?”

Maeve’s hand gripped at Mal’s ring.

“It’s his, is it not?” He asked.

“You’re skipping my questions,” said Maeve.

She reached to pour herself a bowl of stew. Kietel snapped his fingers, and the table cleared.

“We are done with that,” he said. “You answer my questions or you starve.”

Maeve placed her hands back in her lap. A wave of nausea crashed over her. She needed food.

“It is Mal’s ring, yes.”

"I assumed." He held up his hand. This thumb and pointer fingers were burned, blistering bright red.

Relief washed over her. His magic was here with her, even if hers was suppressed.

"How did you do it?"

Maeve's brows lifted.

Kietel was scowling. "How did you get into my officer's mind that night?"

"Impossible to explain," said Maeve.

"That's what everyone said."

"Do they think you killed him for no reason?"

His head turned to the side, and his eyes narrowed on her. "Why do you think he's dead?"

Maeve hesitated. "I felt you kill him. . . It felt like you were. . ."

"Killing you?"

Maeve didn't answer.

"I'll admit I thought he intentionally had you there, that he was a spy, a traitor. But you were in his mind without his permission, weren't you?"

Again. She remained silent.

Kietel laughed softly, no joy in the sound. "You truly don't know how you do it?"

She shook her head.

"Incredible," he said.

"Spare me," she said.

"It didn't take me too long to figure out it must have been you. There's talk of a young witch at Vaukore with the power to jump from mind to mind, to create flawless, false memories. The Orator's Office would have been smart to keep a tight lip about you. Your father should have known you'd be a desired weapon."

"That's what I am to you? A weapon?"

"You are many things, Miss Sinclair. A weapon is among them, yes."

"What terms did you send my father?"

"Simple ones. His Magical Militia are to stand down. He is to resign. I would wager, for you, he'll do anything."

Maeve gazed down at the now empty table. Her appetite gone. "You never answered my first question," said Maeve. "Where is my ring?"

Kietel stood and paced the length of the table. "I sent it to your father. The message should be received clearly."

He went to stalk past her.

"I want a change of clothes," said Maeve.

"Absolutely not." He stormed towards the door. "And you best hope you simply being captive is enough to show your father reason, and we don't have to stain those lovely blue night clothes crimson."

"What's stopping you?"

Kietel halted. She continued.

"He would spiral, and hand over power to you in despair. So why not just kill me?"

Kietel didn't turn towards her and she didn't look at him as she said, "Because you know that I don't bleed crimson. My blood is fucking gold."

Chapter 36

Maeve startled in her sleep as the metal cell door swung open. Nicklefrost stepped inside. He lifted two fingers in the air. Then swirled them sharply.

What felt like a jagged rock slammed into her cheek, busting through the skin and sending her spiraling onto her back. Her eyes squeezed closed.

She groaned as the sharp pain pulsated in the side of her lip and her cheekbone.

"That wasn't as satisfying as I hoped it would be," said Nicklefrost. "Get up. The Commander wants to see you."

Maeve touched her lip. Blood seeped into her fingers from the wound. Maeve stood.

Nicklefrost scowled. "You look disgusting."

"Perhaps you could convince your Commander to let me bathe. Or have a change of clothes," she said. "Maybe a nice satin gown or a beaded dress. Something tight. Those are the ones I always saw you staring at me in."

Nicklefrost lunged towards her. His forearm collided with her neck, slamming her head against the concrete wall of her cell. The room spun. Her legs bent beneath her. She sputtered a cough.

"I wouldn't touch a blood traitor like you," he seethed.

He pushed back away from her and she slid to the floor, arms weak at her sides. She coughed until the tickle in her throat was gone. She looked up at him with a small smile.

"Well, that was fun."

"Get up," he said.

She followed him out of her cell, rubbing the back of her head. They didn't head towards the study or the dining room. He led her somewhere else entirely.

Maeve froze in the doorway. The room was filled with soldiers, all of them in red and black uniforms. Kietel stood at the middle of the room with another man. He frowned upon seeing her.

"Miss Sinclair," he said. He eyed Nicklefrost.

"She wouldn't come without a fight."

Kietel looked ready to reprimand Nicklefrost but brushed it off. He motioned for Maeve to join him at his side.

"Today we jump, Miss Sinclair."

Maeve's mouth fell slightly open. "No," she snapped.

"You're very accustomed to saying that aren't you?"

Maeve looked sideways at the soldiers that lined the room. They all looked up at her, speaking in hushed whispers.

"I figured you'd love to show off."

Maeve looked back up at Kietel.

"I said no," her voice shook more than she liked. "You don't need me-you have your human army and their bombs."

One of the metal cuffs on her wrist snapped loose and fell to the floor with a clang. The room fell silent at once.

"Kill him if you like," said Kietel pointing at Nicklefrost. "I'm certain a Supreme needs only one free hand."

Maeve looked at Nicklefrost. His expression blank.

"He struck you," said Kietel. "Strike him back."

Maeve didn't move.

He circled her. "Come now, Sinclair, my boys are dying to see that Sacred Seventeen power from someone so young."

He stepped towards her. She gasped as he grabbed her free wrist and held it up. The skin was raw over the tattooed three stars. A symbol of her blood.

"See those marks, boys?" Continued Kietel. "Those stars? Some of you here have them." He looked down at her. "Those stars mean something to you, Sinclair?"

Maeve looked up at him. "Usque ad Mortem."

Kietel grinned. He struck fast, and Maeve slammed up a shield, blocking his spell. Her hair whipped behind her.

"Give me both hands," muttered Maeve, pressing her shield against him.

The other shackle fell to the floor with a clang. Maeve drew two fingers at her side.

Kietel released her, stepped away, and nodded.

Bright green light burst from her fingers, shooting towards Kietel. He blocked her with a dramatic wave of his arm.

"I trained with your father, you know," said Kietel. "I was the top Bellator for years."

"I know," said Maeve. "He made you captain."

Kietel fired on her, but Maeve dodged his attack and fired back. His shield slammed up, and Maeve fired again, damaging the shield with fiery red sparks.

The room sucked in a breath.

"We're playing with Dread Magic?" Said Kietel. "Alright then."

He fired on her with deadly red hexes, each one dissipating as it hit her shield. She drew Mal's magic through her arm. It was like breathing after suffocating. A silent sedation and rush of violence.

She pointed at him and pulled all of their Magic together. The curse shot to him at light speed and shattered through his defenses. Blood spewed from his arm, where a thick slice of his uniform had burned up.

Nicklefrost moved towards him.

Kietel held up a hand and then braced his wound. He stared at Maeve. "Well done."

Maeve's heartbeat was fast. Almost too fast. She was certain they could all feel her fear. She pressed her feet into the floor as her legs threatened to collapse. She was nearly drained. She needed a full meal.

"Now that the ice is broken," he said. "Nicklefrost. Felden." He snapped his fingers and pointed at the center of the room.

The soldiers obeyed without hesitation, moving side by side.

"Enter one of their minds and jump to the other."

Maeve shook her head. Panic raced through her.

The soldiers that stood before her didn't look at her. They stared straight ahead.

"Don't be stubborn, I want to see," said Kietel.

Maeve stepped back, still shaking her head. Kietel looked at her shaking hands, her trembling lip.

"You're afraid," he said quietly.

Maeve's jaw tightened. She scowled at him. Rage swelled inside her, fueled by embarrassment.

"You haven't jumped since you jumped to me, have you?"

Maeve cursed herself. And refused to answer.

"At last," he said. "A weakness."

Maeve turned towards him.

"Do it," he said. "Every day that you do not is another day you spend here without food."

Maeve looked back at the two soldiers. Her stomach knotted, sweat pooled at the back of her neck and her palms.

"He'll find me eventually," she said quietly. Then she spoke louder and pointed at Nicklefrost. "I can't get to his- he'll have to open his mind to me."

Kietel nodded.

Maeve stood before them, begging the part of Mal around her neck to keep her safe, to keep her calm.

The only thing standing in your way is you.

Mal's voice rang out over her head. She regretted not letting him push her to jump before. Now she was cornered with the enemy breathing down her throat.

"Are you a Supreme?" She asked Felden.

He nodded.

Maeve looked at Nicklefrost. She didn't ask him if he was ready. She barreled into his mind. Flashes of his life shot before her. Trainings, meetings, attacking Vaukore, a conversation with Headmaster Elgin, a blonde woman with little clothing on.

Maeve called out for Felden. And Nicklefrost's mind bent to her. A memory popped forward and Maeve snagged it. They were training in a facility. Felden and Nicklefrost calling the drills.

Maeve took a steadying breath as the door to Felden's mind opened, and she slipped inside. The darkness beneath her remained steady as the memory changed to Feldens. It looped through once and Maeve pushed deeper into his mind. There was nothing stopping her.

The room filled with soldiers reappeared, blurry at first. And then she saw herself. She did look disgusting. Her days-old dirty and wet pajamas made her look like the prisoner she was.

Her eyes were solid white. She looked to her side, Felden's side, at Nicklefrost. He glanced over. Maeve felt a surge of satisfaction. There was a confused fear in his eyes.

Maeve lunged for him, Felden's Magic bursting from his palms, palms that she controlled. She slammed Nicklefrost's throat to the ground. Curse after curse slicing into his throat.

The room erupted in red light. Maeve screamed. She was yanked from Felden's mind and sucked back into her own. Her arm burned hot. She gripped at it protectively.

She opened her eyes at the ceiling. Kietel stood over her. She hadn't felt herself hit the floor. She pressed into her arm with a wince. She let her head rest on the wooden floor beneath her, panting. The metal shackles reappeared on her wrists.

"That is the problem, isn't it?" Said Kietel quietly. "If you're going to use that trick, you can't protect yourself."

Maeve looked over at Nicklefrost. Blood pooled beneath him. Two healers stood over him, working quickly to seal up the wound.

"He'll be fine," one of them said. "It isn't too deep."

Maeve looked back up at Kietel. Her eyes desperate to close. To sleep. "Satisfied?"

He stared at Nicklefrost. "Unbelievably."

Maeve wasn't given a bath or a change of clothes. She sat uncomfortably opposite Kietel in his study for dinner. Maeve looked down at her plate, attempting to calmly eat. Dinners with Kietel were all she was given.

"You told Nicklefrost to hurt me." She said.

She had realized it hours ago in her cell.

"I have it on good authority you need a little spite to strike."

"I feel strange thanking you."

Kietel stopped eating.

She jumped successfully. Without panic and without falling. And Felden had not pushed back into her mind like Kietel had. She remained in control until Kietel fired on her.

"I would like to make an offer," said Kietel.

Maeve's brows raised.

"Fight with me," he said.

"You mean fight for you."

Kietel broke their gaze, cutting his steak. "I imagine what it would be like to have you at my side, altering memories whenever necessary. Jumping through minds in a deadly manner. I wonder how powerful you could be with training and discipline. Just how far could you bend memory and time?" He sighed. "Makes me regret having taken you in this way. For I know that Pureblood pride will not allow you to join my cause. I fear you will waste that weapon of yours."

Maeve was quiet for a moment. Reeve had called her a Warrior. The Orator's Office had already named her Bellator. And now, Kietel named her a weapon.

Maybe she could be all those things. At Mal's side.

"I read an essay you wrote last fall," she said. "I was so inspired. So hopeful. None of us dared talk about it. Talk about you. Almost like it would jinx your existence."

"I may not be The Dread Descendant, but I still intend to right the wrongs The Orator's Office has done. Magic needs no law. No Officials no Committees."

Maeve's throat tightened.

He pointed a finger at her. "And you agree."

"Of course I agree," said Maeve with slow calculation. "How could I not?"

Kietel leaned back. "Have they picked one for you yet?"

Her eyes slid across the table. She scowled. "No."

"Ah," he said. "When is your twenty-second birthday?"

"In October."

"Very soon then. How will your Dread friend feel to see you betrothed to another? Will he rip them apart too? Like you claim he will do to me?"

Maeve averted her gaze to the centerpiece of the table. Kietel continued.

"I remember what it was like to be your age, decades ago though it was," he said. "I remember how I loved. So carelessly. Without a thought for reality."

"Reality?" She asked softly. "If I am to breed" she spat, "then why not with him? If the goal is strong magical bloodlines. . .whose is stronger than his?"

Kietel stared at her. "I don't need convincing. It is not my thumb you are under."

Maeve placed her hands in her lap and sighed quietly.

"You don't need me. You have your humans and their bombs," she said with a hint of mocking.

"You're so arrogant it's beneath you to utilize their power." His voice softened, "but it's not beneath me."

"What is the end goal? Is it merely power?"

Kietel turned towards her as she spoke once more.

"There was a time I had faith in you. When I prayed, you were the savior. I hoped you would turn out to be so much more."

He scoffed. "You have the Premier as your father and the Dread Descendant at your side, and you hoped I was more?"

Maeve didn't look at him. "It doesn't matter. This will all be over soon. I appreciate your confidence in me, truly. But it is not at your side I wish to stand. And now, now that you have kept me and hurt me, Mal will not hear you. Maeve looked at him now and spoke plainly. "You will die as soon as he finds us and breaks the shields protecting this place." She grabbed the ring around her neck and continued. "It will be the first time Mal has killed for me."

"He has experience in killing?"

Maeve ignored his comment and continued. "My father won't even have a chance. Mal will do it. And it will mark the beginning of his ascent as the Dread Prince, the beginning of his journey to freeing us."

"Freeing you?" Spat Kietel. "Free you from your golden palaces and-"

"You know nothing of-"

"Save your sob story of arranged marriages for one who gives a damn. Tell me, Sinclair, can your slave walk freely away from you? Can she decide she no longer wishes to make your bed and clean your things and serve you forever?"

Maeve's jaw tensed, astonished. "Don't you dare call her that."

"Then what is she if she is not a slave?"

Kietel waited. Maeve had no reply. Guilt dripped down her entire body with a shake.

"You think you're the victim in this tale, but you are the villain."

"I could say the same about you," said Maeve.

"You could." He nodded. "I'm sure that arrogant bastard Reeve thinks he's the victim, too. While his Immortals remain untouched and free to live their lives in the open, Never hiding. They were the ones who screwed over the Magicals to begin with, and they still came out on top."

"What are you talking about?"

Kietel frowned. "Primus and the Gods. I said you needed a history lesson. I suppose it's I who has the honor of delivering it. I had been hoping you didn't know. Your father's winged friend is truly whom you should hate."

Maeve frowned as Kietel continued.

"A century ago in the Shadow War, Reeve's father, who held the Aterna power then, refused the Magicals entry to his kingdom across the Black Deep. The land, which you now know as the Dread Lands, was once ours. Lavish Forests blooming vegetation and powerful magic to match. The Dread Lands were alive, its own Magic present in the daily lives of all who lived there, providing life and nourishment. But as the blight spread, the Magic changed, or it died entirely."

"Yes, I know all that," said Maeve. "But what do you mean they refused entry to their kingdom?"

"Simply that," he answered. "Did you think our ancestors' first choice was to come to Earth? To live in hiding amongst humans and their wars? No. The Immortals-"

"Fought," interrupted Maeve, "they fought the blight back into the shadows."

"Only after that darkness had spread completely to the Dark Peaks, to the edge of those mountains, to the tips of our lands and began poisoning the waters that touched Aterna. Only when the blight threatened to take them, too."

Maeve looked down at the table between them without a word.

"Reeve and the Immortals are not our friends," said Kietel. "The Magicals are on their own."

"You may be on your own, but Reeve and my father have a strong alliance," retorted Maeve.

"Yes," he scoffed. "I was surprised to see him at Vaukore. But he loves stepping in to save the day. Too bad he didn't save you."

Maeve watched him carefully. He spoke with such certainty, such conviction. She knew better than to believe him, but what he said had some truth to it. The Immortals did not offer refuge to the Magicals.

"Sleep on it," said Kietel. "My offer. I don't care who the Dread Descendant is. My purpose is the destruction of our sham Magical Government. And your Dread Prince is welcome in my cause, too."

Maeve shook her head. "Mal will never forgive you. Nor will my father."

"But you might?"

"I am not concerned with forgiveness. My allegiance, however, is not so easily bought."

Kietel nodded. He pointed his fork at her. "Affection will lose you this war, Sinclair."

She looked down. The meat on her plate ran into her vegetables. They were soggy now.

She opened her mouth to speak-

But her hand shot to the ring around her neck-

Her eyes went wide. Kietel's did as well. The windows in the study exploded as emerald green and red swirling night filled the study.

Chapter 37

Mal emerged from the darkness, his eyes on Maeve. She pushed out of her chair and bolted for him. Kietel's chair flew backward behind him.

Maeve slammed into a solid wall of air. She hit the ground, her fists banging against the shield. The wall remained. Kietel obscured behind her and placed one finger at her temple, drawing her to her feet.

Darkness crept from Mal's side of the room. It slithered from the ceiling and across the floors in long tendrils and began penetrating Kietel's wall.

He walked calmly towards her until he was at that invisible barrier. Steps away from them.

Did he hurt you? Mal said into her mind.

His voice caused an audible breath to rise in her chest.

Not badly. She replied.

A pause. Then he spoke into her mind with incredible control.

Did he touch you?

No.

Those bands holding your magic back will snap with his neck shortly.

Maeve had to suppress a smile.

Mal's full lips parted slightly, and Maeve realized they had been apart for only four days, but it felt like weeks since his lips had pressed against hers.

From the red and green swirling nebula behind Mal stepped Ambrose.

"The entire Magical Militia is a portal away, Kietel. At least the ones still loyal to me." He spoke bitterly, his eyes filled with hatred as Kietel held his youngest daughter threateningly.

"I have no doubt, Ambrose. Reeve couldn't deign to join us, or is he spending another week in the form of a beast? I've heard he prefers the scales to skin these days."

Ambrose didn't answer. "Step away from her and let us discuss these terms."

"That deal is off the table," said Kietel.

Maeve's eyes widened.

Ambrose's chin lowered.

"I have a new deal," said Kietel. "Her."

Maeve's heart kicked.

"No," said Mal.

Kietel looked to Mal. "You can join us too, Dread Prince. But that is the new deal. She fights for me."

"In exchange for what?" Ambrose said sharply.

Kietel looked at him like it was obvious. "The lives of thousands Ambrose."

"Kill them all," said Mal. "She is leaving here with me."

Kietel looked at him now. "That doesn't sound very Princely."

"Do you see me in a crown?" Asked Mal darkly.

Mal's Magic was pulsing, pushing out from him. Maeve could feel it around her neck. Winding up, preparing to strike.

"You and I could be quite powerful together," said Kietel.

"I don't need your help," said Mal.

"I am not suggesting you do. Only that it would be beneficial for us to be allies. The real enemy slithers among us, leeching off our power, lining his pockets, and maintaining stolen power."

"You think that after hurting someone close to me, I would want to join you?" Asked Mal calmly.

"Ah, but she's fine, isn't she? And you're going to find that your methods won't gain you much popularity amongst those in power. Or do you plan to usurp them, anyway?"

Mal never broke their gaze. "You will never know."

All hell broke loose then.

The shield wall between them burst with a howling of wind. The finger Kietel had pointed at Maeve snapped in two with a crack. Mal and Ambrose Obscured in a blink. Ambrose toppled Maeve to the floor.

The room turned to pure darkness. Maeve looked up as Mal was a swirling flame of green crackling death, black sparks undulating from the one finger he pointed at the ground.

Maeve was only able to see the look of anguish on Kietel's face before her body flipped over and she was pressed against cool white marble tile. Everything around her fell silent.

She pressed into her palms as her vision focused on the foyer at Sinclair Estates. Reeve stood leaned against the wall, his arms folded over his chest. His eyes slid to her with a gloomy expression.

She leaned back on her knees to catch her breath and looked around. Her father had sent her alone. She ran her fingers across her wrists, where a dullness still lingered, but the moonstone shackles had vanished.

"Are you alright?"

Maeve looked back at the High Lord of Aterna. He was dressed in casual clothes, no suit of armor for war or velvet tux for pleasure. Just a simple pair of pants and a shirt suitable for a human. But nothing about Reeve was human. His face was too glorious. The power in his golden eyes flickered with fire.

Maeve nodded. "Why weren't you there?"

Reeve looked away from her, slightly annoyed. "It was voted best I not attend."

She opened her mouth to speak but sucked in a quick breath instead. Magic lifted around her.

"Woah," she said with a shutter.

"What?" Asked Reeve, and stepped towards her.

Maeve couldn't explain it, but Kietel was dead. The lurking unfamiliar Magic that had plagued her for months was gone.

She looked up at him. He was closer now. His chest sunk and his mouth turned down.

"Who the fuck did that to you?"

Maeve had nearly forgotten her bruised face and split lip. "Who do you think?"

Reeve looked down at her. His mouth opened to speak, but he closed it. He looked down at her in remorse. She held his gaze for a moment.

"The most powerful being in the world," she said softly. "And you let him take me."

His remorse vanished. "You know nothing of controlling something like what is inside of me."

"You hesitated-"

"I calculated," he spat down at her.

With a snap Ambrose and Mal appeared in the foyer.

She was on her feet in a flash. Ambrose slammed into her. The smell of cinnamon cigars warmed her bones. His arms were tight around her. Only when his thick wool cloak turned wet did she realize she was crying.

She unburied her head from his chest, resting her cheek on him. Mal stood only steps away, his eyes locked on her, watching every breath she took.

Ambrose took her face in his hands, forcing her gaze up at him. Small sparks of Magic popped through her cheek, healing the bruised skin with a warm glow. He pressed his thumb into her lip, sealing up the cut.

She looked up at him. He pressed a kiss into her hair and released her.

Maeve stepped towards Mal, stopping as his Magic brushed down her cheek, cool and calming. She felt as though she might burst into tears once more as he smiled softly at her, worry still filled in his eyes.

He had been magnificent. The very definition of divine violence. And he had done it for her.

"How long have you known?" Asked Maeve, looking at her father.

He looked to Mal and then back to Maeve. He answered without hesitation. "I've known since the moment he laid you on that hospital bed in the Healing Hall last year."

Maeve's throat tightened.

Ambrose looked at Mal reverently. "It's time, Malachite."

Maeve looked to Mal.

"I know," he said.

"We need to call a Hexadic," said Reeve.

"I don't know why it's still called that," said Ambrose. "Only four realms truly remain occupied and you know as well as I do we will be lucky if three even attend."

"Lithandrian will be intrigued by him," said Reeve.

"And the other? Do you have contact?"

Reeve shook his head.

Ambrose looked back at Maeve and Mal.

"Reeve and I need to discuss some things."

"No,' said Maeve. "You're not going to exclude us."

"She's right," said Reeve.

Ambrose ignored him. "There is no place for you in a war meeting," said Ambrose.

"That is your blind love for me as your daughter talking and not the mind of the Premier," retorted Maeve.

"Yes," hissed Ambrose as he stepped towards her. "And I shall sleep at night for it."

"Ambrose," said Reeve calmly.

Her father looked towards the High Lord. Ambrose's face twisted. "You are siding with a child."

"I'm not a child-"

"I think it's time we stopped under-estimating power," he replied. "Regardless of its age. You must acknowledge what she and Malachite have to offer."

"You are thinking of her as one of your Senshi Warriors," said Ambrose, his teeth grinding together.

"I am thinking of *them* as strong Magicals, Ambrose. That boy single-handedly held up Vaukore as the magic around it collapsed. Ancient magic. And I am to understand he only killed Kietel only moments ago?"

"His entire army too," said Ambrose quietly.

Maeve loosed a tight breath.

"Fine, then Mal alone comes," said Ambrose.

Mal finally spoke. "No, sir." His voice was velvety smooth. "I'm sorry. Not without her."

A surge of emotion shot through Maeve at his words.

Finally.

Ambrose's face was drained of its usual warm color as he looked at Mal. Mal's right hand slowly turned into a fist, as he placed it over his heart. He looked directly at Ambrose, whose eyes grew large at the gesture.

"I swore to you that I would protect her," said Mal. His eyes slid to her. "I will die before she does."

An electric burst of Magic sliced through her chest. Maeve let out an audible gasp. It tingled down her arms and into her fingers. She held up her hands, observing them, as Mal's Magic shot through her fingertips, becoming one with her own Magic.

"What did you just do?" She asked quietly.

Mal's eyes remained on her, perfectly aware of what he had just done. Maeve's eyes grew large, and she took another step towards him.

The moment between them was silent. Maeve had never wanted to touch his face so badly, to kiss his lips and confess all the bottled-up thoughts she was too scared to say.

Mal would die before she did. It was now written in Magic. Unbreakable Magic sealed in an unbreakable bond between them.

"Zimsy," said Ambrose.

The gorgeous Elf appeared instantly. Maeve tore her eyes away from Mal. A look of relief washed across Zimsy's face when she saw Maeve. Maeve smiled softly at her.

"Help Maeve refresh herself. My daughter won't be attending a war meeting in blood and dirty pajamas."

Zimsy nodded. They ascended the stairs silently.

In her bedroom, Zimsy flung her arms around her. Maeve hugged her tightly back.

Maeve pulled away as a knock came from the door. Zimsy turned the knob and Mal stood, his eyes glazed over at Maeve.

"Could you give us a moment?" Mal asked.

Zimsy bowed her head and slipped past him into the hallway.

Mal stepped inside and the door clicked shut behind him.

Maeve sighed into the sedating feeling of his presence. "Why did you do that?"

He studied her face closely.

"Because I mean it," was all he said.

Maeve's breath hitched, and her mouth hung open.

His hands reached for her face.

At last.

His cool, smooth hands fused with her flushed cheeks.

"I'm filthy Mal-"

"When the castle began falling, and you looked at me like you were going to die, I nearly couldn't bear it. I don't think I could have done what I did if that fear hadn't been there. I was determined that you would live, or I would die trying to save you."

Tears pooled in the corners of Maeve's eyes. He wiped each of them as they cascaded down her dirty cheeks.

"I realized then," said Mal, looking back and forth at her tears, "that while I will always save you, I was meant to save us all. I was meant to save the Magicals, or die trying."

"I'm scared of what's coming," said Maeve, her voice catching. "I'm scared I'm not strong enough. I'm not like you. I don't have your iron reserve."

"You don't have to be like me," he said quietly. "Your strengths are not my own, either. I need you to be you."

"I jumped," she said.

Mal's eyes lit up. "What? When?"

"Kietel made me," she said. "But I did it."

Mal's chest rose and fell in a steady rhythm.

He pulled her head to his chest, and she snaked her arms around his torso, palms flat against his back. He kissed the top of her head and spoke calmly.

"I am going to reform the Dread House and reclaim our place as Magicals in the promised land."

Maeve nuzzled closer to him. "I knew you would."

"And you will be my second, Maeve."

She looked up at him, pride building in her chest. Not his High Lady. Not his Queen. Not his wife.

His second in command.

"Does that make you happy?" He asked with a subtle smile, one that showed he already knew the answer.

Maeve nodded, her own smile blossoming. "Yes," she breathed.

His eyes traveled down to her lips as his hands shifted lower on her body.

Her stomach flipped.

"I thought it might," he said, barely above a whisper.

She pushed onto her toes and he met her halfway, bending down to press his lips into hers. He held her waist firmly as she tipped backward, his tongue quickly finding its way into her mouth.

She let out a soft moan as his tongue played with hers. The sound turned him hard against her. Maeve smiled into their kiss, knowing how quickly she excited him. He pushed them backward until she hit the writing desk. He nipped at her bottom lip and pulled away from her. Maeve's breathing was fast, the heat between her legs growing intense.

His hands moved to the dirty pearl buttons of her pajama top, working from the bottom up. When the fabric fell loose. His expression softened into a dull look of hunger.

Maeve gripped the desk on either side of her hips. Her body was hot. Too hot. Her cheeks were burning from the intense vulnerability she was trapped in under his gaze.

Mal's eyes traced over every inch of her chest. His long, slender fingers reached out and caressed the side of her breast.

A slow breath rose up through her. His fingers were icy and smooth. She was stuck. Paralyzed from his touch.

"I thought about you ceaselessly," he said. "I don't think I quite understood the meaning of your presence until I was forced to endure your absence."

His hand moved down her stomach, slowly, sending ice across her skin. She gripped the desk harder and willed herself to stay still and not push every inch of herself towards him.

"I wondered if he was hurting you. . . touching you."

Maeve gasped as his hand slipped between her skin and the top of her pants. His fingers danced along the band, teasing her.

"I only hate that I didn't see you end him," said Maeve.

Mal took a deep breath. "I will end each and every one of them that tries to take what is mine."

"The Dread Lands?" She asked as his hand pulled out from between her stomach and her pants.

A darkness formed on Mal's face. "You." His eyes bore into hers with a lethal rage so calm it should have been unsettling. "You are mine."

Maeve couldn't hold herself still any longer. She pushed off the desk and stepped towards him hastily, eager for more of his taste, his bite. His hand caught her throat, gently squeezing and keeping her back.

"Bathe, Sinclair." He grinned in satisfaction. "You are positively filthy."

Chapter 38

It was difficult to listen to The Disintis ramble on endlessly when Maeve's thoughts continuously drifted back to the way Mal's hands felt across her chest. Especially when Mal seemed equally bored and kept sending little wafts of magic winding up her legs. Each one growing higher and higher.

No one objected to their being there. Everyone knew what Mal had done, and soon they'd know who he was.

The Disintis was a Magical. Each of the realms in attendance had rolled a die in order to see who orchestrated the meeting and held the title of Grand Disintis for the duration of the meeting. The Magicals won the roll. And so Orator Moon's Press Secretary stepped forward.

Maeve learned that The Orator and her father had an agreement: as soon as the humans dropped those bombs, they stopped all communication between the legal and militant sides of the government. Reeve had been right. Kietel and his rebels were watching and attacking the fires and Portals. It was better that Moon and her father were in the dark of one another's moves.

The Queen of the Elven Realm was in attendance. She brought with her an audience, as did Reeve. Their inner circles and courts and high-ranking officials all came.

Ambrose Portaled Mal and Maeve personally to The Dark Planet, where Shadow Magic once flourished and thrived. It was now an unoccupied realm, completely deserted.

Neutral ground.

They gathered in what once was an amphitheater, with open air and stacked seating. The sky above was in a perpetual state of twilight. The Dark Planet's star system was nothing like Earth's. Multiple moons and foreign stars.

Finally, Reeve interrupted Moon's secretary.

"Grand Disintis," said Reeve in a bored tone. "Do you have a point?"

He looked at Reeve incredulously. "I think the point is that we cannot afford to compromise our forces any further."

Two men sat on either side of Reeve. One Maeve recognized from the Summer Solstice Party. He was part Elven. His long white hair lay flat down his back. His tipped ears were covered with piercings that looped through one another. He watched the room with careful caution. His hands crossed in his lap. His sword a grab away.

To Reeve's left was an Immortal, like himself. He looked years younger than Maeve. His hair was chocolate brown. The sides were shaved completely. He, like Reeve, wore a set of Vexkari tattoos, on the shaved parts of his head. His bow and arrows slung around his back. He reclined against the stone seating with his legs crossed.

"How many have you lost, Premier?" A musical, childlike voice said.

Lithandrian, Queen of the Elven Lands, sat next to her husband. Her skin glowed like moonstone and her delicate features were like Zimsy's, like those of a bird. Her hair was golden with spirals of white running through it. It was braided intricately atop her head. Elves were not Immortal, but they lived far longer than Magicals, hundreds of years sometimes.

"A third," replied Ambrose.

Arman was at his side. Rowan was there too, his usual scowl was present rows behind Ambrose, along with the top Bellator. Orator Moon and his cabinet from The Double O were next to them.

"You called this meeting Ambrose," said Lithandrian. "I hope it was worth traveling to his forsaken planet." She smiled at him.

Ambrose smiled back. He stood and addressed the room, his hands behind his back. "My duty to Magicals is clear: protect. The vows I took as a Bellator, then as a Magical Militia, then as a Captain, and then as The Premier were not taken lightly. I will always do as my conscious dictates to protect the innocent from any evil power that seeks to corrupt or destroy. It is my honor as The Premier of the only Magical race of people left to introduce you all to Malachite Peur."

Ambrose gestured to Mal. Maeve looked up at him.

Mal stood. Abraxas had picked his attire. It was modest and simple, almost plain, as to not draw attention to himself, but to his words.

"My name is Malachite Peur," he said, calculated charm and just enough humility oozing out of every word he spoke. "I'm honored to sit among you, the most renowned and powerful leaders, minds, and fighters across our worlds."

"You are the boy who held up Vaukore," said Lithandrian. "And who killed Kietel."

Malachite nodded. "My mother was a Human-born Witch. And my Father was descended from Artemis Orion the Dread. I am the last of House Dread. And the first in three hundred years to wield their Magic in my veins."

The shift that slammed through the room caused pride to well up in Maeve.

Maeve looked to her father, expecting a smile. But Ambrose was not. He sat straight up and his gaze drifted slowly throughout the room.

When his eyes landed on Mal, he gave him a small nod.

"The Premier and I have discussed these matters at great lengths. I have no intention of running from my destiny," said Mal. "But there is an order. I do not wish to throw our world out of balance."

"Balance?" Said Lithandrian. "From where I am sitting there is nothing but chaos on Earth." Lithandrian observed him with watchful eyes as she said, "What says the High Lord of Aterna?"

Reeve was kicked back with his hands behind his head.

Reeve was silent. In fact, he ignored her completely. The Grand Disintis cleared his throat softly. Reeve looked at him and then at Lithandrian.

"Oh, doth she speak to me?" He asked in an affected tone. "I thought surely after three centuries of the silent treatment you'd have something more interesting to say than that."

Lithandrian's tongue ran across her top teeth.

Reeve stared at her casually, his head resting on the back of his seat and his arms folded across his chest. His voice returned to its normal timbre. "The High Lord is gladly and dutifully remaining in alliance with the Magicals."

Lithandrian looked towards Ambrose. "And what say you?"

"I must be missing the part where you were put in charge of this meeting," said Reeve.

Lithandrian did not look to him again.

Orator Moon answered defensively. "Malachite is well aware The Orator's Office supports his claim. I will do my duty as an elected official to the people."

"Premier-" Lithandrian started.

Reeve groaned.

"I am merely curious about the state of things, High Lord. Do not forget it is I who was begged to attend this meeting today. It is my realm whom you desire alliances with."

"It is not just alliances that are desired," said Maeve, the words slipping from her mouth. "It is about returning to a Magical utopia, where all realms lived in harmony."

At last, her gaze fell upon Maeve. She studied her for a moment, as though she hadn't noticed her presence yet.

"I don't believe we've met."

"My name is Maeve Sinclair," she answered without hesitation.

Lithandrian's eyes widened slightly.

"Can I see?"

Maeve didn't move.

"Come now," said Lithandrian. "I've heard rumor you are capable of ensnaring the mind entirely. I want to see."

"No." Ambrose spoke with authority. "This is the most important meeting in a century. She can show off for you later if that is what you desire."

Lithandrian smiled at Ambrose.

"And why is your daughter present?" She asked with no condemnation in her sing-song voice.

"Maeve is to be my second," answered Mal.

Lithandrian looked over at her husband. He sat to her right, just as Maeve was at Mal's. She smiled knowingly. "Entangled, aren't we?"

"Actually, I am confused about why you were begged to be here," said Reeve. "What does the Elven land offer us? You have no magic." Reeve shrugged.

"My army is thrice the size of your Senshi Immortals," she replied with a laugh. "Perhaps I misheard you just lost a third of your Magical Militia, Premier?"

"I thought the goal was harmony," said Reeve. "What do we need armies for?"

"The blight," said Mal. "I will need armies to fight that darkness."

The room was silent for a moment. Reeve's all too casual demeanor vanished. "Indeed, you will."

"You are not the first to claim the Dread Lands," said Lithandrian. "How can we be certain of your Magic? I believe your Magical Government was nearly overturned not a fortnight ago."

"Kietel did not come close to overthrowing the Magicals," said Mal with a soft smile. "And I do not wish to overthrow. My only goal is to return my people to their planet, where their magic can flourish. I do not wish to seek power by force or topple governments. I desire to restore Dread Magic and our home," said Mal.

The Magicals in the room stood at once, their fists placed over their hearts in a motion of honor. Maeve watched Lithandrian. Her brows flicked up.

"It seems you have already moved some of your kind. But it will take time for change to be accepted," said Lithandrian. "I wish you the best, Malachite Peur."

Mal bowed his head at the Elven Queen. "I do not take your affection lightly. Your allegiance would mean a great deal in writing the wrongs of the past."

"Stay the course," said Lithandrian. "And you shall have it."

Mal smiled at her with reverent charm.

Lithandrian looked back to Ambrose. "Did you receive a reply from the Hiems?"

Ambrose shook his head.

"To be expected. Kier and his ice planet have cut all contact with the other realms." She looked back to Mal. "You should travel to him, young Dread Prince. I promise he would open that wall of ice for you."

Kier and his people lived in a realm Maeve knew little about aside from the fact that it was perpetually a frozen land, and Kier, a human, had been King there for years. He closed their planet from all other realms the day his father died and he was crowned.

Giants, werewolves, goblins, centaurs, and all sorts of winged human-like creatures occupied Kier's ice planet called Hiems.

"Thank you," Mal replied to Lithandrian.

"You ended one war just to begin another," she said softly. "I was a child when that shadow overtook the Dread Lands. My father was a picture of strength. I never saw fear in his eyes until that shadow came for us. Rest assured, young wizard, it is still there, lurking in the Dark Peaks, sinking in the Black Deep, and buried in the vines and roots that snake across the land."

Mal nodded at her.

Ambrose spoke now. "Mal's coronation will be on the thirty-first of December in four months' time. We have all been given a choice. The Dread Lands are neither your burden Queen Lithandrian nor yours, High Lord of Aterna. But should you decide to aid us in our fight, that is the day to pledge yourself as allies."

Chapter 39

It had been Maeve's idea to hold Mal's coronation on his birthday. He would be twenty-two on New Year's Eve.

They had four months to find the Dread Armor and charm the Magical World.

Ambrose brought them back to Sinclair Estates after the meeting with the other realms.

"That went well," said Ambrose lightly.

Mal looked to her father. "I think so."

Ambrose stopped and turned towards him.

"Regardless of your speech, which I think you truly mean, you threaten to destroy the power that is already in play," said Ambrose. "It will not be given to you without a fight."

Mal nodded.

"But Lithandrian like you," continued Ambrose with a chuckle. "Which is unheard of."

"Why doesn't Reeve like her?" Asked Maeve.

"The High Lord," he corrected, "and Lithandrian have never gotten along to my knowledge."

"They both turned their back on Magicals three hundred years ago," said Maeve. "It seems like they are perfect company."

Ambrose stared at her for a moment and then spoke. "Reeve's father and Lithandrian's father were responsible for that. Reeve is our greatest ally. If you are to be Mal's second, you need to learn to forget the past and make moves calculated towards a future."

Maeve nodded.

"You can continue to stay here Malachite," said Ambrose. "Until we secure you a place of your own."

"What about the Hapswitch House?"

"The flat in London?"

Maeve nodded. "It's been vacant for years. Since Uncle A died."

Mal looked to Ambrose.

"I can take you to see it today," said Ambrose.

Mal nodded. "Thank you, sir."

"And," said Maeve tentatively. "While we are gone, it can be prepared for Mal to move in."

"Gone?" He asked.

Maeve looked to Mal.

"So," said Ambrose, looking back and forth between Mal and Maeve, "you'll be leaving in a few days to track down this Dread Armor?"

Maeve hesitated. "We don't want to waste any time."

"Tomorrow then?" Her Father asked as he understood.

"Tomorrow," answered Maeve.

Ambrose's face fell flat with disappointment that he attempted to hide. "You're really not going to finish school, Maeve?"

"Really not."

Mal had saved Vaukore. And it was being pieced back together and new Magic poured into it every day. Rowan resigned as Headmaster and Larliesl took his and Elgin's place as interim Headmaster. Elgin was alive, but Maeve's Dread Magic had paralyzed her spine. She was a permanent resident at The Restoration, the Healing hospital where Alphard and Astrea's mother worked. Elgin was a medical prisoner there and would face charges of conspiracy and attempted murder.

Most Magicals were too afraid to send their children back to Vaukore. But Mal had plans to remedy that.

Ambrose clapped his hands together and nodded. He moved to step away from them.

"We'd like to discuss something with you, sir," said Mal. "Privately."

"Of course," said Ambrose, making for the stairs to his office.

"Actually, Daddy," said Maeve, "we need to go downstairs."

Ambrose stopped suddenly. He turned towards them slowly with a mischievous grin developing.

"Say no more," he said. "Meet me there in thirty minutes."

When his footsteps disappeared around the corner, Mal looked over at her. Maeve exhaled under his piercing gaze and leaned against the wall behind her.

"You don't want me here?" He asked quietly, a taunting in his voice.

"No," whispered Maeve, looking up at him and tucking her hands behind her back. "I want a place far from this house where you and I can be."

"Clever girl."

Maeve bit her bottom lip.

Maeve followed Mal and her father down into the basement. It had been a long time since she visited there.

The main corridor was lined with portraits of every patriarch from the Sinclair bloodline. At the very end was Antony, peacefully sleeping in a large armchair. Next to him was an empty portrait, meant for her father. On the other side of her father was Grandfather Alyicious and so on.

The corridor opened into the large basement room, with the giant dragon skull and skin as the room's centerpiece.

Maeve had not been exaggerating when she recounted her childhood memories of the Sinclair Estate basement to Mal. With its vaulted ceiling, carved statues, a hundred shelves filled with nothing but dark artifacts, glass jars filled with strange potions and materials, illegal potions made centuries ago, trunks and cases that seemed to whisper things as they walked by, it lived up to her description.

It was like a glorified antiquities store, only it was filled with much more dark magic than was allowed under current legal regulations.

Ambrose had stacks of books that were enchanted just to hold themselves up. In the center of the room was a seating area with a large mahogany table in the very middle.

Maeve began walking around, looking inquisitively at all the artifacts. She didn't understand many as a child, and many she still did not understand.

"The stone you spoke about last summer, the broken one," said Mal.

"Ah, yes," said Ambrose excitedly. "You need it?"

Mal nodded. "And we're prepared to find the other half."

Ambrose's face turned serious.

"Maeve," he called.

She looked at him.

"You know what's in those caves?" Asked Ambrose.

Maeve nodded and gave her father a confident look. Ambrose nodded back and turned back to Mal. They didn't stand a chance of finding the Dread Crown across miles of heavily forested terrain without it.

Maeve reached for a small leather-bound book that was high on a shelf. She pulled it down and began flipping through its pages. She heard Ambrose rummaging through wooden boxes.

"Here it is," said Ambrose, turning and dropping the stone into Mal's palm.

Maeve replaced the book and made her way over to them. They examined the stone while Ambrose was pulling maps out of a long, thin drawer.

It was a small obsidian-colored stone with a few faded carvings that Maeve couldn't make out.

Ambrose rolled out a hand-drawn map on the table near them.

"This is the map my father drew," said Ambrose. He pointed to a grouping of mountain ranges. "These caves are where Uncle Alian admitted to storing all of the treasures he stole." Ambrose turned the map slightly. "These three are the only ones we never fully explored."

Maeve took a seat in one of the armchairs and scrutinized the map.

"This one," she said, pointing to one spot in particular, "is the only one that worries me. Based on the terrain in the area and the waterfalls, I believe there's a chance it has already flooded."

"It's been a few years since I was there," said Ambrose.

"We won't know until we're there," said Mal. He turned to Ambrose. "Thank you, sir."

Ambrose grinned. "Which one is first on your list?"

Mal smiled. It was feline. Captivating. Deadly. "The Crown."

On the morning of their departure, Maeve and Mal walked past the front gates of Sinclair Estates, beyond its Magical borders, Ambrose close on their heels.

Maeve charmed the pockets in their cloaks to hold everything they needed for their trip.

"Ready?" Ambrose asked.

They nodded and grabbed hold of him.

He counted to three and the tree line blurred out of view as he Obscured them to The Alps.

The bright orange morning sunlight at Sinclair Estates twisted into hues of grey and blue. They landed on slick ground, steps away from a large cliff, overlooking a dense forest. Tops of green trees shot out of swirly grey fog. Clouds were brewing with a distant rumble.

Ambrose and Mal clasped hands.

"Thank you, sir."

Ambrose kissed Maeve's cheek. "Be careful, please," he said with raised brows.

He twisted out of view before Maeve could ensure him she would.

Mal pulled the map out of his cloak and pinpointed where they were. They began walking along a makeshift trail of rocky terrain; the paths were overgrown and steep. They passed the entrance to a cave that Ambrose and Maeve's grandfather had already explored a decade prior. They walked silently for half an hour.

Thunder clapped behind them, and they picked up their pace. Within another half hour, light raindrops hit her face. They pulled up the hoods of their cloaks, and soon after, the sky fell out.

"It's not much farther," called Mal from ahead.

They traveled for another few minutes before coming to a large river that ran fast and deep. Boulders and rocks jetted out from the crashing, swirling stream. Maeve looked in the direction the water was coming from, and there was a large opening.

"This is the first cave," yelled Mal over the storm.

"This is what I was worried about," shouted Maeve.

Mal cast his right hand forward and sent a giant light beam into the cave. It hovered in the cave for a moment then exploded like a firework before it disappeared.

"There's a dry landing in there. I can see it," yelled Mal.

Several lightning strikes followed a large boom of thunder.

"It's too dark!" Replied Maeve.

Obscuring without fully being able to see your destination was incredibly dangerous.

Mal took Maeve's hand and exhaled loudly, preparing himself. The sound of their disappearance couldn't be heard over the storm. Maeve's stomach twisted in a knot, and then they landed safely inside the cave, soaking wet. Her lux charm illuminated at once.

She looked up at Mal. His brows flicked up. She nodded in admittance of being wrong. She snapped her fingers, drying them both instantly.

Maeve cast small flames ahead of them, lighting their way and attempting to stay warm as they ventured into the cave. Much of the cave was flooded, as Maeve expected. She lowered her hood.

They Obscured from dry landing to landing, going deeper into the mountain. The cave walls split off in two directions, creating two paths. One was dry, and one continued like the path they were already on, where small patches of rocks peeked out above the water.

They decided to explore the dry path first. This path turned narrow quickly. After some time it opened into a large cavern with many openings and crevices. There was a giant, pitch-black lake at the center of the chamber. It was so flat and still that it looked like slick grease on the ground.

Many of the openings were small dark holes in the walls, with nothing in them. They walked through the larger opening, exploring each smaller cave inside. They continued deeper into the cave. The pathway became wetter the farther they traveled.

Maeve was getting too cold for her liking. The bottom few inches of her cloak were continually soaked, and the farther they traveled, the colder the cave became.

They searched all morning and all afternoon. It was likely dark outside by now. Their path turned back to deep-running waters, and they Obscured to small rocks that emerged above the water.

They came to a fork in the cave that looked familiar.

"Is that the way we came in?" Asked Maeve.

She followed Mal in the opposite direction from which she was pointing. It opened up into the large cavern with the dark lake in the center.

"We've made a circle," said Mal.

Maeve took off her cloak and dried it quickly with a spell.

"Now what?" Asked Maeve.

Mal thought for a moment before answering.

"I want to be sure all of these caves in here have been thoroughly searched, and I'll go check the conditions outside."

Mal disappeared with a POP. Maeve threw back on her dry cloak, wrapping it tightly around her. He reappeared a moment later.

"I don't think we'll be able to travel to the next cave in this storm tonight. The rain and wind are washing out the path, and I can't see enough ahead to Obscure," said Mal.

"So we're staying here for the time being?" Asked Maeve.

Mal nodded.

"I'll start searching again over here then," said Maeve.

She made her way over to some of the caves. Mal went in the opposite direction. They called it quits after carefully searching for any hidden holes or areas, to no avail.

Mal seated himself on the ground and crossed his legs underneath him. He studied the map, playing with the stone in his other hand. Maeve pulled out a tiny glass plate and placed it on the ground between them. She pointed two fingers at it and it grew in size. She kneeled down and placed her palm on the glass. She yanked her hand away just as a fire burst forward, traveling to the edges of the plate.

She seated herself next to it on the floor of the cave and watched Mal intently.

The ground in the cave wasn't comfortable to sleep on. Maeve didn't actually remember falling asleep. She rolled over onto her back.

A low, strange sound was coming from somewhere in the cave. Maeve sat up.

The fire was out, and Mal was gone. His cloak was draped over her.

The strange sound grew louder. She sent a ball of light into the air above her and turned behind her. The black water of the lake that had previously been sleek and still now had small bubbles popping across the surface.

Maeve's breathing quickened. She placed her hands behind her and began to scoot away from the lake. The gurgling sound became loud now. Something was in the water. Maeve stood to her feet, still backing away from the pool.

She was afraid to call Mal's name for fear of disturbing whatever was lurking in the dark water. The bubbles along the surface grew large as the creature rose higher in the water. The opening out of the chamber was farther than Maeve would have liked.

The noise from the water grew in pitch, getting louder and louder. Maeve quickened her pace. The sharp noise grew and grew until water soared into the air and the cave filled with the shrillest and most unsettling scream Maeve had ever heard.

Maeve jumped and her heart stopped as a giant creature burst forth from under the water, with eight octopus legs flailing about. It was pale green, at least twenty feet tall, with a large mouth and razor-sharp teeth. Two wiry arms with scaling long fingers slammed into the ground. Its glassy eyes locked on her.

She had seen its picture in school, but never imaged they grew this large. The Water Demon towered above her in the cave.

Grendel. Grindylow. They were called many names. But Maeve knew one thing for certain: as terrifying as its teeth and claws were, it was going to try to drown her.

She shot a stunning spell at the beast. Blue light sparked from her fingers. But the water demon screamed and pulled itself fully out of the water. She turned and ran towards the opening. One of its long tentacles slammed into the ground next to her, the impact knocking her over, and the floor of the cave shattered.

She scrambled to get back up, but the Grindylow grabbed her ankle tightly, and it started pulling her towards the water.

Maeve took aim and pointed directly at the tentacle wrapped around her ankle.

The water demon screamed as Maeve scorched it with fire. Maeve cried out too as her skin burned.

She pushed off the ground and started running towards the way out once more, desperately shooting defensive spells behind her. Mal appeared at the entryway, a ball of green light swirling at his hand. His eyes went wide upon seeing the Grindylow, and he ran towards Maeve.

But he was far. So far.

One of the tentacles grabbed ahold of her leg this time, sending her crashing to the ground. She strained and aimed for the demon's face, but a second muscular tentacle wrapped around her waist, crushing her.

Her mouth opened in silent agony as her ribs caved in and the Grindylow dragged her towards the water.

"Maeve!" Mal screamed, but he was too far away.

His screams disappeared in an instant as the Grindylow pulled Maeve under the black water. The Grindylow jerked her down further and further until her head felt like it was going to explode. She mustered up what Magic she had and sent it barreling towards the monster.

It howled and gripped her harder. Pink and white spots appeared in her vision.

The Grindylow stopped suddenly. Maeve managed to open her eyes, but she could barely see through the murky water. The creature was horrific. Its oblong mouth hung open, exposing hundreds of teeth.

Maeve couldn't hold her breath any longer. She knew she wasn't supposed to, but her body betrayed her. She sucked in. Water poured in through her mouth and nose.

The Dread Ring, which hung about her neck, floated up into her line of vision. The Grindylow extended one tentacle slowly towards the ring. Before the tentacle touched the ring, it began pulsating, sending ripples out into the water. Slowly at first, then larger bolts of energy.

Maeve felt a surge of hope.

The Grindylow frowned and tightened its grip on Maeve. She winced and more water filled her lungs. The ring fell still for a moment, and Maeve's heart dropped.

Her body became nothing. Everything faded into blackness.

Chapter 40

She was drowning. He could feel it. Her heart was beating faster than he knew a heart should beat.

Pure fear overtook her senses.

She's screaming. She's drowning.

She's going to die.

It was just like at Vaukore. Just like when Kietel had her. This feeling. On the edge of losing her was unbearable. His lungs constricted. His hands went numb.

Water filled her lungs.

Water shouldn't be there.

He fell to his knees with his fists balled up at his sides.

His magic was beating against his head. Against his hands. Tearing at his skin. It screamed at him viciously, just as it had the times he lost control before.

Like those times at the orphanage.

I can't lose her. I can't.

And that time with Valeria.

I can't lose her.

And with Kietel. He hadn't just killed him and his traitorous army. He had shattered every bone in their bodies. Drained them of every drop of blood.

It was breaking through the walls of his mind, overtaking his senses, his ability to see and breathe. It pounded through him, in synch with his heart.

Let me destroy let me rip let me go, it screamed. *I can save her.*

His eyes closed. And he took one last controlled breath.

And then he let go.

Magic flooded into his mind.

Bring her to me, he commanded that power.

Dark and dirty and free magic poured out of him. It slithered across the wet stone and dove into the water.

The Grindylow's piercing scream was short. Its tentacles loosened around Maeve's body. The pale green water demon suspended in the water. His own Magic circled her and drew her to the surface.

She didn't gasp for air as her face broke the water.

Those black streams of magic carried her to him. He took her body in his arms, laying her across his lap. She wasn't breathing. He pushed the hair out of her face.

"Maeve."

His voice shook. His Magic swirled around them. It flew from behind Mal's shoulder, straight to her mouth. Her eyes flew open, and she shot up. Mal held her firmly on his lap.

Water poured from her mouth. She was soaking wet. Her hair was stringy and clinging to her cheeks and down her back. She was frantic. Her gaze darted around him, her breathing everywhere with violent water-spewing coughs.

He held her, and she tried to push away. The cold water seeped into his own clothes.

He reached for her face, his hands shaking, as Magic trickled across his fingertips. Magic he rarely allowed himself to access. She shook him away violently as more water poured from her mouth.

She was a wreck. She was hyperventilating.

Get control, he told himself, as Magic pushed freely through him.

The alternative was unknown. But last time he didn't, he hurt Valeria.

He grabbed her face once more, his hands slipping across her skin.

Anger was welling up inside him, manifesting from his fear. It swelled inside him like a rip current. He pushed back. Tight. His chest was so tight.

Get control of yourself, he begged.

Maeve's agonizing cry filled the cavern. The sound ripped through him like lightning. He gripped her tightly in response. Too tightly.

But she was too frantic to know he was hurting her, too distressed to feel the Magic pouring from his hands involuntarily.

Control, goddamit-

He pushed down and down and down but that darkness pushed back with every jagged breath she took.

She was crying now. It was a cry he had never heard from another human. Pain. Fear. Relief.

He couldn't bring himself to look at her leg. He was too afraid the sight of her injury would create a burning inside him strong enough to take the entire mountain down.

If I could just see her eyes-

He grabbed her forcefully now, hands shaking. Leaving her no room to thrash away.

There.

Her face was dripping wet. The whites of her eyes were pink. Her black lashes clumped together wetly.

But her eyes. Those sapphire blue eyes sparkled up at him despite all else. They would be the end of him. He had been captivated by them since the first time she glared at him.

And then the first time she smiled at him. It had not been a smile of joy. She smiled at him like a cornered lion, ready to play. No one had ever looked at him that way. Like they were up for the challenge.

But she was his challenge.

He stroked her cheeks and placed his forehead on hers.

"Breathe," he said to both of them.

And they did.

His hands stilled. The veins in his arms and neck retreated.

And they breathed in synchrony. In and out. In and out.

"It hurts," she cried, sniffling sharply.

"Your leg?" He asked.

In and out. Inhale and exhale.

"My ribs," she said. "It hurts to breathe."

In and out. In and out.

Mal's hands moved to her ribs. She winced as he pressed into them. He was no healer. But he could get her breathing properly.

He pressed a healing spell through his palms and fingertips. Magic wrapped around her. She relaxed ever so slightly.

"Better?"

She nodded up at him.

Mal breathed deeply. That darkness in him fully retreated. He was in control once more.

Mal stroked her face, gently wiping away her tears. "That's it," he said, encouragingly. "We need to get out of here. Hold on."

She wrapped her arms around his neck, holding him tightly.

With a tight twist and flip of his stomach, they Obscured outside of the cave. Maeve bent forward and vomited as he supported her.

The storm had died down.

He settled her against the stone, cradling her head back against the rock. He pulled from her coat pocket two small vials of potions they brewed for their journey.

"I don't want-" she sniffled with a shiver.

But he was already pulling out the glass stoppers. He placed his free hand under her chin. "Drink," he said, placing the rim of the first vial at her lips.

She obeyed.

And Mal poured the contents into her mouth. She grimaced and her jaw tensed against his hand. The sedative hit her quickly. Her face fell into his hands. He quickly assisted her with the second vial for the pain, but Maeve's eyes were already fluttering closed as she swallowed the smooth liquid.

He pulled her to his lap and brushed her hair out of her face, cradling her head against his shoulder. Her body was still cold and wet. He placed his hand on her chest, drying her clothes and hair instantly.

Warmth was another issue. Creating heat had been one of his only struggles in Charms Class. Fire was nearly impossible, at least one strong enough to help her body get warm.

She shook against him.

He held her close.

"Maeve," he hummed. "Give me warmth and I'll sustain it."

She groaned. She was barely conscious.

"Maeve," he said again.

"Take it." Her voice was hoarse and quiet.

She sighed, and he felt it a moment later: the walls of her Magic slipped open for him completely. Her magic lay there for the taking. Completely vulnerable. Unprotected. Alive. Deadly.

And massive.

She hadn't harnessed a fraction of her power, he knew at once. She merely had a toe dipped in her pool of Magic.

He closed his eyes and willed her fire. At once they were toasty warm. Mal leaned back against the cave wall. The walls around her Magic weaved up the open seam, closing him out.

He looked down at her. Her mouth hung slightly open as her chest rose and fell in an even rhythm.

"You have no idea do you," he whispered. "No idea what lies waiting inside of you."

His hand traced along her jawline.

"I will show you."

Chapter 41

Their journey into the second cave was not as easy. Maeve's ribs were severely bruised from the Water-Demon attack. The bright side was that the second cave was not flooded at all. They illuminated their path and began the journey deep into the mountainside. Maeve's lux charm was enough to light their way. The second cave system was tighter, with a low ceiling. Mal ducked many times under the low stones.

Within the hour, they found signs that Alian Sinclair had used this cave to store some of his treasures. There were numerous wooden chests shoved in smaller caves, all of which were empty.

"I wonder if they were filled with gold or rubies," said Maeve. "And someone, or something, ransacked the cave."

"Let's hope they had no attraction to a broken obsidian stone," said Mal, as they continued deeper into the cave.

They reached the back of the cave and could continue no farther. In the farthest corner was a large oak trunk with the faint marking of the Vaukore crest on it. Maeve kneeled in front of it and unlatched the brass clasps.

There were textbooks, essays, and even a few detention slips. One detention was for setting fireworks off on the grounds. Maeve laughed softly to herself, picturing it.

"What possessed my uncle to hoard all his things away like this?" She muttered.

She picked up an essay for Charms class. Within the first few sentences, she knew her Uncle Alian could not have cared less about Charms class.

She removed a Vaukore embroidered scarf and placed it aside, shifting through the papers. There was no broken stone.

She sat back on her heels and sighed, then began placing all of Uncle Al's things back inside.

"I found it," said Mal from a few feet away.

Maeve struggled to her feet with a groan. Sharp pain shot from her ribs through her leg at her quick movement.

In the middle of the cave was a pile of things covered in brown scraps of paper.

"I think it must have been inside something valuable, and all of this was discarded for the box itself," said Mal, referring to the assortment of objects that appeared to have just been haphazardly thrown to the ground.

Mal held in his hand a very purposefully broken piece of obsidian stone. Maeve recognized the same faded markings from the other stone. He pulled out the stone Ambrose gave them from his coat pocket and held the two together.

"It's a perfect match," said Maeve.

Mal laid the stones next to one another on a high-standing rock, and Maeve pushed her floating light high so they could see.

He ran his hands over the stone, a soft lavender glow emitted from his palm.

They didn't budge.

He tried again, with a stronger, darker repairing spell. Still, nothing happened.

Maeve had the feeling all along they wouldn't be able to repair such a strong Magical object with their own Magical knowledge.

"Those idiots," whispered Maeve, referring to her uncles who broke the stone.

"Looks like it's plan B," said Mal, pocketing the stones. "Take my hand."

Albania was just turning to fall. The climate was cool, which thrilled Maeve greatly having just spent the past two days cold and freezing. They rented a room on the top floor of an inn called Cobbler's Cabin.

They were somehow, as if by Magic, the only guests.

They were forced to make a quick trip to London, to use the fires there to travel to unknown Albania territory. They opted not to stay in an area full of Magicals and retreated south, closer to a more impoverished area of town. Less chance of a familiar face.

Mal insisted that Maeve rest for a day before they continued their journey. She laid on her back, with her head propped on a red pillow, while Mal used a healing charm over her injured ribs and burned ankle. Her shirt was unbuttoned halfway up, exposing the damaged areas.

Precise circular bruises ran the length of her leg from the Grindylow's octopus-like grip.

Mal ran his hands along her ribs and focused his healing on where she said hurt the most. It was difficult to focus on relaying any information to him. His hands across her skin were mesmerizing.

Maeve's eyes were closed. He pressed into a particularly severe area. Maeve whimpered and shot up.

Mal's stare was intense. He watched her endure the pain without complaint. Finally, his Magic dulled the area, and the pain softened. She laid back down with a large breath and a shiver.

His cool fingers moved further down, pressing into her lower ribs.

"I shouldn't have left you," he whispered.

Maeve stared into the fire. "I shouldn't have panicked," she said. "Number one rule, right? I could have killed it with one Dread spell, one you showed me. But. . . Fear overwhelmed everything I thought I knew."

Mal moved his hand slowly back and forth over her ribs, the silvery spell penetrating her skin. Each stroke was like a refreshing gulp of water. She was certain her cheeks were flushed red from his touch.

"I promised your father a safe journey," said Mal.

"Well, that was foolish of him to ask for, knowing the kinds of creatures that lurk in those caves."

"I wasn't aware those things grew so large," said Mal.

"Nor was I," said Maeve, playing with the carpet beneath her.

His hands traveled down her to her leg, cupping her knee in his grip. She peeked down at him. He studied each circular bruise carefully.

He moved tauntingly slow, his smooth fingers gliding across her skin. His fingers wrapped around her calf, grazing the back bend of her knee.

Her hips involuntarily pushed upward.

Mal bent her leg, positioning her knee close to his face. He pressed a slow kiss into her leg, along each bruise. The ache that lingered in each one lifted with every touch of his lips. Maeve was certain he could feel every sensual wave that crashed over her.

She pushed up on her elbows, straining less at the pain in her ribs. Mal gently placed her leg back on the plush carpet.

"Thank you," said Maeve quietly.

"Get some rest," he said. "We still have a long journey."

Chapter 42

They waited four days for the mysterious woman who could repair broken magic to present herself. Ambrose wasn't even sure if she was alive when he proposed their plan B option.

Mal had begun to doubt her existence, but Maeve assured him her father did not entertain fantasy.

They sat at a dusty table on the bottom floor of the Cabin, drinking what Maeve considered a disgrace to the good name of tea after their dinner.

The Innkeeper set down a fourth cup of tea before her, with a hopeful look as he gestured for Maeve to try it. Maeve pretended it was perfect. After The Innkeeper shuffled back to the kitchen happily, she pushed it away.

"Just tell him you don't like it," said Mal, not looking up from his book.

"I did," she said incredulously, gesturing around them. "Three times."

The door to the Inn creaked open slowly, and a tall woman with long black hair stepped through the threshold. She was covered in dark tattoos and colorful piercings. Well-dressed, with lavish jewelry hanging from her neck and running along her fingers.

The woman made her way straight to Maeve and Mal and took a seat at the table. Her eyes were rimmed with dark makeup.

"I am Ismail, young travelers," she spoke with a sensually thick, regional accent, like the Innkeeper. "You travel with something broken that was once strong. Are you in need of mending it?"

Maeve was so surprised, so enthralled by her ability to know such a secret, that she didn't see Mal's face turn cold.

"How did you find us?" Asked Mal, suspicion dripping from his voice.

"Don't fret, young wizard," said Ismail with a smile. "I am drawn to the broken Magic in your pocket."

"That's amazing," said Maeve.

Ismail gave her a smile and a nod.

Mal was still not entirely convinced. He didn't take his cold eyes off Ismail.

"Are you in need of my services?" Asked Ismail, looking directly at Mal.

He contemplated for a moment.

He nodded.

"Come with me," she said, standing.

They did as she asked and followed her out of the Inn, pulling up the hoods to their traveling cloaks. She led them around the corner to a shadowed alleyway, and they passed a plethora of homeless Humans living in makeshift houses in the back alleys.

Ismail turned down another completely vacant alley. She held out her hand silently. Maeve and Mal took her hand, and they Obscured with a faint SNAP.

Maeve's stomach flipped, and they twisted quickly to another alley. Ismail turned and pushed open a small iron gate, leading them along a brick pathway until they reached a small house.

Mal was on full alert next to her, his Magic prepared to strike at any moment.

Ismail held open the front door, extending her hand into the house.

Maeve stepped into the dimly lit room. The walls were lined with potions in all colors. There were giant vases around the room with perfumes leaking from their openings. It was clean and stylish on the inside.

Ismail discarded her coat and walked to the center of the room, to a tall, round table.

"Please," said Ismail, gesturing to the table.

Mal stepped forward and placed the two pieces of the stone on the table. They lowered the hoods of their cloaks.

Ismail leaned over the stones, closing her eyes and inhaling loudly. She did this three times before looking up at Mal.

"I can do it."

"How much will it cost?" Asked Maeve.

Ismail adverted her gaze to Maeve with a strange look on her face.

"How much money?" Clarified Maeve.

"Ah," said Ismail, nodding. "To be clear, young travelers, my flat fee is one hundred rubies or two thousand gold pieces. But this Magic is dark, and it will cost you more than precious stones."

Maeve turned to Mal, who gave her a slight nod. She pulled the money from her pocket and placed a purple drawstring bag on the table.

Ismail poured the contents out and counted each piece. She smiled. She slid one chipped piece of gold to the side, separating it from the rest.

"Ambrose Sinclair sent you?" She asked with a glittering grin.

Mal's magic whipped to attention.

Maeve laughed and sent a soothing bit of her own Magic his way. "Yes. I am his daughter. You can tell that from the coin?"

Ismail picked up the chipped gold piece. "Magical objects hold memories. Things Magicals touch hold memories. When they are damaged and broken, I can see everything." She placed the chipped gold coin back with the rest. "This is his gold." Her eyes flicked up to Maeve. "I know who you are then. Why pay me when you could trick my mind into thinking whatever you want?"

Maeve thought carefully on her response then said, "How do you know I already haven't?"

Ismail grinned at Mal. "Then that makes you The Dread Descendant. I heard a rumor you had appeared."

"From who?"

"Not, who, young wizard. What." She ran her fingers across the broken stone pieces. "I've heard many rumors from the Magic that speaks in only whispers I can hear. I heard rumor that the Premier's daughter cannot enter the minds of others anymore. Quite a disappointment to the Orator's Office. You were on track to be their favorite weapon." Ismail touched the broken stone pieces and inhaled sharply. "Or," her eyes flicked up, "it seems that has changed. You are no longer afraid."

Maeve stared her down for a moment. "Have you ever?" She asked quietly.

"No, little witch, I have never been in another's mind."

Maeve nodded. "That's because you aren't capable. You have no idea what it's like. To make you think a lie is one thing. But to alter one's mind memory and matter is entirely another."

"I imagine you are mighty witch to achieve such a thing. I meant no offense, small Sinclair." She took a deep, exaggerated breath. "Let's begin," she said.

With a wave of her hand, the seals on the vases popped off, and colorful perfumes began quickly filling the room.

She began chanting in a language Maeve didn't understand or recognize, taking the stones in each hand.

The Witch inhaled the perfumes through her nose, extending her arms forward. She opened her eyes with a snap. Her pupils were gone and her eyes were pure white.

"This Magic is ancient," said Ismail. Her voice had changed into something strained: deep and rough. "It will cost you three times."

"What will it cost me?" Asked Mal.

Smoke surrounded Ismail as she placed the stones in the center of the table and inhaled the smoke again, her long tattooed fingers grazing over the stone.

"Three marks," she said. She continued to inhale the colored smoke. She gripped the edge of the table, bending over in a contorted way.

"A mark on your soul," she said, beginning the spell.

Damn. There was only one thing that put a mark on your soul. It wouldn't be Mal's first.

Ismail was chanting in another language between each direction.

"A mark on your body," she continued.

An offering of blood. Painful, but he could handle it.

Ismail's voice flattened out. "And a mark on something pure."

Maeve's breath caught in her throat.

Ismail's hands broke away from the stones. The room grew brighter. She stood to her full height and addressed Mal.

"Do you accept?"

"A life. My blood. And. . ." Started Mal.

Ismail's brows lifted. "Another's innocence. Dirty Magic," said Ismail with a wicked look. "And in that order. You have seven hours to complete the spell. With each cost, you must repeat the incantation 'hoc aliquid do' three times. Once you have completed the cost, my Magic will take hold, and what you seek will be returned to you. Do you accept?"

Mal hesitated.

"Yes," answered Maeve. She didn't look at him. "He does."

Ismail's eyes and the smoke began to turn dark.

"Go," she said.

They left without question or pause, pulling up the hoods to their cloaks. Silently, they made their way back up the pathway to the main road.

Mal kept walking and walking.

"We aren't going to Obscure?"

"I need to think," said Mal.

They turned down empty back alleys and back streets. They passed shops and bakeries. Each block turned darker, shabbier, and more broken. Windows boarded up with wood and covered in bars, glass shattered along the sidewalk and shops lay empty. Maeve stayed in line behind Mal. His pace was quick.

They stopped at the opening of a tight alleyway. Mal pressed his palms against the faded bricks. His head hung. Three figures from the unlit gap between buildings made their way closer.

Maeve opened her mouth to assure Mal that they'd find another way, or that she could figure out a loophole to complete the Magic costs.

"Hello, princess."

The voice came from the alley. The man's speech was broken. Nothing like Ismail's fluid and elevated voice.

"You look near to royalty I would say."

All three of them laughed. They were close now. Almost in the light of the street. Maeve ignored them.

"I've only ever seen such a face on a girl I overpaid for." The light hit their faces. They were older. Poorly dressed with dirty hands and ripped trench coats. He addressed Mal now. "How much for her?"

Mal was still facing the wall. "Get on." He said with a sigh.

"I'd pay a pretty price to see what's under that coat."

"I said to leave," said Mal. His voice was low and tired.

The man in the middle stepped towards Maeve.

"How about I just take her, then?"

The other two sniggered at one another. Together they pulled an assortment of second-hand human weapons out.

The man's eyes never left Maeve as he pulled a knife from his pocket, pointing it at each of them. "I'll fuck your pretty guts out and make him watch. And then slit his throat and make you watch. And then my boys will fuck you too."

Maeve nearly laughed.

Mal's magic stilled. Like deep waters.

He dropped his hands and turned towards Maeve. She raised her eyebrows.

Mal turned his attention to the man. The man faltered slightly. Mal was taller, yes, but against three there was no competition to humans. Except Mal was not human. And the power of Magic could be felt by all. Even the lowest of humans.

"Apologies," Mal said. "She's all yours."

Chapter 43

The man swallowed and nodded. "That wasn't so hard. Follow me, princess."

He stowed his knife back in his pocket. The others put away their weapons as well.

Maeve stepped towards him. They retreated into the dark alleyway. Mal stayed back with the other two.

She rounded a corner, following the man. He stopped and turned towards her.

"Take off your coat."

"May I try something?"

His face scrunched together. "What-"

Maeve stepped closer to him. "It's just that you're going to die soon anyway. And I've struggled to enter minds for months now. Only once recently but I was, truthfully, under duress. But you. . . You're scum. I don't feel guilty. If I accidentally hurt you with this little experiment, it won't matter. Because your time is up."

"You're fucking crazy. I enjoy them a bit-"

Maeve snapped her fingers, sending jolts of Magic through her whole body. She pushed into his mind. She had never been in a human's mind before.

And this one was a horror show. The alleys there were littered with his sins. Crimes no man should be permitted to commit even once. Let alone over and over. He sold poison and murdered men and-

Mal appeared there with her. Gently pulling her out of his mind. She had done it. And she was fine. Just like with Kietel and Nicklefrost. But the things she saw. . .They prevented her from celebrating.

The human stood there, hunched over, his hands on his knees. Mal appeared behind him, circling to his side. He bent to the man's ear.

"Now what was that you said you were going to do to her?" His voice was sinister and slow.

The human couldn't speak.

"Your friends are already dead," said Mal. "Funny. I needed only one. Now I'll have two."

The human dropped to his knees, his hands in a prayer motion, shaking them up at Mal. "Thank you," he cried. "I -I promise I won't speak a word of their death-"

"You misunderstand," said Mal. "Just because I'm not going to kill you, doesn't mean she isn't going to ensure you live a horrible half existence."

The human trembled. He turned towards Maeve, falling over onto his elbows. "I beg of you."

Maeve looked up at Mal. His hands were in his coat pockets.

"You know what to do," he said. "You've been thinking about it for a long time. You're capable."

She swallowed. "How do you know?"

"Because I see you, Maeve. We are going to ensure all of that Pureblood of yours is harnessed."

Maeve looked down at the weeping man before her. "Can you imagine what it must feel like? To be broken in such a way? I wonder what it will do."

The ally was silent save for the human's prayers. She pointed two fingers at him.

"Frangere," said Maeve.

The word rolled off her tongue like silk. A spell that had never been used to her knowledge. But spells were merely the will of Magic. The possibilities endless. And Maeve's will was strong.

She slammed through his mind, like a sharp blade slicing through butter.

He didn't scream. He didn't jerk forward or even fight. He fell limp to the ground, over on one shoulder. His fingers jittered. His chin shook back and forth. His eyes were wide, glossed over as he stared into nothing.

He was breathing. His body was alive. But his mind was shattered and his soul was trapped existing between life and death. Never finding release.

Maeve sucked in a sharp breath. Her hands trembled and her legs dipped. Mal was in front of her suddenly, his hands on her arms as he Obscured them to his room at the Inn. Maeve broke away from him and turned her back.

The floor felt soft beneath her. The fire in the corner was too hot.

"What did you see?" Asked Mal.

Maeve didn't meet his gaze. Her mind looped at the image of the man's broken body. "All the women he's raped. The children he hurt. The innocent he sold disgusting substances to and the dying families he stole food from." She took a moment and turned towards Mal. "He never will again."

"Congratulations on your new Magic," said Mal.

"You were right," she said. "I have wanted to try that for some time."

Mal nodded. "A Magical's mind will not break so easily."

"I know."

He stepped away from her and discarded his cloak across the back of a chair.

"It was difficult not to kill him too," said Mal. "I can't imagine letting anyone live after speaking to you in such a way." He ran his fingers through his hair and looked up at the ceiling. "Even now, I want to return and finish him."

She jumped at a knock at the door. Mal's fingertip swarmed red. Maeve recognized the Inn Keeper's voice.

"No," she mouthed, motioning for him to relax his hand.

He shook it out, and the red sparks vanished.

She opened the door, and the Inn Keeper stood smiling. He had an arm full of blankets for them.

"Thank you," she said, taking the blankets from him.

"Naten e mire," he said with the bow of his head.

"Goodnight," said Maeve.

She placed the blankets on the chair and turned back to Mal. He was preparing himself for the second cost.

He brought his pointer finger to his hand. Without hesitation, he sliced open his palm.

"Hoc aliquid do," said Mal three times.

Bright red blood splattered as he cut deep across his palm. The Magic took hold as three spiraling strands of blood wrapped around the others, twisting above his palm. They turned black.

Mal's focus was strained, intense, as he gripped his palm.

The fire in the room evaporated with a hiss. The walls began to crawl with black vines, inching their way from the corners.

Maeve didn't dare step towards him. The last time she stepped forward to intervene in dark Magic she was slammed back against the wall at the Peur family home.

Blood was pouring and pooling at his feet.

His jaw tightened. The veins along his arms and neck protruded. The black swirls of blood retreated towards his palm as he pulled his fingers closed around them and the wound. With a shake, the room swirled back to life. The fire puffed back into existence.

Mal breathed heavily and his arms dropped to his side.

The second cost was done.

But the wound wasn't healing; it was only pouring blood from his palm faster.

"It's not going to stop, is it?" Asked Maeve.

Mal stared at the blood running down his fingers.

"No," he replied.

Maeve stood silently. They were both fully aware of the implications of Ismail's instructions for the third and remaining cost.

A mark on something innocent. There were many ways to get it done.

But there wasn't time.

And there was only one thing left about Maeve that was innocent. She had broken sacred Magical laws. She had offered her blood for Magic. But the part of her that had never-

"I can find another way, so you don't have to-"

"I want to," said Maeve, the words escaping her lips before she could stop them.

She did want to. She had wanted to for some time.

Mal's head turned slowly to her.

She willed her legs to not falter, and they did not betray her as she crossed the room towards him. Each step felt like wading through honey. Chills blistered across her arms. Their eyes never broke away.

She took his hand in her own, examining the wound. Blood spread over onto her pale skin, dripping to the floor.

Mal's bloody fingers wrapped around her wrist.

She anticipated the tug that followed. But he hesitated. He searched Maeve's face for any sign of second-guessing. She looked up at him, darting between his eyes. She swore they were darker.

"Don't worry," she whispered.

She boldly reached up and grazed her free hand across his face. Magic, icy and electric, trickled at the places where their skin met. She had longed to touch his face so tenderly. His perfect face with a jawline made for treachery.

His skin was smooth as cool stone. His cheekbones rolled sharply under. She ran her finger across the dip slowly.

Blood now soaked the sleeve of her dress.

She peeled her eyes away from his mesmerizing skin and looked up at him. "I come willingly, My Prince."

His grip on her wrist tightened, and he pulled her close as his other arm tightened around her. She winced as his arms pressed against her bruised ribs. His nose brushed across hers, and she opened her mouth for him. Their bottom lips grazed one another as they lingered on the edge of temptation.

"Take me," she whispered into that temptation. "Take all of me."

And then his lips pressed into hers fully. She immediately opened her mouth wide, begging for more. His kiss was intoxicating. Reviving. Thrilling. It pulled her to the tips of her toes. His lips parted from hers only for a moment, pushing her hair away from her face.

Blood, warm and slick, slid across one cheek as his hands held her in his grip. She looked up into his eyes, his mesmerizing eyes that constantly swirled with a wicked desire.

Her fingers wrapped through his raven hair, tugging his lips back to hers. His hands moved across her chest, down her back, soaking her clothes in blood. Her skin shot to life. She gasped into his mouth as his cold fingers found their way under her blouse.

He gripped the waistband of her skirt and whirled her around to his other side. The back of her knees hit the edge of the mattress. In one swift movement, he pushed her down onto the bed.

She crawled backward, and he stalked over her, forcing her flat on the bed. His eyes were on hers as he slowly lowered himself onto her, pressing his chest into hers.

Their lips met. And her legs spread.

He pushed against her, and Maeve swelled beneath him. She pushed herself into him as heat rose between her legs.

She moved her hips across him, selfishly. But Mal responded in full. He grew hard beneath his clothes. A soft moan slipped from her as his bulge pressed against her. His hands moved to her face, spreading more blood and holding her in place as they writhed together.

He nipped at her bottom lip as he broke their kiss and pulled up from her. His hands, bloody and calm, slipped apart every button on her blouse until it fell open.

His eyes raked over her chest as a dark expression took hold. It was hungry. Predatorial. It spiked her adrenaline, and her heartbeat increased. He held his hand over her breasts, letting blood fall across her. His other hand moved to his cock, still concealed beneath his pants, and gripped what he could.

Blood dripped down her ribs and onto the bedding.

"Open your mouth," he commanded.

She obeyed.

Mal's sliced palm pressed against her parted lips, blood spilling over her tongue, dripping over her chin. The metallic taste of him sent icy shivers down her arms and spine.

She swallowed.

She swallowed his blood.

He pulled his hand back and watched her.

Something new settled in her own Magic, strong and unyielding.

Her eyes tightened, and her lips parted. She craved more. Perhaps it was how wrong it was. How dirty and taboo.

But she knew it was because it was his. Blood was powerful to Magicals.

She looked down at her bloody body. Deep shades of crimson flickered in the dim lights.

His hands slid around her lower waist, pulling her off the bed and arching her back. He licked across her blood-stained breast, sucking at her nipple. Maeve's head fell backwards with a groan as her stomach tightened. He licked broadly across her chest, blood smearing across his lips, his chin, and his cheeks. And then up her neck until their lips molded together once more and she tasted him again.

"Mal," she moaned against his lips.

He pulled away, holding her steady. His eyes shot back and forth between hers, searching for distress.

"What is it?" He asked quietly.

Her hands moved to the collar of his shirt. With two fingers, she traced down the buttons of his shirt. They opened one by one under her touch. She slipped her hands down his shoulders, loosening the fabric. His chest was smooth, just like she imagined. His lean frame was toned with faint lines of his stomach muscles.

Her hands moved to his pants and gripped the buckle of his belt. Her fingers shook at she pulled the leather from its metal clasp.

The button was next.

Then the zipper and-

His arms slipped between hers and pushed them away. She fell back onto the bed. One calm and cool hand pressed into her stomach. Mal breathed deeply, his eyes on her.

But her eyes were on his other hand. His other hand that stroked his hard and considerable length she had released. Maeve's chest rose and fell hastily. She licked across her lips, where the lingering taste of Mal's blood remained.

Mal's hand brushed down her stomach to where the fabric of her bloodstained skirt rested just above her knees. He balled the fabric in one hand and tugged. Maeve lifted her hips as the skirt slipped across her thighs and down her legs. Mal discarded it.

Blood dripped into her ivory panties, spreading across the satin fabric. He hooked two fingers around the band of them along her hip bone. Cold ice pressed into her skin. He removed his fingers as the ice traveled across the fabric. Maeve shook beneath it as it disintegrated the only thing left between them.

She was completely bare. Her legs shook. Mal ran his hands down them and moved himself closer to her entrance. His cock pressed against her gently and her eyes rolled back. She gripped the sheets beneath her. Electric magic shot between them, cool and sharp, where their skin met in intimacy.

"Look at me, Maeve."

She obeyed.

She opened her eyes. Light marks of blood still smeared across his mouth, some against his chest. His jaw was relaxed and his lips slightly parted. His hair fell halfway across his face, a perfect picture of fearlessness.

It nearly drove her mad, the perfection he oozed. She had to have it all. Every inch of him. The head of his cock rested at her entrance. She opened for him further, a silent plea to become one.

Mal obliged. He guided himself into her, barely moving. She immediately grabbed his forearms as he slowly stretched her open. He pushed further, his hungry eyes on where their skin fused. Maeve winced. A low groan in her throat. He was being so gentle, so calculated.

"Fuck," he said slowly as he exhaled. He pulled slightly out and then back in. "You were made for me."

Maeve reeled. Her stomach flipped over. Her brain went fuzzy. Pressure built just above where he eased in and out of her. She wanted to reach for it, satiate that burning. She squirmed under him, pushing her hips up.

Mal's eyes moved to her own. He moved deeper inside of her, maintaining that slow and steady roll of his body. His hand slithered across her thigh, right to that burning she wanted so badly to release.

His thumb grazed over her clit and Maeve's insides twisted. She pushed into his gentle touch desperately. His hand moved away.

She looked up at him, her eyes protesting. His hand moved to his face. He licked across his thumb with a delicate precision. Maeve felt herself melt into the bedding.

His thumb moved into his mouth, his tongue flicked across it once more before lowering back down to her.

"Here?" He asked as he placed his wet thumb over her once more.

He was so close, just lower and-

He moved lower.

Maeve sucked in sharply and whined.

There. Yes fucking there.

His thumb began a torturous motion, running over the tight nerves that demanded more and more. She tightened around his cock. Which brought a hefty exhale from him.

His pace remained steady, pushing further inside her every few thrusts, pushing against her core. She only had half of him, and she was whimpering beneath him. Shaking. Doused in the exhilarating and euphoric feeling that he was inside of her. Tears formed in her eyes.

Mal's head cocked to one side. "Maeve," he said softly.

She shook her head. "I'm fine. I'm more than fine. I-I-just. . ." Her fingers traced up his stomach.

Mal hushed her tenderly. "You don't have to explain, Little Viper."

Maeve spoke before she could stop herself. "It feels like I have known you for a lifetime, and I am only just remembering."

Delight flickered in his eyes. "I know."

Mal continued to push and pull inside her tenderly. A tear slipped down Maeve's cheek as she smiled.

"It's as though I've been suffocating and you are-"

"The very air I need to breathe."

Maeve nodded and a small laugh of relief escaped her lips. "Like calls to like."

Those powerful words caused his pace to quicken. And he stopped himself. He rested his head against her shoulder. He released a long and controlled breath. Her fingers moved across his back, running down the dip of his spine.

Mal's back arched as he pressed deeper into her.

He lifted himself back up. His arms braced on either side of her. Shadows dipped into the muscles of his arms. A crescent moon shape on his bicep and a system of rivers running down his forearms in his flexed veins.

"I want all of me inside you," he said with a quiet desperation.

Maeve could form no response other than a broken, "please."

In one swift movement, he plunged into her fully. Maeve latched onto his back as her mouth fell open in a silent scream. Mal moved faster, pumping in and out of her with his full length.

His hands moved to her waist as he held her in place. His eyes closed. He stilled. His skin was paler than she'd ever seen it.

"You've lost too much blood, Mal," said Maeve. "You need to finish the spell."

His eyes opened, and he nodded.

He held her firmly and thrust fully into her. Her hands dropped above her head as she tried to keep her eyes open.

"Hoc aliquid do," said Mal, his voice dark and low.

He thrust into her again. Mal's head fell backward towards the ceiling as his grip on her tightened. He repeated the words a second time. The room shifted. Shadows along the walls grew. The candlelights flickered.

He looked down at her, his eyes hazy and hooded.

"I want you to go over the edge with me," he said, his movements slowing.

Maeve reached up and stroked his face, brushing his hair back. "There isn't time, my Prince."

Frustration shot across his exhausted face. The spell was taking its toll on him as it neared completion.

Maeve reached down and her fingers grazed against his exposed shaft. He stiffened against her touch. She tugged on him, bringing him further.

"I want you to find release," she whispered up at him. "And I want it all inside of me."

His cock twitched, and his thrusts resumed. A low moan began building deep in his chest.

She laid back down. Mal fell into her chest as he expanded her further. Her knees pulled back. His breath panted into her neck as that moan turned into a whimper. His hands lifted her arched back slightly off the bed, wrapping around her fully. She twisted her fingers through his hair, their cheeks pressing together.

Shadows broke from the walls and hovered across the room, across the bed, blocking out the light. They were in complete darkness.

His hands moved to her ass. He pulled her up as he slid in and out, never pulling his cock from her completely. In and out and in and out and-

Magic slipped from him. It was pure, almost unbearable, as it infiltrated her. Her skin was dirty now. Her body was his.

Mal repeated the ancient words to complete the spell once more, just as his whimper turned into a low grunt and he pumped inside her with force one last time, releasing every drop she had asked for.

Dark magic, lethal and unfamiliar, pierced into her blood like needles. She twisted beneath him with a scream. His hands shot to her face and held her against his chest.

It barreled through her body, scraping across every part of her. She pushed against Mal, desperate for the pain to ease. The darkness in the room swirled, creating a cyclone of shadow around them.

Maeve's cries faded into silence. Her heartbeat disappeared. The room slowed.

Her face turned warm. Hot tears of panic and pain fell down her cheeks as he pinned her in place. She jolted under him, violently shaking.

The dark magic lifted only once she was drowning against its presence in her body. The vortex around them shifted into breathable air. The candles on the side tables flickered back into flames.

Maeve gasped and heaved a cry, limp under Mal.

"I've got you," he hummed in her ear, his voice velvety smooth. "It's over."

Her Magic was wounded completely, pierced by that darkness. Mal rolled off of her and pulled her close. She didn't shake or move. Her body was drained. He tucked his head atop hers, entangling their legs and draping his arm around her.

The third cost was complete. The Finders Stone appeared on the bedside table. Neither of them noticed. They were already asleep.

Maeve Sinclair would never be satisfied with just his lips again.

Chapter 44

The Finders Stone was fully repaired, and even when it was just in Mal's pocket, it was leading him toward the Dread Crown deep in the Black Forest.

The length of their journey through the forest was unknown. Neither had any idea of how close or how far they were. They Obscured when they could see far enough ahead of them but mostly traveled on foot.

Ismail had left a note with the stone:

Beware of the moon in the forest, young travelers.

And so they covered ground by day and camped by night, throwing up plenty of protective enchantments while they slept beneath the stars. Ambrose had given them the most fantastic traveling gifts. He was particularly skilled at shrinking charms. They slept on cozy, plush mattresses and had tea each night.

Mal marveled at the tiny teapot in her pocket that expanded to full size. Maeve was jealous that he still got to experience Magic for the first time. She would love to go back and feel those moments of awe again.

As they traveled mostly in silence, Maeve had plenty of time to reflect on the events of their final evening at Cobbler's Cabin. Her stomach twisted every time the memory made its way into her head. The way his fingers crawled across her skin. The way she had driven him over the edge.

They slept separately at night. Though one night Maeve dozed off by the fire, and when she rolled over in the morning, she was in Mal's bed, covered in extra blankets. He was already up.

On the seventh day, early in the morning, Mal stopped walking suddenly.

"Just ahead," said Mal, "there's a clearing. It's in a tree there."

An excited breath welled up in Maeve's chest. They were so close.

After a little more than a week of traveling through a massive forest in a foreign country, she was finally about to put her hands on the long-lost Dread Crown. The crown that would be atop Mal's head.

They entered the clearing.

"We found it," said Mal.

"Where is it?" Asked Maeve.

"It's the strangest thing," he said. "It's not the stone now. I can feel which tree it's in out of these hundreds. It calls to me."

Maeve looked up at him. He wasn't making a move for the tree.

"There's only one problem," said Mal. "We've been followed."

"Miss Sinclair!"

Maeve whipped around, her fingers ready at her side.

Walter Brighton laughed heartily. "So jumpy."

Maeve's face scrunched. "Mr. Brighton?"

"What are the chances?" Brighton laughed.

His older sons, Remy and Bill, and two other men emerged behind Brighton.

Walter was a large framed man, his sons were no different.

"What are you doing here?" Asked Mal, with little charm in his voice. He, too, knew this was no coincidence.

Brighton laughed, "I've been researching these forests for decades, boy. I should be asking you that question. What brings you so confidently to this grove?"

"He knows," muttered Maeve.

"I know," replied Mal.

Maeve tensed as the other men slowly encircled them.

"It is not yours to take," said Mal.

Brighton laughed. "But it's yours?"

Mal smiled softly. "Yes."

"Please," he spat. "You're a child. Even if you are The Dread Descendant who's to say you're owed that crown? Who's to say the Magicals even want to see you wear it? It belongs in the museum. We have our government. We picked it. We didn't pick you."

Mal laughed hollowly. The noise seemed to unsettle Brighton, but he quickly regained his composure.

"True," said Mal. "But that is not of consequence or concern to me."

"You know you would have been smarter to wait until we had actually retrieved the crown to make yourselves known," said Maeve.

Mal smirked and looked down at her. "She's right."

Walter spit at Mal's feet.

Maeve and Mal stared down at the ground between them.

Maeve inhaled slowly. Disgust swelled inside her. Before anyone could react her arm shot out towards Remy. With a low thudding sound, his eyes popped white.

Swirling colors appeared at everyone's fingertips, but Mal clicked his tongue.

"Don't," he said.

Walter looked at his son, his eyes wide.

"They said you-you-couldn't enter minds anymore. They said you-"

"Did they?" Interrupted Maeve. "So strange." She held Remy on the line, he was unconscious, but she wasn't in his mind. He was fighting her. And fighting hard, but she was hard to fight. "Everyone seems to be having discussions about what I can and cannot do and no one bothered to ask me."

Her hands tensed, sending a convulsion through Remy's body where he hovered.

"Merlin," said Brighton. "That man in Albania. That was you."

Damn. She hadn't expected that.

"The Times printed about it. The Orator's Office said the Magic was unknown. But you did something to his mind."

Remy tensed again. He was fighting hard now. Maeve would either need to let go or fully infiltrate his mind to keep her hold.

"Alight," said Brighton, pressing his hands down in a calming manner. "We can discuss this."

"There's nothing to discuss," said Mal.

Brighton shook his head in anger. "No. No," he said. "I will not give up my life's work for an illegitimate usurper, and a Sacred Seventeen bitch."

"Father," said Bill.

"Shut up," he snapped at his other son.

"You will give it up," said Mal. "I am sorry, sir. Truly. I know in your heart what you desire is virtuous, but I will have that crown. I will receive the magic it holds. Magic my blood calls to."

Mr. Brighton's breathing was quick and heavy. His eyes on Maeve. Mal continued speaking calmly.

"I am not quick to anger like Maeve here. Her temper is truly to be feared." Praise rang out from his voice. "I keep a very tight leash on my temper, Mr. Brighton." Fear was pounding from them all. "But make no mistake, you step towards her and I will use it with joy."

One of the men spoke then. "You really are him."

Mal gave him a nod.

"I'll be dammed."

"Apologies, gentleman," said Mal.

With a snap of his fingers, they all fell unconscious, slumping to the ground.

"Wipe their memory," said Mal plainly.

"What?" Asked Maeve.

"The only people that get to know the moves I make are the people I choose."

"Wipe their entire minds, Mal?"

"That's what I said."

Maeve stammered. She pointed at Brighton. "That man holds more knowledge about Magicals and our history than anyone on Earth."

"Well, I hope he wrote it all down."

"Bill and Remy have children- they will forget-"

Mal's eyes slipped to hers and her mouth snapped tightly shut.

"Don't look at me like that," he said softly. "Please. Everyone in the world is going to look at me like that at some point. I can accept that. But not from you."

Maeve's jaw loosened. Her body relaxed and she heaved a sigh. She nodded and turned back to where the five men lay unconscious.

She started with Remy. She pointed two fingers at him, but she didn't erase his mind. She dove into it, searching for the memory of their encounter.

She had never done it before, but she knew it must be possible. She grabbed onto Remy's memory of being in the Yatir Forest, of their encounter. She held up her hand, preparing to destroy just that memory.

She snapped her fingers. A cracking sound echoed across Remy's mind. Maeve held her hand up to her eyes. Blinding white light surrounded her.

She pulled out of Remy's mind, prepared to be satisfied with another accomplished new spell. But her face fell gaunt as she saw Remy.

He was convulsing like the man in the alley in Albania. His body shook and his mouth foamed. His eyes rolled into the back of his head.

Maeve's hand shot over her mouth.

"What did you do?" Mal said.

"I-" she stammered.

Mal crossed over to Remy, pulling him up by the collar. He wasn't dead, but he may as well have been.

Just like that man in Albania.

"Answer me," said Mal.

"I just- I don't know- I just-"

"I told you to erase their minds." He looked over at Brighton and the rest. "Not shatter them."

"I didn't mean to," said Maeve. "I was trying to do something else-"

"That's not what I instructed you to do," said Mal, dropping Remy to the ground.

"I was trying to erase the specific memory, alter it-"

"Again," said Mal, "I didn't say practice a new idea on him I said-"

"I know what you said!"

Maeve's ribs were throbbing now. Her leg pulsating. The numbing spells and potions were completely worn off.

Mal inhaled slowly. Maeve swallowed.

He looked back down at Remy.

"Erase his mind now," said Mal with calculated control. "If there is any mind left."

Maeve dropped her hands to her sides and nodded.

"And then wipe the rest clean, too."

The forest stilled as Mal's slender fingers pulled the Dread Crown from a hollowed out spot in a tree. It shined like it had just been polished. Not a single bit of dirt or tree bark, dust or debris, touched its radiating silver color. Serpents ran, twisting and biting, across the sparkling crown. Their eyes were set with emerald stones, and their flared tongues of rubies.

Magic radiated from it, surging the longer Mal held it.

"It's beautiful," said Maeve.

He frowned. He reached into his pocket and pulled out Finders Stone. It was snapped down the middle once more, laying in two equal pieces in his hand.

"Well now we know your Uncles weren't idiots," said Mal.

"That is still up for debate," said Maeve. She ran her fingers over the stone. "It must break after each use."

Mal's gaze returned to the crown. "Take my hand."

Chapter 45

Maeve couldn't stop staring at the crown. The crown that Mal insisted wouldn't touch his head until his coronation. It remained in a glass-topped box inlaid with white satin and black trim on his dresser.

There were still five Dread artifacts left to find. Mal and Maeve Obscured to Ismail to have her repair the Finders Stone once more. To their dismay, she was gone. Her house was stripped of its glamor. It looked like the rest of the alleys. It lay empty.

In the center of the room was the gold they paid her. Every last coin accounted for. With no explanation.

"Maybe something happened to her?"

Mal's shoulders pulled up slightly.

"Maybe it was a gift to you, the Dread Descendant."

Mal said it didn't matter. He couldn't stop now. He changed his focus then to searching for the goblet and its mysterious auction buyer.

After a visit to Mrs. Mavros, Alphard's mother, Maeve's ribs, burned ankle, and black and blue spotted leg were mended entirely. Astrea, the oldest Mavros child, and Alphard's older sister, who inherited her mother's skill, observed only.

Ambrose had turned a ghostly shade of white upon seeing her, even though she assured him everything looked worse than it was. He nearly fainted when she told him about the Grindylow water demon attack.

Abraxas stayed with them for much of the fall since Mr. and Mrs. Rosethorn were vacationing in Italy. Abraxas was never one who enjoyed solitude.

Maeve, Mal, and Abraxas sat outside on the balcony having a lovely breakfast when Ambrose burst through the terrace doors.

"I hope you'll forgive my interruption," said Ambrose, his voice panicked. "Maeve, I completely forgot to tell you-Seven Realms, your mother is furious at me. Gods!" He muttered.

"What is going on?" Laughed Maeve.

Seeing her father, the Premier, in a panic over his wife was always humorous.

"Your Mother's very best friend and her daughter are staying this week. You remember them, yes? Her daughter is about your age," said Ambrose.

"No, absolutely not," said Maeve, dropping her toast and pointing a finger at her father. "I will not be babysitting that snotty French girl for the whole week."

"Actually, that sounds like fun," said Abraxas with a flick of his brows.

Maeve scowled at him.

"I'm terribly sorry, Maeve," said Ambrose. "You don't really have a choice."

The terrace doors swung open once more, and her mother Clarissa stepped through, closely followed by two of Maeve's least favorite people.

The first was Marguerite St. Beveraux, her Mother's oldest friend, who married a Frenchman and now spoke with an affected French accent, even though Marguerite herself grew up in Oxford.

The second was Marguerite's only offspring, Ophelia St. Beveraux. Ophelia was a small-framed girl with olive skin, golden brown curls, and an annoying voice. Once when they were twelve and Ophelia had not gotten her way, she screamed until Marguerite did her bidding.

Ophelia was stunning. Beautiful in all the proper ways. Even her round-framed glasses made her look effortlessly elegant.

"Here they are!" Exclaimed Ambrose cheerfully with a nervous laugh.

"Ambrose!" Mrs. St. Beveraux grabbed him and kissed both his cheeks. "And Maeve, oh look at you! You're all grown up."

Mrs. St. Beveraux blew Maeve multiple kisses from both her hands.

Maeve smiled and scrunched her nose.

"How could I have forgotten the fake accent," whispered Abraxas from behind his napkin.

Maeve smirked.

"Ophelia. Good to see you again," said Maeve.

"Si pleasur'zis all mine," said Ophelia.

Ophelia bounced to the table and set herself opposite Maeve, next to Mal.

"Let the children converse," said Clarissa, taking Marguerite's arm. "We'll have tea in the sunroom."

Ambrose followed them inside.

"I'm Ophelia," said Ophelia, turning to Mal and extending her hand.

"Malachite."

"I know," said Ophelia, her gaze starry-eyed. "You are the Dread Descendant."

Mal smiled diplomatically. "Guilty as charged."

"My mother and father can't wait to meet you zemselves. When they got word of you, they cried!"

Ophelia turned to Abraxas and extended her hand once more, though Abraxas didn't take it.

"We've met," said Abraxas, incredulously. "Many times."

"Oh!" Exclaimed Ophelia, her voice rising into an even more annoying octave. "I'm zo sorry I don't remember."

His eyes narrowed, and he returned to The Starlight Gazette, wounded, without another look her way.

"You were at Vaukore with Maeve?" Ophelia asked Mal.

"I was. I assume you attend grade school together?"

"Oh, yes. It was a lovely school. Though I 'ave always been jealous of Maeve going to Vaukore."

"Why's that?" Asked Maeve.

"Oh," Ophelia blushed. "Mother considered secondary Magical education I waste of my time. She said my talents lay elsewhere."

"I thought you didn't get in," said Abraxas dryly.

Ophelia's cheeks drained of their color.

Mal ignored the comment. "Well, maybe we can give you a taste of Vaukore while you're here," smiled Mal.

He was being entirely too nice.

In the coming days, Maeve attempted to avoid Ophelia at all costs. Ophelia, however, had no issue bursting into Maeve's bedroom unannounced to see what she was doing.

Maeve and Abraxas were left to fend for themselves at Sinclair Estates as Mal's new flat was ready and he moved in. Maeve was eager to spend time there with him and escape her busy and listening home.

The penthouse suite sat seven floors high, with mahogany plank floors and scrolling windows that looked out over Westminster in London. Mal had his very own study on the East side of the apartment, where he spent much of his time. It was furnished with its own library, large working desk, and potion-making station.

He was given a bottomless budget for furnishing and outfitting his new home.

"I cannot accept this freely," he said as they toured the lavish apartment, filled with deep woods and leather, plush rugs and linens.

His face was sad.

Maeve recalled his first week at Vaukore when the Head Boy and his gang of fourth year senior boys decided to mock Mal's secondhand uniform and books. They all learned quickly, though. He may have had little to no money, but the first time he dueled all their lips were tightly sealed thereafter.

Her throat tightened. Her eyes felt glossy.

Maeve placed her hands on his face and forced his gaze at her.

"You deserve it all," she whispered with a desperate expression. "Anything you desire. You'll never go without again."

Mal looked down at her. A single brow ticked up. "Anything?"

Maeve pressed her hands into his chest. "I'm serious, Mal. I want you to be comfortable and taken care of I-"

His hands wrapped around her own as he hushed her gently. "I know." He brought his lips to her temple, inhaling deeply.

Despite being offered a top spot amongst the Bellator, Mal took an unadvertised and unopen job as a curator for the Magical Antiquities Museum, working directly with auctioneers and Magical antique stores. It took little work on Maeve's part to correct the fact that the Museum wasn't hiring.

His choosing to work for the Magical Museum, and not pursue a career in combat, had been an unexpected move to most, except Maeve. She knew he was there to collect treasure. The Dread Armor was essential in taking back the Dread Lands.

Maeve's mother sent her to the Magical Shops in Paris to ensure that Sabrina's Sweets Shop had all the correct instructions for the cakes she ordered for the Autumn Gala. As if her mother wasn't difficult enough, having her host the two largest parties of the year back to back and plan Arianna's wedding did not help.

Maeve decided to do some window shopping while she was there, a perfect excuse to escape Ophelia. With an armful of bags, she slipped into The Daydreamer, an antique store, where Mal was working on a few deals for the Museum.

The shop shelves and displays were filled with a variety of items, some expensive, rare, and one-of-a-kind. Mal's job was to convince them to sell.

"Miss Sinclair," said Mr. Gims, the grey-bearded owner, as Maeve walked through the door. "What brings you here?"

He spoke with a slight annoyance in his voice. The last time Maeve had seen Mr. Gims prior to Mal's employment, her father was practically throwing him out of their house.

"Finally come to sell you some precious family heirlooms, Mr. Gims," said Maeve sweetly.

He almost dropped the overfilled box he was holding.

"Gods, are you serious?" He asked, his voice quivering.

"No," said Maeve, smiling.

His face fell flat, and he mumbled something foul under his breath.

"Maeve."

Mal appeared from the other room wearing grey tailored pants and an offset grey button down. His sleeves were rolled back. A fact which Maeve greatly enjoyed. She tore her eyes away from his arms.

"Hi," said Maeve.

"You know this one?" Asked Mr. Gims, gesturing at Maeve.

"Yes, sir," replied Mal.

The shop owner scowled and shuffled into the next room.

"Why doesn't he like you?" Asked Mal as he crossed behind the counter.

"Daddy won't sell him anything," said Maeve.

Mal nodded. "He would make a fortune off that basement."

"Indeed," agreed Maeve. "Anyway, I stopped by to say dinner tomorrow is at six o'clock, and there's unexpected company."

"Who?" Asked Mal.

"Grandmother Agatha and Grandmother Primrose," grimaced Maeve.

"Come now, Maeve," said Mal playfully, leaning on the counter towards her. "You fought off a giant Grindylow. Surely two old ladies don't scare you."

"You fought off that demon," corrected Maeve, mimicking his movement as she played with his ring around her neck.

Mal's gaze dropped to the ring around her neck. "I am not afraid of them. In fact, I am ready to woo them," he smirked up at her.

"Are you?" She asked with a smile. "And how is the wooing going here?"

"As good as expected. Those who know who I am think it's remarkable that I would take such a humble job, working alongside the everyday Magicals in pursuit of Magical preservation."

Maeve bit her lip and shook her head. "I bet they do."

Mal dipped his face closer to hers. Maeve heard footsteps creaking down the stairs of the shop.

"I'll see you tomorrow," she whispered.

"What about tonight?" He insinuated with a devilish calm.

"I have training tonight." Maeve pushed off the counter and called to Mr. Gims in the next room.

"Mr. Gims, I'm going to use your fire!"

She heard muffled cursing from the other room. Mal shook his head.

Once she was back home, Maeve spent the rest of the day avoiding Ophelia, who had pestered her multiple times, ensuring that Mal would be attending dinner the following day.

She ducked into her father's study, quietly closing the door behind her.

"Mal coming tomorrow?" Ambrose asked.

Maeve laughed and sighed. "Yes."

"Are you ready for tonight?"

Maeve nodded.

"Are they giving you a hard time?"

"Of course they are," said Maeve. "And I don't even blame them."

She sat in one of his oversized armchairs.

"Which ones in particular?"

"No," said Maeve, unwilling to divulge which fellow Bellator in training were being rude to her. "Distance, remember?"

Ambrose raised his hands in surrender.

"Tonight will determine the Optimum," said Ambrose. "They will see that you are not merely there because you are my daughter."

And Ambrose was right.

The Optimum was placement for each level and class of Bellator. It was a series of duels with only one winner per rank, who would earn the titles of Optimum. And in three weeks, be challenged once again by those in their fellow rank.

It wasn't about age. It was about power. It was likely Maeve and Roswyn, who had also been offered a spot in the Bellator, would move into the higher ranks quickly.

Ambrose didn't even smile when she won that night. He pinned the new badge on her black high-collared vest without any emotion. Right next to a bright shiny S. She placed her fist over her heart and looked up at him. She couldn't help but smile. Her father's eyes sparkled despite his reserved manner. He gave her a nod and strolled away. Arman walked at his side.

“Congratulations, Sinclair,” said Hennington, Captain of the Bellator in training, and her direct officer. He was a few years her senior. A true Supreme, and a decorated Wizard.

“Thank you,” she said.

She looked down at the matte black pin with optimum written across it.

“Best of luck hanging onto it,” said Hennington, no condemnation in his voice. He was merely stating facts. “No cadet ever keeps the title of Optimum longer than six weeks. Most of these Magicals haven’t harnessed a fraction of their power in school.”

Maeve looked up at him. “Nor have I.”

His eyes narrowed. She had no intention of letting her status as Optimum go.

“If I may sir?” She asked.

He nodded once, and she stepped away, leaving the arena without meeting eyes with the rest.

“Suppose I should have seen that coming.”

Roswyn stood leaning against the smooth pillars outside of the Bellator training arena.

Roswyn lasted nearly to the end of the trials. But a boy named Mumford from America beat him. Leaving Maeve and Mumford at the end.

Mumford had been privately trained his entire life. He was two years older than her. They had only just become acquainted, but Mumford scowled at her like he had hated her for years. And he wasn’t the only one.

They hated her for her last name. For her Pureblood. For being better. For being close to Mal.

Mal was the reason many of them joined. Most of the recruiting class of Bellator cadets he also trained personally. Many of them had heard of his valiant return and were desperate to fight in his war to come. Mumford came from America to join Mal’s cause.

Mumford appeared from the doors behind her.

“Don’t ever get inside my head again,” he grumbled as he walked by.

“Don’t let me,” she replied.

He stopped on his heel and turned towards her, his nostrils flaring. Roswyn appeared at his side, grabbing his shoulders before he reached Maeve.

"Come on," said Roswyn. "Mal wants to meet you."

Mumford shook Roswyn off.

"He wants you there too, Sinclair."

Mal looked at the Optimum pin on her black simple uniform.

"Well done," said Mal, as she crossed the doorway of his flat.

They didn't touch. Or embrace. Maeve walked to the fully stocked bar she was certain Mal would never partake in and poured herself a glass of sparkling water.

She leaned against the windowsill as Mal and Mumford shook hands.

"This is a great honor," said Mumford.

Mal smiled softly.

Mal gestured for Roswyn and Mumford to sit.

"Would you like a drink?"

Mumford nodded. Mal personally poured Mumford and Roswyn a glass of Bottomless Bourbon.

They clinked their glasses together and Mal took a seat in a large throne-like upholstered chair.

"Congratulations on second place. You'll have to get used to Maeve beating you if you want to file in my ranks," said Mal.

Mumford nodded once. "How do I stop her from getting in my mind?"

Mal smiled softly. "I don't know that you can. Maeve's abilities with the mind are quite a mystery."

Mumford took a sip of his drink. "May I ask you something?"

"Yes," replied Mal.

Mumford hesitated. "Why aren't you a Bellator? Why don't you wear that badge?"

Mal looked over at Maeve. "She is my second. When I am crowned as The Dread Prince she will be the rock against which the waves crash. The mountain standing against the storm. Everyone must know now that she is something to be feared." He turned his attention back to Mumford. "Even you fear her."

Mumford looked like he was prepared to argue, but Mal held up his hand.

"You should fear her," he said. "I don't want stupid men in my court."

Mumford straightened.

"So tell me," said Mal, his voice dipping into a dark hum, and letting some of that lethal Dread Magic slip from him. The firelights in the room dimmed. "Are you stupid enough not to fear what is more powerful than you?"

Mumford's skin flushed. He shook his head sternly.

"Do you feel the Magic that slips threateningly from her?"

Mumford nodded. Mal's eyes sparkled.

"Magnificent, isn't it? Such a power."

"What of your power?" Challenged Mumford. "Dread Magic is surely to be more feared."

"More?" Asked Mal. "Magic is not quantified in more and less. My Dread Magic is holy and divine. It is deadly and catastrophic." He smiled. "I will admit to you that even I fear it. It's as though part of me is not my own. It lies dormant. Until needed."

Mumford looked to Maeve. "I've been fighting my whole life. And I've never fought anyone like her. It was like she was ahead of me, in my mind, like a shadow slipping around me."

"That is what she needs to be."

"I want to be a part of your team," said Mumford.

"Good," said Mal. "In the coming weeks Maeve will need your support, both of your support," his eyes slipped to Roswyn. "Stand by her as she wins. The rest will follow your example."

Roswyn looked at Mal and spoke carefully. "They don't like her."

Mal's eyes were carefully on Roswyn. "Then make them."

Mumford nodded. Roswyn downed his Bourbon with a hefty sigh.

"The three of you must be a united front as you move up in the Bellator ranks."

"Belvadora was there too," said Maeve. "She did not return to school."

"She needs work," said Roswyn.

"She learns quickly," said Maeve.

"She came in last today," seethed Roswyn. "That's what happens to the enlisted and not the recruited."

"I didn't get much time with her at Vaukore," said Mal. "Don't let her fall behind Roswyn. Push her, work with her outside of trainings if you must. Any of them that need it."

Roswyn looked directly at Mal and nodded.

He and Mumford finished their drinks and left.

"Well done," said Mal.

"They hate me."

"They envy you."

"Same difference," she muttered.

"What did you tell me once? None of it will matter in the end?"

Maeve glared at him playfully. But his eyes sparkled in dark swirls of brown with flecks of red.

The sun was beginning to rise across the city. Blues and greens pressed into the stone and stucco buildings, illuminating their cream coloring, turning his flat into a grey hazy dream.

The leather couch behind them called her name.

"Roswyn made it to the end?"

Maeve nodded as a yawn escaped her lips. "He did well."

"You held back."

"How do you know?"

"He said it took you forty-seven seconds to beat him," said Mal.

"He's strong. His Magic is wild."

"But your Magic is certain. You could have defeated him in half that time."

"Duels are cumbersome," said Maeve. "I can't move with haste. I can't slam into their minds. I can't slice through their bodies. It takes control to beat and not kill. Killing would be easier."

Mal chuckled. “Indeed.”

Chapter 46

Everyone sat around the Grand Dinner Table in the Dining Hall the following evening. Much to Maeve's happiness, Ophelia's father had shown up that morning and whisked Ophelia away a day early.

Grandmother Primrose and Grandmother Agatha had fawned over Mal through drinks and appetizers in the sitting room. Mal had both old ladies eating out of the palm of his hand. Abraxas and Maeve watched them from across the room.

Agatha cried twice telling Mal how much she wished her late husband Alyicious could have met him.

"He always knew you would come," said Agatha as she bowed her head.

Mal took her hands in his own and thanked her for her support.

At dinner, Agatha asked lightheartedly, "Have you given any more thought to that Orator's Office job, Maeve?" Asked her Grandmother Agatha. "Or are we certain of the Bellator path? I heard you made Optimum. Will you join the Magical Militia?"

Maeve had been dreading this topic of conversation but knew it was bound to come up.

"No, actually. I haven't. And no I'm not."

Agatha frowned slightly. "So, what are you doing, darling?"

Maeve smiled at her grandmother sweetly. "Figuring it all out, I suppose."

Mal smiled softly.

"What's there to figure out?" Said Primrose, nastily. "Get married and start producing heirs."

Maeve grimaced and looked to Agatha, whom she knew strongly disliked her daughter-in-law's mother.

"Prim," said Ambrose. Primrose looked down at him. "Maeve will be Malachite's second."

Agatha slammed her fist on the table. "Now that's more like it."

Primrose's eyes moved to Maeve. "His second."

Mal nodded. "Maeve is an excellent fighter."

Primrose looked to Clarissa, her daughter. "And her betrothment to Alphard Mavros?"

Abraxas choked on his drink, and Maeve's stomach plummeted.

The room fell cold. Silent.

"My what?"

Clarissa avoided Ambrose's gaze. Maeve's head whipped to her father.

"My. What?" She said, biting into each word.

Ice was radiating from Mal next to her. The entire room dropped in temperature. Significantly.

Primrose laughed. "Primus and the Gods, Ambrose. She doesn't even know?"

Abraxas's eyes darted between them as they spoke. Arianna stared at her plate.

"Things are changing, Prim," said Ambrose. "The agreements we had with the Mavros-"

"-Are suddenly void because she is to be the Prince of Darkness' second in command? Can she still not produce heirs and continue strong Magical bloodlines? Speaking of," said Primrose, "Arianna. What's the hold-up?"

Clarissa's eyes rolled. "Mother, I don't think a dinner party is an appropriate place to discuss such things."

"When should we discuss it? Morning tea?" Asked Primrose. "By the time I was her age, I already had two." Primrose turned to Maeve. "And by the time I was her age, I was already with child," said Primrose proudly.

"We aren't even married yet," said Arianna, looking to their mother for support.

Primrose shrugged. She and Agatha began arguing. Their voices drained from Maeve's ears.

She was arranged to marry Alphard. And no one told her. Alphard knew, it only made sense. He had probably known for years.

"Well obviously that's not happening," she blurted out.

Their conversation halted.

"You think you are special?" Primrose set her drink down. "You think you can skip the traditions of this family, and the duties of a Sacred Seventeen-"

"I don't give a damn about those duties," said Maeve.

Primrose's eyes slid to Mal. "Do you."

"Of course I do," said Mal calmly.

Maeve's stomach twisted around. Her throat tightened and her jaw seized up.

"Magic is dying here on Earth. Creating and preserving Magical bloodlines is crucial."

Primrose looked to Maeve with a satisfied expression.

"However," continued Mal. "Once I return us to the Dread Lands Magic will flourish. We will no longer need such desperate arrangements."

"And until then?" Pressed Primrose.

"Until then, you will walk by your conscious and I by mine."

Primrose glared at Maeve over her spectacles. "Not one single Pureblooded woman with that mark on her wrist has fled from her duties. Do not shame those of us who came before you."

Alphard Mavros.

There are only so few names on the list, Mal had once said.

"Are you not still affectionate for the boy?" Asked Primrose. "Or has that void been occupied by another?"

"Primrose," warned Ambrose, who had been incredibly restrained for the entire evening so far.

Every head at the dinner table turned towards him. Ambrose's face was stern.

"I believe you've pestered my daughter and our honored guest enough for one night," his voice danced on casual annoyance.

"Yes," said Primrose with a sneer. She turned towards Mal. "I hope you do not misinterpret my disappointment in my granddaughter as disdain for you. I am honored to have lived to see the prophecy brought to life."

She toasted Mal and sipped the rest of her drink in silence. Mal watched her casually for a moment.

Maeve's mind was looping on one thing: Alphard Mavros.

"And if I asked of you to refrain from your opinions of disappointment?" Questioned Mal.

Primrose swallowed and set her drink back down. "Are you asking as The Dread Prince or as her lover?"

Maeve may as well have been spread on the table naked.

"Enough," said Ambrose, his voice sounding more like The Premier.

Mal held up a reassuring hand to Ambrose. "It's alright, sir. I am prepared to answer."

He was calm, entirely too calm. They all sat rigidly still at the table.

"Let me make something clear, Primrose Rosethorn. If you ever speak of my second again in such a vulgar and disrespectful way I will ensure your right to The Dread Lands is denied. And anyone with your blood as well. Save for Abraxas, who luckily did not inherit your lack of poise. I will see to it personally that you are abandoned here of Earth, with not a scrap of clothing to your name."

Magic snapped taunt between them. He was serious.

Primrose's eyes grew large. Her mouth opened slightly.

Agatha grinned and raised her glass. Abraxas' jaw was practically on the floor with glee in his eyes. Ambrose eyed his mother-in-law and Clarissa stared at Ambrose, disdain running through her.

Arianna watched Mal. And Maeve stared at Grandmother Primrose, who was speechless for the first time.

"You would see Magical bloodlines preserved, huh?" Maeve asked Mal at the Gates of Sinclair Estates, feet away from the magical boundary.

"You are not everyone, Maeve." He answered quickly, ready for her questioning.

"Did you know?" She asked after a moment.

Mal exhaled. “No.”

Maeve looked away from him. “No.” She repeated.

The question was begging at the tip of her tongue. Did he expect her to marry Alphard and create strong Magical bloodlines? Fear of the answer kept her lips closed.

Mal spoke softly, in that intoxicatingly calm way he did. “If I was not the Dread Descendant, if I was not to assume power, what would you do?”

“I don’t know,” she answered honestly.

“Then figure it out,” said Mal. “Because it cannot be me that excludes you from the standards of your blood while I perpetuate them for others.”

The words slammed into her. He may have threatened Primrose for talking down to her, but he had said it plain as day. He expected Purebloods to continue to marry and produce heirs, just as Primrose and the Committee wanted.

And he made no indication that he would stand in the way for her. It was hers to fight. To decide.

He made no alternative suggestion.

His second. That’s what she was.

That night in Albania was for Magical purposes, that much was clear. They hadn’t spent a night together since.

He reached out and ran his thumb along her jawline before they bid one another goodnight.

Maeve didn’t sleep at all.

In the early morning hours, she shot up from the bed, clutching her chest. Air moved tightly through her lungs.

Zimsy appeared at once.

Maeve rubbed at her chest. The air was squeezing her from the inside. Zimsy grabbed her shoulders just as the pain passed.

Maeve sighed and leaned back, against the pillows, bracing her hands on the bed.

"What was that?" Asked Zimsy.

Her hair was loose. Not in the Elven braids she normally wore intricately weaved across her head and down her back.

"I have no idea," said Maeve, running her fingers across her chest.

"Could it have anything to do with Alphard Mavros?"

Maeve's eyes shot to hers.

"Nothing happens in this house the servants don't know about."

Maeve groaned and laid back on the bed. Zimsy crossed the footboard to the other side and climbed onto the plush velvet bedding.

"What does he have to do with it?" Asked Maeve.

"I've heard stories about your human counterparts having chest pains when they are overwhelmed."

Maeve frowned. "Human counterparts?"

Zimsy smiled.

"You know you look like a human too," said Maeve.

Zimsy's smile dropped. "I most certainly do not."

She was right, of course. The ethereal glow of the Elven people rivaled that of even the Immortals. Her eyes were larger than theirs, her hair shiny as silk and her body glimmered like moonstone in the right lighting. Her ears were delicately drawn to a tip at the top.

"No," said Maeve with a soft smile, rolling onto her side. "You most certainly don't."

A week later, her chest tightened again. This time a wave of pain overcame her, making her head spin dizzy.

She excused herself from lunch.

"I think I need to go lie down.," said Maeve as air constricted in her lungs.

"Oh darling, send Trudy if you need me," Clarissa called after her.

The artificial sound of her mother's caring voice only fueled her nausea. This spell lasted longer, the pain in her chest was tighter.

"I think I should call Mrs. Mavros to see you," said Zimsy as Maeve splashed her face with cold water.

Maeve commanded her not to tell anyone about the incident and to bring her a pain potion.

Zimsy frowned and left her be. Maeve never gave her direct commands.

"Zimsy said you were sick all night," said Ambrose.

"Did she?" Asked Maeve dryly.

"Don't be angry," replied Ambrose. "I commanded her to tell me. Magic obeyed."

Ambrose's command superseded Maeve's as head of the household.

"Why?" Snapped Maeve.

"I worry something is wrong with you, Maeve."

"Nothing is wrong.'

"You've barely touched your breakfast, and I can see it all over your face." Ambrose pointed out. "If you're dabbling in unknown Magic, which I know you are, don't lie to me, you must be careful."

Maeve, truthfully, was reeling and felt as though she could drop to the floor at any moment.

"I'm fine," she lied. "I can handle it."

Pain lurked low into her stomach, tight and twisting and writhing.

She shot her father a look when he tried to push the subject further. He was ultimately proved right when Maeve vomited shortly after breakfast.

This frustrated her greatly as Ambrose put her to bed.

"But Mal is visiting today," whined Maeve. "And Abraxas leaves tomorrow."

"Good," said Ambrose. "Maybe he'll tell me what you're doing that is causing this."

"I'm not doing anything."

"We shall see. At any rate, you'll be laying in bed resting," said Ambrose. He closed the curtains in her room with the wave of his hand.

Maeve protested as Ambrose conjured a glass of water on her bedside table and pulled out a small vial. He emptied its clear contents into the water.

"Drink," he ordered.

She didn't protest.

Maeve downed the water. Her throat turned dry and her head hit the feathered pillows before she could even complain.

Chapter 47

"Premier Sinclair," started Mal but was quickly cut off.

"I've told you a hundred times, son, call me Ambrose."

That term hit Mal square in the chest.

The Premier smiled cooly at him. He saw Maeve in that smile. He relaxed into his chair.

Mal gave him a soft smile back. "May I be candid with you, sir?"

Ambrose puffed on his cigar and laughed. "What have you been so far?"

Mal chuckled softly.

"Firstly," started Mal, "I am sorry for dinner last week. This is your house. I worry I overstepped my bounds speaking to your Mother-in-Law in such a way."

Ambrose puffed on his cigar. "Do you know what delights me?"

Mal raised his brows.

"My daughter being protected."

Mal's stomach turned.

He hadn't seen her in a week. Not since he found out Alphard Mavros was to be her fiancé. Every time he pictured her face, he was on the brink of losing control. The foyer hallway in his flat had taken the brunt of that anger when he returned home that evening.

Maeve had no desire for Alphard. She desired power and glory.

Wealth maybe. . . Vain little thing that she was. And the Mavros were the richest Purebloods.

Perhaps that thought alone is what caused his anger to linger.

But that didn't change the simple fact that he wanted to crush Alphard's skull with his bare hands at the thought of their engagement.

Ambrose's voice pulled him from his thoughts. "She has always been rebellious, you know? Could never just do as she was told."

Mal smiled softly in agreement. His eyes traveled to Ambrose's mantelpiece, where a small photograph of Maeve was framed.

"What did you truly come here for today?" Asked Ambrose.

Mal wasted no time. He set aside the cigar he had only accepted purely to appeal to Ambrose. "What can you tell me about Di Inferi? I came across the term in a banned book, in connection to the underworld. It alluded that centuries ago necromancy was prevalent in the Dread Lands."

Ambrose answered at once. "They were called many things according to history. Dead Walkers. The Dreaded Dead. They were an army of undead used in the Shadow War, or as Reeve calls it: The War of Shadows."

"Is that what I am facing in those lands?" Asked Mal fearlessly.

There was a slight twitch in the corner of Ambrose's mouth. He looked away from Mal and took his time finishing his cigar. Finally, after many long moments, Ambrose looked at Mal with a twinkle in his eye.

"This isn't a Study conversation. What say you and I visit my basement?"

Mal eyed the tapestry on the far wall. Ambrose saw his gaze and answered before Mal asked.

"Dragon skin. The last Ironclad there was. My great-great-grandfather killed it himself on the Dark Planet. Killed him too."

Ambrose nodded to the giant dragon skull at the center of the room.

The scales on the dragon skin glittered in the light of the torches that wrapped the hall.

"What do you think of my collection?" Ambrose plopped himself in a black leather armchair and pulled another cigar from his pocket, proudly gesturing around the basement.

"I think it will take me quite a bit of time to read all those books." Mal smiled charmingly. "And that," he pointed to a particularly tattered trunk, "one reminded me about a recurring nightmare I had as a child."

Ambrose laughed. "Yes. You'll get many repressed memories from that one. Best not to open it when you're feeling vulnerable."

Mal strolled around the circular room, hands in his pockets, taking in everything as though he would never be granted access again.

"How did you come to all these things, sir?"

"Most of it's been in my family for hundreds of years, and some of it I sought out on my own. There's a scroll Merlin himself wrote. I paid a pretty penny for that one-an essay on familiars. He never completed his studies at Vaukore either. So enamored by those Humans."

"I read that."

"Ah," said Ambrose, as he puffed a ring of grey smoke inside another, larger circle.

Mal stopped in front of an emerald green velvet box. It reminded him of Maeve.

"How's she feeling?" Asked Ambrose. "She just lies to me about it. Hides it from me."

Mal wondered if it was a coincidence that Ambrose brought Maeve up at the exact moment he, too, thought of her.

"Fine, I believe. Better." Mal ran his finger along with the box. "Though she tries to hide it with me too." He looked up at the tall shelves, filled with the knowledge he knew he had to get his hands on.

"How do you know she's lying?"

"I infiltrate her mind," said Mal calmly, turning back towards Ambrose.

The Premier chuckled and turned his head to the side, unsure if Mal was joking or serious.

"Does that alarm you?" Asked Mal.

Ambrose took a puff off his cigar. "Does she know?"

Mal nodded. "I wouldn't invade her private thoughts if she didn't wish me to, Ambrose. She taught me how. I only have access if she allows it."

"Her shields are strong."

"Stronger than any other Pureblood I have tried on."

Mal strode over and took a seat by Ambrose, and continued.

"But your daughter and I share a strange connection too," said Mal in a low voice, staring across the hall. "I don't always have to be in her head to know what is happening to her."

Ambrose nodded, obviously intrigued by the idea. "She's mentioned."

"Would it be alright, sir, if we visited here regularly?"

Ambrose nodded. "You can take a few at a time home with you as well," said Ambrose gesturing to the endless library.

"I'd like to tell you something, sir," began Mal, his voice dropping to a low tone.

Ambrose shifted in his seat, placing his finished cigar in an ashtray.

"I hope it's not too bold," started Mal.

Ambrose shook his head. Mal looked at him. Maeve's father. The only person she worshipped more than himself. Mal spoke with a calm conviction.

"She will not marry Alphard Mavros."

Ambrose didn't move. He listened to Mal carefully with a vacant expression. Mal continued.

"She will be sworn in as my second in two months time. And on that day, any obligations to The Bellator, The Double O, or Committee of the Sacred will be null and void. If she is forced to uphold those obligations, then I will step in after my coronation."

Ambrose laid his head back in the armchair, the hint of a smile on his lips. "She won't go down without a fight."

"I am certain of that," said Mal. "But you warned me, neither will they."

Ambrose inhaled slowly. "They won't." Ambrose reached for a dark mahogany box and pulled out another cigar. "Any closer with another artifact of the Dread Armor?"

"The records for the auction of the Goblet are closed, but I am perusing a hopeful path towards it."

"Good," said Ambrose. "I was certain one of those rich disasters that come to my home would have it."

Mal nodded. "I believe you were correct. Though getting to it has presented an entirely different set of obstacles."

"Oh?" Said Ambrose.

Mal looked across the basement at the dragon's skull. He grinned. "I've never had a problem with persuasion."

Ambrose laughed heartily. Mal smiled at the sound and met his eyes. The Premier looked at him pridefully.

"Are you ready for The Autumn Gala?" He asked.

Mal crossed his legs. "I think you have prepared me as well as I can be. Do you think Lithandrian will come?"

"There are always surprises at these things." He puffed on his cigar. "Now," said Ambrose. "About those Dreaded Dead."

Chapter 48

Hundreds of guests arrived at Sinclair Estates for the Autumn Gala. Clarissa spent weeks planning this party. Ambrose ensured the Highest Orator's Office Officials were there and The High Lord himself was on the guest list.

Mal had extended an invitation to King Kier from The Ice Planet Hiems and received a gracious acceptance. They had not set foot on Earth in quite some time.

Kier was in attendance with his wife and two young children.

Mal also extended the invitation to The Elven Queen, though they knew it was unlikely she would leave her realm for a party. Her visit to the meeting Ambrose called was the first time she had left her realm in three hundred years.

"Maeve," Abraxas came bursting into her bedroom, his voice casual. "Could you- oh dear what's happened?"

Abraxas stopped abruptly and looked about the room after seeing the distressed look on Maeve's face.

She stood in one of the large windows, looking grim. With one finger, she motioned for Abraxas and pointed down at the gardens.

There was Ophelia and Mal, walking back towards the house.

"That won't do," said Maeve.

Abraxas clicked his tongue. "Poor girl," he said darkly. "Fix my bowtie, will you?"

Maeve sighed and assisted him. "Why is she even back here? They never come to these parties."

"Thank you," chimed Abraxas as he admired himself in the mirror before following Maeve out. "Mal invited her."

Maeve stopped. She took a long inhale. Then an even longer exhale. "I'm going to wring her neck with my bare hands- not even my Magic!" Maeve hissed to Abraxas, who laughed. "It's not funny."

"Oh it most certainly is, cousin."

Maeve's face dropped.

They made their way downstairs together, watching as guests were now arriving in droves through the ivory doors. Ambrose placed a charm in the foyer, and tonight the theme seemed to be butterflies. Glowing orbs shaped like the tiny winged creatures fluttered through the halls like floating ice sculptures.

She and Abraxas made their way onto the balcony, and Maeve grabbed a glass of sparkling water off a floating tray. Abraxas grabbed something stronger. The sun was setting over the horizon. The late fall blooms in the garden complemented the color of the sky beautifully.

Abraxas laughed to himself, then said, "You could duel her right here right now- that'd send her home crying."

"That would be a start," said Maeve sourly.

But Abraxas hadn't heard her at all.

"Gods.," he said. "Look at that."

"What?" Maeve followed his gaze over to the garden stairs where her father was walking down with an incredibly well-dressed blonde young man. His face was long, his ears were tipped to a small point. She recognized him. He sat behind Lithandrian at their meeting.

"Who is that?" Asked Maeve in amazement.

He was Elven. Dressed in the finest cream satin formal wear.

Abraxas nearly choked on his drink.

"Amaranthine Maeve Sinclair. I have failed you."

Maeve shot him an incredulous look at the use of her full name. "It's your job to know all these pricks and all their secrets, not mine."

"That's Olympium Xander. Prince of the Elven Lands. And hand to Queen Lithandrian."

"They came," she whispered, and her heart swelled. "Her little brother?"

Abraxas nodded. "He's pretty."

Truly, he was. Light beamed off his smooth skin, just like it did Zimsy's. The Elven people had a feminine and light air about them.

Mal and Ophelia had now made their way up to the balcony.

"Good evening, Maeve," said Mal, the evening sunset liquifying his molten dark eyes. His eyes trailed up and down her body.

Maeve's stomach flipped. She had still not grown used to the sight of him in a suit.

"Mal was jus' giving me some last-minute pointerz in case I get picked tonight to duel. I honestly sink I stand a chance now!"

Ophelia giggled in a shrill way that caused Abraxas to recoil.

Mal took a glass off a floating tray and leaned in close to Maeve's ear.

"Helpless," whispered Mal.

His hand glided across her back. She relaxed.

"Did you see?" Maeve whispered, jerking her head towards Xander.

"I did," he murmured into his glass. "Would you like to join me?"

"Later," she said. "Let him see you and you alone."

Mal looked down at her, tucked a loose strand of hair back into one of her braids and whispered, "Yes, Little Viper."

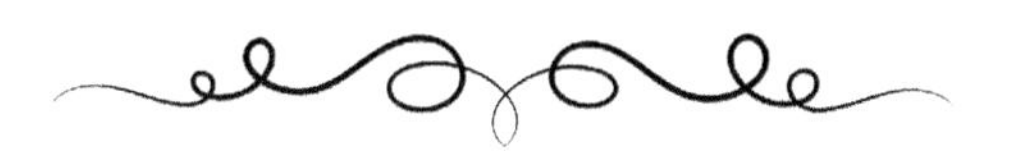

Xander seemed delighted to meet Mal. Maeve and Abraxas took to the bar inside for most of the evening and let Mal work his magic on Kier and Xander.

Maeve's chest tightened.

"Excuse me," said Maeve suddenly to Abraxas and Juliet, a stunning blonde whom Maeve attended primary girl's school with. Her parents were loaded with money and with Pureblood back as far as the first Magicals. Abraxas happily took Maeve's seat next to Juliet and moved in closer to her.

Juliet's cheeks flushed.

Maeve barely made it out the balcony doors and around the corner before she vomited into the bushes. She clutched her stomach as sweat pooled on her brow. Her chest was icily tight. Once again.

Zimsy appeared with a SWISH. She handed Maeve a small bottle and opened her tiny mouth.

"Zip it," said Maeve.

She downed the pain potion and Zimsy shook her head. She snatched the bottle back from Maeve and disappeared.

"One too many?"

Maeve turned over her shoulder and suppressed the breath that rose in her chest. Abraxas was correct. He may have been the most handsome man she'd ever seen. His dark hair hung casually at his shoulders. His sharp and earthy scent slammed into her. His tan face wasn't completely shaved. His light shadow of stubble caused her eyes to linger on him for longer than she would have liked.

Damn.

She recovered quickly. "I don't drink."

Reeve looked her over, his eyes narrowing slightly across his otherwise casual demeanor.

His black leather top fitted him perfectly, dipping open into his chest. Three tiered necklaces hung from his neck. Each with a symbol she didn't know the meaning of. It was no language she had studied. But she had seen it before. In books about Vexkari, and carved into the hollowed tree in The Black Forest.

"You should see a Healer," he said.

Maeve mustered the strength to scowl at him. A playful glimmer danced across his face at her annoyance.

His eyes were a sunset to themselves.

"I'm fine," said Maeve. "And I've already seen Mrs. Mavros."

"I don't mean a Witch Doctor," he replied. "I mean a Healer."

"Same difference," said Maeve as nausea rolled through her.

"Not at all," said Reeve. "A Healer has power ordained from the Gods. Irma is merely a good nurse. And you're not fine. There is dark Magic hurting you that you did not create."

"Fuck you," snapped Maeve cooly.

"My, my," said Reeve with a slick smile. "You're spicy this evening. All guards down."

"Would you prefer me to engage with you in the forced and fake manner that I spend nearly all of my interactions at such events as these?"

Reeve's smile met his eyes. "No. You're much more fun this way."

Maeve rolled her eyes with a quick shake of her head.

"I'll go fetch Mal for you then," said Reeve.

"No," said Maeve quickly. "No, thank you."

"Hiding something, are we?"

"Can you mind your own business?"

Reeve gave another small chuckle.

"I don't mind sending my own Healer to see you, or you can come to Aterna to see her. I'm sure Ambrose would love a visit to my city again."

"You will say nothing of this to my father," said Maeve.

Reeve's face twisted in confusion, with a hint of pity. "I don't know why you're hiding from them, or from the reality that something is wrong, but if you change your mind-"

"I won't," said Maeve carelessly.

Reeve downed the rest of his drink and shrugged, the concern on his face gone. "Have it your way."

The moon was high when Mal and Ophelia disappeared into the crowd as she stole him from speaking to Kier's wife. Maeve attempted to hide that she noticed this, but there was very little hiding from Abraxas.

"You're overthinking," murmured Abraxas.

Maeve sighed and ignored him.

"Primus and the Gods," whispered Abraxas, his glass of brandy dropping from his lips.

Maeve followed his gaze across the hall. Reeve, stood shaking hands with her father. He gave her mother's hand a kiss.

"Ugh," said Maeve, rolling her eyes. "I don't know what the fuss is over with him."

Abraxas grimaced. "First, he's the most powerful being alive. Second, I didn't realize you went blind, cousin. Look at him."

"No," said Maeve, turning back to the bar.

"He's coming this way," said Abraxas hurriedly.

"No, he's not," said Maeve.

Abraxas pulled his drink to his lips and murmured, "Yes, he is."

"Mr. Rosethorn," came Reeve's voice. "Maeve."

"You don't intend to address me formally as well?" She asked dryly, turning towards him.

"I feel more aquatinted with you than, what is it, your cousin?"

Abraxas smiled brightly at Reeve and nodded. Maeve rolled her eyes and turned fully towards Reeve.

"Abraxas, this is the High Lord of Aterna, the Shadow Slayer, and Senshi Warrior. High Lord, Shadow Slayer and Senshi Warrior, this is my cousin Abraxas."

Reeve eyed her humorously. "You honor me, little kitten."

Abraxas choked loudly on his drink, spilling it across the front of his suit. He turned towards the bar and hastily dried his attire with the snap of his fingers.

Maeve smiled at Reeve. "The honor is all mine, your *majesty*."

Reeve tilted his head back and nodded slowly, sizing her up. He exhaled loudly.

"Abraxas," said Reeve. "Do you enjoy cigars?"

Abraxas turned towards the High Lord. "Sinfully."

"Come," said Reeve. "Ambrose and I have a new box to break open. It looks like your cousin has more brooding she'd like to do. Let's leave her to it."

Maeve bit her bottom lip and shook her head with a suppressed smirk. Abraxas quickly kissed her cheek and followed Reeve off without so much as a goodbye.

She made her way out of the hall, attempting to look for Mal discreetly. She drifted through the ballroom nonchalantly. There was no sign of Mal or Ophelia.

"Have you seen Mal?" She approached Mr. and Mrs. Mavros and unapologetically interrupted their conversation with January Jones, the senior editor of The Magical Times.

"No, darling, I'm afraid not," replied Mrs. Mavros, sweetly tucking Maeve's hair behind her ear.

Maeve moved past them without a reply before whipping back around and interrupting them once again.

"Have you seen Ophelia?" She asked.

They all shook their heads, slightly confused.

"Right," Maeve smiled charmingly, "carry on."

She stuck her head in the dining hall and abruptly turned around on the ball of her foot when she realized it was vacant save for Alphard Mavros and a red-headed Pureblood girl she had met only a handful of times that was his age. Victoria was her name.

The grandfather clock in the foyer chimed a quarter to seven o'clock, meaning dinner would soon be served.

Maeve found Mal and Ophelia in the library. It was dimly lit, and she spotted them across the room between two rows of books. Mal was showing Ophelia something in a book.

A deep wave of nausea passed through her from watching them stand so close together in private. She observed them for a moment, hating the way he smiled down at Ophelia.

She backed away on the tips of her toes and walked across the marble floor as quietly as possible, leaving the library.

She wanted to smack herself. And then smack him. And then really smack Ophelia.

"There you are."

Maeve was drawn from her thoughts by Daniel Rodriguez.

"Mr. Rodriguez," said Maeve, as politely as she could, given that she felt like punching something.

Mr. Rodriguez had a punchable face. Good enough at least.

"I was just on my way out, rather early morning tomorrow, but was hoping I'd run into you."

"Still haven't filled that Assistant Junior Undersecretary Position?" Maeve wondered if perhaps too much sass had slipped into her tone, but Daniel smiled at her.

"I'm so curious about you."

Maeve cocked her head to one side. Daniel continued.

"Clement Parsons on the Committee of Experimental Charms said they offered you a higher position and higher pay. You didn't take that either. Wilkinson at the Creation of Magic office said the same."

"Perhaps you lot do not understand the common factor among you," said Maeve.

"Come now," said Daniel, laughing. "You joined the Bellator. The Double O is not so bad. Your Father loves it."

Maeve knew that wasn't completely true, but smiled sweetly at Daniel all the same. Her Father tolerated his job because of the power and position he held.

"I believe dinner is starting soon, Mr. Rodriguez. I'll trust you can see yourself out."

Maeve walked past him and back into the main hallway. She entered the Great Dining Room, where the table was set for nearly one hundred people.

A few had already taken their seats. The enchanted butterflies from the foyer fluttered their way into the room. Maeve found the card with her name on it to the right of the head of the table and next to her father. Mal's name was beside her.

Maeve contemplated moving his name card further down on the table, away from her.

He arrived in the Hall a few moments later, with Ophelia on his arm. Maeve's jaw snapped shut as she watched them walk across the room together.

Touching.

A group of women seemed excited to see Ophelia, and much to Ophelia's dismay, pulled her away from Mal, who was heading towards Maeve.

She looked down at the name card on the other side of Mal's.

"Of course," muttered Maeve bitterly, snatching up Ophelia's name card and swapping it with one much further down on the table.

"Maeve, darling," she heard her father's voice call out.

She jumped, and he was striding towards her quickly. Ambrose was in a cheerful mood, it seemed. He came closer and spoke in a hushed voice.

"The Elven Hand would like to sit across from you. Next to me."

"Who?"

"The Prince. Xander."

Maeve blinked. "Alright."

"The Prince is staying for dinner?" Mal appeared next to her now.

"Yes, well, you would know that had you not been holed up in the library for the past half hour."

She smiled at him sweetly. Mal gave her a reproachful look, knowing her sweet demeanor was fake.

"Are you alright?"

"Fine," she replied hastily.

"Finally! Maeve Sinclair."

Maeve and Mal looked across the table. Xander took his place behind the chair across from Maeve.

"We meet at last," he said.

Maeve thought this was possibly the worst time to have to put on a show. She would rather be anywhere else at the moment, especially not having to charm an Elven diplomat and brother of the Elven Queen.

Maeve plastered on her most charming smile. "It's lovely to finally meet you, sir."

"Sir?" Xander laughed. "I've only just celebrated my thirtieth birthday. I hope I'm not old enough for you to call me 'sir'."

"Apologies," said Maeve. "I'm sure 'my Prince' will suffice, then?"

Mal's magic tensed up next to her, which brought her great satisfaction.

"Xander will be fine," said the Elven Queen's brother playfully, eyeing Maeve with a flirtatious look.

On his breast pocket was a pale blue butterfly.

Kier appeared at Xanders' side.

The ice.

The decor for the evening made sense now.

Everyone stood behind their seats at the Grand Dinner Table, and Ambrose took his place at one head of the table and Clarissa at the other. Once they were seated, the rest of the party pulled back their chairs and followed suit.

Mr. Iantrose sat down on the other side of Mal. Mal looked to Maeve with a curious brow raised.

"Oh, Merlin," muttered Maeve, placing a hand on her temple as Iantrose began barking some incoherent nonsense loudly. She had not paid attention to whose card she swapped with Ophelia's.

The food was delicious, and it was served on the finest treasure. Clarissa saved the real crystal only for the most important guests. And their home was currently full of them.

The conversation flowed lightly, but Maeve was more reserved than usual, granting her many looks from her father. She was completely in a daze, swirling around a bit of soup. She snapped back to reality when she heard Xander bring up a particularly touchy subject.

"I hear you are half human," he said to Mal. Xander laughed, but an awkward silence fell amongst those around them. "Then I am with great company! My cousin is half human. Down there by Reeve. His second in command, Eryx."

Maeve looked down the table where Reeve and Eryx sat. Abraxas sat across from them. The three of them having more than their fair share of fun. Abraxas poured them all another round.

Reeve's eyes lifted to Maeve. He looked to Xander and then winked at Maeve. She rolled her eyes and brought her attention back to the conversation at hand.

Maeve knew the last thing Mal wanted was to be reminded of his parents, even if Xander was wrong.

She spoke, so he didn't have to.

"Actually, Xander, both of Mal's parents were Magicals. But I am curious," said Maeve with a drawl, as though hanging on his every word, "does it feel strange to be the only non-Magical being here?"

Ambrose's eyes shot to Maeve. Abraxas had told her everything. He was the son of royalty, yes, but what little Elven power their kind possessed, which was usually that of battle, Xander was gifted with no skills besides his politics.

Xander didn't miss a beat. "Only as strange as it feels to be the only member of the Royal Elven Family here."

Maeve replied with a charming laugh. "Ah- of course. Well, I hope you'll volunteer for tonight's duel. I know we're all dying to see such royal abilities."

Ambrose kicked his youngest under the table. Maeve bit her lip and didn't take her eyes off Xander.

"You are every bit as ferocious as I had hoped," said Xander. "You studied at Vaukore, correct?"

Maeve nodded.

"What prestige," continued Xander. "Your Father tells me you studied Practical Magic, were Head Girl, and best in your year."

Maeve smirked at her father, already haven forgiven him for kicking her. "Head Girl, yes, however, I was second best. Mal was the best in our year. My Father is kindly biased."

"Mally and Maeve are quite the pair," slurred Mr. Iantrose. "I remember when I taught them in school!"

"You never taught us, Mr. Iantrose," said Maeve.

"Never taught school at all," muttered Ambrose with a grin.

"Of course," said Xander. "The Dread Descendant would be at the top."

Maeve looked up at Mal. "Where he belongs."

Mal looked over at her, smiling softy with humility.

"I don't mean to pry," said Xander. "Our worlds have just been apart for so long." He turned his attention to Ambrose and raised his glass. "Here's to new alliances between The Orator's Office and the Royal Elven Family," Xander turned his glass to Maeve, "and to new bloodlines."

Maeve's stomach dropped about a hundred feet.

That was bold.

Too bold.

Quite a few heads turned their way. Ambrose held his composure well, but for the first time all evening, Maeve thought perhaps her father wasn't genuinely fawning all over The Elven Prince. Perhaps he was caught between a rock and a hard place.

To new bloodlines, she repeated over and over to herself, each time growing more panicked and nauseous.

He hadn't just come for an alliance with Mal or the Double O. He came, with that stupid smile he must have thought was charming, to win her.

Maeve hadn't realized how fast her breathing had become until Mal's long, slender fingers rested on her leg underneath the table. His thumb traced cool, calming circles across her thigh.

Ambrose gave Xander a small nod and met Maeve's eyes for a moment. He couldn't hide his expression of shame from her.

After dinner, Maeve and Mal took their places at the center of the Dueling Hall. Mal had been picked to duel Arman, but Arman fell too ill after Maeve saw Ambrose whisper hurriedly to him just before the duel.

Ambrose then suggested Maeve and Mal show them all what Vaukore was teaching their children. Maeve noted to herself that none of what they were about to see was learned from any Professor at Vaukore.

Everyone was eager to see what The Dread Descendant and the young Bellator Optimum could do.

Maeve and Mal danced their duel as usual. Nowadays, most of their time spent practicing was no longer with dueling formalities, and they were freer.

She enjoyed herself nonetheless. Mal let her show off, showed himself off, and they both put on a show for the crowd. Maeve held on longer than Mal meant for her to.

She was growing stronger.

She sat back on her knees, breathing heavily as Mal stood over her with his finger pointed at her throat. Ophelia cheered for him above all the rest.

He smirked down at Maeve.

"Well done," said Mal extending his hand to her, pulling her to her feet. "You held on longer than usual."

Hand in hand, they took a bow. Mal was swarmed at once as Maeve slipped through the crowd. She headed for the bar, where her father leaned, bragging on her loudly. She needed refreshing after that performance.

She overheard one of her father's friends say that they had never seen a boy so young with so much strength.

"Dread Magic is ancient," said Ambrose. "Not unlike pureblooded magic, but something else entirely, too."

Mal had one more duel, of which she knew he would win. The crowd never grew tired of watching him beat elite soldiers twice his age in a duel, though. They were just as captivated by him now as they were over the summer when he arrived.

Maeve was on the back balcony with Abraxas, admiring the illuminated butterflies that now lit up over the gardens.

"They were my idea you know," said Abraxas.

"I should have known," she replied.

"Maeve, darling," said Ambrose, appearing at her side.

"I'll give you a moment," said Abraxas.

"No," said Ambrose. "Stay. If you are to be Malachite's hand, it is crucial you understand the game." Ambrose wasted no time getting to the point and spoke openly to Maeve. "I need you to go thank Xander for being here tonight and offer to see him out. It would mean a great deal. . . for appearances."

"A game indeed," shot Maeve. "So it can appear that I'm remotely interested in this nonsense?"

"I know you don't want Xander. I know you don't want Alphard."

"Is that so terrible?"

Abraxas opened his mouth to speak and then closed it.

Ambrose gave him a nod.

"It's not that it's terrible, Maeve," said Abraxas. "It's that things are delicate right now. And everything we can do to ensure that Mal is crowned and we return to the Dread Lands is critical."

Maeve looked to her Father. He inclined his head as if to say Abraxas nailed it.

Maeve found it difficult to argue. After she chewed her lip for a moment, she sighed. "Fine."

Maeve pushed past them both and headed to find The Elven Prince.

"It was incredibly kind of you to have me tonight," said Xander.

"Oh, I believe we're the ones lucky to have you. We are overwhelmed by the Queen's willingness to communicate and join forces."

"I do hope we can see one another again. You turned out to be a pleasant surprise."

"Oh?"

"Yes! That duel!"

This brought a genuine smile to Maeve's face. But as quickly as it arrived, it vanished when he continued speaking.

"You looked beautiful."

Maeve scoffed and couldn't help but shake her head.

"Were you impressed with the duel itself?" Asked Maeve.

"Oh yes," said Xander flippantly. "I was hoping to see some of that rumored mind work. . ." He said it like he didn't believe she could do it. He came to a stop at the gate as it opened for him, taking a step towards her. "But you looked so-"

"Beautiful yeah, you said," sighed Maeve coldly. "Goodnight, Xander."

She turned on her heel without waiting for a response and returned to the house. He may have been an Elven Prince, but he was a shallow one. She couldn't bring herself to play the game. It only took her a moment to find Mal sitting in the study. He spoke first, not looking at her.

"Where did you get off to?"

"Just doing us all a favor, apparently."

"That's all?"

"That's all it would ever be."

The silence between them was thick. Mal wasn't reading the book in his hands. He stared straight at the wall. Maeve studied him for a moment before asking where Ophelia was.

"He is going to pursue you," said Mal, ignoring her question. "Lithandrian sent him for that reason. You for her army." His voice dropped to a whisper. "And the world looking at us would love to see that happen, wouldn't they?"

It wasn't a question, but a statement.

Maeve knew it was taking all his strength not to explode right there.

"Well, it depends on who you mean by 'they'," replied Maeve. "The Double O- oh yes. My father- completely torn over his political duties and my own happiness. The Elven Royals, obviously my blood status is the appeal. The common Magicals would eat up such an affair, yes. My mother- through the moon for one of her own to marry someone so powerful, only I'm sure she wishes it wasn't me. Part of her whole campaign for my unhappiness, I suspect."

Mal didn't laugh at her joke. "And you?"

She sighed, impatient now, frustrated with how the entire evening had gone.

"Goodnight, Mal. You are welcome to see yourself out." She paused, needing a moment to muster the courage for what she was about to say. "My bedroom fireplace will be open to you tonight, should you really need an answer to that question."

She walked away without waiting to even gauge his reaction. She began climbing to the third floor as the last few guests were stumbling their way down to the foyer.

"Goodnight, Maeve!" January Johnson hiccuped.

"Safe travels," replied Maeve weakly.

Once inside her bedroom, she locked the door with a wave of her wrist. It wouldn't be the first time a drunken guest had stumbled in mistakenly, looking for a bathroom or a closet. She walked into her bathroom and began undressing. The oversized, circular tub was already filled with hot water and what appeared to be lavender, as bright purple bubbles were escaping the edges. Zimsy's doing. Maeve thanked her audibly. The bubbles turned pink.

With a soft snap of her fingers, her hair was down, and she ran her fingers through it, massaging, frustrated. As the hot bath water hit her skin, her mind drifted.

It drifted deep into the memory of Mal's hands on her, inside her. The feeling of their bodies pressed together, all the while knowing they shouldn't, had been an intoxicating thrill.

But it had been weeks since that night in Albania. He had not pulled her close that way since.

Perhaps it was no more than a spell for him. A necessary duty to repair the Finders Stone. Maeve didn't want to admit the pang in her heart at the thought. But it remained all the same.

Ophelia had his attention all night.

They didn't dance. He didn't kiss her before any of the guests. Abraxas was right. They had to do whatever it took to get Mal on that throne. Whatever it took to restore the Dread Lands.

She hadn't realized it would come with the cost of her sanity, though. She allowed herself to soak until all the bubbles had long gone and resigned herself to go to bed.

She laid her head back and looked up at the night sky twinkling across her enchanted canopy bed, rattling off the names of constellations in her head. Her mind was too busy to fall asleep.

A loud crackling sound filled the room, and her sapphire room flashed bright green. She sat up to see Mal stepping out of the fireplace.

Chapter 49

Mal moved across the room swiftly. Before Maeve could speak, he was at her side, pushing her back onto the bed with a firm kiss. His hand slid around her back and pressed their bodies together. He sat up and pulled Maeve with him so that she sat straddling his lap on the edge of the bed.

Her cheeks flushed and her body shook with adrenaline at his sudden appearance. She pressed her forehead against his and tried to calm her breathing as his hands glided across her satin nightgown. She placed her trembling hands on his shoulders.

She pulled away and looked at him as his eyes traveled down her chest.

"He has some nerve," whispered Mal, as his finger trailed along her collarbones.

She felt him growing hard between her legs. Maeve tilted her head back and tried not to become overwhelmed.

"Why did you wait so long?" She whispered.

Mal was silent. She opened her eyes and looked down at him. "Why now?"

His eyes darkened. "You know why now."

She pushed away from him. His hands held her in place. "Because you are jealous?"

Mal's head cocked to one side as he let out a controlled breath. Maeve pressed on.

"Then why the first time? You've had me convinced it was all for that spell, nothing more. That my virginity was a tool you kept in your back pocket until you needed it." The honest words poured from her before she could stop them. "And now, seeing her on your arm-"

Mal's hands moved to her cheeks and pulled her lips to his. His kiss was softer this time. Supple and gentle. Maeve kissed him back tenderly, moving her hands to his hair.

He kissed her until her breaths were long and even, and once they were, their lips parted. He held her face between his hands.

"Your purity was important to me because I knew once I had you, that a line would be crossed we could never take back. I knew I would see you as mine and mine alone. That it might inhibit your future. I dreamt about corrupting your sweet body long before I did. But I waited for you to come to me. To decide to be mine."

She gasped as he flipped her onto her back on the bed, his chest pressing against hers.

"I have taken many. That night in Albania you gave yourself to me," he whispered. "That is what I was waiting for."

He slid off her and whisked the limp bowtie off his neck, swiftly unbuttoning his shirt and discarding them both. Maeve pushed herself up as he crawled back on top of her. His slender chest was perfectly sculpted, smooth as stone.

Their lips were inches apart and Maeve desperately wanted to kiss him.

"Tell me what I want to hear, Little Viper," said Mal as their noses brushed.

Maeve swallowed hard and tried to keep her composure. She couldn't bring herself to speak. He sighed, but a wicked glimmer shot across his eyes.

His hands gripped her throat tightly and pinned her to the bed. Maeve's hands instinctively shot to his, tugging on them.

"I want to hear you say it."

Maeve looked up at him with wide eyes. His expression was fierce and feline. His grip tightened until Maeve relented. Her words were shattered and hoarse.

"I have no desire to marry him," said Maeve hastily.

Mal released her throat as Maeve coughed and breathed deeply. He brushed her hair out of her face.

"And why is that?" Asked Mal slowly and meticulously.

Maeve looked up at him, panting, the skin on her throat hot and pulsing. "Because I'm yours."

Mal nodded serenely. "Because you are mine."

Those words swimming from his lips caused her body to push up towards his and her legs to spread impatiently. He smiled hungrily and ran his hands down across her satin nightgown, to her exposed thighs, his eyes raking over her whole body. His hand moved in between her legs and she gasped as his thumb pressed into her, moving in slow circles. He positioned two fingers at her entrance and stopped.

Those chocolate eyes were the color of night in the darkened bedroom. They landed on her own. "Every inch of you is mine."

Then those two fingers slipped inside her so slowly it hurt. She wined as he pulled them out, and back in again, each time pressing further inside her.

"Do you understand?" He asked.

Maeve nodded. Unable to form any sound other than a small moan.

"Good girl," said Mal as he pulled his fingers away from her and lowered his mouth to where they had just been. She pushed herself towards him.

"Greedy little thing," he said as he pressed a kiss against her thigh.

His lips trailed closer and closer to the warm, raging spot between her legs. He stopped as they nearly brushed against her clit.

His eyes were the most beautifully wicked orbs of darkness.

"Say it once more," he hummed against her.

She obeyed.

"Every inch of me is yours," she replied desperately.

His head reeled back at her words. His mouth was cool as it pressed into that pulsing bundle of nerves between her legs. His tongue flicked out over her, and Maeve jerked beneath him.

His hands moved to her hips, holding her in place as his tongue explored her with precision. She writhed underneath him, desperate to be closer. Her hands wound into his hair, a silent plea for more.

More and more and more until that wasn't enough.

"I want all of you," she said.

Mal's paralyzing tongue pulled away from her, and he stood. He removed his pants as Maeve propped herself up on her elbows. Her stomach flipped when she saw he was fully erect. He stroked himself a few times, his eyes locked on Maeve. She felt herself completely ready for him.

He crawled towards her, and she stilled.

He positioned himself back between her legs, his cock poised and ready.

"I was nice the first time. I won't be nice tonight," said Mal.

Excitement shot through her, and her hips pressed towards his. His hand moved down and positioned himself at her entrance.

"When it hurts," continued Mal, "remind yourself who you belong to."

He slammed inside of her fully, and she cried out.

He wasn't lying.

The night they shared in Albania had been different. That night he eased into her, his thrusts were slow and sensual. Now he was buried fully inside her and he pumped in and out.

Fucking her.

She began to protest as his movements spread her but Mal's hand covered her mouth and pushed her off her elbows, slamming her back onto the bed.

His movements were rough as their flesh fused. She wined against his hand and gripped his arms. Mal's eyes rolled to a close as his head tilted back. His hand moved away from her mouth.

And then something sparked inside Maeve. A realization washed over her, one she probably should have realized before. It wasn't just jealousy or possession that drove him in and out of her. It was his own pleasure she was seeing. Pleasure at her body, her skin. Her.

"Are you mine?" She asked.

He sucked in a sharp breath. "In every meaning of the word."

She relaxed against him. And the pain turned to pleasure. Mal's hands moved to her waist. As he pushed into her, he pulled her down. He smirked as her pain returned. She grabbed his face and pulled his lips down to hers. Their mouths moved in perfect rhythm, breathing through their noses.

Mal pulled away from her lips and nuzzled into her neck. Maeve's knees pulled up towards her as his lips worked their way down her chest. His teeth grazed the thin fabric, cupping her breast. He tugged on it until her entire chest was exposed and her satin straps fell off her shoulders.

Her fingers gripped his raven hair as he nipped at her breast. His tongue swirled and teased until she was groaning.

He was suddenly very tight inside her. He pulled from her and rested back on his knees.

His cock was dripping with herself, the veins that ran through it pulsing slightly.

"Turn around."

She obeyed.

Once her back was to him, he wasted no time slipping back inside of her. The sensation was different, and she felt herself wanting to push back to have more of him.

Heat, tight and pressing, rose up between her legs. She tossed her head back as his smooth hands slid across her spine.

"Mal I-" she started as the pressure built where he slid through her.

It rose and rose, gripping her insides in wet all-consuming euphoria. She gasped as that tension slammed and spiraled out of her, releasing in a shaking and uncontrolled way. Maeve cried out helplessly in her release.

"There we go," he said triumphantly as she orgasmed.

Mal's hands moved to her hips, pulling her back against him as he thrust forward.

"He thinks he stands a chance," said Mal, "but if only he could see you now."

Mal's hands snaked down her back and tightened around her throat, causing her back to arch downwards. The tighter his grip around her throat grew, the harder he became inside her. The asphyxiation heightened all of her senses.

He thrust in and out of her in a primal way. Maeve lost all ability to hold herself up. Only his grip kept her in position. She felt nothing but his cock buried inside her and the fuzziness in her mind. His grip quickly became so tight that Maeve couldn't breathe. She clawed at his hands, but there was no moving him.

Just when she felt herself blacking out, Mal felt the biggest so far. Maeve gasped for air as he released her throat.

"Tell me again who you belong to," commanded Mal.

"You," gasped Maeve, her voice broken and hoarse, between thrusts. "I belong to you."

He grew quiet for a moment, inhaling loudly. Then his gasping, whimpering, satisfaction filled the room as he thrust inside of her one final time. His swollen cock pulsed, spilling every drop of himself deep inside her.

The warm feeling of his satisfaction dripping out of her brought her eyes to a close. He slipped out of her.

The first time, she didn't think about much. Mal had been soft, and most of her mind was occupied with worrying about him. But now, she was invigorated by the idea that she could make him do that. That she could bring him over the edge and that a part of his body had been given to her.

Mal stood beside the bed with long breaths. Maeve turned to face him. He took her chin in his hand.

"I will kill him if he ever touches you," said Mal, his voice humming between pants. "I don't care if it means the Elven Queen never opens her borders again. I'll do it with my bare hands."

Shadows pulled across his face. She moved to her knees on the edge of the mattress and traced her fingers down his chest, along the toned lines of his slender frame.

"And what of Alphard?"

Mal dropped his hand. "I told you that was yours to fight. Ensure it's done."

Chapter 50

Abraxas' voice pulled Mal's thoughts out of his daydream. Though it was less of a daydream and more the image of Maeve's helpless body as he conquered her the night before.

"You named her your second," said Abraxas. "Not your betrothed. We were foolish to think Maeve wouldn't be sought after. She is one of the only remaining Purebloods unwed-"

Mal held up his hand. And then placed it on his temple. Rain pattered against the slanted windows in his penthouse suite.

Abraxas took a moment, then pulled a cigar from his coat pocket and used the tips of his fingers to light it. He drew in a large pull and took his time exhaling. He looked out over the city below. Mal's penthouse sat high. "You are the Prince of Darkness. Not King of the Seven Realms. Everything else continues to turn, despite our plans to return home."

"I cannot see her married off to some Elven Lord," he said tensely.

"Then make her yours, Mal," pressed Abraxas. "There is little else to be said."

"It is not that simple," retorted Mal. He relaxed back into his study chair, his legs crossed.

"How?"

"Because your cousin does not desire such a thing," he said quietly. "She is validated as my second. She doesn't want the title of wife. It cheapens her as a warrior. She wants the respect that comes with being my Dread Viper. Not my Lady."

Abraxas sighed. "Then the pair of you will have to accept the reality that while all of that is true, The Mavros family and Lithandrian seem to think she can be your Dread Viper and reproduce Magical heirs with their men all in a day's work."

Mal's eyes slid to Abraxas.

"Only the messenger," said Abraxas. "But as your messenger, let me also say: Maeve is not the only one being vied for."

Mal's brows rose.

"The Walthons have suggested their daughter to you."

Mal almost grimaced. "She's a child."

"They are willing to wait. And provide a gracious donation to the crown."

Mal opened his mouth to speak but came up short.

"And," said Abraxas. "The St. Beverauxs."

"Ophelia?" Asked Mal.

Abraxas nodded.

Mal sighed.

"Again," said Abraxas, taking another puff of his cigar, "we clearly didn't calculate for this."

"Clearly," said Mal. "Isn't that your job?"

Abraxas didn't look at him. "I would urge we not decline them just yet."

"I believe I am in agreement but may I ask why?"

"Because," started Abraxas. "We need their support. We can't isolate any families right now. Which is what I told Maeve when she refused to escort Xander out."

It had been Abraxas' persuasion. For his benefit.

Mal nodded after a moment.

"I'll simply prolong any talk of a decision," said Abraxas. "However-"

"I know," said Mal. "I can handle Maeve."

"And Maeve?"

Mal laced his fingers together. "Maeve can handle herself."

"Wonderful," said Abraxas, pressing his cigar into the bronze ashtray on Mal's table. "Now," he turned towards him, "who is handling Alphard?"

Mal's teeth slid together. "Maeve is."

Abraxas's brows pulled together. "That was your doing?"

"Yes," said Mal slowly.

Abraxas looked away from him.

"You doubt my judgment?"

Abraxas looked back at him. He sighed. "I'm going to speak as your hand and your friend now, Mal." Abraxas folded his arms across his chest, his tone conversational. "Maeve doesn't want Alphard, but make no mistake," Abraxas hesitated, "she loves him."

Mal looked up at Abraxas as the corners of the room flickered darkly.

"You weren't there," Abraxas continued calmly. "Antony and Alphard were inseparable. They were the class favorites, the cut-ups, and the misbehaviors. They crashed Sacred parties and got kicked out of dinners. Antony and Alphard were bonded from a young age. Maeve loves him because Antony did."

Mal resisted the urge to sink his fingers into the arms of the chair. "I know that. But that has nothing to do with her ability to ensure that their engagement never happens."

"I am certain my cousin is capable of anything she sets her mind to," said Abraxas with admiration. "But that is not my concern. I'm asking why make her do it? When it will only hurt her to have to? Any affection between them is in memory of her dead brother and I suppose I don't agree with tarnishing it at her hand."

"What would you have me do? I cannot fight every battle for her Abraxas, she must come into her own."

"Tell him that," said Abraxas. "Tell him to refuse. We all know he wants Victoria, anyway."

Mal was quiet for a moment. His hands relaxed, and he folded them in his lap. "I will consider it."

Abraxas smiled. "That is all I can ask."

Mal was eager for the subject to change. "What else for today?"

"We need to go over the guest list for Arianna and Titus' wedding next week. I have the list stacked. Much smaller than the Autumn Gala Party, so you'll have more time with those that really matter."

"I thought you said they all mattered," said Mal dryly.

"They do," said Abraxas with a nod. "But some more than others. Those that oppose the Orator's Office are those that supported Kietel. You need them. But I also invited Dillon Shelby, who ran Moon's campaign. You need those whose ear he has as well."

Chapter 51

Maeve's two least favorite guests returned to Sinclair Estates shortly after The Autumn Gala and she was forced to entertain Xander and Ophelia once more.

"Heads up," said Abraxas quietly.

Maeve looked inside the house and groaned.

"Damn," said Maeve. "I lost track of time. I could have run and hid upstairs-"

Ophelia threw her arms around Maeve as soon as she walked onto the balcony, and Maeve pushed her away gently with a smile. Ophelia turned to Abraxas and kissed his cheek. Abraxas wiped his face with his hand when she turned her back.

Xander walked onto the balcony shortly after Ophelia, and he was not alone. To his side was The Senshi Warrior. He was Reeve's second, Commander of the Aterna Army.

Eryx was his name. Xander's half-human cousin.

Ambrose and Mal rounded the corner together, and Ophelia bounced on her heels when she saw Mal.

"Eryx," said her father. "Xander."

"Ambrose," they responded in unison.

"Are you about to go riding?" Asked Ophelia with a smile.

"Yes," said Maeve.

"I don't sink I've ever zeen you wear pants," said Ophelia with a repressed giggle.

"I wear trousers all the time," said Maeve.

Ophelia shrugged and looked over at Mal adoringly. Maeve and Abraxas exchanged a quick look of confusion.

"I would be honored if you would escort me around the estate," said Xander. "I ride well."

"Oh," said Maeve. "Well, I-"

"She'd love to," said Abraxas with a smile.

Maeve glanced at Mal, whose expression was casual.

"Wonderful," said Xander happily.

Ophelia bounced in front of Mal, and Maeve felt her stomach burn.

"Would you care to escort me?" Asked Ophelia with a smile.

"I have business to discuss with The Premier and Abraxas," said Mal sweetly. "Though I'm sure Xander's company would love to accompany you."

Ophelia's face dropped as Eryx offered Ophelia his hand. He didn't look too pleased. But Eryx had a perpetually stern look on his face.

He was dressed more casually than the last time she saw him. But still, the Aterna didn't have the same sense of style that the Magicals on Earth did. There was nothing worldly about his or Xander's attire.

The horses were brought up from the stables, and Xander extended his hand to Maeve.

"I can ride myself," said Maeve.

She had no intention of getting on a horse with him.

He tried to hide his look of disappointment as Maeve mounted her own horse. They rode along silently, shortly behind Eryx and Ophelia. Maeve thought Xander wasn't terrible company when he was quiet, but soon after this thought, he ruined her peaceful ride.

"May I speak candidly, Miss Sinclair?" He asked.

"Of course," replied Maeve, bracing herself.

He looked out over the cliffside as they rode along the trail.

"I know you've only just turned twenty-two-"

Maeve cursed Abraxas for being so wicked and forcing this interaction. Xander continued.

"I understand it's crucial to your family to maintain strong magical bloodlines," said Xander. "And it's crucial for mine to be reinstated."

Maeve tensed up and stared straight ahead. He cleared his throat when she didn't reply and sat up straight.

"You're young, but-"

"I am aware of why you are here," said Maeve, her voice quiet.

He was silent for a moment. "I've noticed you are close to the Dread Descendant. I have heard you are to be named his second. Though I can't imagine he is looking to marry his right hand."

Maeve looked over at him, and her eyebrows drew together.

"I meant no offense," he said.

"And yet," said Maeve dryly, "I am offended all the same."

Xander laughed. It was a beautiful, empty laugh. Like his face. His eyes. "Your father warned me you would be difficult."

Maeve looked away from him and watched as Ophelia pouted at the lack of attention Eryx was giving her. Maeve rolled her eyes.

"I hope you'll consider my offer," said Xander.

"Consider?" Maeve laughed. "You are not aware that I have no say in the matter? That I am expected to marry whomever I am instructed to? You are not aware I have a nonconsensual agreement with the Mavros to marry their son?"

Xander didn't answer and pretended to look confused.

"I could have sworn I saw you all over Leslie Loxerman at the Autumn Gala," said Maeve. "Or were you also not aware she is the head of The Committee that decides such arrangements?"

Xander sighed and smiled.

"Difficult was an understatement," he said.

Maeve didn't return his smile.

"I hope you're enjoying your time at Sinclair Estates," said Maeve. "And I trust you are smart enough to follow the trail back to the house."

Without waiting for a reply, Maeve squeezed her legs together, and her horse broke out of its leisurely pace and into a gallop. She rode quickly past Ophelia and Eryx.

When she arrived back at the house, Maeve dismounted her horse and made her way up the stone stairs to the balcony. Her Father had just nailed the punchline to a joke as everyone laughed.

Mal was seated beside Ambrose, looking quite relaxed.

"Back so soon, darling?" Asked Ambrose as Maeve tossed her riding gloves on the table.

"Where are the others?" Asked Clarissa.

"Still on the trail, I suppose," said Maeve in a huff. "Lucky for me, I know a shortcut."

Maeve winked at her father and took the glass of water he offered her.

"That's not the point, dear. It isn't a race," said Clarissa with a forced smile.

The tone of her mother's voice made Maeve want to vomit.

"It's an escort through the cliffside to show our guests the estate," continued Clarissa.

Maeve looked over at her mother and shrugged. "Xander couldn't keep up."

Mal smirked, and Abraxas covered his mouth with his drink.

Clarissa eyed her with a frown. "Dinner will be served soon. I suggest you change."

Maeve's eyes met Mal's before she took her leave without another word.

She hastily changed from riding clothes into a dress and short heels for dinner. With one hand on her canopy bedpost, she picked up the pale blue sling back and raised her foot.

The door to her room clicked quietly open and Maeve whipped around, nearly falling over and dropping the shoe. She sighed with relief as Mal closed the door quietly behind himself. He strode across the room with a satisfied look on his face.

Maeve picked up her shoe just as he reached her. He snatched it away and tossed it across the room. His lips found hers quickly. And he took her on the writing desk, one hand hoisting her leg high, and the other over her mouth, to keep from being heard.

When Maeve arrived in the dining hall, her father was waiting for her.

"So I'm difficult, huh?" Asked Maeve as she walked toward him.

Ambrose laughed.

"I believe I said 'he would have difficulty,' which is entirely different."

"Please don't make me sit next to him," said Maeve.

"He's already asked to," said Ambrose solemnly.

Maeve took a deep breath.

"What about Iris?" Asked Maeve.

"She won't be of age for another year," answered Ambrose.

"Natalia or Victoria?"

"She and Marcos are set to be married after the New Year, and Victoria is under a bidding war currently."

Maeve rolled her eyes. "As if the Mavros family can't afford her."

"They want you," said Ambrose carefully. "We agreed to that years ago."

"I didn't agree to anything."

Clarissa's voice came from behind Ambrose. "Technically, you did."

Ambrose turned. "Not now."

"Look at your wrist," her mother said coldly.

Maeve swallowed. She didn't obey.

Clarissa nodded, her upper lip curled. "When those honorable stars were burned into your skin, you took a vow as a Pureblood Witch."

"I was a child," said Maeve. "I don't even remember that."

Clarissa looked at Ambrose. "Neither do I."

She walked to the Dining table and began straightening the place settings. Ambrose watched her as he spoke quietly.

"Just play the damn game, Maeve. If not for yourself, then for Mal."

Maeve rounded her father and sat in her seat with a huff. Dinner was shortly served, and Maeve ate her food silently for most of the meal.

Xander was much too close to Maeve all evening, and judging by the look on Mal's face across from her, he felt the same.

"Your attire, Miss St. Beveraux," said Eryx. "It's quite unique. I've not seen such fashion on Earth."

Ophelia dressed like all the spoiled girls in Paris. Over-the-top frills and ornamentation.

"Thank you," said Ophelia.

She turned towards Mal.

"Do you agree, Mal?" Asked Ophelia sweetly.

"It's lovely, yes," said Mal with a smile.

Ophelia's face brightened, and she bit her lip. Maeve's grip on her knife tightened.

"Back home," said Ophelia, "zis is all the women wear. Eet is quite fashionable. I see none of zat here. All embroidered collars."

Maeve was well aware the collar of her dress had embroidery on it. Arianna looked away from Titus and frowned at Ophelia's comment. Embroidered collars and sleeves and shoes were Arianna's favorite.

"You'd look lovely in such a style, Maeve," said Xander.

Maeve looked down at her plate as she felt Xander's eyes burn into her.

"Oh, pleaze," said Ophelia with a giggle. "Maeve n'a aucun style."

Maeve has no sense of style.

Ophelia yelped, and her hand flew to her face as a small incision appeared across her cheek.

"Oh, dear," said Xander, reaching for his handkerchief and attempting to help Ophelia from across the table.

Eryx's eyes grew wide for the first time. He looked at Maeve with the smallest hint of approval.

Ophelia's eyes shot around the room as she avoided Maeve's gaze.

"It's alright," muttered Ophelia as her cheeks flushed. "I - I- must 'ave hit a branch earlier of ze 'orse an' not noticed."

"Oui," said Maeve coldly . "C'est ça."

Shock rang across Ophelia's face as she realized Maeve spoke French.

Maeve looked across the table at Mal. Who stared back at her emotionlessly. A calming sensation resonated from the ring around her neck, and Maeve relaxed in her chair with a deep breath. Ambrose cleared his throat quietly, and Maeve tilted her head towards him. His whispers were covered by the fuss everyone was making over Ophelia.

"No physical magic?" Asked Ambrose curiously.

Maeve shook her head subtly. "Some Dread Magic is silent and swift."

Ambrose picked up his brandy with a satisfied look on his face.

And Maeve realized, feeling only the slightest bit of guilt, that the mark on Ophelia's face would scar. As all Dark Magic did. As all Dread Magic did.

Chapter 52

Arianna and Titus' wedding was the 'event of the decade,' according to Leslie Loxerman. Clarissa and Titus' mother had thrown quite the party. Every important Magical alive was present, and Mal made sure to impress them all.

The real event of the century was in exactly one month- Mal's coronation. The beginning of a new age.

Mal slowly danced Maeve around the ballroom while they talked.

"How are you feeling?"

"Better," said Maeve.

She spent the majority of the morning feeling lightheaded, the compressions in her chest heightened once again. The feeling had come and gone since their travels three months prior. Her father had gotten Irma Mavros to examine her many times, but the skilled healer found nothing out of the ordinary.

Still, she was lightheaded more often than she ever had been. Her breath would turn tight in her chest. And then it would fade. She refused to acknowledge what the High Lord had told her. That there was dark and unwelcome Magic in her. She continued to take pain potions and denied any negative symptoms.

Maeve watched Arianna and Titus dancing. Her own time was running up. Soon it would be Christmas and the Sacred Seventeen Party where customarily Maeve's betrothal would be announced.

But no one was saying anything. Not even Mal. In fact, he told Primrose he thought the preservation of Magical bloodlines was vital. How was she to stand at his side and be an exception to his policies?

Mal, always in her thoughts, whispered to her.

"Don't fret, Little Viper. You have time to set things right."

Maeve looked up at him. "They are watching us," she said, her smile never faltering.

"They are," said Mal.

Leslie Loxerman and The Committee of the Sacred were just across the ballroom.

Maeve continued to stare up at him adoringly.

"You're good at that," said Mal, as he pulled her closer.

Maeve tilted her chin up towards him.

"Not yet," said Mal, smirking down at her.

He danced them around until they were back in a good line of sight.

"Now," said Mal, slowly bringing his lips gently to hers.

This kiss was the opposite of how she was greeted when she arrived at his flat early that morning. When he pushed her against the wall in the darkened hallway with demanding and paralyzing force. She didn't mind that kiss at all.

Nor did she mind the way he delicately and loosely kissed her now. But that wasn't what she wanted them to see.

With a sharp inhale, she pushed to her toes and wrapped her fingers through his hair. She spread her mouth open and ran her tongue across his lips.

Mal tensed under her and then relaxed with a chuckle into her lips.

Maeve looked to Leslie Loxerman. Disdain curled at the old witch's lip.

Maeve bit into his bottom lip, her teeth raking across the skin as she lowered back down to her feet, never breaking her gaze with Loxerman.

Maeve didn't smile. The song ended, and she looked up at Mal. His hands slid behind his back.

"Always the rebel," he said darkly.

"You said to get it done," said Maeve innocently.

She left Mal to charm the guests and went into the Dining Hall to get a drink and look for her father. The room was empty save for Abraxas and a boy she recognized to be Alphard's friend who were seated at the bar. They were sitting so close Abraxas was nearly in his lap.

A few seats down were Reeve and his Commander, Eryx.

Maeve smiled softly.

Abraxas' cheeks were flushed. Maeve put her arm around him.

"Maeve, darling," drawled Abraxas. "Have you met Hugo Septum?"

Hugo extended his hand to her, and she took it.

"Pleasure," said Maeve.

She turned to Abraxas, who was clearly very drunk.

"Are you dreading it, Maeve?" Asked Abraxas.

"Dreading what, Brax?"

"This," said Abraxas, gesturing about the room. "The wedding, the whole thing- I know I am." Abraxas burst out laughing, and Hugo followed suit. Hugo was as drunk as Abraxas. Her cousin rested his head on Hugo's shoulder. The two were familiar.

Maeve snagged a glass of water from the bar. Her father's favorite glass of brandy appeared. The Estate was quick and smart.

Maeve finally looked over at Reeve. His eyes were already on her.

"Good evening, Miss Sinclair," said Reeve with a grin.

"Good evening, Your Imminence," she said with a dramatic bow.

"Gods, don't do that again," he said with feigned offense.

His eyes flickered with confidence. Bridging on arrogance. He took a swig of his drink and Maeve raised her eyebrows.

"What?" He asked.

His voice was challenging.

"Nothing," said Maeve with a playful shrug. "Just thinking about that time, you couldn't save me from Kietel."

Eryx clapped a hand over his mouth and turned away. Abraxas howled with laughter.

Reeve slammed his drink down on the bar and rounded on Maeve. He licked across his teeth. Something about the motion sparked a fire in her stomach.

"Listen here-"

Maeve was smiling so triumphantly that a real laugh escaped her lips.

"You got yourself captured that evening," said Reeve.

"Is that so?"

"Yes," said the cocky High Lord. "You would have made it to Malachite and Obscured had you not been staring at my incredibly fearsome form."

Maeve rolled her eyes.

Even though he was right.

"Someone thinks highly of himself, doesn't he?" Asked Maeve dryly.

"You have no idea," said Eryx. "Though from that display at dinner a few nights ago, I'd say you are equally as vain."

Maeve smirked.

"You'd speak to a lady in such a way?" Asked Maeve.

Reeve laughed now. "You only play that card when it suits you."

Maeve dropped her voice and leaned in close as she addressed him. "That is the only time one should be playing any cards, Your *Grace*."

"Stop that," said Reeve, with a growl in his tone. "Or my patience will run thin."

"Does your grace only extend so far?"

Reeve licked his lips and leaned towards her. "I can show you exactly how far it extends."

Maeve's mouth fell open. Abraxas' attention flew from Hugo and his wide eyes landed on Reeve. A wicked smile at her cousin's lips.

"I find it hard to believe such crass words have warmed your bed for the last hundred years," said Maeve.

"Why don't you tell me in the morning?"

He was so bold, so brazen, so ridiculous, that she laughed.

She tried to find a smart remark to wipe his smirk off his face, but she knew one would not come, and The High Lord was too confident to be swayed by any blow.

"Don't play the game if you're going to get your feelings hurt," said Reeve. "I will always win. I have centuries of a perfected quick wit."

"More like you're a perfected prick," muttered Maeve.

"I have that too," said Reeve with a wink.

"Set yourself up for that one, cousin," said Abraxas.

Reeve smiled at him cunningly. Abraxas blushed.

"Fine," she said. "I yield."

Reeve and Eryx shared a triumphant toast, slammed their goblets on the bar, and downed their drinks.

She snagged her father's drink from across the bar. "He who knows all," she said and turned to Abraxas, "do you know where my father ran off to earlier?"

Abraxas swallowed his drink hard and nodded.

"He's in his study with the Orator," said Abraxas.

Maeve thanked him and made her way out of the dining hall.

She rounded up the stairs and headed towards her father's study. Maeve knocked lightly on the door.

"Enter," said Ambrose.

Maeve pushed open the door. Her Father and Orator Moon were seated in two large armchairs, smoking cigars.

"I hope I'm not interrupting," said Maeve.

"Not at all, dear," said Moon. "I actually have a message for you."

Maeve sat down with them.

"Let me guess, it's from Daniel Rodriguez," said Maeve.

Ambrose laughed, and Moon chuckled.

"Yes," said Moon. "He said he'd give you Junior Undersecretary."

"Oh-ho!" Cheered Ambrose.

Maeve smiled. "How many times do I have to decline this job?"

"I don't think I've ever heard of anyone turning down a Junior Undersecretary position right out of school," laughed Moon. "Primus and the Gods, child, what position could you possibly want? I know you must hate it in the Bellator Sector, all that rivalry isn't good for the soul."

"My father's job," said Maeve, without missing a beat. "Or perhaps yours."

Moon choked on his cigar, and Ambrose smirked subtly, pride in his eyes.

"I'd expect nothing less from the daughter of this man," said Moon, jerking an elbow toward Ambrose as he tried to relight his puffed-out cigar.

Maeve stood and turned to her father. "I only wanted to say goodnight, Daddy. It's getting late for me," said Maeve with a yawn.

There was a knock at the ajar door. She turned. Mal and Abraxas, Reeve, and Eryx filed into the room. Others behind them. Important people Abraxas made sure had the opportunity to meet Mal on a personal level, over drinks and cigars.

"Goodnight," said Ambrose as he kissed her cheek.

Maeve walked past Mal. He snagged her arm gently. "Stay," he said.

"Oh no," she gazed up at him. "It's past my bedtime. They're all yours."

He smiled softly and brushed his thumb across her lip. For a moment, they forgot where they were. They forgot Ambrose and the others.

"Goodnight, Little Viper," he whispered.

"Goodnight, My Prince."

Mal's chest rose dramatically and then fell, his breath was cool down her face and neck. He dropped her arm.

And they remembered they weren't alone.

And for the first time, neither of them cared.

"Goodnight," she said to the rest.

She closed the large, rounded door behind her and headed back down the hall. Her fingers lingered across her bottom lip. His touch was captivating. Addicting.

His fingers were scared with death and yet she trusted them completely. She craved them.

She made her way down the back set of stairs and down the long corridor to the third-floor landing when a voice came from behind her.

"I was beginning to think I'd never get just a moment with you again."

Alphard Mavros emerged from the darkness, staggering slightly. His wild hair was down to his shoulders. Maeve smiled.

"Well, lucky for you, here I am," said Maeve. "Unlucky for you, though, I am heading to bed."

"Need any company?"

Maeve's face fell flat at his comment. He wasn't provoking her. She wasn't the butt of a joke, like Reeve's crass comments. Alphard was serious. And he was disgustingly intoxicated and inebriated.

"Mal's got you all wrapped up, huh?" He slurred his words.

She looked back at him with a raised eyebrow in complete confusion. "What are you talking about?"

Alphard stepped in towards her, and before she could stop him, he kissed her.

Maeve jerked away. "What are you doing?" Maeve pushed hard on Alphard's chest.

"Don't-don't pull back from me now," said Alphard.

"What?"

"I've missed your touch, your lips-"

"Hush," hissed Maeve.

She placed one hand on his chest, keeping distance between them, and looked him dead in the eyes before choosing her words carefully. She studied him. Her eyes darting back and forth between his own.

"You're drunk," she said.

"I'm not," growled Alphard.

He grabbed her arm firmly and pulled her close. Maeve was flustered, terrified of someone seeing them.

"Where is your redhead?" Asked Maeve quietly. "Where is Victoria?"

"Otherwise occupied. The Damario's gold seems to have caught her attention."

"You have more money yourself than the entire Damario family," said Maeve. "Just buy her and be done with it."

Alphard's nostrils flared. "I don't want to buy her, Maeve." His voice was sad. "I want her to pick me. Like you've picked Mal."

"Let go, Al," she said. But her voice kicked.

And he disobeyed. He tugged her closer.

Electricity tingled down her arm. Ready if needed.

"Don't you dare do this to me," said Maeve lowly. "Don't you dare put me in a position to lose him, Alphard." Her voice shook. "Don't ever think that anything we had one fleeting summer is more important than our Dread Prince. Than my allegiance and dedication to him. That I would ever go behind his back- with another of his own cause much less. Or have you changed your support of him?"

"Bloody hell, that's so pathetic, Maeve," said Alphard, laughing as he dropped her arm.

She shook her head at his ridiculous behavior and continued down the corridor. Alphard was hot on her heels.

"Is that how it feels when he kisses you? Might as well be pissing all over you."

Maeve's jaw dropped at his vulgar comment.

Alphard stumbled slightly. "I know you're smarter than to-to-to think there are any feelings there- that you are more than a prize to be claimed to him or that his possession over you has anything to do with love."

She didn't look back, but that didn't stop Alphard from lashing out at her further.

"But if you do think any of that, you're a fool, Maeve. And I feel sorry for you."

She stopped and turned on him. Ice, angry and tired, slammed down her arm. She pointed two fingers at him, the tips swirling with blue light. She stared him down coldly.

"Either go back to the party, Mr. Mavros, or go home. Your inebriated shortcomings aren't welcome."

Alphard looked at her and chuckled grimly. "Your loyalty never fails."

"You're damn right it doesn't."

His eyes bore into her in a way she hated. He had never looked at her with disgust until this moment. He had always been her friend and Mal's friend. One of his boys.

But then she remembered. Before he was one of Mal's boys. . .he was Antony's best friend.

A dull numbness wafted over her arm. The blue light faded and her arm fell to her side.

"Even when you're mad, you're beautiful," said Alphard.

"Beautiful?" Maeve gave a frustrated groan. "Do you know how tiresome of a compliment that is?" Maeve looked at him incredulously. She was beyond disappointed in his behavior, and drunkenness was her least favorite state in which to interact with someone. "Beautiful is the lousiest and laziest compliment I could possibly get," said Maeve. "Yes. Of course, I am. Do you have anything else that draws you to me? Besides my beauty and the fact that you cannot have the one you love? Is that enough for you to deny me the one I do?"

Alphard ran his fingers across his face and through his hair. "Gods-you two were made for each other," he spat. "For all your intellect and brilliance, you have let him completely take your mind, your reason and logic."

"I'm not going to apologize for knowing my worth, Alphard. I can't help but resent anyone who thinks all I have to offer is my looks. And you chastise me for choosing him when I've never once thought he was shallow enough to think that way. I am by his side because of my abilities, what I have to offer. Not as arm candy."

A wave of nausea overcame Maeve, and her hand shot to her head. The hall spun. The fire lights lining the hall blurred. The bones across her torso and chest constricted.

"Not your last name?"

A sharp breath caught in her chest, and she glowered at Alphard.

"Oh," seethed Alphard. "That had never occurred to you, had it?"

Maeve swallowed hard.

"Or," continued Alphard, "maybe it has occurred to you, and you just deny it. That's the part you don't let yourself see. It doesn't matter what he's using you for. You need to admit that he is using you. I bet he can't wait for you to have his child. Solidify his claim over you."

Maeve laughed. "You are so behind. Jealousy isn't very becoming on you either."

Alphard staggered slightly. Maeve continued. Her swift sickness vanished.

"I am beyond you in ways you can't even fathom. But you want to play the name game? That's a joke. What's your last name?" She folded her arms across her chest and closed the gap between them cooly. "Isn't it your family that has the darkest and purest bloodline of us all? Isn't it your name being used just as much as mine? The letters your parents get from Mal, you think they're out of the goodness of his heart?" Maeve laughed. "But here's the difference, Mavros, between you and I, and I'll spell it out for you since you obviously can't comprehend it on your own. I offer The Prince of Darkness more than you. I offer him a discipline in charms that the Orator's Office and even the Immortal High Lord recognize as bloody brilliant. I offer him unfaltering trust and unfailing loyalty. I've proved it. And if you want to be realistic about it, yes, I offer him a Pureblooded inheritance, access to my father's world, and the continuation of a strong Magical bloodline. And as you stand here, having failed him, ask yourself this: what besides a name do you have to offer?"

She left him standing in the corridor, and without looking back, made her way across the landing to her bedroom.

Arianna came out of her own room.

"Are you alright?" Asked Arianna.

Maeve was taken aback by her sister's comment but kept walking down the hall to her bedroom.

"Yes," said Maeve. "I just want to go to bed." She passed her and then turned around. "Congratulations."

Arianna had already changed out of her wedding dress. She looked back at Maeve without a reply and then continued back to the party.

Maeve had hardly made it to her room and closed the door when there was a swirl of wind and Zimsy stood in front of her.

"A bath?" Said Zimsy.

"No," said Maeve. "I just want to sleep."

Zimsy nodded and extended her arms open wide. Maeve walked into them as Zimsy guided her to the bed. Maeve plopped down and grabbed a pillow.

"Thank you," said Maeve, resting her head on the soft velvet. "Do you want to stay with me and talk about all the annoying guests tonight?"

"Say more," said Zimsy as she climbed into bed next to Maeve.

Chapter 53

No sooner had Maeve shut her eyes that the sun was pouring through the tall windows in her bedroom. A familiar voice rang through the room.

"Breakfast on the balcony, come on," whined Abraxas. "I've been waiting on you for an hour."

Maeve didn't open her eyes. "Why are you still here?" She groaned as she tossed a pillow over her face.

She heard the door snap closed behind him and willed herself out of bed. Zimsy was gone.

Her mind immediately replayed the previous night's events. She frowned, thinking about how stupid Alphard was.

And what she feared most of all was Mal's disappointment.

Fifteen minutes later, she joined Abraxas on the balcony overlooking the gardens. The sun was sharp in her eyes. She had stayed up too late. And slept too little.

Despite the thick snow that coated the ground, the Estate was still enchanted to remain warm.

"Did you stay the night?" Asked Maeve.

Abraxas nodded. "I fell asleep in your father's study around three."

Maeve smiled. "Did you really? What about Mal?"

"He went home around four, I believe. Your Father says they were up until the early hours of the morning with some of the others, so I assume he is resting," said Abraxas.

"But you felt the need to disturb me?" Asked Maeve sourly.

"I do not fear you the way I fear him," said Abraxas, simply. "Where did you get off to anyway?"

Maeve groaned, then recounted her heated argument with Alphard to Abraxas as they poured orange juice and piled pastries on their plates.

"Mal won't be pleased," said Abraxas plainly. "But he's been very understanding. Things are changing quickly. Not everyone will adjust right away. Besides, we know Alphard, and that wasn't him."

"Wasn't it, though?" Asked Maeve. "You know as well as I do, he's got a nasty side."

"You're being thick," said Abraxas, smearing jam across his toast and shaking his head.

"What?"

He paused for a moment and sighed. "You can't honestly tell me you didn't realize your parents and his parents have had the pair of you picked out your whole life?"

"Come off it," said Maeve.

"Maeve," said Abraxas. His voice was more solemn than she could ever remember seeing him before. "That's been decided."

"No, it hasn't!" Shot Maeve.

"By your families, it has, and you and Mal are re-writing things to your own accord, rightfully so, and of course, Alphard feels cheated and betrayed, especially with Victoria likely being betrothed to Damario in just a few weeks."

"I never pledged myself to Alphard," said Maeve.

"No," said Abraxas calmly. "But do any of us pledge ourselves in an arranged marriage? And how many times have you kissed him? How many parties did he take you to?"

Maeve's mouth fell open. "None of that means I agreed to marry him."

"I'm not arguing it does. However, maybe you can see why, in a drunken state, he lashed out at you. Why he came to you for comfort in the first place. When comfort was once what you provided one another. Especially when Victoria was all over Damario last night."

Maeve frowned. "She was?"

Abraxas nodded.

"Oh."

She sat back in her chair and sighed.

Spinel jumped on the table and began lapping up porridge. Maeve folded her arms across herself and stared away from Abraxas.

"It's truly burdenous knowing everything," he said.

After breakfast, Maeve tucked herself away in the observatory on the East side of the house for the rest of the day. Spinel was ripping up frayed bits of carpet while she lay in the window reading. It was late afternoon before Mal came to the house and found her. He leaned in the doorway, studying her predatorily.

She felt his presence the moment he appeared outside the gates. The ring around her neck ensured that.

"Good afternoon, Sinclair?" Asked Mal.

The formal use of her last name did not go unnoticed.

"Fine," she replied, avoiding his gaze for longer than necessary. He crossed the room smoothly and took up in one of the velvet armchairs, crossing one of his long legs over the other.

"If I didn't know better, I'd say you were hiding from me up in this tower."

"Don't be silly. Congratulations are in order, I believe." She set her book aside, giving him a weak smile. "You had quite the night."

"You heard?" He smirked, propping his feet up in the chair adjacent. "Couldn't have gone better if you ask me. Reeve was eager to hear my plans."

"Good," said Maeve. Fear of the potential backlash that was coming kept her from meeting his gaze. "I fell straight to sleep."

"Not before having a run-in with Alphard, though," said Mal emotionlessly.

Maeve stared straight ahead, and then slowly her eyes moved to him. He was difficult to read at the moment. His eyes were sharp, unyieldingly piercing.

How could he possibly know about their argument?

He answered her unasked question. "I could feel it." His gaze traveled to his ring, which lay flat against her blouse.

Maeve stared at him, waiting for an explosion. Waiting for that temper to break loose. If Xander's attention had brought him to anger, surely Alphard's actions would too. His eyes bore into hers so intensely that she swallowed.

"Interesting," commented Maeve, as she played with the ring around her neck.

"So tell me," said Mal, his voice cool and calm. "How did that go?"

"Not well," answered Maeve.

He nodded and intertwined his fingers across his chest. "So when I told you to handle it, instead, what you did was ignore it to the point that Alphard Mavros thought he could put his hands on you." Mal's jaw tightened. His voice dangerously low. "His fucking lips on yours."

Maeve sucked in a slow breath. "He was drunk."

"Was he drunk the times you allowed him to kiss you?"

Maeve's jaw tightened.

"The times he danced so close to you?"

"Alright," said Maeve tensely, getting the point.

Mal nodded subtly. "It isn't about The Committee or an agreement between your family and his. When I told you to handle it, I meant handle him." Mal looked away from her. "He loves you. Truly. Maybe it's only out of the love he had for your brother, but it remains all the same."

Alphard's love had always been there. That was true. And she didn't doubt Mal could feel it, but she'd never be able to explain that love to him. That it was childlike. Blind. Comfortable. It was Antony's death that brought them together. Two spiraling, collapsing stars that needed one another not to burn up. It was a bond rooted in despair. One she no longer needed.

"It was naive of me," said Maeve.

His face was blank, devoid of emotion.

"Your heartbeat was rapid, uneven," he said. "You were a range of emotions, and I could feel them all. Fear. Disdain. Pity. . .Guilt."

Maeve tucked her hands under her legs and spoke hesitantly. "I was afraid of it. I was afraid to tell him. I didn't want to hurt him-"

"Hurt him?" Mal's eyes darkened and flicked to hers. "That is your concern?"

Maeve sighed. She stood from the window seat and walked towards him, kneeling beside his chair.

"Do you doubt my loyalty?" Asked Maeve, her voice soft.

Mal took her chin in his hand, running his finger along her jawline. "I doubt my ability to ever trust again a man who kisses you knowing full well you belong to another."

"And what about your trust in me?"

Mal hesitated, his eyes racked over her face as if looking for an answer. "Tell me you are mine."

It was a command like many he had given her before. She had never disobeyed him and didn't intend to start now.

"I will show you," said Maeve.

He didn't hesitate to enter her mind. It only took a moment for him to witness the altercation from the previous night. A smirk tugged at his lips as he finished watching the memory unfold.

He withdrew from her mind.

"Very good, Little Viper," said Mal, his face only inches from her own.

Chapter 54

Maeve knocked on the door to her father's study. His voice called for her to enter. Maeve sat down in one of the armchairs and waited for her father to finish reading the piece of parchment in front of him. His desk was strewn with books, newspapers, and proposed military legislation in the Double O.

Ambrose looked up at Maeve. Then at the book in her hands from his personal collection. She was researching for any information about the Dread Armor's whereabouts.

"You found something?" Asked Ambrose, looking back down at his papers.

"He's a pathokenesis," said Maeve.

Ambrose looked up at her, loosed a laugh, and nodded. "I don't know how I didn't see it."

Maeve nodded. Ambrose's smile faded as he realized Maeve's expression was one of worry.

His eyes narrowed slightly. "He doesn't know?"

"Oh he knows," said Maeve. "He just doesn't. . . know. He is aware of his effect on others. But. . ."

Ambrose's brows lifted.

Maeve exhaled slowly. "I don't know if he's doing it to me."

Her father nodded in contemplation and looked away. He retreated into his thoughts for a moment before he finally spoke. "And you never will."

"I've considered telling him. And asking him not to manipulate me that way."

Ambrose looked back at her. "I don't think there's any harm in that."

Maeve's stomach filled with acid as the adrenaline of penitential confrontation kicked. And just after she had narrowly avoided his disappointment with Alphard.

Ambrose gave her a sympathetic smile and softly said, "If you don't want him to manipulate your emotions, then make it so Maeve. You need not rely on his word alone."

"Put up a shield?" She asked with a frown. "I don't want to have to do that. I'm not even sure it would work."

Ambrose nodded. "Then you're back to your original idea."

Maeve slipped through the study fireplace into Mal's flat. He was behind his desk, writing with a long, black quill. She crossed towards him and placed the book down in front of him, not bothering to wait for him to finish his writing.

"What's this?" Asked Mal.

"It's a book," she replied plainly.

Mal frowned and looked up at her, annoyed. Maeve smirked.

She slid the green leather-bound book across the desk towards him. "It's a text about the power of pathokenesis."

"Pathokenesis?" He asked with a raised brow.

He took the book in his hands and flipped open the front cover.

"Yes," said Maeve. "The ability to sense and manipulate others' emotions."

Mal glanced over the first page.

Maeve said, as if it were obvious, "You're one."

Mal's eyes flicked up at her. "What?"

"You have pathokenesis abilities."

Mal flipped through a few pages, his eyes scanning quickly. He closed the book and looked up at her. "I didn't know there was a word for it."

"I don't want you to use it on me," she stated plainly, their eyes locked together.

Mal shook his head. "I won't."

Maeve didn't hesitate. "Swear to it," she said.

Mal's eyes softened. He stood and crossed around the table. Maeve turned towards him. A small smile was pulling at the corners of his lips as he brushed her hair behind her shoulders.

He spoke lowly. "You think a bright and clever Witch like yourself wouldn't know if I was manipulating your emotions with Magic?"

Maeve looked up at him. "I have no idea."

Mal nodded subtly, his thoughts far from Maeve's request.

"Thank you for telling me. Now," he said, his fingers traveling up her neck to her cheek, "when I master this, Maeve, there is nothing we won't have."

His hand moved to the back of her neck as he pressed a kiss to her forehead.

Maeve spoke as he moved away from her back towards the book. "Mal."

He looked over at her.

"Swear it."

Mal's face twisted slightly, scrunched into a confused expression. "You don't trust me?"

"I don't think even you know when you're doing it," she answered gently.

Mal's jaw tightened. "No. Right now I don't. But," he tapped a slender finger on the book between them, "I soon will."

"Alright," said Maeve. Mal moved to sit back down. "Then swear to it until that day comes."

Mal gripped the edge of the desk, his knuckles turning white. Maeve pretended not to notice.

She spoke again before all nerve abandoned her. "I'm not asking for much, wouldn't you agree?"

"No," he said, his voice low, "I don't."

Maeve's mouth fell open slightly. "Why not?"

Mal braced himself on the desk, his head bowed. "Don't do this, Maeve."

Maeve laughed nervously. "I am asking you to promise me, with Magic, that you won't-"

"I know what you are asking," said Mal. "And I won't do it."

Maeve fired back quickly. "You understand the implications of your resistance to do so?"

"And what of your implications in asking me?"

Maeve scoffed. "I came to you honestly. I didn't want to have to protect myself with Magic. I wanted us to come to an agreement."

"You think your shield would stand a chance against my Magic?"

Maeve's eyes narrowed. "The one in my mind would."

Mal couldn't disagree. He was only able to slip into her thoughts and speak to her silently because she allowed it. Her mental shields were impenetrable if she wanted them to be. Her mind was a fortress of Magic that was unlike any other.

Maeve turned on her heel and headed for the fireplace in his penthouse. She didn't bother asking if he'd be at the Christmas Party the following evening.

Maeve watched Mal from the bar at the Rosethorn's Christmas Party. He was surrounded by the Bellator that worshiped him, and Abraxas at his left.

She frowned more every time he laughed.

"Lover's spat?"

Maeve licked across her teeth and didn't look over at the High Lord of Aterna as he leaned against the bar. "Have you ever considered minding your own business?"

"Unfortunately, it is absolutely my business what the second and third most powerful beings are doing."

Maeve glared at him.

Reeve smiled as he said, savoring the insult, "You're third."

"How generous of you," she muttered.

"You are in a fine form tonight if I must say so, kitten."

Maeve slammed her crystal goblet into the bar sharply and she turned towards him. "Don't call me that."

Reeve's eyes traced over her face and his head cocked to one side. "Then how will I provoke you?"

"I am certain you'll find a way."

Reeve's mouth hung slightly open as he studied her from head to toe with royal ease. His playful expression faded as his eyes sparkled with flecks of fire.

"You are a magnificent creature," he said slowly.

Maeve's eyes widened at the change in his tone. She looked up at him. Panic flooded her mind, chilling her skin and kicking her heart into motion.

"Must be terrible though," he said, his eyelids heavy and his voice raspy. "To fear compliments from another man."

"I don't know what you mean," she said tensely.

"You think I can't feel your Magic? I don't need to be in your mind to feel your anxious heartbeat. It's practically screaming at me." Reeve looked down at her chest, his voice low. "We Immortals have heightened senses you know. I smell your fear as it seeps from your pores." His eyes lifted back to hers. "So pretend all you want, but I know that deep, deep down, buried beneath your delusion and pride, that you are afraid of him. . .deep. . . deep down. And you should be."

Maeve couldn't speak. She settled for glaring at him.

"Hmm," said Reeve. "All that Magic flowing freely. It's intoxicating."

Her stomach dropped.

Reeve smirked at her, satisfied.

The prick.

Maeve slammed the rest of the sparkling water before her and wiped the corner of her mouth delicately with a finger as she slid off the bar stool, careful to remain close to him, but not to let their bodies touch.

"Let me ask you something, High Lord," she whispered, looking up at him. He did not meet her gaze but stared behind her at the bustling party. "If the second and third most powerful beings alive are joined together and you, the most powerful, stand alone, wouldn't you say that makes Mal and I the most powerful force alive?"

Reeve's smirk never faltered. He merely looked down at her and said, "Your faith abounds."

She slid around him and left him without another word.

Maeve stalked out of the party. She felt Mal step into the foyer behind her.

"Going so soon?" He asked as she headed for the fireplace.

The Rosethorn's Elf servant appeared with a light misting sound and handed Maeve her coat. Maeve thanked her and slipped it on.

"Yes," was all she said in reply to Mal.

Mal slipped his hands in his pockets.

"I have better things my time could be occupied with other than these endless and ridiculous parties."

"These parties are buying me a crown, Maeve."

"Then go buy it," she gestured back towards the party.

"What did Reeve say to you?"

"What does it matter? Why don't you just manipulate my emotions to your desired outcome?"

She turned and stepped into the fire without even looking at him.

Books from her father's collection were strewn across the sitting table in her room. She was no closer to finding the Dread Armor now than she was months ago.

She blinked rapidly as the words on the page blurred. It was late into the night. The only light in her room came from the firelight candles floating beside her chair. Her thoughts kept shifting to Reeve. He had said she was the third most powerful being alive.

No one had ever called her that.

Her room flashed green. She didn't look over her shoulder at the fireplace. Mal stood behind her. His face lowered to the side of hers.

"I will not use my pathokenesis abilities on you," he whispered in her ear.

A trickle of cold Magic moved down her neck and slowly infiltrated her chest. She shuddered and closed her eyes as his promise took hold. Her head tilted backward.

After a moment, heat returned to her skin. She turned in the chair, the book in her lap sliding to the floor, and sat on her knees facing him. She took his face in her hands and kissed him tenderly.

"Thank you," she whispered as she laid her forehead on his.

"You're so spoiled," he said dryly.

She laughed softly. Mal spoke quietly.

"I did not try to see your perspective. I will not fail to do so again."

Chapter 55

Christmas was within the week. And then it was New Year's Eve, Mal's birthday and Coronation.

Maeve was in London looking at townhouses with her father.

"It's close to Mal," she said, her voice echoing across the black and white marbled living room. "And it's gorgeous. But I don't need this. I can stay at home until Mal secures the Dread Lands and we move there."

Ambrose shrugged. "Whatever you want, darling. I just wanted to show it to you."

Maeve smiled. "It's a lovely thought. Thank you. But I don't need it."

Ambrose took her arm as they ventured out onto the chilly street. Ambrose quickly cast an invisible shield charm around them, keeping out the harsh weather and keeping them warm.

Sinclair Estates was lavishly decorated for Christmas. As soon as Maeve stepped through the door with her father, the strong scent of pine filled her nose.

"It's giant," said Maeve, referring to the oversized tree in the foyer. It was decorated with blush and red-colored ornaments and silver garlands. "Much bigger than any I can remember."

"Yes," said Ambrose. "Your mother insisted this year. Something about the Mavros having one last year," said Ambrose with a wink.

Maeve smiled, taking off her coat.

Trudy appeared and took Maeve's things from Ambrose.

The holiday season at Sinclair Estates included very little quiet time around a fire opening gifts and much more chaos. Her Grandmother Agatha had already chastised Maeve and Arianna for not helping her pick out new holiday drapes for the dueling hall.

"Last year, the Mavros family had gorgeous drapes," huffed Grandmother Agatha. "It would be a disgrace to the Sinclair name to have the same drapes in the dueling hall that we did in October."

Agatha turned from Maeve and Arianna and began discussing tablecloths with Trudy.

"I hate when we host this party," muttered Arianna.

Maeve, who was often at odds with her older sister, couldn't agree more. She managed to slip out of the hall while Agatha was preoccupied.

"No." Maeve turned the page of her book without looking at him.

Mal spoke plainly. "I didn't ask."

Maeve tossed her book to the side and stood. "So I have no say?"

"I didn't say you had to go. You are welcome to stay at home this evening. But I am going."

Maeve's mouth fell open. Mal crossed the room towards her.

"Why don't you want to go? You love parties."

"I don't love them anymore. Besides, only my mother and Arianna are going. Father won't even be there. Why should we go?"

"Because they are wealthy and influential. I need their support."

"So it's only political?"

Mal's brows pulled together. "What else would it be, Maeve?"

She swallowed. "I don't know."

He reproached her with his eyes and spoke lowly. "Speak your mind, please."

Maeve shook her head. It was too silly to say out loud. She would swallow her feelings about Ophelia and the St. Beverauxs and attend their Christmas party. "Never mind. I'll go. But I won't enjoy myself."

The corners of Mal's lips tugged up ever so slightly. "Have I come to bore you already?"

Maeve stopped. "That's not what I meant."

Mal stepped around her and on the sofa appeared a large flat black dress box with a cream velvet bow sprawling across its top.

"For tonight," he said, pressing a kiss to her temple.

The gown was fully beaded, deep crimson red to the floor with matching satin gloves to her elbows and a long, flowing bow for her hair, which she used to fasten her hair neatly pulled back.

Despite the attire's beauty, Maeve gripped the edge of Mal's dressing table.

Once again, her throat was tight. Her chest ached and her mind spun fuzzy. Deep in her stomach, something strange moved, creating a quick wave of nausea.

"Something's wrong," she whispered to herself, but Mal didn't miss it.

"Something's been wrong," he said, plainly.

Maeve raised her eyebrows questioningly.

"You've been fatigued for weeks now. Months before that, you've been ill. You're dizzy and you can't breathe."

She sighed. "Maybe the dress is too tight," said Maeve. "I just think I need to lie down for a moment."

She made her way over to the sofa and threw herself on it. Mal stood over her.

"I don't think I've ever seen you sick," he said.

"I'm not sick!" Snapped Maeve. "Magicals don't get sick."

He gave her an annoyed look. She laid her head back.

"I'm sorry. I just mean. . ."

"You don't even know what you mean, Maeve," said Mal. "And your refusal to see Mrs. Mavros again irritates me endlessly."

"I have seen her. Many times," she muttered.

Her arm draped across her eyes.

"I don't think you should go tonight."

Maeve shot up off the sofa. There was no way she was letting him run off to Ophelia all by himself.

"I'm fine. I just need to finish getting ready."

She pushed up off the sofa as a larger wave of pain hit her across her sternum. Mal steadied her as she became weak.

He placed her back on the sofa. Mal took her chin in his hand, forcing her to look up at him. He examined her for a moment as if searching for what plagued her, before dropping his hand.

"You're not going."

Maeve pouted.

Shortly after he departed, without hesitation, which annoyed her greatly, she fell asleep on his sofa.

Something dark deepened in her stomach, forcing a moan to escape her throat.

Her eyes were still closed as panic swarmed through her body. Her cheeks flushed hot, but her body was ice cold. Long slithering trails of frozen magic pushed through her. The pain in her stomach was worse than when the Grindylow crushed her ribs.

With a ragged and sharp breath, she pulled herself upright, gripping the carved wooden arm of the sofa. The sensation moved quickly to her legs.

Maeve let out an agonizing scream.

She conjured every bit of strength she had and tried to combat the rough magic flowing through her. But she was weakened. And it was strong.

She needed help.

Her legs gave way beneath her as she attempted to stand. She fell into Mal's dressing table and saw her own reflection.

Snaking up from the beaded neckline of her gown were thick black lines, her own veins, but they were dark as a starless night's sky.

And they were moving.

Something in them was moving.

Her panicked and shaking hands fought with the back laces of the dress, loosening its grip on her. But the ice running through her veins constricted still. She pulled the dress up and to the side, exposing her legs and stomach.

Thick black veins ran all across her skin. As they traveled up towards her collarbone, they also dipped down, wrapping her legs.

"Fuck," gasped Maeve as terror set in.

. . .Somewhere in a marbled ballroom miles away, The Prince of Darkness looked slightly over his shoulder, as though someone had called his name.

"Mal?"

He looked down at Ophelia as they danced. Her voice was muffled.

The hair on the back of his neck stood up. His hands slipped from her body, falling to his sides. . .

Maeve's knees buckled beneath her, slamming her to the floor. A charmed tree ornament from Abraxas was chiming across the room. It was nearly midnight. Nearly Christmas Day.

She cast out her magic once more. But the blackness swarming through her surged and depleted her own instantly. Mal's flat was freezing, her own skin was iced to the touch.

"What the fuck," she whispered, her voice cracking as she shivered.

She needed Mal. But he was in Paris, sucking up to Ophelia and her family.

Her father's face flashed before her- dark magic was his specialty. He was the Premier.

The sensation was spreading quickly into her chest. Breathing was next to impossible as Maeve's lungs felt like they were collapsing under an enormous weight. Each breath strained and tight.

She pulled herself to the brick fireplace on all fours, straining and gasping.

The flames engulfed her. A moment later, her knees hit the old mahogany floors in her father's office. Ambrose flew around his desk towards her.

His face instantly drained of its color.

A wave of pain hit her, and she doubled over, unable to make a sound, gripping at her stomach and her chest.

"Maeve?" Ambrose kneeled in front of her, pushing her hair back and cupping her face. "Maeve- tell me what's happening!"

Looking at her father was not comforting; she had never seen his face terrified.

"Tell me, Maeve, I don't know what to do," said Ambrose, his voice struggling to hide his fear.

His Magic wrapped around her as he tried everything he knew to pull the darkness swimming through her out. Magic isn't always perfect. If Ambrose cast the wrong spell or something too strong, she could be more weakened or wounded in the process.

But it didn't matter. The darkness inside her wasn't affected.

She looked down at her trembling hands. They looked as though someone had traced all her veins in black ink. The room was becoming hazy, but her eyes found her father's. It only took a moment for her to realize he was helpless.

The room went silent until all Maeve could hear was her own heartbeat, thumping loudly, growing slower. She couldn't even hear her father's agonized pleas.

It was barely a whisper, hoarse and broken, but from her lips escaped a final desperate attempt, and she called to him.

"Mal."

The veins across her chest ran black, spreading rapidly now through her neck. Maeve gripped her throat as tears began to stream down her cheeks as she suffocated.

Ambrose gripped her face, desperately screaming her name. As the whites of her eyes, too, flooded with black pigment, green flames lit the room.

Mal appeared from the fire, his eyes wild.

Ambrose stumbled backward as Mal swooped Maeve under one arm and placed his palm flat on her chest.

With a guttural noise and an ancient tongue of Magic, a green jet of light shot from the tips of Mal's fingers and hit Maeve square in the chest.

The walls of the study shook. Pictures and artifacts fell from high shelves and shattered on the floor.

Mal's counter-curse took full effect as he continued to speak in a foreign tongue. His fingers traced up towards her throat, slowing, meticulously with each word, his voice grew deadlier. Darker.

So did the room.

Maeve's scream was bloodcurdling as Mal drew a long, black, ghostly substance from her mouth. It broke away from the tip of his finger and hovered above them ominously.

Big Ben struck Midnight outside Ambrose's enchanted office window. Maeve was losing conciseness now. Mal's grip around her tightened as she slipped limply.

His finger remained pointed at the dark swarm of Magic, which looked as though it was cowering from him.

"A container, Ambrose," said Mal darkly. "Something laced with wolfsbane."

A glass jar flew to Ambrose's hand with a flick of his wrist. Mal's eyes narrowed and forced the ghostly bit of dark Magic down towards Ambrose's outstretched arm.

"Keep the lid on tight, Ambrose, and I'll seal it myself in a moment," commanded Mal.

He returned his gaze to Maeve now, who was barely conscious. In a few strides, he laid her on the large leather tufted sofa.

"Rest, Maeve. Sleep now," hummed Mal as he brushed her hair to the side. "You are in no danger anymore. I came when you called."

Chapter 56

A tall slit of sunlight spilled onto Maeve's bed, forcing its way through the closed velvet curtains. They hadn't been drawn Magically that morning. She felt Spinel curled up in the crook of her knees.

There was a tray of pancakes next to the bed. Maeve pushed up and looked at the small paper calendar next to her bed.

December 26th, 1945

"No," she whispered, reaching for Mal's ring around her neck. But it was gone. He must have taken it.

She had been asleep for days.

She looked on the nightstand and food tray for a note or message from Mal, but there was none. Maeve laid her head back down, exhausted.

Whatever it was that tried to kill her nearly succeeded, and she was still recovering. Her eyes became too heavy to hold, and she rolled over, falling back asleep.

Another day later, Maeve was on her feet. She was weak, but she was moving.

She sat on the stool of her vanity in complete disbelief at her reflection. Her fingers traced the black lines that shot up her neck like bolts of lightning. They traveled down her arms, and into her fingertips.

No part of her was spared except her face.

Maeve wiped the tear that silently dripped down her cheek.

Zimsy's hands brushed through her hair, gently weaving it into a braid.

"It isn't fading," she said softly from behind Maeve.

Maeve wiped another tear with the back of her hand.

It wasn't going to.

Dark Magic leaves traces.

Zimsy took her downstairs, where she opened her presents from the Christmas festivities she missed. Ambrose was careful not to comment on the now permanent marks on her skin.

She hadn't seen Mal at all. However, he had sent her a Christmas gift, which was a vintage pearl layered necklace wrapped in silver and emerald paper with a cameo brooch. It was perfect.

There was a short note as well.

Lucky for you, I purchased this weeks ago. Otherwise, saving your life would have sufficed as a gift itself.

Maeve missed the Sacred Seventeen Party, for which she was grateful. She found out from Abraxas that the Committee announced no engagements at all. He speculated the current state of affairs prevented them from making any movements currently.

Later that evening, Zimsy walked into Maeve's bedroom, where she sat up in bed reading a book.

Zimsy smiled.

"You have a visitor."

Maeve threw the book aside, knowing from Zimsy's smile it was Mal. Without his ring, she couldn't tell if he was close or not. She tossed the covers aside and grabbed her dressing gown.

She nodded at Zimsy, who left and returned a moment later, much to Maeve's happiness, with Mal. Zimsy bowed her head at Mal and left them. Maeve stood from the edge of her bed, and Mal reached out to assist her.

"I'm alright," said Maeve, slightly lying, holding up a hand to Mal. "Please." Maeve gestured to the armchairs in her room.

He seated himself in the chair, keeping his eyes on her the whole time as she walked his way. Maeve noticed the Dread Ring on his finger.

"I'm glad to see that you are," said Mal.

"What happened?" Asked Maeve bluntly. "What on Earth was that and how did you know exactly what to do?"

Mal sighed, being equally blunt. "That was something similar to Vexkari I did not intend to make."

Maeve's mouth dropped. "What?"

His eyes swam with remorse.

"I believe when we were in Albania, and I killed those men, and I was doing so much dark magic, some things got crossed, and when you and I…."

"Oh," whispered Maeve.

"I also believe that's why you spent months feeling ill," said Mal. "I suspected for a while that something may have accidentally rooted in you, but nothing drastic ever changed. You were ill, and then fine, and ill, and then fine. I kept feeling for something foreign attached to you. I never felt anything strange. Because it was me."

Maeve bit her nails, looking down at the floor, disturbed that a part of him had nearly killed her.

"I don't have all the answers," said Mal. "But I am terribly sorry, Maeve."

He spoke with sincerity.

"You saved me, though."

Mal gave her a small smile that didn't meet his eyes. "Each time you have been in peril over the past year, it was because of gross negligence on my part. It won't happen again."

Maeve knew better by now than to argue with him. She owed him her life three times now. It wasn't his fault.

"Thank you for the gift. And the gown, even though I didn't get to appear in it," said Maeve.

Maeve knew he had purchased those things with his own money earned from working at the museum.

He smiled softly at her, "Here."

He slid his ring off his finger. Maeve held out her hand.

"Where's the chain?" Asked Maeve.

"You won't need it anymore," he said. "I've bewitched the ring to fit any finger that wears it."

Maeve commended him. That this was a brilliant idea. She slipped the ring onto her left hand, and it fit perfectly.

"Speaking of the gown you didn't get to wear. I got the loveliest bit of information from Ophelia the other night."

Maeve frowned.

"Stop that," he said and ignored her pouting. "She introduced me to her Great Aunt Vetus Willus. Claims she's a descendant of a broken Sacred Magical Bloodline."

"Oh?" Said Maeve, intrigued. "That is interesting."

"More so," continued Mal, "is her boasting her possessions and collections."

"Such as?"

"A rather personal artifact of King Siris, two Dread Kings ago. A goblet."

Maeve sat up. "She bought it in the auction?"

"Yes," said Mal. "She keeps a tight lip on her treasures, though. Ophelia only speculated Vetus might have something of interest to me. I finally was able to meet her at the St. Beveraux's Christmas party and get her to open up to me. I've been writing to her for weeks."

A sinking feeling of embarrassment washed over Maeve.

"What's the matter, Little Viper," said Mal tauntingly. "Realizing my only interest in Ophelia was her Great Aunt's collection of treasure?"

Maeve bit the inside of her lip and suppressed a smile. "You could have just told me."

Mal leaned back in his chair. "I'll admit I like having leverage on your infatuation with me."

Maeve laughed and played with his ring on her finger. He watched her for a moment. His expression content.

"I'm glad to see you feeling better."

They sat in silence for a moment. After a long inhale, Maeve spoke.

"So, I am assuming Ophelia's Great Aunt what's her name took a liking to you?"

"I'm meant to have tea with her tomorrow morning."

Maeve smiled at him. He continued.

"Do you feel strong enough to alter memories?"

Maeve nodded.

"So we'll meet close by and go together," said Mal.

Maeve had not been expecting an invitation.

"Don't you think it would go better if she has you to herself?"

"Probably. I'll need your expertise, though."

Maeve understood. She would be there for memory clean-up.

"I wonder what other things she has in her collection," said Maeve.

"I thought something very similar."

"Your coronation is in five days," said Maeve. "And your birthday. What better present than a piece of The Dread Armor."

Mal's eyes traveled down her neck, then shifted to her hands at the black veins. He placed his elbow on the arm of the chair, cupping his chin. He looked at her with uncertainty.

"I'm sorry," he said finally, a guilty sadness in his voice.

"It's not important," she lied quickly.

Mal took a long breath. "Maeve, those marks don't mean-"

Maeve shook her head, and he fell silent.

She didn't want to think about it. She didn't want to look at herself.

Chapter 57

Maeve met him precisely where he instructed at eight AM sharp. She wore a high-collared shirt, covering the black veins that shot up her neck.

When she Obscured to his location, she landed gracefully. Mal was already waiting for her.

"You're getting much better at that," he commented.

"Better when I have full strength."

Mal turned on his heel and exited the shadowed alleyway. Maeve followed suit. They walked along a row of giant, well-maintained, lavish Parisian mansions before stopping at one that was pale pink.

The cream-colored stone steps were embedded between rows of colorful flowers all the way to the front door. Mal pulled on a golden rope. A bright melody began to play.

The door was opened quickly by a scrawny and ancient Elf. She looked nothing like Zimsy. She was short. Her skin was less radiant and sagging. Her hair was silver and stringy, exposing bald spots across her delicate skull.

Despite her haggard appearance, her voice was bubbly and she still held an elegant beauty.

"Mr. Peur! Miss Vetus will be delighted you are here," she said and shut the door behind them.

Maeve thought her grandmother Primrose's taste was gaudy, but Ophelia's Great Aunt Vetus took the cake on tacky decor. There were colorful ornate tapestries and curtains all along the walls, even those without windows. The carpet and most pieces of furniture were a thick shag fabric, and everything that could have fringe did. In every color.

"May I ask Mistress' name to introduce to Miss Willus?" the Elf said.

"This is my good friend, Maeve Sinclair," said Mal.

"Thank you so much, Mr. Peur, and welcome, Miss Sinclair. Please wait while I announce your arrival."

The small Elf tottered into the next room, leaving them in the foyer.

"Lovely taste," said Maeve under her breath.

Mal smirked.

"Malachite!" A loud cry came from the next room. "Do come in, darling dear!"

Maeve followed Mal into Vetus' drawing room, which looked no different from her foyer, except for the many glassed shelves and pedestals showing off her collections. All were guarded with Magical enchantments. Ophelia's aunt was sprawled across a lounging chair.

"Now, I didn't say you could bring a guest, Mal," she said reproachfully.

Mal smiled at her charmingly. "My apologies. This-"

"Maeve Sinclair, yes, I know who she is," said Vetus. "To think I wouldn't know The Premier's daughter- Heavens!"

Mal waltzed through the mayhem of the room, dodging each of the tables piled with antiques, and kissed Vetus on the hand.

"Sit down, dears," instructed Vetus.

Maeve took a seat on a gold and pink tufted stool.

Ophelia's great aunt Vetus Willus was a plump French woman, with bright red ringlet curls spiraling from behind an ornate headband.

"Descendant of Merlin? Or is zat hogwash?" Vetus asked Maeve as she admired her manicure.

"My Father says hogwash, though the books say otherwise," said Maeve with a smile.

"Sacred Seventeen, though?" Vetus asked, a bit of disdain in her voice.

Maeve nodded.

"Well, surely Malachite, the darling boy he is, haz told you about my bloodline?" Vetus raised her eyebrows at Mal.

"Of course, ma'am," said Maeve. "How impressive."

"I know the Museum has sent you here to persuade me to sell some of my treasures," said Vetus, eyeing Mal.

Mal smiled at her. "I am only here per your gracious invitation," said Mal, charm oozing from his words.

Vetus' chin dipped down as she relished his attention.

"May I?" Maeve interrupted, pointing to the large shelves of antiques.

Vetus looked annoyed and waved her away. Maeve stood and made her way through the room as she and Mal continued their conversation.

Her house was packed to the ceiling with ornaments and knickknacks and treasures. Maeve thought she might as well be in her father's basement, or the Magical Museum itself. Only Vetus' collection was much more curated to her specific taste Everything was lavishly Magical.

"I have a gift for you, our soon-to-be Dread Prince," said Vetus.

She had dropped her voice, Maeve assumed, for her not to hear their conversation easily.

"You honor me," said Mal.

"It is you who honors us, dear boy," said Vetus. "I can only hope there is a place in your Dread Kingdom for an old Magical like me."

Maeve rolled her eyes. She bent over to examine a gold-plated mirror with ancient ruins engraved along the handle. The inscription was hard to follow. It was a spell of sorts.

Maeve turned around just as Vetus presented him with an ornate golden goblet. His eyes lifted to hers.

"I'll bet you didn't believe my sweet niece, did you?" She squealed. "And now, it is my gift to you."

"I cannot accept this," said Mal.

"Of course you can! You must drink from it on the night of your coronation!"

She pushed the goblet towards him. He took it gently in his hands. A wave of relief washed over Maeve. Mal ran his fingers over the two serpent handles.

"Thank you, Vetus," Mal uttered with meaning. "This Magic is ancient Magic. My family's Magic. Thank you."

She kicked her feet and smiled. "Jema will wrap it safely for you, won't you Jema." The fragile Elf appeared at Vetus' side. "I wrote you a card as well. Jema, place it inside."

Jema bowed and took the Dread Goblet from Mal. She glided away silently.

"I don't know how to repay this kindness," said Mal.

Vetus threw her stubby hand in the air. "My darling boy, never you worry about that."

Mal smiled at her.

"Now," said Vetus, rubbing her hands together. "I'd like to show you around my collection before tea is served." Vetus rose from the lounging chair. Mal extended him her hand, which she took with pink cheeks. Maeve followed them in silence as Vetus bragged and baited compliments from Mal. She lowered the protective Magic around her possessions as they perused the tables and shelves.

Maeve moved ahead of them, browsing a set of swords and daggers.

She stopped before a shining metal dagger on a bed of ruby silk. Magic slipped from the tip, calling to her. Taunting her. The hilt was a steel serpent with ruby eyes. It was familiar somehow. Vetus' voice faded to nothing as Maeve's hand gravitated towards it. Her fingertips brushed the cool steel.

She sucked in tightly, recoiling from the dagger as pain flooded into the top of her thigh.

Mal's attention snapped to her. He was at her side a breath later.

"Mon Dieu!" Exclaimed Vetus. "Did not your mother teach you it's improper to touch others' zings without prior approval?" She clicked her tongue.

Maeve's attention remained on the dagger. She knew.

He knew.

Mal's Magic pressed into Maeve's mind.

The Dread Dagger.

"What's caught your eye, Malachite darling?" Asked Vetus as she appeared at his side. "Oh yes," she said, observing the Dread Dagger. "Quite a collection. A betrothal gift."

Maeve looked up at Mal. His eyes slid to hers.

Vetus was unaware of the Dread Magic that radiated off that dagger. She had no idea it was an artifact of the Dread Armor.

"Centuries old, I am told," continued Vetus. "Ze ruins say 'forever wounded.' Ze dagger's inflictions cannot be healed with Magic. They must heal naturally if not fatal."

Jema returned with the Dread Goblet wrapped in a bright pink shiny bag with yellow tissue paper flowing from the top and placed it nearby.

Are you alright? Mal said into her mind.

Maeve nodded subtly, assuming the pain she felt was merely another protective charm on Vetus' collection.

Vetus urged them along into the next room.

"I'm sure you know Walter Brighton, at the Museum," said Vetus.

Maeve's stomach tightened as Vetus continued.

"Shame what happened to 'im," she said, little concern in her voice. "This was his favorite room before he lost 'is memory."

Vetus' second installment of antiquities was made up entirely of jewels. Sunlight poured from the glass ceiling, sparkling across the finery.

"Come, come," she motioned excitedly. "This one above all ze rest, I cherish. No Magic has ever called to me ze way it does."

At the center of the room was a slender pedestal with a glass case on top.

Mal stopped, a lengthy exhale slipped from his lips. Vetus continued on ahead of them.

"I've only had it for twenty and some odd years," said Vetus. "Fought for it in a bidding war, you see, at the Museum." She laughed. "Walter Brighton would not speak to me for years over his loss."

Vetus moved aside, granting them a view of her most prized possession.

Suspended in the glass case was a shining golden locket.

Maeve had only ever seen it once before. It had been around Orion the Dread's neck in his portrait that hung in Mal's father's home.

Vetus snapped her fingers, and the glass case lifted. "A marvel of Magic," she whispered.

The room stilled. Magic filled the air with a soft, pulsing song. Like a burning heartbeat. Maeve stepped beside Mal, both of their gazes on the Dread Locket.

Vetus looked back at Mal in awe with no idea or understanding that this locket had been meant to protect Mal. To protect his mother.

Mal did not wait for Vetus' permission to touch the jewelry. He took the locket with gentle and controlled fingers, holding it in the morning light.

Maeve's heart skipped multiple beats.

Golden vines wrapped the oval-shaped frame. A small marking was etched on the front. An ancient and holy mark of power.

They had seen it before. A symbol of divine Magic. It wasn't always the same. It was like a scar. Just a reminder of the Magic there.

Vexkari had been on the tree in the forest where the Dread Crown was. It was on the Dread Ring on her finger. She had seen it on Reeve too, tattooed up his skull and on his jewelry.

It was across her neck and down her body permanently.

"At last," said Mal quietly, as the sunlight bounced off the ornate serpent clasp.

Vetus had no idea she held three of the seven Dread Armor artifacts. Nor that she was about to lose them all.

She clapped her hands together at Mal's fixation. "The auctioneer told me a little secret about zis necklace, you know? Only after I paid more than was logical did he laugh and gloat before me, saying he'd swindled it off some pregnant whore."

Maeve audibly gasped as Mal's eyes flashed red. His grip on the locket tightened. Vetus was still rambling, but Maeve was focused on Mal, and he was focused on the locket.

"-she would have taken a single human penny for it being scum and all-"

A soft hissing sound began to fill the room. Vetus was unaffected. Her rambling continued. It grew in intensity. The language was foreign to Maeve. But Mal. . .

It was clear he understood every word of the Magic resonating from the Dread Locket. It was finally back in the hands of its blood.

"I was only sour he had swindled me!" Continued Vetus. "Can you imagine human filth like that running the back alleys with vermin and a Magical jewel so beloved about her neck?"

Vetus' laughter filled the air.

Her hand reached for the Dread Locket casually. When Mal did not return it, her bright face looked upon his curled lip and dangerous demeanor.

Vetus' hand reached further out, grasping for the locket, but Maeve knew she was never getting it back. Maeve was slowly pulling her fingers together at her side.

"Are you all right, Malachite, darling?" Asked Vetus as her smile faltered. "You look. . ."

"Make short work of this, Maeve," said Mal, all sweetness in his voice long gone.

There was a flash of blue light, and Vetus slumped to the floor, unconscious.

"How dare she speak of her that way," said Mal darkly.

Maeve knew what was coming next. Vetus' life would have likely been spared, and her memory simply altered, had she not made those nasty comments about his mother while dotting on Mal and flaunting her fortune. They were going to steal the Dread artifacts she possessed, but her fate had never been planned with deadly intentions.

"Jema," called Mal.

The Elf came tottering back into the room.

Bright white light shot from the tip of Maeve's fingers. Jema froze and Maeve Obscured to her at once, catching her bony frame before she crumbled to the floor.

Mal continued to stare at the locket.

"You cannot make it brutal, Mal," said Maeve. "I have to be able to cover us. It will need to be believable."

Mal didn't respond. He took the long chain and placed it around his neck. His eyes closed. Clouds covered the sunlight pouring from the ceiling and darkened the room.

He raised his hand silently. The Dread Dagger flew into the room and into his grip.

His eyes opened as he looked at the shining blade.

"Do whatever you must," he said.

Maeve looked back down at Jema, the wheels in her mind turning. She wondered if she could get the Elf to safety, if somehow she could find another way to explain Vetus' death. She looked up at Mal, prepared to argue that Vetus' life needed to be spared. Selfishly she didn't want the framing of Jema on her conscious.

But she altered the Elf's memory, ensuring she and Mal would be in the clear for stealing Vetus' Dread artifacts and her soon death.

Maeve had implanted many memories by now, but this was the first time it wasn't for practice. This was an invasion of the mind, unconsenting and unwilling. Her arms tingled weakly as she finished. Her full strength was not yet restored.

"I'm sorry," said Maeve. "If I could, I would break yours too."

She laid the Elf gently on the shag carpet and turned her attention to Mal. He was staring down at Vetus dangerously.

Maeve's heart kicked at his expression. She hadn't seen him kill Kietel. She hadn't witnessed the revenge in his eyes. The hatred. She had seen him kill, but even in killing his father he was calm and calculated. Emotionless.

Rage resonated from him.

"To sit here, on a pile of gold, and still be so unworthy of possessing it," said Mal, raising his pointed finger.

The room flashed red, and Vetus lay dead.

Chapter 58

"What do you make of it?"

A camera flashed brightly behind her, photographing Vetus Willus' crime scene of a house she and Mal had fled only twelve hours before. She had been called there to verify Jema's confession.

Maeve looked away from Jema and to Doggbind, Head of Magical Law. He was a stout man with a full grey beard. Older than her Father.

"She poisoned her," said Maeve, having just run through Jema's mind. Her memory work was perfect. "Would you like to see?"

Doggbind shook his head. "I've seen it. She showed me."

Maeve stood from where she kneeled in front of the short Elf.

"I'm sorry to have caused you any grief, Miss Maeve."

Maeve looked down at Jema. "You've done no such thing. I'm sorry you were treated poorly enough to feel killing her was the only path to relief."

Doggbind stiffened. Purebloods weren't the only ones with Elven people for servants.

"Am I excused, sir?" She asked.

Doggbind nodded.

Maeve slipped behind him and made for the door.

"Sinclair," he called after her, his eyes never leaving the photographer and inspector as they made their way around Vetus' house.

"Sir?"

"Give my regards to Ambrose."

Vetus' murder made the front page of all the Magical newspapers. An unexpected byproduct of their wrongdoings- Clarissa cracked down on every Elf Servant in the household.

Including Zimsy.

Zimsy sat in the corner of Maeve's favorite reading nook, legs pulled together, the side of her lovely face brutalized with a thin slice.

She gazed out the window with a dull, broken expression. Maeve kept her distance.

"Your mother said I needed reminding of what would happen if I ever tried such a thing," said Zimsy, her voice hollow, absent of all its normal lively timbre.

"Fucking bitch," muttered Maeve as her stomach turned to acid.

She walked towards Zimsy and took a set opposite her on the window seat, leaning into the wall and curling her legs towards her in a similar fashion.

Zimsy looked at her now. Maeve met her eyes, red and swollen, and cursed swiftly under her breath.

"I promise, Zimsy-"

Zimsy looked away and shook her head. "Don't." She tucked her chin on her knees. "Don't promise me something you can't keep."

"Once Mal is-"

"Don't," she said softly.

Maeve pressed on. "In the Dread Lands there won't be any servant curse-"

"Don't!" Snapped Zimsy. She had never spoken to Maeve like that. Her expression wilted. "Don't."

Maeve's head hit the wall behind her. Her Magic drifted over, gently healing Zimsy's face. She breathed deeply and moved towards Zimsy. She pulled her into her arms, and for the first time, let herself feel the wicked curse that bound Zimsy to her Mother.

It was a solid steel wall, cold and unyielding, that stretched in every direction for miles.

She then felt for the strand connecting Zimsy and Maeve, which would be weaker, as Maeve was only Clarrisa's daughter. But there was nothing.

Not even a thread of Magic lingered there.

An Enslavement Curse was considered unbreakable by a third party. No one had ever managed it.

Solid steel walls of magic were nearly impenetrable.

But so was the mind. And Maeve shattered those just fine.

Mal wore the Dread Locket every day, concealed under his clothes. She argued with him about Zimsy's enslavement curse. And they argued about the locket. Mal was set on adding more Vexkari to it.

The locket already had Dread Magic, someone else's Magic, stowed in it. It was dangerous to entangle with it. But Mal, confident in his wealth of power, felt the opposite.

He wanted to feel close to his mother if part of her Magic still lingered on that locket. He wanted Maeve to be protected with the locket in his absence.

Maeve argued she could break Zimsy's chains with his help, and Mal said it was possible, but not soon.

"You are not strong enough for that Magic," said Mal. "Not yet. But I have told you, once we are in the Dread Lands there will be no such curses."

"What if my mother doesn't come?" Asked Maeve. "What if she keeps Zimsy here?"

Mal stood close, packing a small black leather shoulder bag for a short journey into the Dread Lands. No one but the pair of them knew he had been traveling there alone. His coronation was planned to be in the restored Hellming Hall of Vaukore Castle, but Mal had a surprise for every Magical that would be in attendance.

They would all be visiting the Dread Lands in just a few days. Mal had nearly finished restoring the Magic of Castle Morana in The Dread Lands where his coronation would actually take place. Maeve couldn't accompany him in preparing the throne room. She still couldn't breathe there for as long as he needed to stay to ensure it was ready.

He slipped the serpent-tip Dread Dagger into his bag. Contemplated for a moment and then slid it back out. He crossed around the table and held the hilt towards her.

"Keep it on you at all times," he said.

"I wish I could come with you," she replied.

"Soon," said Mal with a nod.

Soon.

That was his answer to everything lately.

Maeve took the dagger in her hand. It was hefty. The serpent's fangs were bared, its eyes made of crimson ruby stones.

The blade was tapered to a fine point. And just as Vetus said, the inscription read 'forever wounded.'

"Will a wound on a Magical heal?"

Mal opened his left palm to her. Where a fresh red incision was barely closed up. "Magical blood will heal at the rate a human heals. But I imagine a human would never heal."

Maeve looked back down at the dagger. Her hand crept up to her neck. Concealed beneath her sweater were her own markings that would never heal. Her veins ran black from Mal's dark magic.

Mal took a seat next to her on the edge of his bed.

He closed her hand around the dagger. "On you at all times." He grabbed the back of her head and brought their foreheads together. "When I return, I will be the Dread Prince, and you will be my Dread Viper."

Maeve's heart swelled. She pushed herself closer to him, their noses brushing.

Their lips pressed together in a silent goodbye.

Chapter 59

Maeve sat in a comfy, ornate wooden lounging chair in the back sunroom of her Grandmother Agatha's lavish cottage, preparing her mind for a conversation she had avoided for months.

Her father's mother had a way of getting hard truths out of Maeve and was considered the only Witch alive who could talk some semblance of sense into her young rebellious granddaughter.

The doors to the main room were open, letting sunlight pour onto the old dark walnut floors. A pot of tea and two teacups appeared on the table between them.

"So," said Agatha in a business-like voice. "I hear you nearly died."

"Which time?" Asked Maeve, with the hint of a smirk on her lips.

"Some dark Magic you're dabbling in," said Agatha. "Though I expect nothing less from my youngest son's offspring."

Maeve didn't respond and let Agatha speak.

"Speaking of death," said Agatha, waving her hand to pour herself another cup of tea. "I heard Vetus Willus died."

Maeve turned her head to her Grandmother slowly and said calmly. "You knew her?"

"Hated her. Too much money and no class," she huffed. "She wouldn't shut up about all her favorite collections."

"Funny," said Maeve. "Mal had just met her at the St. Beveraux's Christmas party. But you didn't introduce them."

"Funny," said Agatha. "Was it Ophelia St. Beveraux who did?"

"You sent him to that party to meet her? You told him to get close to Ophelia?"

Agatha sipped her tea. Maeve leaned forward in her chair. "How did you know I've nearly died three times this year? Did Father tell you or did someone else?" Asked Maeve, beginning to understand that Mal and Agatha were communicating with one another more than she realized.

"I don't really need to answer that question, sharp as you are," said Agatha.

Maeve loosed a laugh.

"Did you get it?" Asked Agatha gruffly.

Maeve nodded and studied her grandmother with appreciation. She nodded. "And then some."

Agatha smiled.

"Why don't you ever come to parties anymore?" Asked Maeve.

"Ambrose, keep me informed."

"Don't you miss it?"

Agatha chuckled, "No, dear, it was a welcome relief, truth be told. Not having to face all those arrogant bastards all the time."

Maeve laughed. "I can't disagree. I've grown tired of pretending to smile at them."

Agatha raised her teacup, toasting Maeve.

Maeve's attention was drawn to the giant portrait of her grandfather, who had just stood up from his armchair and began walking in the field of wildflowers around him.

"So," said Agatha. "Malachite. Our soon-to-be Dread Prince of Darkness."

Maeve felt a flush in her cheeks at the mention of his name. And the twinkle in her grandmother's eye.

Agatha continued, "Though I hear you call him so already."

Maeve remained silent. The conversation had arrived.

"Well?" Pushed Agatha.

"What would you like to know?" Maeve asked calmly.

"Well, for starters, I'm wondering how I missed the addition of the name 'Peur' on the list of suitable pureblood men for you to marry."

Maeve placed her teacup down, folding her hands into her lap. "You didn't."

"And so I'm to understand you're aware he is not of pureblood. Regardless of his blood heritage from centuries ago, on paper he is not fit for a Sinclair. You need strong Magical bloodlines."

"You think our child wouldn't be strong?"

Agatha's eyes narrowed. "I think he has no need for future descendants. The last Dread King reined for an eternity before the blight. Malachite will be no different."

Maeve chose her words carefully, wondering if Mal would ever see this moment through her memories.

"His blood means nothing to me," said Maeve.

Agatha frowned. "Then what of him does mean something to you? Besides his future throne?"

Maeve smiled softly. "Oh, where to begin? There's so much more at play here. Grandmother. Bigger things are happening."

"Thank Primus for that. But what are you to him? Will you stand as his second, and marry like expected? Bare children that continue a Sacred line? To repopulate our Promised Land? I know my son has raised you to be fearless. However, I wish you could foresee the regret you may have one day. If you stand beside a ruler who has no desire or need for a family of his own, will you waste your life for that title? Better yet, will you give up your life? You've truly known this boy a little more than a year and you've nearly died three times, my girl."

Agatha's eyes drifted to Maeve's neck. To her gloved hands. She knew about the marks Maeve was concealing.

"I do fear regret, Grandmother," said Maeve gently. "I fear the mundane. I fear sitting in a mansion all day with more gold than a God waiting for a man I despise to return home. A life of redecorating the same rooms over and over again. I fear a life lived without thrill. I fear growing old and regretting the life I wasted doing what was expected of me. I crave excitement." Maeve sighed. "I crave him."

Agatha nodded slowly, her face a mixture of remorse and pride.

Maeve leaned back in her chair. "I have been mesmerized by him before I knew who he was. No one understands. It's as though our Magic is one already."

"Even on the brink of death again and again?"

Maeve gave her grandmother an understanding look. Agatha looked over her spectacles, her lips in a thin line.

"I will gladly die a hundred deaths if it is he who breathes life back into me."

Agatha didn't respond.

"I know why I'm here," said Maeve. "I know you're meant to convince me to marry Alphard Mavros or that insufferable bit of Elven Royalty."

"And?"

"Oh, Grandmother. You already know. I can't."

"Every Sacred Seventeen woman before you, myself included, has risen to the occasion Maeve, and done her duty to her family. A duty that the Dread Prince will continue to enforce."

"I know that," said Maeve sincerely. "But who will stand in opposition to him after his coronation in two night's time? No one stands in opposition to him now."

They sat in silence for a few moments. Alyicious wandered back into his portrait, smoking his cigar. The same ones Ambrose smoked. Both Maeve and Agatha studied him.

"You know," started Agatha. "It breaks my heart that Antony won't continue the Sinclair name. My sweet Alyicious would be so devastated."

Maeve contemplated her grandmother for a moment as Agatha stared longingly at the portrait of her late husband.

"Did you love him?" Asked Maeve.

Agatha smiled softly. "Oh, yes."

Maeve leaned toward her earnestly. "I don't love those men."

"No," said Agatha. "And Malachite has all but made it clear to me, that if they forced you, those men wouldn't live to see their wedding day."

Maeve smiled. Mal's ring sent a trickle of Magic down her fingertip.

Agatha let out a small sigh. "Here sits my youngest grandchild, master of charms and confounding witches and wizards twice her age, pleading with an old bitty to get her way."

Maeve chuckled softly at the compliment. "I could never confound you."

"I will tell The Committee of the Scared that you are not moving forward with Mr. Mavros or Xander. And if they have an issue, they can take it up with our new Dread Prince."

A large sigh of relief escaped Maeve's lips. Her heart felt like it was going to burst. "I have one more thing to ask Grandmother. Something you must make happen. I cannot ask Mal for it. He won't understand."

Agatha raised her brows.

"Convince the Committee of the Sacred that Victoria Deaveros is not going to marry Damario. She will be Alphard's."

Agatha eyed her for a moment.

"And the Mavros will not pay for her," said Maeve. "No more bidding war."

Chapter 60

Clarissa hosted a charity ball to raise money for the Opulentos Society, for which Maeve had very little care. But Abraxas insisted she attend. The society would be providing major contributions to reestablish a thriving society in The Dread Lands. They had planned restaurants and shops and the restoration of mansions and palaces.

Maeve was seated at the bar in the main hall. Mal was still far off, unreachable, in the Dread Lands. She didn't expect him to return until the last second before his coronation.

"How did you squirm your way out of it?"

Maeve looked to her right at Arianna, disappointed to hear the disdain return to her sister's voice, given that they had been on agreeable terms lately.

"I've been trying to tell you for a while now. I take what I want."

"I cannot believe you used Magic on our ancient grandmother to get your way!"

Maeve scoffed. "I did nothing of the sort."

"You lie," seethed Arianna. "It's all a lie. I'd love to see you duel without that pretty little ring."

Maeve's heart skipped a beat. Arianna wasn't stupid.

"I'm not sure what you're getting at," said Maeve grimly. "I didn't trick Grandma Agatha, and I don't appreciate the assumption that I did. And I will gladly kick your ass any day without it."

Arianna pushed away from the bar, but Maeve was on her heels, unable to let it go.

"Jealous, are we? Jealous that you're too scared to venture out of the box created to keep you confined?"

Arianna didn't stop as they entered the ballroom. Patrons and donors were eyeing them awkwardly as they continued to argue.

Maeve continued. "I'm sorry you did everything you were told, and now you're miserable for it."

Arianna turned in a flash, and Maeve whipped out her hand just in time to deflect a hefty curse sent her way.

A large collective gasp came from the room, and a few guests quickly shuffled away from them.

"Oh, my, Arianna," Maeve mocked her sister. "I must have hit a nerve."

Arianna screamed in anger, sending bright green beams her way. Maeve blocked her once more.

"You're making a scene," said Maeve cooly.

"How do you always get your way? How is everyone else making concessions except for you?"

"Are you joking?" Laughed Maeve darkly. "You have no idea the sacrifices I've made, the things I've endured to ensure Mal is crowned and we are able to return home."

"That's rich."

Arianna sent another spell her way, which Maeve blocked with ease. Arianna's spells were weak. Her anger was fueling them, which, for Arianna, was not a powerful enough source.

"It's not my fault I fight for what I want and you don't, Arianna."

"And what you want is that dirty-blooded boy," hissed Arianna.

Thin strands of weak, green lightning swarmed at Arianna's fingertips. But Maeve didn't notice the rare Magic coming from her sister.

A surge of hatred rose in her chest. She barely had time to think before her body reacted.

Anger was a powerful source for her.

A jet of black light burst from the tip of her fingers. Arianna screamed as it was deflected with a deafening crash, though not by herself.

Ambrose Sinclair stood between his daughters, looking at Maeve in complete shock.

The room was deadly quiet. The band had stopped playing, and the usual chatter and clanking of glasses had ceased. All eyes were on Maeve and Arianna.

"Come with me. Now," commanded Ambrose as he strode past Maeve.

She looked at her sister, whose face was white with fear, and she dared not look at anyone else in the room. Ambrose was silent as they ascended the stairs to his study.

"What is the matter with you?" Ambrose spoke darkly once they were behind a closed door, which he slammed.

Maeve wasn't even aware her father had spoken. She made her way to the sofa and sat, shaking out her hand.

"Are you aware of what you just did?" Asked Ambrose, louder now.

"I used illegal Magic," said Maeve, her voice dry. "Deadly and unforgivable Magic."

There were only a handful of spells that produced black light. None were permitted under the Orator's Office.

"Deadly." Ambrose searched her expression, confused. "On your sister!"

Magic Ambrose blocked. Maeve often forgot his power.

"She insulted me. She said Mal had dirty blood. He's about to be The Dread Prince!"

"I don't give a damn what she said. Maeve Sinclair, none of my children have ever embarrassed me like this."

Maeve reclined in the sea, genuinely stung by his words.

Ambrose sat behind his desk, one hand rubbing his chin. "You are aware that you did that in front of at least a hundred people?"

Maeve was speechless. Conflicted by the way her father was looking at her and the knowledge that Arianna had deserved it.

"You have nothing to say?"

Maeve looked blankly at her father. "I am sorry to disappoint you."

Ambrose shifted in his chair.

Maeve continued. "I have lived under her torture for a long time. She has always pushed me when I was down and made it clear she viewed herself as superior to me. And now that she is the one envious of me, she wants to be nasty still. She threw four curses at me before I countered. I blocked every single one too, and I think that only made her madder. Do you remember when her curses brought me to my knees? She isn't above me anymore and she can't stand it."

"She is your sister and my daughter, too." Ambrose lowered his head and spoke tenderly. "You could show her some compassion."

Maeve's mouth fell open. "Compassion? Where was her compassion towards me my entire childhood?"

"Stop dwelling on the past, Maeve!" Ambrose raised his voice. "Can you not see the strides your sister has made toward you? Did you not witness her concern for your safety after Christmas? Her empathy? Newfound as it may be, it is there."

Maeve chewed the inside of her lip.

"Of course, she is envious of you," continued Ambrose. "You have the whole world ahead of you, whatever you choose for it, and she does not. You are about to stand at the side of The Dread Descendant-there is no greater honor I could wish you."

"But that's not-"

"Whose fault that is remains irrelevant," interrupted Ambrose. He shook his head, lowering his voice. "If anything, it's my fault."

Maeve's face scrunched. "How's that?"

Ambrose leaned back in his chair, looking up at the ceiling. "I told myself, after Antony, I would put an end to it. That no more of my children would suffer at the hands of the Committee. I promised your sister that even, did you know?"

Maeve shook her head.

"Oh, yes," said Ambrose. "As she sat where you sit just after Antony's funeral, she sobbed, terrified, of these people that were capable of such a thing. She's smart. She knew it was no accident. I promised her refuge. When the time came, I fought for her. But there are consequences to going against The Committee and their influence in the Orator's Office, and I feared there were already too many marks against me. I relented, and they picked Titus for her without a second thought. And the promise I made her was broken. Just a year ago." Ambrose sighed. "I can't imagine how cheated she feels to know you are the benefactor of the promise I made to her."

They sat silently. Finally, Maeve said, "I'll fix it. I'm sorry I embarrassed and disappointed you."

"You can't erase it, Maeve," said Ambrose. "What's done is done."

"That's true," said Maeve, standing and running her left-hand fingers down her index and middle fingers on the other. "But that doesn't mean they have to remember it."

Ambrose's eyes glittered for a moment.

"Would you like to see it?" Asked Maeve.

Ambrose contemplated what she was saying.

"You're certain you can do that?"

Maeve smiled. "I've already done it."

They made their way back down to the party, Ambrose at Maeve's side.

"You're going to forget the duel between Arianna and me. I can't help that, and I can't control one person not forgetting," said Maeve. "But you'll remember the rest of our conversation and that we are standing here because of it. Make of that what you will, I suppose."

Maeve stood in the center of the foyer. Party guests were in the ballroom, singing hall, and bar, scattered through the house. She raised her two fingers to her temple and closed her eyes. She extracted the memory of her argument with Arianna from only moments ago. It lingered at the tip of her fingers, swirling around in a silver mass.

The silvery strand of memory began to grow and turn a glittering gold color. In an instant, golden streams exploded from the tips of her fingers, traveling in all directions at the speed of light.

It didn't take long for the cloud to return to the tip of Maeve's hand, where it turned silver once more. Maeve popped the memory back into her head.

Maeve looked up at her stunned father.

"I-" stuttered Ambrose. "I had no idea."

"Do you know why I haven't taken that job with Daniel Rodriguez, Daddy? As beneficial to our Magical world as it may be? And why they pester you about it constantly still?"

"Because the Orator's Office will want to weaponize this spell you've created."

Maeve stared at her father intensely and nodded. "I don't intend to share it."

Chapter 61

The preparations for Mal's coronation were going perfectly, according to Abraxas and Maeve's grandmothers. They were two of the oldest Magicals alive, and held the distinct honor of ensuring Mal's ascent to the throne was a memorable one.

He was still traveling and was set to return late tomorrow evening or early in the morning on his birthday.

She entered her father's study. "You wanted to see me?"

Ambrose leaned against the enchanted window. A stormy twilight brewed through the glass. Movement to her right caught her eye.

Reeve sat on the black leather loveseat. No claws. No wings. Just the handsome High Lord whom she had exchanged unpleasant words with last they spoke.

His chin lowered. "Sinclair."

Maeve looked back to her father. The air was tense. "What's this?"

"Have a seat, darling," said Ambrose.

Maeve crossed the room and sat opposite Reeve. They were quiet. Maeve shook her head.

"Wonderful," she said. "It's the eve of his coronation and let me guess," she looked to Reeve, "you've come up with some reason it shouldn't happen."

Neither of them spoke. A sinking feeling washed over her entire body.

"I knew it. You're moving against me?" Asked Maeve in a shuddering whisper. "Against us?"

Ambrose's eyes shot to his daughter. "No," he said darkly.

"Then what is this?" She pressed.

Ambrose sighed. "I am sorry, darling. I have told you before there are aspects of war you know nothing of."

She looked to Reeve. Not a flirtatious flicker in his firelight eyes. This was The High Lord of the Immortal Realm. He spoke now.

"There are whispers. Whispers that have happened before. A darkness growing stronger in the Dread Lands," said Reeve.

"Of course there is," said Maeve. "The Dread Descendant has returned."

"It's more than that," said Reeve. "The darkness there is growing."

"Mal can handle-"

"Tell her Ambrose," Reeve interrupted.

Ambrose was reclined back in his chair. His arms draped down the arms of his chair. "I am afraid for you, Maeve. I am afraid of what lies there. Afraid it will corrupt you before Malachite even has a chance to defeat it. I took an oath to protect all Magicals. I called you here, and Reeve here, because I need you to understand why I informed Reeve about your spell."

She looked back and forth between them.

"Excuse me?" Maeve said in disbelief, certain she had misheard him.

"Maeve," said Ambrose, his tone dismissive. He didn't even so much as glance at her. He turned his chair towards the window.

But Reeve's eyes slid to Maeve as Ambrose continued talking. After only a moment Reeve's expression swiftly shifted, as he realized Maeve was on the edge of her seat. Shock spread across her face.

"You didn't," said Maeve. "Tell me you didn't-"

Ambrose rounded on her. "You know nothing of wartime and the sacrifices that must be made-"

"I know plenty of sacrifices," snapped Maeve, her voice growing dark. She pulled at the fabric of her high-collared sweater and then pushed up her sleeves, exposing the marks of proof.

Ambrose ignored the gesture and continued. "We are on the verge of another catastrophic war, this time we may not survive."

Maeve's throat burned hot. She couldn't believe it. "So you betrayed my secret to him, for your own gain?"

"For all our gain," corrected Ambrose.

Maeve shook her head. “I told you what the Double O would do with this power, you agreed the danger-”

“I am not your corrupted government,” said Reeve.

“Shut up,” said Maeve.

“You think you are the only one with loved ones to protect,” said Reeve.

“Spare me,” said Maeve. “You don’t give a damn what happens to the Magicals, so long as your precious and perfect society stays tucked away from harm. When was the last time your schools were attacked? Your lands destroyed?”

“He has been to the Dread Lands, Miss Sinclair,” spat Reeve, his voice sharp and low. “Malachite has traveled into The Dark Sacred Lands that sit across the Black Deep from my lands. Immortal lands.”

“So what?” She said.

They were silent for a moment. Ambrose and Reeve exchanged a glance.

“You knew,” said Ambrose.

“Of course, I knew,” she answered. “I am his Second.”

Reeve nearly rolled his eyes. He stood and walked past her to gaze at the artifacts along her father’s mantle as if looking for a distraction, his breathing slow and controlled.

But Maeve could feel that temper ready to whip from him. Fire danced and pushed across the floor towards her.

Maeve looked to her father, who ran a hand through his darkened silver hair. “He’s there now, isn’t he?” He asked her.

“And so what if he is? Those lands, the Magic in them, is his.”

“True,” said Ambrose gently. “And I advised him that I fully supported his desire to travel.”

“But?” Pressed Maeve.

Reeve turned from the mantel now, Maeve looked to him.

“But those lands have been sealed for centuries for a reason. We had a plan. Armies of Magic to take back those lands.”

Maeve scowled. “You’re so arrogant. You think he isn’t capable of handling the power?”

“No, I think he’s going to fail miserably and bring all of us down with him.”

Maeve's jaw tightened. "Ah." She looked to her father. "And there lies the real reason he wanted my spell. Speaking of things failing miserably," she looked back at Reeve, "good luck casting it right."

"Now look who is arrogant."

"I do not hide my arrogance behind the guise of diplomatic alliances and humanitarian generosity. I will be feared for my arrogance."

Reeve was closer now, towering above her. So close she could see a bright white scar that ran across his neck, surrounded by ink. Those same three necklaces hung from his neck.

Vexkari markings.

"I don't doubt that," muttered Reeve.

Maeve turned back towards her father. "So what if the humans start another war? We will be moving from this realm soon."

"How soon?" He asked gently.

Maeve didn't have an answer. Ambrose pulled a cigar from his pocket and handed one to Reeve. The tips of them lit instantly.

"You wanted to be in the room, Maeve. You begged me not to be excluded. Now here you are, having the real conversations."

"So I am to accept the Premier gave away my most prized secret, not that my father did."

Pain glimmered across his eyes. "Yes."

Maeve swallowed and accepted his point, horrible as it was.

"Fine. I can accept that reality. And to answer your question: tomorrow."

Ambrose's cigar dipped from his fingers. "What?"

"His coronation won't be at Vaukore. It will be in the Dread Lands. In just a few short months, he has restored Castle Morana. And then soon the rest of what was once a great city will be ready for our return."

Ambrose's eyes were wide with joy. "Incredible."

Maeve's throat tightened. "Do not tell Mal what you've done. Do not tell him you doubted him," she spoke directly to Ambrose. "You are the closest thing to a father he has. Do not devastate him in this way."

Ambrose looked at his daughter with remorse.

"I need a moment alone with my daughter, Reeve."

The High Lord didn't argue. He didn't look at Maeve as he passed by her and left the study.

Maeve and her father sat silently for a moment. Ambrose finished his cigar and then stood. He moved around the desk and pulled one of the armchairs towards her. He sat with their knees almost touching.

She didn't look at him.

"Maeve," he said gently, his voice warm and calm.

She looked up at him. His face was content.

"A year ago we sat in this office and I had to beg you to even tell me Malachite's name. Now here we are, and you are fighting to protect him still." Ambrose reached forward and held her face in her hands. "You are going to be the most fearsome and dedicated second." His eyes traveled to her neck and then to her arms. "Do not fear these marks, Maeve. Show the world what you have done to earn your place tomorrow."

"I worry that he won't find me beautiful anymore." The brutally honest words slipped from her before she second-guessed them.

Ambrose exhaled. "You will always be beautiful, my darling daughter. He could be blind and I know he'd still choose you. The connection you share goes beyond the physical. Like calls to like."

She calculated what to say next, but as the person she loved most in the world bore into her, she couldn't hold a facade.

"I didn't expect this to happen," said Maeve weakly. Then she laughed, almost with a cry. "Especially when I know it will never be anything more."

Ambrose was quick with a response. He squeezed her hand three times. "It already is something more." He held Maeve's hands in his own. "I know that he brings you more excitement than you've probably felt in all your life, and I know you are drawn to the same dark Magic he is, and I can't blame you there. It's in your blood. I have watched you do great things since making his acquaintance. Things I hoped for you even as a just a child. That's all I can hope you continue to do." He looked at her tenderly. "There is nothing you weren't born to do. It is all yours for the taking, Maeve. I pray you take it all."

Maeve pushed off her chair and threw herself into her father's arms where he sat, wrapping her arms around him. He held the back of her head and kissed her hair.

"My plus jeune serre-livre," he murmured. "My littlest bookend."

Chapter 62

The sun was still down, nowhere close to breaking the horizon. Maeve couldn't sleep. The anticipation of Mal's coronation was heavy. She propped herself on one side and read A Witches Guide to the New World, with Spinel curled tightly at her stomach. Her new favorite read wasn't enough of a distraction. She read the same lines over and over, her mind drifting to Mal and his crowning.

An unmistakable cold tingle shot down her spine. She sat up with a gasp that sent Spinel running. Her heartbeat kicked loud as a drum in her ears, and her head spun for a moment. She tossed her book and went bolting for the bedroom door. Spinel was still chaotically running about.

She made her way across the landing and began her descent from the third floor. Halfway down the stairs, she came across Trudy, who jumped upon seeing her.

"Oh! You have a visitor, Miss-"

"I know." Maeve interrupted her without even a glance.

She tried to slow herself as she flew down the main staircase to the foyer.

"Hi," said Maeve, out of breath.

"Hello, Maeve."

She sighed with relief and hopped from the stairs, throwing her arms around Mal's neck. He caught her with both arms wrapped around her waist.

A small chuckle escaped his lips. "Three days and this is how you behave?"

He slid her down to the balls of her feet. She looked up at him.

"Happy birthday," she said, nearly beaming. "Tonight, everything is going to change."

His eyes traced over her entire face. "Not everything."

His cheeks were slightly more sunken, or more prominent, she didn't know. All she knew was that it suited him nicely. He looked like the Prince he was.

"Would you like to sit in the drawing room?" Offered Maeve, trying to sound calmer, but her heartbeat was pounding even louder now that she was close to him.

He released her waist and nodded once. They stepped across the foyer and Maeve closed the doors to the drawing room behind them.

"How have you been?" Asked Mal as he took a seat.

"Skip the pleasantries, shall we?"

Mal smirked.

She sat across from him. "You did it. I can feel it."

Mal watched her for a moment. "Does that disappoint you?"

Maeve shook her head. "It amazes me. You are-"

"Perfectly fine," he said. "As I told you I would be."

"Perhaps one day I'll stop doubting you," she said quietly.

"I doubt it. So," he leaned forward, "I have something for you."

He pulled a small black box from his pocket and ran his fingers over it. "I was hoping you would keep this one as safe as you have my ring."

He opened the box and ran his fingers over its contents.

Inside was the Dread Locket.

"How did it go?" Asked Maeve, looking up at him.

He stared at the locket. "Like the others."

He pulled it from the box and held it in the light, standing and crossing towards her. He sat next to her.

"It's gorgeous," said Maeve, staring at the fine detailing. "Even more so now, it's. . . It's glowing with Magic."

He placed the box on the table and turned to her. "May I?"

She turned her back to him and pulled her hair to the side as he placed the locket around her neck, fastening it. His fingers were cold and sent a quick chill down her back. A wave of deep magic came over her, so strong that she had to breathe deeply to counter it. She gripped the cushion beneath her. Her vision went out of focus, and when it re-entered, she could have sworn the room's colors seemed different. Her mind swam through a few thoughts she couldn't quite make out.

The ring didn't have nearly such a profound effect as the locket.

She turned back to him and looked down at the locket, which was glistening in the light.

Mal ran his fingers down the chain and grasped the locket. His touch brought heat to her cheeks. He ran his thumb up and down the new emerald markings and spoke in his perfect velvety voice.

"Time is strange in those lands. It feels like weeks. I've missed you."

She looked up, and his eyes were already on her.

Mal continued before she could say anything. "How does it feel?"

"It... It feels like you."

He smirked at her and let go of the locket. "Good."

His hands moved to her wrists, pulling her with him as he relaxed back on the sofa. Their chests pressed together as she lay atop him. He brushed her hair to the side.

"Tonight you shall wear them," he whispered, their noses nearly touching. "Do you have your gown?"

"No," said Maeve with a small smile, thinking about the custom dress. "Grandmother Agatha wouldn't let me even see it yet."

"Mmm," he hummed, his thumb tracing over her cheek. "That won't do."

"Why?"

"Because I want to see you in it now," he murmured, his voice smooth and delicious.

And he did.

The sun was barely rising, the sky a pale shade of blue, when they Obscured to his flat. Mal opened the doors to his armoire. And Maeve's heart soared.

It was every hue of sapphire blue and silver, like an early evening cosmos. Satin and beads and tulle and sparkling fabric draped elegantly across the hanger.

"It's stunning," she said.

Mal moved behind her and put his lips close to her ear. "Put it on."

He left the room. She obeyed.

Moments later she emerged into his sitting area. The sight of him stopped her feet and her breath all at once.

He was in an emerald green brocade suit, head to toe, with black trim and embellishments. In the subtle floral print were serpents intertwined with thorns and branches and leaves. Pinned at his shoulder was a black and emerald cape that fluttered royally to the backs of his knees.

He was a vision of nobility. A prize.

His eyes traced leisurely down her entire body. Even her black lightning bolt-like veins. "Perfection."

Maeve's head kicked back, and she balled the fabric of her dress in her fists and moved swiftly towards him. He strode towards her and their bodies collided with a magnetic slam. His hands tucked around her neck, pulling her face up towards him. She kissed him hard, her tongue begging his mouth for entry. He obliged and heat surged between her legs as their tongues moved as one.

Mal kicked her legs from beneath her, swooping her into his arms. She threw her arms around his neck, refusing to break her lips away. He brought them down the hall, pushing his bedroom door open with his back.

Maeve gasped as he dropped her on her knees at the edge of his bed. His hands gripped her hips and held her steady as he slowly moved his lips to her throat. His tongue moved tauntingly across her skin. Maeve shuddered and gripped his arms, pushing herself against him.

His mouth trailed down, licking across her collarbone. She moaned and tilted her head back. She reached forward, finding the band of his pants, and ran her hand down to feel him. She cupped her palm around him and smiled widely.

Mal pulled his mouth away and brought his hungry gaze to her. His eyes swam with a paralyzing darkness. Darker than she'd ever seen them. They were the night sky now. She didn't pull her hand away from the hardness that pushed against her palm.

"Does that please you?" He asked, his voice sensual and dripping with pride.

"Very much, my Prince."

A surge of Magic swelled up between them. In one swift movement, Mal flipped her around. He pulled the silk laces of her dress open with calculated precision. Each ribbon snapped from the corset one by one. The dress loosened and fell down her arms. The bed shifted behind her. He pressed against her back, snaking his hands across her shoulders. One hand moved over her chest and the other moved to her throat, sending icy wafts of his magic down her body.

Mine, it whispered.

"Yours," she replied.

His grip around her neck tightened and then pushed forward until the side of her face pressed into the black silken duvet.

He hovered above her, letting their breaths return to a slow and steady pace together. He traced lazy circles across her skin, up and down her darkened veins. He pressed his palm just above her breast on her left side. Over her heart.

"What?" She asked softly.

"I want the world to know who you belong to."

"They will know after tonight," she said.

Mal shook his head ever so slightly. "Not like that."

"Then how?" Asked Maeve.

"I've been thinking on it for a while. My ring on your finger is a symbol. So I thought, maybe another jewel? Something with my own symbol on it, perhaps? But then I realized this needs to be a mark no one can ever escape. A permanent trace of magic binding me to my most loyal. Vexkari." Mal kissed her skin just over where her heart lay. "Right here."

"I'll do it," said Maeve at once.

He looked up at her. Maeve ran her fingers through his raven hair.

She was always quick to please him.

"I'll do whatever you ask of me. I will take my vows tonight as your second in front of them all, and if you want it written in Magic across my heart that I am yours so be it."

Mal sat up and she followed suit.

"You will be the first to receive my mark," said Mal.

"An honor," she said.

"This Magic will mark you and bind you to me permanently, Maeve-"

Her fingers moved over his lips gently. "I do not volunteer lightly."

She lowered her hand and swiveled her knees beneath her. Mal placed one hand on the back of her neck and his right hand over her heart.

Their eyes locked together.

"Amaranthine Maeve Sinclair," he began, his voice hummed low with authority. "I mark you as a Magical of The House of Dread." Shards of ice shot into her skin where each of his fingertips lay. "I mark you as my own."

Magic pierced her skin. She cried out, snapping her eyes tightly shut. Mal held her firmly. She bent forward, grunting against the pain. Tendrils of shadowy black magic crept from his fingertips, crawling into her skin one by one, like metal, stinging spiders. Her cheeks were stripped of color. She wined, and he pushed deeper into her skin.

The candlelights next to the bed flickered.

With one last painful scrape, he pulled his hand away from her chest.

On her chest was a bright inky green two-headed serpent, snaking its way through the mouth and eyes of a skull. One viper's mouth was closed. The other had its fangs ferociously bared, ready to strike.

Maeve ran her fingers over the tattoo. It was already healed. Mal tucked his fingers under her chin, bringing her gaze up at him, and cocked his head to one side. Her cheeks flushed with warmth under his sultry gaze. The corners of his mouth turned up.

"We'll be late for my breakfast banquet if you don't get dressed."

"What's the alternative?" Maeve asked mischievously.

"I have you again."

Maeve dropped back onto the bed, flinging her arms above her head. "So be it."

Chapter 63

"Listen to me carefully," said Maeve as Zimsy brushed through the matted wet hair falling to Maeve's shoulders as they prepared for Mal's Coronation.

Zimsy's eyes popped to hers in the mirror, and Maeve continued in a whisper.

"You are not magically bound to answer to anyone in this house except my mother or me anymore."

Zimsy's hands froze and her eyes grew large.

"However," she continued quietly, "until the time comes when I can break your chains completely, you will need to obey them perfectly all the same. No mistakes."

Zimsy nodded quickly and bit her bottom lip. "You are playing a dangerous game."

"I have been for quite some time," said Maeve with a half-hearted smile. "Might as well stay true to character."

"It is illegal for one to break the enslavement curse on another where Elves are concerned. They could imprison you."

"Do you think I would let that happen?" Maeve's smile turned into a smirk, trying to calm Zimsy's nerves.

"No," said Zimsy contemplatively. "Nor would the Dread Prince."

Maeve nodded and reached back for her hands. "Don't worry about me. Just stay on your toes. With the Magic gone, if a command slips your mind, my Mother won't be happy and she isn't stupid. This is my world now, Zimsy. And I won't be leaving you behind."

Thousands of Magicals gathered in teary-eyed awe at Castle Morana. The throne room's floor shone with dark emerald and silver oversized tiles. The smooth stone pillars along the room towered over them, jetting up into an enchanted ceiling of the cosmos.

Maeve smiled. It was like her bedroom window only massive. Her heels clicked across the floor as she and Abraxas walked arm in arm towards the Throne Room.

"I can't believe it," he said. "We're here."

They stopped and watched as not just Magicals took their places lining the long hall. Reeve and Eryx stood with a handful of Immortals. Lithandrian and Xander brought a number of Elven citizens and royalty too. King Kier stood with his wife and children and his court.

All of the remaining realms came. All of them were prepared to move forward with their plan of unity.

Ambrose stood at the head of the room, beside an ornate throne of crimson red. Maeve and Abraxas stayed at the back of the hall, behind the archway. Music began playing from the throne room, its provoking melody flitted across the hall.

Mal appeared at their side in his emerald brocade suit. The three of them stood alone.

Mal looked at each of them. "Thank you," he said, his voice dripping with gratitude.

He stepped forward. The Magical lights of the throne room glistened across his beautiful face. Maeve couldn't help but smile. Abraxas's arm tightened in excitement, pulling her closer as Mal stepped onto the shining tiles and began his promenade down the hall toward his throne.

Every magical on Earth was invited. Not just Purebloods. Anyone with Magical blood was offered a place in the Dread Lands. Some dropped to their knees as he passed. Some dabbed their eyes. Some tossed flowers and tokens of magic at his feet. Children looked up at him, captivated by his princely stride.

Mal reached Ambrose near the throne and climbed the stone steps. At the top of the platform, he kneeled on a dark velvet pillow, his eyes staring above the crowd, not meeting any one particular gaze.

Ambrose placed the Dread Crown on his head with careful ease. Mal's chest swelled noticeably as the golden serpents made contact with his skin. His eyes fluttered to a close. His fingers reached up and brushed along the crown.

"Arise," said Ambrose, his voice echoing across the hall with power. "Malachite no longer his name. He is reborn as the Prince of Darkness. The Redeemer of Magic."

The solid tapestries spanning the height and length of the hall burst to life with black sparks. Burned into them with dark smoke was the Dread Mark: the decaying skull and winding two-headed serpent that now decorated Maeve's chest.

The Hall moved as one.

As one they bowed their heads to him.

As one they waited for his command to look up.

With an outstretched arm, he pulled their attention up. He smiled fully. And dropped his hand.

The hall erupted in thunderous cheers and exclamations. Applause rattled the very floor. Mal took his time accepting their accolades.

He looked to Ambrose. Who nodded once in approval. Mal took his seat on the throne. Maeve's legs wobbled slightly at the sight.

"My turn, cousin," said Abraxas, giving her a quick peck on the cheek.

Abraxas dropped her arm and strode down the hall towards Mal. His suit was a deep shade of emerald, nearly black velvet. His blonde hair was styled back fashionably.

Abraxas stood before Mal. He bowed at the waist, a grand gesture of his adoration and allegiance to his new Prince of Darkness. He rose and placed his fist over his heart.

"Abraxas Flint Rosethorn," said Mal. "I name you Hand of the Prince."

On Abraxas' chest appeared a silver brooch. It was a serpent missing its twin. It's mouth closed. One of the serpents of Mal's Dread Mark.

Mal motioned him forward, towards the throne.

He took his place to Mal's left. He looked out and met his Mother's eyes. His face beamed with pride. Her cousin had never looked so at ease, so perfectly in place.

It was Maeve's turn.

She took a steadying breath and stepped forward into the hall.

Time froze. Her slow footsteps echoed across the Hall. Mal sat on his new throne with collected dignity. The perfect balance of confidence and humility. Like he knew he didn't deserve to be there, but all the same, it was his.

The crown atop his head was designed for his perfect face. He looked older. More profound. With the slightest incline of his chin, that serpent crown gleamed across the hall, bouncing light across the shining stone floor.

His Magic found her a blink after. It stopped her in her tracks as it slithered up her legs and around her waist. Up to her chest and around her neck. Cold and deep magic.

He was more powerful.

The crown held Dread Magic. Just like the locket and the ring.

But more. Much more.

It was incredible. Threatening. Deadly. Alive.

It was fear and death and desire and ambition all bottled up into one man.

In this place, in the Dread Lands, he was holy with power.

Her Prince of Darkness. Her savior.

All eyes were on Maeve as she fell to her knees.

It was quick, but satisfaction shot across Mal's eyes.

"I do not deserve this honor," she said, bringing her fist slowly over her heart, where his mark was. "But I will spend the rest of my life fighting for your reign. For your crown. For your life. For you."

The spell snapped between them like a whip.

Mal's magic swelled across the Hall between them, sliding her backward onto her feet, her sapphire and silver gown swished across the floor, flecks of light glittering around her. She braced herself against the power and allowed his gift to circle her completely.

It swirled around her, dripping her in ancient and reverent magic. She could taste his power. It was electrifying.

Her skirt transformed into fitted pants of a dark emerald brocade, like his, and her satin shoes shot up her legs, swirling with Magic. They were now shining boots laced to her knees. The fabric of the bodice unfurled itself, creating a trench coat that matched the dress with a high-collared tunic underneath. Her hair swirled around her until it was intricately braided down her back.

On her breast pocket was the serpent twin to Abraxas'. Its fangs bared and ready. She looked down at it. At herself. A warrior. A fighter.

This was the uniform of a second. Of his Dread Viper. Of a deadly Witch with agility.

She crossed the hall between them with confidence. In three short steps, she stood before his throne. A decaying skull brooch appeared on his own breast pocket. The final piece of his Dread Mark.

She and Abraxas were the mouth and the sword. He was Death incarnate.

Chapter 64

Ambrose had been the first to bow and swear his allegiance and his army of Magical Militia to their new Dread Prince.

Mal didn't break their grasp. He looked across at Ambrose reverently. His eyes glassed over, and when Maeve looked to her father, she realized his eyes were the same.

They stared at one another with what Maeve could only describe as… love.

Pride swelled in her chest.

"Premier Sinclair," said Mal.

Ambrose's grip tightened. "My Prince."

The hall burst into applause.

The throne room at Castle Morana transformed into a reception hall. Long tables of food and refreshments and more liquor than could possibly be consumed lined the hall. Music played serenely across the hall.

Mal pulled forth the Dread Goblet and presented it to Ambrose.

"A gift," said Mal. "For your allegiance and dedication to my cause."

Ambrose took a hefty exhale. He hesitated to grasp the goblet's serpent handles.

"Bring us some wine," called Ambrose. He looked up at Mal. "Our new Prince deserves a toast."

The wine was poured. Floating trays of glittering goblets delivered them around the hall. Ambrose stepped onto the stairs of the throne and raised the Dread Goblet high.

"A toast! To the new age of Magic, to the end of living in the shadows and hiding from the world. To our Savior and his Viper, my darling daughter. I knew from the moment the pair of you stepped into my home that this day was soon to come barreling forward."

There were a few clamors of excitement. Maeve and Mal locked eyes. That new Magic slipped from him, taunting her with every breath he took, filling his eyes with otherworldly implications.

"To the Dread Prince!" Cheered Ambrose. "May your reign be true!"

Ambrose raised the goblet to his lips, and everyone followed suit. Light conversation began flitting through the room. Ambrose stepped past Maeve and clapped her shoulder, heading towards her Mother and Arianna.

Maeve watched as each Magical came, desperate to grasp Mal's arm, to feel some of that divine violence resonating from him. He smiled at all of them with unbeatable charm.

Abraxas was already playing the game. He was in deep conversation with King Kier.

Maeve placed her glass of wine on a floating tray.

An unsettling feeling slipped into her spine. She ran her thumb across her fingers and then slowly flexed them. There was an unfamiliar Magic in the room. Her eyes moved slowly to Mal.

He was fine. His Magic at rest.

She followed the feeling. Unfamiliar- no.

Wrong-yes.

She looked across the hall and hit her mark.

Ambrose lifted the Dread Goblet to his lips once more.

Maeve's whole body went cold.

"Daddy-" she started, but he didn't hear her over the music and the crowd.

He coughed.

"Daddy!" She shouted as she pushed through the guests.

Ambrose brought the Dread Goblet to his lips, drinking quickly, in an attempt to satiate his coughs.

Alphard's father whipped his handkerchief from his pocket and handed it to Ambrose. Her father coughed into the bright white cloth.

Red spattered through the fabric instantly.

"Irma!" Screamed Mr. Mavros as Maeve broke through the crowd to him.

Ambrose faltered. The goblet fell from his fingers. Maeve didn't hear it clatter on the emerald and silver floor.

She gripped his shoulders and forced his gaze to her. He took her down to the floor with him. Something sinister slithered through his body, its power hot and lethal.

Blood slipped from the corners of his eyes.

From his nose.

From his ears.

Irma was at Maeve's side, her hands over his face, which was turning a yellow shade of sickness. Bright red lines shot from his lips, spreading across his cheeks.

Ambrose's eyes went black. Empty.

Then the whole world stopped.

And he collapsed forward into Maeve's arms.

Maeve's frantic eyes looked to Irma. She was ghostly white, her shaking hands still raised before her.

Ambrose was limp against her. His body was cold as ice. Maeve moved her hands to the back of his head, cradling him, feeling for his Magic. He didn't blink. He didn't meet her eyes. He stared past her at the ceiling with collapsed black eyes.

She found no heartbeat. No Magic flowed from him.

Maeve's eyes burned. Her chest tightened. Pressure built up in the back of her jaw.

Arianna appeared before her. Her knees slammed to the floor. Her hands moved to hold their father's face. His head was limp in her grasp.

"No," cried Arianna, tears spilling onto her face. "No, you can't." She was shaking Ambrose's shoulders now, desperately attempting to wake him. "You can't, you can't," she cried, touching his face again.

She continued to beg her father to wake.

The room was terrifyingly silent, save for Arianna's sobs. Her voice bounced high into the hall, echoing across the room. No one moved away. No one stepped forward. They kept their distance, creating a large circle around the Sinclair sisters and their father.

Maeve's heart was slow and steady. But something electric and deep in her began to swell. It was barreling forward like a hundred-year storm.

Maeve tore her eyes away from where her father's cold, dead body lay in her arms. And looked to Mal.

He was a few feet away. His arms limp at his sides. His eyes were wide and his mouth hung slightly open. Pure horror plastered across his beautiful face as he looked at Ambrose.

More electricity rushed through her.

Mal's eyes darted to Maeve as he realized-

He stepped towards her with one long outstretched arm. But it was too late.

Magic, uncontrolled and unyielding, shattered through her. She sucked in a sharp breath as darkness erupted from her.

Chapter 65

Black cosmic swirls of night burst from her entire body. No corner was spared as the room plummeted into a void of light.

Mal darted for her as screams of pain, and frantically fast footsteps filled the hall. Burning hot tears streamed down her face through sobbing, sharp breaths. Arianna was collapsed over on their father. Guests hurled themselves past them, scrambling for safety.

Slender, cool fingers wrapped around her arms, attempting to move her. She ripped from his grip. Hot electricity slammed through her fingertips, uncontrolled and of its own will. It was too much to hold. The force caused her vision to blur.

Reeve appeared before her, wings fully out. With a blast of air, he wrapped them around Arianna and her father, swirling into darkness, and disappearing with them.

The pressure exploded through her body. She screamed, extending her arms fully out at either side. An agonizing, bloodcurdling, and monstrous scream. Deadly bolts of green lightning illuminated the dark hall, shooting in every direction. Even towards Mal.

He threw up his arm, blocking and shielding himself from nearly all of them. Nearly.

A single bolt slammed into the side of his face, slicing open the skin from his jaw up his cheek, and staggering across his eye.

He recoiled and his hand flew to his face. Blood stained his fingertips.

And then he dove for her.

His arms wrapped tightly around her middle and slammed her to the floor. Her head cracked against the marble tile. He straddled her stomach and pinned her wrists to the floor with brutal force. His own Magic slammed into her, attempting to sedate her.

"Control!" He bellowed.

Maeve wailed once more. Green bolts of lightning continued to spiral from her trembling hands, shooting flat across the floor of the Hall.

"Maeve!" Mal growled. "Stop!"

Blood dripped from his face, landing across her cheeks in little pools.

There was no control within her reach. The tether had snapped on whatever wall had been inside her, and it could not be repaired.

"I don't want to hurt you, Maeve," begged Mal, his breathing quick.

He didn't speak again. He kept her pinned until she exhausted herself, pushing his Magic into her in an attempt to sedate her. Every ounce of Magic she had poured from her. She was drained entirely. Empty.

Light returned slowly to the hall as the clouds of darkness dissipated. They were alone in the hall. Mal's grip on her wrists loosened, and he leaned back, still straddling her.

Long exaggerated breaths slipped from him.

The Hall was desecrated. The once swirling marble pillars were chipped and cracked, now a pallid grey stone. The floor too. The windows in the hall were wide open, the glass previously in them scattered everywhere. The ceiling was bare. The tapestries had burned into nothing.

Maeve's arms moved across her eyes and face.

"Take me away from here, Mal," she cried.

Without argument, he Obscured them from Castle Morana.

She folded her arms across her chest in the long corridor that led to her father's basement where the portraits of her family hung. The previously empty portrait between her Grandfather Alyicious and her brother Antony now held a portrait of her father sitting behind his desk, smoking a cigar.

She had been to this portrait many times in the past two days. It was the only proof her mind accepted that he was truly gone.

Someone had poisoned the person she loved more than anything. Whose heart beat closest to hers. Whose dazzling and mischievous smile was the cure to all her ailments. He would never come strolling through a set of doors, swagger in his step and a cigar in hand.

His body was decaying already. Buried on the cliffside in Northern England, on Sinclair land, where all the Sinclair family were buried from the past three hundred years. Many came to honor her father. Hundreds of Magicals. The entirety of the Magical Militia was in attendance. Every single soldier. Past and present.

Several people felt compelled to speak at Ambrose's funeral. Maeve heard none of their words.

Everything felt empty. Nothing struck her emotions, nothing made her smile or feel angry. She was numb. Even as she replayed the image of his body passing in her arms, nothing swelled inside her.

Her Magic was sharpened somehow, but it was exhausted, even days later.

She knew there were those who opposed them. She knew The Committee and all those who were sitting fat and happy from the power she and Mal threatened to usurp were angry. But she never dreamed Ambrose would be the target. She was prepared to fight, but it was not Maeve or Mal who had been betrayed.

Her Father had warned her about a rebellion. Those who would have never seen Mal return. Those that benefited from the current class status and structure would not accept their new way without a fight.

He had been painfully right.

Mal had not left Maeve's side since. Not to sleep, not to eat. Even now, he was waiting for her at the top of the stairs, watching her carefully.

Maeve knew they wouldn't kill her yet if they planned to at all. This wasn't just a warning. It was to incentivize her to rethink her choices. To marry Alphard or Xander and produce heirs and do her duty.

There were only so many Sacred Seventeen women of age who were free. Arianna was already married. Victoria was engaged to Damario, possibly soon Alphard. Iris was two years away from turning twenty-two and Juliet's parents had families offering a fortune for her betrothal. Emerie was promised to Roswyn. Their wedding was a month away.

The rest of the Sacred Seventeen girls were still children in their primary studies. But there were a dozen or more Sacred Seventeen men without wives.

They wanted her still. They had no other choice.

Maeve took a steadying breath and tore her eyes away from her father's portrait.

Mal was waiting for her at the top of the stairs. He was in relaxed clothing. Black slacks with a thin pressed seam and a dark blue turtleneck. The locket hung freely around his neck. No crown.

His face now had a pale red and white jagged scar, courtesy of Maeve's unexplained lightning. Magicals didn't produce lightning. The mark ran from his chin, jagged and broken, up across his cheekbone and through his eye.

"Will it scar?" She had asked after Irma healed him the day before.

Mal nodded. "Dark Magic leaves traces."

Maeve ran her fingers over the black lines that shot across her own neck. "I'm sorry." She had said.

Maeve reached the top of the stairs. They walked silently to the Dining Hall. Mal pulled out Maeve's chair, and she sat across from Arianna. Her mother sat at the head of the table. Mal stood next to her, looking down.

She felt him pushing into her mind. It took little effort and she let him slip inside.

I am a word away, he pushed into her mind.

It had taken much convincing, but Mal agreed to leave her for an evening with just her mother and sister. He brushed her hair behind her ear and looked to Arianna. Her sister looked down at the table and back up in respect.

Mal didn't address Clarissa as he took his leave.

Maeve didn't touch the food on her plate, and neither did Arianna. Clarissa cleared her plate.

The evening was primarily silent until Clarissa finally spoke.

"You are aware that your father purchased you that ridiculous townhouse in London?"

"No, I wasn't."

Clarissa reached for her glass of wine. "Yes, well. You're welcome."

"I don't believe you purchased it," said Maeve darkly.

Clarissa's eyes shot to her. "How dare you."

Arianna sat with her head bowed, staring at her full, untouched plate.

Trudy appeared in the doorway.

"A Prince Xander, ma'am," said Trudy with a low bow to Clarissa.

Maeve merely looked across the table at Arianna. Her sister returned her exhausted expression.

Xander sauntered into the room. "My deepest condolences for your husband, Mrs. Sinclair," he said, placing his hand over his heart. "Though I must admit, I was grateful to receive your letter of reconsideration for my marriage to your daughter."

Maeve sighed and shook her head. "Don't do this," said Maeve weakly.

Clarissa eyed down her youngest ruefully. She swished the wine in her glass around in a circle before taking a long sip.

Maeve's hollow laugh echoed in the silent dining hall. "Daddy would have never. . ."

Clarissa raised her eyebrows. "Ambrose isn't here." Her thin lips pulled up at the corners.

A surge of hatred rose through Maeve. The first emotions she had felt in days. The crystal glass in Clarissa's hand shattered. She jumped as wine poured onto the table and into her lap.

"Let me make something very clear," said Maeve calmly. "I don't obey you. I stand beside the greatest dark Magical of all time. A man with talent beyond your feeble comprehension."

Clarissa stood wiping her dress with a cloth napkin, staring Maeve down with disgust. "Your blood earned you that spot."

Maeve looked over at her and said plainly. "My talent earned me that spot. My loyalty, my abilities, my mind earned me that spot."

"You think he would have ever given you the time of day if you'd been a half-blood or even worse, a human born? Don't think for a second if your blood was dirty, you'd have this disgraceful attitude towards marrying royalty."

"But it is dirty, isn't it?" Said Maeve, her brows raised.

Clarissa's face faltered. She stammered.

"And I don't give a damn about marrying royalty. In fact, I don't give a damn about marrying at all. They've already taken the only thing that could hurt me besides Mal, and do you truly think that would be successful?"

"I always knew you'd turn out to be so horrible, just like-"

"Oh heavens, yes, just say it," seethed Maeve. "You think I don't already know I don't belong to you? That you didn't carry or create me? You think there are any secrets of Daddy's left for me to find?"

Arianna covered her mouth in shock as Maeve unveiled the secret she had known for months.

"I spent the past four months scouring every corner and crevice of his mind while he let me work my memory charm experiments on him. I know everything. I know you did not bear me and were disgraced into pretending that you did. And I know that my real mother died at the hands of the Committee just like Antony and just like Father."

Clarissa spat. "Don't you dare speak about my son and that trash your father lay with in the same sentence."

Maeve scoffed. She dropped her napkin on the table and stood. She looked to her sister. "I'm sorry, Arianna. I'm sorry for everything." She meant it. "I'm sorry you lost your father too."

Arianna's eyes swelled with tears. "It's your fault."

Maeve swallowed and spoke softly. "I know it is."

She turned on her heel. Clarissa called after her.

"Always ungrateful for everything I have given you. And how will you fare then?" Shot Clarissa. "How will you get by without all the wealth that would be handed down to you if you had stayed in line?"

Maeve didn't stop. "While you dangle your precious gold above me, I know that when you married my father, the Rosethorns had nothing left. The Sinclair's money was their saving grace, delivered in exchange for you. You, who had nothing when you married him, dare to lecture me on what you have given me! When it was never yours in the first fucking place."

"I have grown tired of you." Spat Clarissa.

Maeve stopped and turned back towards her. "Fuck you."

"Go and marry your Prince boy then. Your blood is perfect for him."

Maeve shook her head. "You still don't get it, do you? I don't care about marrying him. I don't care about losing my inheritance. You can keep your precious blood money."

She turned once more and walked out of the dining hall.

The house was filled with eerie silence as she made her way to the third floor. She pushed open her bedroom door, and there stood Zimsy, carefully packing all of Maeve's belongings into a trunk.

"You're leaving," said Zimsy quietly.

"Yes." Maeve strode past her to her vanity, which she found empty. "You already. . . "

Zimsy nodded. "All of your personal and private things are tucked away. Your favorite books, all your clothes." She gestured to the trunk.

"You fit it all in there?"

"Easy Charms work," said Zimsy softly.

"Of course," said Maeve awkwardly.

They stood silently for a moment. Zimsy took a step towards her. Maeve took a step back.

She swallowed hard. "You're free to go."

Magic severed between them, like a solid steel bar snapping in two. It felt easy to break the rest of Zimsy's enslavement curse. Like tugging at a loose bow.

Zimsy shook her head and grabbed her chest, her eyes wide.

"No," said Zimsy, her voice concerned.

"It's not a trick," said Maeve. "If I'm leaving, you should leave too."

Zimsy's mouth quivered. "I could come with you-."

"No," said Maeve plainly. "Leave. That's an order, Zimsy."

Zimsy rubbed her hands together nervously.

"But-"

"No!"

"I want to come with you!"

"I don't want you to!"

Pain spread across Zimsy's face as she Obscured with a swirl of Magic.

Maeve sighed and ran her hands across her face. A lump rose in her throat as she made her way out of her room to gather the rest of the things from the house that she wanted.

She didn't look back at it. She couldn't look back at it.

Ambrose Sinclair's study lay untouched, as though he would walk through the door at any moment and pick up his unfinished brandy. But many books and pictures were gone. Magical items had a way of presenting themselves to their new owners in death. Ambrose had likely promised many of his readings and trinkets to others who now possessed them.

The basement of Sinclair Estates lay empty.

Maeve sat behind his desk, staring across the room. She would never be here again. And she was glad of it. This room harbored too much happiness. Joy. It was a burden.

Two books sat in front of her. One she was taking for herself and one for Mal. Across the desk were strewn article clippings, letters from several different officials, and handwritten notes by Ambrose himself.

There was a brief knock at the door. Xander stood in the doorway. "May I come in?"

He didn't wait for her response but strode across the room and stood in front of Ambrose's desk, where Maeve had just finished off a bottle of her father's Dragon Whiskey. There was not much left, but it burned Maeve's insides all the same.

She didn't look at Xander but continued to stare at the notes on his desk.

"That was quite a display down there," said Xander. "And at The Dread Prince's coronation."

"I'm glad you enjoyed it," said Maeve emotionlessly.

"I'm terribly sorry about your father. Lithandrian sends her regrets as well. Everyone adored the Premier."

Maeve didn't speak. He continued.

"You're an incredibly powerful witch to create magic like that, just from your emotions." He laughed.

Maeve looked him over. "Why are you still here? Didn't you hear? I am not of the blood status you think I am."

Xander eyed her. "That doesn't matter to me. No one knows that, and our alliance would still be strong. Even more beneficial for you now, given the circumstances. The Dread Prince might agree if you asked him. His court would have an immediate bonded alliance with another powerful realm. The realm he is so desperately trying to grasp."

Maeve stared at him for a moment.

"You know what's incredibly clear to me now, Xander?" Maeve leaned back in her father's chair. "No one has anything to offer that is beneficial to me. Marrying Alphard, no benefit. Your offer was never beneficial for me. I was so confused as to why my mother would fight for something seemingly good for me." Maeve stood and looked out the large window. "And then I realized my Mother pushed for it because she'd win either way. If I agreed, I'd be a blood traitor and embarrass myself by marrying you. And if I refused, I'd be disowned, lose my inheritance and all. She got to get rid of me either way."

"I think you're discrediting me too quickly," said Xander.

He was suddenly closer than she realized, standing directly behind her.

"I think you'll find I can be of use to you and Malachite," he continued. "My blood, the people I know. . . And your father, I think he agreed it would be a strong realistic choice for us."

Xander speaking of her father as if he knew him caused a wave of nausea to pass through her.

He brushed her hair off her shoulder and trailed his finger down her arm. Her stomach didn't flip. Her skin didn't flush.

She looked out over London as the enchanted window began to fog over.

"Could it be so terrible to be Elven Royalty too?" Xander's voice now had that slimly quality again. "We would create an entirely new line of Magic."

He brought his lips down to her neck. She didn't stop him. It sent nothing down her spine. His fingers continued to trail down her arm, and he laced his fingers with hers. He brought their hands up and examined them.

"See? That's not so bad." He brought his lips down to her fingers and kissed them tenderly. Just as his lips brushed Mal's Dread ring, he winced and pulled away from her.

He chuckled nervously and touched his lips, confused. Maeve watched him for a moment in their reflection.

"That was odd," said Xander, feigning laughter again.

Maeve looked down at the ring on her left hand ring finger. She brought it to her lips for a moment before turning around in the chair.

"If I know Mal, and I really and truly do," said Maeve, relishing her words, "it's only going to get worse."

He scratched at his lips in a panicked manner as they began to inflate and turn bright red.

Xander began to panic as the curse flared and spread across his face. Maeve waved her hand and effortlessly gathered the readings and books of her father's she intended to take for now.

"What's happening to me?" Screamed Xander, pathetically, dropping his facade.

"I believe, put simply, you tried to take something that is not yours. Consider it a parting gift from The Prince of Darkness," said Maeve. "And by all means, please tell Lithandrian just how it was you ended up in such a state."

Maeve headed for the fireplace and vanished as Xander screamed.

She stepped out of the fire in Mal's penthouse suite. Ambrose left it to him. His name was now scrolled across the deed. Ambrose left Mal a number of things.

Mal crossed towards her and took her hands in his own. Her Sinclair family ring shone on one hand and his Dread ring on the other.

"I need to prepare the Dread Lands. I need to get my people out of here as soon as possible. I have so much work to do."

"I need-"

"I know what you need," he said softly. "And you will have it." He brought his lips to her forehead. "I will give you time to grieve and mourn. But when our kingdom is ready, I will come back for you. And you will be at my side once more."

He took her hand again and balled it into a fist. He placed it over her heart, where his Dread Mark lay beneath her clothes. She held her chin up proudly.

"Pour toujours," she said.

Forever.

"À tout jamais," he said in reply.

And always.

Maeve's eyes darted between his. Her voice shook as she said-

"I'm going to kill them all."

Mal brushed his free hand across her quivering bottom lip.

"No, Little Viper. We are going to kill them all."

end of book one

ABOUT THE AUTHOR

Lauren Cate Leake is an artist from Mississippi. After decades of devotion to training and exploring the performing arts, she shifted her focus to bringing The Dread Descendant to life on paper. She began writing fan fiction at a young age and loves reading. She has two cats: fourteen year old Merky (Mercutio) and seven month old Charlie. She loves to travel and perform when she can. She encourages everyone to pursue a better future for themselves regardless of their academic record.

Thank you so much for reading! It means the world to me to have gotten Maeve's story into your hands. Follow along for book antics and updates!

Xoxo LC

TikTok @thedreaddescendant
Instagram @writer_lc